KINGSTEEL

The Dragonkin Trilogy: Three

MICHAEL MEYERHOFER

Kingsteel
The Dragonkin Trilogy™ Book Three
A Red Adept Publishing Book

ISBN-13: 978-1-940215-59-4
ISBN-10: 1940215595

Red Adept Publishing, LLC
104 Bugenfield Court
Garner, NC 27529
http://RedAdeptPublishing.com/

Cover and Formatting: Streetlight Graphics

*This book is dedicated to all the lovely people who
are currently reading this sentence.*

Wintersea

Sorocco

Dhargoth Peninsula

Ivairia

Phaegos

Lotus Isles

Dead Shores

Syros

Quorim

Cassica

Simurgh Plains

Lyos

Cadavash

The Red Steppes

Godsfall

Hosod

Stillhammer Mtns.

Armahg's Tears

Ash'bana Plains

Atheion

Wytchforest

Quesh

Dendain

Runn

PROLOGUE

THE CLOAKED MAN HALTED. AHEAD of him, in sharp contrast to the snow-covered Simurgh Plains, lay a gaudy temple and a sea of tents and wagons sprawled before a great torch-lit gorge. Horses whinnied and pawed the snow, probably agitated less by the cold than by the ominous chanting and weeping coming from the tents. He felt a surge of pity for the animals. Lowly though they were, they deserved better. Granted, Humans were lowly, too, but they could blame no one else for their own wretched lot in life.

The man grimaced, not at all heartened by finally reaching his destination. Despite all he'd gained, arriving at a place like Cadavash was hardly something to celebrate—and he'd taken far too long to get there.

Chorlga chided himself. After entrusting the Sylvan king to kill Silwren, the Shel'ai-turned-Dragonkin, he had made the decision to return and once again bolster his own magic with the aid of Namundvar's Well—just in case the king failed. He could have teleported himself all the way from Sylvos to Cadavash, but that was risky. Few uses of magic drained body and spirit more thoroughly than teleportation, and Chorlga had already nearly exhausted himself reaching the forests of Sylvos—much too weary to risk facing Silwren himself.

He'd told himself that he was just being cautious. There was no sense risking death just to avoid a few days' walk. But Chorlga knew the truth.

Gods, I hate this place…

Though most of the dragonpriests were asleep, several still milled about the temple and the adjacent gorge, wailing theatrically and slashing their own bodies with ceremonial knives. Their madness washed over him—right before he reminded himself to wall off his mind from their emotions. He was tempted to slip unseen into the deepest, secret vaults of Cadavash and head straight to Namundvar's Well, which the foolish dragonpriests did not even know existed.

The thought of what he was about to do turned his stomach, but he had no choice. Delving into the magic of Namundvar's Well was dangerous. He needed to be at full strength for that.

Chorlga paused a moment, laughing at the absurdity of his situation. He had to make himself stronger before he could undertake a ritual that would make him stronger still. At any point, the slightest misstep might kill him.

He drew in a deep breath of winter air. He wondered what it would be like to feel *truly* cold, like those who had nothing of dragons inside them. Exhaling, he started forward. He walked past the temple, in full view of a handful of bone-worshippers, making no attempt to conceal himself.

As he passed an open tent, he paused, glanced inside. A group of naked worshippers—male and female alike, some little more than children—sat in a circle, rocking themselves and muttering feverish prayers. All had red, swollen eyes. He wondered if they were drugged or simply exhausted. In one direction, with slow reverence, the worshippers passed what looked like a dragon's wingbone. In the other direction went a thin ceremonial knife, with which they took turns cutting their own legs.

Chorlga shuddered and looked away. Even by Human standards, bone-worshippers were loathsome. Still, he marveled that they could live in such a state. He almost pitied the young ones, born into such a life, until he reminded himself that they were still Humans.

In the next tent, a richly dressed merchant counted coins. A pair of muscular, armored bodyguards scowled in Chorlga's direction. One warned him to keep walking. Chorlga resisted the sudden impulse to burn the men to ashes and continued toward the temple. Before he had made it halfway, two more armed men blocked his path. Unlike the bodyguards, the men had a green emblem sewn into their thick wool cloaks and painted onto their shields: a naked man with wings and a dragon's head. The soldiers waved silently to a third guard, who raced back to the temple.

Biting back his impatience, Chorlga waited. Late arrivals were apparently an anomaly at Cadavash. Moments later, a squad of guardsmen descended the temple steps and headed in his direction, led by a dragonpriest. They smelled of sweat, incense, and ale. All wore the same green emblem, though in place of a cloak, the priest wore an extravagant robe.

While the dragonpriest appeared to be unarmed, the guards wore mail and shortswords and carried footmen's spears tied with strips of green silk. Two of the soldiers carried bronze-collared torches.

The priest bowed stiffly. Scars from self-inflicted cuts covered the man's wrists and hands, as well as his young, otherwise-handsome face. "Greetings, traveler. You are most welcome in this holy place… though a gift of twenty cranáfi is required before you may approach. If you're paying in iron crowns, we have reduced the cost from thirty to twenty-five, as a sign of respect to the Dhargothi prince."

Chorlga frowned. He wondered at the dragonpriest's choice of words, then remembered seeing Dhargots on the plains the day before, massed some distance away, under a telltale cloud of smoke and screams. He realized that in the dark, he might have been mistaken for one of them. The thought made him laugh.

"I am no Dhargot." He threw back his cloak, letting the soldiers' torches reveal his long, tapered ears and violet eyes. He smiled at the men's surprise. A few reached for swords. "Nor am I a Shel'ai."

"You look like one. Those eyes…" The priest's face tightened with fear. He gestured, and the soldiers formed a protective ring around him. "In fact, you look like the one who came here a few months ago and killed—"

Chorlga undid the clasp of his cloak and let it fall onto the snowy plains. He waved his hand, and the soldiers' torches flared to life, turning from yellow-orange to violet, blazing so fiercely that the soldiers threw them down. On the ground, the torches continued to blaze, brighter and brighter. The blaze did not push back the darkness so much as brutalize it.

A few soldiers screamed and stepped back. Others turned to the dragonpriest, anticipating an order to attack. But the priest stood paralyzed, his eyes locked on the plains. Chorlga traced the line of the man's sight and realized the priest was gawking at Chorlga's shadow, which had suddenly grown enormous. Chorlga studied the priest's expression of horrified astonishment. He did not need to delve into the mad priest's mind to know that he was trying to figure out how a cloaked man could produce a winged shadow.

Mad, this one… but not stupid.

"As I was saying, I am not a Shel'ai. Nor have I come to buy dragonbone." A few soldiers had drawn their swords.

Chorlga waved, and those swords flew from their hands. Chorlga drew closer, edging around the guards. Though he faced the dragonpriest, whose eyes were wide and wet with fear, he spoke loudly enough for all to hear.

"For years, you have prayed that your lamentations and self-imposed suffering would reanimate the bones of dead dragons... that the dragons themselves might return, burn you, *devour* you, and thus make you part of them forever." He paused. "Followers of Zet the Dragongod, rejoice! For this night, in my blood... in *me*... that wish shall finally be granted."

Without further ceremony, Chorlga pressed one hand to the dragonpriest's scarred face. The young man's jaw dropped. His eyes grew wider still. He might have screamed had Chorlga permitted it. Instead, Chorlga drained the man's essence, absorbing it into his own. He sensed both the man's terror and his dreadful willingness. Chorlga grinned at the familiar, welcome rush of exhilaration, even as the draining of a Human, rather than a dragon, turned his stomach. When he let go, the dragonpriest's eyes were black and blistered. The corpse slumped quietly to the ground, where it steamed in the snow.

Chorlga turned slowly, surveying those around him. In addition to the guards who were still paralyzed by his magic, their swords glinting in the snow, other priests, worshippers, and a few simple tradesmen had come closer to see what was happening.

They all stared.

Chorlga released the guards from his spell. Tendrils of wytchfire ignited from his fingertips, racing back and forth along his arms, leaving his clothes unburnt. Chorlga turned again, slowly. "Who else wishes to bathe and burn in the legacy of dragons?"

No one moved. Then an old dragonpriest limped forward, moving slowly. His scarred, wrinkled face was damp with tears. The old priest knelt before Chorlga, speechless, head bowed. His narrow shoulders trembled, though Chorlga could not be certain without probing the old man's mind whether it was from cold, fear, or anticipation.

Chorlga smiled. "Good choice." He pressed one flaming, open palm to the old man's face. Like the first priest, the Human did not scream. A moment later, another corpse slid to the snowy earth, its eyes burnt out, the sockets blackened and smoking. The flames coursing along Chorlga's arms grew slightly brighter, as did the torches still blazing on the ground.

Chorlga took a deep breath, held it, let it go, then turned to find the next volunteer. He expected to find only one or two, so that he would have to compel the rest by force. Instead, he found a dozen men and women already kneeling.

Others ran, spreading word of his arrival. Dragon-worshippers began to shove, eager to reach him. Some cried out in wild exaltation. Within minutes, nearly all the souls in Cadavash stood before him.

When they saw the haze of unearthly violet light, a few people backed away, aghast. A handful, mostly merchants, ran. Chorlga let them go. After all, in less than an hour, he already had a small army of joyous, weeping figures, so many that he had to fight back the urge to teleport elsewhere or burn his way to freedom, just so he could be away from them.

So many wanted to join him. So many had waited and prayed all their lives—not for this moment, exactly, but near enough. Praying, crying, and pleading, the throng pressed in on him. Though his senses whirled and he had to fight to keep from retching, he forced himself to hold his ground until he had welcomed them all.

Soon, the corpses piled around him like walls. Then Chorlga had an idea.

CHAPTER ONE
FLIGHT FROM THE FIRE

IT WAS SUNSET NOW, BLOOD-GOLD light spilling through the trees behind them. All of them shook with exhaustion. Still, not one of the cloaked figures slowed to glance back over their shoulder, let alone rest—none save Shade. The ragged band of Shel'ai had been fleeing since dawn.

Shade turned to scan the forest for signs of pursuit. Hours had passed since they'd blundered into a war band of Wyldkin. For all their magical senses, the Shel'ai had somehow been utterly surprised. Two Shel'ai had died in a hail of arrows, another from a thrown spear, before a blaze of wytchfire had driven off the rest of the Wyldkin.

I should have been more careful. Three more dead—because of me.

Though it further weakened him, Shade had used his magic to enhance his senses. He expected the Wyldkin to call for reinforcements and pursue them, but the only sounds he heard came from faraway battles. He reminded himself that most of the Sylvs were probably still trying desperately to drive the Olgrym out of their homeland.

As they drove us out... He shook his head. *No, it wasn't the Sylvs. It was that Isle Knight, the one with* Fâyu Jinn's *sword. And Silwren...*

Though a surge of grief threatened to bring tears to his eyes, Shade turned and rejoined the others, who had slowed but not stopped. Four men still carried the litter, their faces slick with perspiration, while two more, both women, scouted ahead. As quickly as he had squelched it, Shade's feeling of grief returned. *Gods, only six of us left!*

"We do not stop until we are clear of the forest," he said.

The other Shel'ai did not protest. Shade did not have to use his magical aptitude for mind reading to tell that they could not keep up the pace much longer. He hoped they would not have to.

In the distance, the forest began to thin. Here and there, the towering wytchwoods gave way to the sickly trees of the outer world: oaks, yews, and even a few dogblossom trees that must have been brought from the Isles, then forgotten centuries ago. Beyond these trees, snow-flecked hills rolled on beneath a naked blue sky.

Shade shuddered. Already, he missed the shelter of the wytchwood branches soaring hundreds of feet over his head—though even they paled before the World Tree into which the Sylvan capital had been carved.

The city we failed to take.

Memories of the battle washed over him. It had seemed at first as though they had won. The Sylvan forces—a mixture of Wyldkin and a handful of Shal'tiar, plus a frightened multitude of hastily armed conscripts from Shaffrilon, most of them women and children—had been routed. Olgrym swept through the smashed gates, their hulking bodies painted with the blood and entrails of their victims. The Shel'ai followed, led by Fadarah himself.

Between the Shel'ai wytchfire and the Olgrym's sheer strength, they had decimated the Sylvan armies, thrashing the once-mighty Shal'tiar and burning every fort and village between the capital and the Ash'bana Plains. All that remained was to surge up the walkway into the city and find and slay the Sylvan king—then centuries of injustice would be set to right. The Shel'ai— driven out of the forest, hunted for their innate ability to work magic, and hated for their perceived similarity to the despotic Dragonkin who had ruled a thousand years earlier—would finally have a home.

Then *he* had appeared.

The thought of Rowen Locke caused Shade's lip to curl in disgust. He clenched one fist, wytchfire smoldering between his fingers, before he felt the magic draining what little strength he had left. He forced himself to relax. Still, the image haunted him: that red-haired Human, the lone Isle Knight, stalking toward them, Knightswrath in hand. The sword's blade was wreathed in flames... the flames that meant the sword's ancient power had been rekindled and that Silwren was dead.

"No..." Shade choked on the word then shook himself again, glad the others had not heard. He shifted his attention to the litter the sorcerers were carrying. Hastily constructed out of wytchwood boughs fused by magic, the litter was strong enough to support three grown men. Still, the boughs bent and strained under the weight of the wounded man.

Shade was tempted to check for Fadarah's pulse since he had not done so for hours, but that would mean stopping. They had already sacrificed as much magic as they could spare, urging healing energies into the Sorcerer-General's body. They could do nothing more for him. If Fadarah had already died, at least he'd died in the shade of the trees.

And if he's alive...

Shade's mind reeled at the thought of what lay ahead. They'd lost their army. They didn't even have horses. They would have to carry Fadarah for days and days, through savage lands, all the way back to Coldhaven on the perpetually desolate Wintersea. Even the famed Sorcerer-General would never survive such a journey.

Once they rested, the Shel'ai might be able to defend themselves against the Human raiders they would surely encounter along the way, but beyond the magical shelter of the forest was winter. Though the fire in their blood protected the Shel'ai against the cold, they would be forced to forage for food. Shade did not think the Sylvs would pursue them beyond the boundaries of the forest, especially with so many Olgrym left behind, but the Shel'ai had plenty of enemies. No one had forgotten that it was Fadarah's army, the Throng that had ravaged the Free Cities in the first place.

But since then, they've been conquered again by the Dhargots.

Technically, the Dhargots were Fadarah's allies. But they'd failed to send forces to help Fadarah against the Sylvs. Besides, the Dhargots were the worst of all the Humans. They valued only strength and prestige but nothing else, not even family. In that, they were even worse than the Olgrym. When they saw the great Fadarah's army reduced to a mere seven sorcerers, ragged and exhausted, assistance would be the last thing on their minds.

No, we'll have to traverse the Simurgh Plains undetected. That will mean avoiding thousands of Dhargothi warriors, plus everyone they're fighting.

Shade glanced at Fadarah. Even with the gray tinge afforded by the Sorcerer-General's half-Olgish parentage, he was too pale. Shade would have expected the big man to be feverish, bathed in sweat, but the Sorcerer-General's face was frightfully calm.

Panic rose within him, and he ordered the Shel'ai to stop. Grateful for the chance to rest, they gently lowered the litter onto the forest floor and stepped back, all of them collapsing. Shade knelt and held one fist over Fadarah's armored chest. Ignoring the ghastly, blood-splattered rend in the Sorcerer-General's armor, he slowly opened his fingers and closed his eyes. Igniting his magic, he probed the Sorcerer-General's body for a heartbeat.

He searched as though searching for a spark in a pile of wet leaves. At last he found it, though it was weaker than before. Though Rowen's blazing sword had mostly cauterized the wound, it had sliced through one of Fadarah's lungs, nicked his heart, and carved a path all the way down to one kidney. Only the other sorcerers' magic, coupled with Fadarah's incredible will, had kept him alive. But both had limits.

Shade withdrew his hand. He felt the others' gazes, though he trusted his tears to answer the question they'd been about to ask.

They should leave him and save themselves—as Fadarah would wish them to do. Shade gestured. Without hesitation, the men picked up Fadarah's litter again. With renewed strength, they hurried through the trees, as though help were waiting for them beyond the forest. But that was impossible. Even if they got Fadarah to Coldhaven, even if a dozen Shel'ai came sprinting over the hill right then to assist them, it would make no difference. The great Fadarah would die. Shade pushed the thought from his mind and quickened his pace.

An hour later, they passed the final wytchwood tree and set foot on the plains. Shade tugged at his white cloak. The ground was snowier than he'd expected. The snow crunched beneath his boots. A wild hope rose within him.

Humans won't fight in the winter. If they've holed up in their cities, we might be able to slip past undetected.

Then, as though to mock him, a wisp of smoke appeared on the horizon. Too big even for a burning village, it could mean only one thing: an army was camped nearby. Shade fought back a wave of despair.

That's Prince Ziraari. It has to be.

Like all Dhargots, the crown prince, Karhaati, was paranoid about potential rivals—particularly among his own family. But he also wanted to be close to Lyos, one of the richest cities on the plains. So he'd given his strongest brother, Ziraari, the dubious task of helping the Shel'ai take the Wytchforest. With Fadarah's host vanquished, Ziraari had no reason to help them. In fact, Dhargots distrusted sorcery as much as other Humans did. Ziraari might well kill them for sport.

Unless…

Shade glanced at Fadarah's still face. He steeled himself then addressed the others. "Take our father east." He pointed at a copse of trees in the distance. "Guard him well. If I can, I'll return before dawn. If not… stay with our father until he breathes his last, then make your own way to Coldhaven. From there on, your lives are your own."

The others started to protest, but Shade cut them off.

"If I'm not back by dawn, don't plan a rescue. I'm already dead." *Not necessarily.* The thought of the Dhargots' favorite method of slow torture—

impalement—sent a shiver down his spine. "What happens to me isn't important. Stay with our father. When he... when he *dies*"—he choked on the word—"your new responsibility will be to get back to Coldhaven and protect the other Shel'ai, especially the children. Do you understand?"

One by one, the others nodded. Shade faced them for a moment, feeling as though he should say more but lacking the words. After a final glance at Fadarah, he started in the direction of the smoke.

Once Shade was alone, he felt his exhaustion even more profoundly than before. He looked west, staring directly into the setting sun. *I am a Shel'ai, descended from Dragonkin, who gained their power by conquering beings that soared on six wings and breathed fire into the face of the gods. If it's my will to stay awake, I will do so.*

Nevertheless, his steps grew heavier and heavier as he trudged northeast across the snowy plains. He was glad his cloak matched his surroundings because he would eventually encounter sentries. Then he reminded himself that the sigil of the crimson greatwolf sewn into his cloak would be visible from a half mile away. He cursed. Undoing the clasp of his cloak, he let it slip from his shoulders and land on the snowy ground. A chilly breeze made him shudder.

I feel cold. That's a bad sign. He loosened his sword in its scabbard and continued in his just his fighting leathers.

He felt a mixture of trepidation and relief when he realized that the Dhargots were making no effort to hide their presence, though little could be done to conceal an army of ten thousand men. Shade could hear the drunken laughter of Dhargothi soldiers mingling with the cries of women being raped. He also heard what sounded like a single man screaming in pain.

How did we ally ourselves with such people? Shade shook his head. Resisting the urge to turn around, he rested one hand on the hilt of his sword. The sounds grew louder, especially those of the screaming man. An hour later, in the thickening blue-black haze of twilight, he spotted the first two sentries. Both wore scale armor decorated with tassels of black silk. One leaned on a spear. The other leaned on a stake, onto which a naked man had been impaled. Like the sentries, the impaled man had painted eyes and a braided goatee. He was weeping in agony, pleading for help. The sentries laughed.

Must be a deserter.

Shade stepped behind a tree, glad his superior Sylvan vision had allowed him to spot the sentries before they saw him. Crouching low, he slipped from one tree to the next. When he ran out of trees, he surveyed the twenty feet of snowy grass separating him from the sentries. He came up with three options: he could circle around them; he could step out from hiding, present himself to them, and demand that they take him to see Prince Ziraari; or he could kill them. He tapped the hilt of his sword.

The sentry leaning against the stake munched on an apple. When he was done, he threw the core at the impaled man's head. Though the impaled man hardly seemed to notice, the other sentry laughed then quickly flipped his spear and jabbed the impaled man in the ribs. Blood spurted from the wound. The man screamed but did not die. Shade realized the wound had not been intended to kill but merely to add to the man's torment.

Not that he can suffer any more than he already is.

Shade felt an unexpected pang of pity. True, the man was a Dhargot and had probably visited this same agonizing death on others, but his cries rang out in the encroaching night, piteous and shrill—a warning to any who dared defy their prince.

The same prince I intend to ask for help. Shade straightened, took a deep breath, and stepped out from hiding. He approached with open hands raised. The sentries spotted him at once. The one with the spear leveled it at Shade's chest while the other fumbled to retrieve a crossbow.

"No need for that," Shade said in Common-tongue. "I am a friend of Dhargoth... and of your prince." Hiding the fresh surge of exhaustion it caused, he summoned violet tongues of wytchfire, letting them course along his arms before sending them away. Both sentries backed up, awed. Shade was glad the one had not loaded the crossbow yet, or else he might have shot him by accident.

"My name is Shade, champion of Fadarah, the one you call the Sorcerer-General. I have drank the Red Emperor's wine and shed more blood than both of you combined, times ten. If you have any sense, you'll lower those weapons and take me to your prince. *Now.*"

The sentries exchanged glances. The weapons came down. Both men kneeled.

"Your excellency," one said.

"Great one," said the other, "we will take you to see Prince Ziraari."

Shade resisted the impulse to order them back onto their feet, marveling that they would bow before a creature they probably mistrusted and would like to kill, if only for the challenge.

"Good. Be quick about it. The prince and I have urgent business to discuss."

The sentries exchanged a quick, hushed word. Then the one with the spear said, "Avaaji will take you to the prince, Excellency. I must keep my post."

Avaaji bowed. "It will be my honor." He fit his foot into the stirrup and spanned his crossbow before loading a bolt. Then he gestured for Shade to walk in front of him.

Biting back a smirk, Shade shook his head. "After *you*, sentry."

Avaaji blinked. "Pardon, Excellency, but I must protect you. These lands are dangerous, full of Lochurite berserkers and Noshan raiders. It's a quarter mile to the prince's tent. If anything harms you, the prince will see I end up like this one!" He hooked his thumb at the weeping man on the stake beside him.

"Oh, I think this one can watch our backs just fine." Shade forced a smile and nodded at the other sentry.

The sentry with the spear did not return the gesture. "Please let Avaaji protect you, Excellency. It's our duty and honor to do so." He tightened his grip on his spear.

Shade forced a smile. "As you wish." He took a step. As he was passing Avaaji, he drew his sword, spun around, and flicked his blade over the sentry's throat. Avaaji's eyes widened. A gurgle passed his startled lips.

Shade felt a familiar exhilaration within him at the sight of blood. He thought of all those Humans he'd killed years ago to avenge the death of a Shel'ai friend. He thought of all the Humans he'd killed since. Shaking off a rush of bloodlust, he reached out and slapped the crossbow before Avaaji could fire it. The arrow flew by and vanished in the darkness.

The other sentry howled. Shade cursed at the noise. Using Avaaji as a shield, grasping the man by a necklace of dried ears that hung around his neck, Shade raised one hand, fingers splayed. Wytchfire burst forth, catching the other sentry full in the chest, bearing him down.

Shoving a dying Avaaji to the ground, Shade approached the other sentry, scanning for reinforcements. He half expected to see a squad of Dhargots charging toward him. Instead, he saw only darkening, snowy fields.

They probably just thought it was the impaled man screaming.

At that moment, though, the impaled man had fallen silent. Shade wondered if he'd died or was merely stunned by what he'd seen. Shade could not see his face in the darkness as he attended to more pressing matters.

The sentry he'd struck with wytchfire had been badly burned but was not dead. The man fumbled for his spear. Shade stepped on his hand and knelt, pressing the edge of his bloody sword to the man's neck.

"You meant to kill me. Why?"

The sentry's painted eyes swam with fear and pain. "The prince gave orders. Kill any sorcerer on sight. He said that himself."

So much for our alliance.

"You said it's a half mile to the camp?"

The man tried to look at his own scorched chest to inspect the wound, but Shade pressed with his sword, forcing the man to meet his gaze. The sentry nodded. "Half mile. Lots of guards, though. Palisades and traps, too. I can show you the way, if you use that fancy magic to heal me!"

Shade scanned his surroundings again. "Thank you. But I can manage." He dragged his sword across the sentry's throat then wiped it on the man's sleeve before sheathing it. He heard a whimper from the impaled man. Shade straightened, took a deep breath, and let it go. His breath fogged in the air.

That was too close. This isn't going to work. I should just get out of here.

He picked up the fallen sentry's spear and turned in the direction of the camp. As he passed the impaled man, he thrust the spear up under the man's ribs, as high as it would go, and left it there. He thought he heard the man gasp *thank you* before he died.

Shade shuddered, wishing he had not left his cloak behind.

A night breeze blew a fresh misting of snowfall into Shade's face as he crept toward the camp. He stopped often to crouch behind a tree and listen for sentries, using his magic to heighten his senses. Twice, exhaustion made him retch. Still, he avoided two more sentries before he almost ran straight into a third. Cursing himself, Shade pressed his fingertips to the man's forehead just as the Dhargot's eyes widened and he fumbled for a sword. In his weakened state, Shade could produce only a single jolt of magic straight into the Dhargot's brain: enough to merely render the man unconscious. Shade caught the man's body and lowered it quietly to the snowy ground. He hesitated.

If I don't kill him, he'll wake up in less than an hour. Or else he'll be discovered before that. Then again, if I can't convince Ziraari to help us, I'm never getting out of here alive, anyway.

Shade decided to let him live. He crept on. He was close enough to the camp that the reek of charred meat and filth overwhelmed him. The cold made him curse his own foolishness for discarding his cloak instead of simply turning it inside out to conceal the sigil of greatwolves. Dismissing the magic that heightened his senses, he continued until he spotted a great sea of campfires ringed by a trench and a palisade. He heard more drinking and the protests of savaged women. He touched his sword hilt again.

Despite the foul merriment within the camp, plenty of guards strolled about, armed and armored. A few crude bridges that led over the trench and through gaps in the palisade were heavily patrolled and lit by torches. He considered trying to crawl through the trench and climb the palisade then reminded himself that the trench was probably full of caltrops. The wooden stakes of the palisade glistened in the torchlight, probably smeared with animal fat to make them more difficult to climb.

Shade crouched behind a tree to consider his options. If he'd had time to rest and recover his strength, he might have used his magic to confuse one or two sentries, but that was impossible in his current state. And he had no hope of fighting his way in.

He considered giving up. Then he remembered the sentry he'd incapacitated earlier. He doubled back and found the man still unconscious. Careful to watch for other sentries, Shade stripped off the man's armor. He fumbled wearily with the buckles and straps, unaccustomed to handling armor—let alone armor that was too big for him. Moments later, though, he figured he made a passable Dhargot. He ungirded his own sword and took the Dhargot's weapons. He took the Dhargot's helmet, which was uncomfortable and too big for him, but at least it covered his tapered ears.

So long as nobody looks too closely and sees the color of my eyes, I should be fine.

He returned to the palisade. This time, he forced himself to walk out in the open. He tried to lumber, approximating a Human's gait. He waved lazily to the sentries as he approached. They hardly acknowledged him. Shade crossed the crude bridge and passed through the gap in the palisade. His heart leapt into his throat, but he forced himself not to slow down or grip his weapon.

"See anything out there?"

Shade turned to the speaker, glad it wasn't an officer. "Just what I left in the snow. Still out there if you want it, though it's probably frozen by now."

The Dhargot laughed and waved him on. Shade quickened his pace, grateful he'd been around Humans enough to emulate their accent. He passed a campfire, beside which two men were drinking wine while a third had his way with a naked, dirt-covered woman. The woman's eyes were without spark, as though she'd long since given up. One of the men offered Shade some wine.

Shade forced himself to smile as he waved them off. As he passed, the woman's eyes met his. If she noticed their violet color, she gave no indication.

Fighting back pity, Shade made his way through a stinking sea of tents toward the center of the camp. Though he was careful to keep his eyes down in order to avoid eye contact, it was impossible to miss all the standards jammed into the ground. Most depicted the Dhargothi sigil of a dragon impaled on a bloody spear, but others, also done in black and crimson, showed a flexing naked warrior with an enormous phallus. He concealed a sneer.

Ziraari the Potent, indeed.

When he reached a tent thrice the size of the others, wreathed by its own trench and palisade, he knew he'd reached his destination. He circled the tent slowly, pretending to be bound for elsewhere. He counted ten guards—too many to kill. He doubted he could bluff his way in, either.

Cursing, he returned to searching the camp. Soon, he found another tent that was bigger than the others but still smaller than Ziraari's, with a gaudy standard showing the impaled dragon planted beside a tent flap sewn with brass toggles. Only two guards stood outside.

An officer. A general, maybe.

Nodding, he searched the camp a third time before he found what he needed: a cart heaped with sacks of grain. The cart had already been fixed to a mule but abandoned, as though the driver had wandered off and gotten drunk. Shade climbed into the cart as casually as he could, grateful for the chance to sit, and drove the cart back toward the second large tent. He stopped the cart at the rear of the tent. Luckily, the guards either did not hear him or did not care. Still, he wandered off, in case anybody else happened to be looking.

He waited at least a quarter of an hour then circled back. Using the cart as a shield to block what he was doing, he crouched, drew his sword, and cut his way into the tent. He stepped in, sword drawn. His Shel'ai senses allowed him to see as well as an animal. He spotted a single sleeping Dhargot inside the dark tent. The man was snoring, probably drunk. Shade approached him stealthily, covered his mouth, and cut his throat. The man's eyes widened.

Sheathing his sword, Shade looked at his hands, shaking in the dark. Then he washed off the blood using a nearby water basin and searched the tent for the dead man's armor. When he found it, he removed his borrowed armor as quietly as he could and donned the officer's armor. It looked more impressive but was also more complex, with a frustrating overabundance of buckles. He guessed the general often had extra help. When he thought he had it right,

Shade threw a black silk cape over his shoulders and fixed the dragon-shaped clasp beneath his throat.

The general's helmet was an equally extravagant thing with a high, sharp crest exploding into a weave of black-and-crimson plumes and precious stones lining the nose-guard. The helmet reeked of sweat, but he put it on anyway. Then he slipped out the slash in the tent, back into the camp.

Ziraari's tent was well lit and smelled of lamp oil and strong wine. A bear of a man, naked and muscular, the prince stood before a table, studying a stack of reports. He did not look up as Shade entered. The guards had not challenged him, but they were still just one shout away. Careful to keep his eyes low, Shade approached the Dhargothi prince, bowed, and removed his helmet. He waited until Ziraari looked up.

"If you scream, I'll burn you to cinders."

To Shade's surprise, Ziraari answered with a cold sneer. "Ziraari never screams out of fear. Only when he runs out of enemies or women does he scream." Ziraari straightened, not bothering to cover himself, and crossed his strong arms. "You are the one who calls himself Shade. Haven't seen you in years. You've grown balls of solid brass since then, to come into my camp like this." He looked Shade over. "I trust General Cafaari is dead, since you wear his armor. How many more did you kill?"

"Two sentries and a deserter."

"My thanks for the deserter, but you should have let him suffer." Ziraari looked down at the table, openly eyeing a ruby-encrusted bastard sword. "You really think you can burn me before I cut your head off?"

"Whether or not we find out depends on you."

Ziraari's grin said he approved of Shade's answer. "You look tired, Sorcerer. I think you burned through whatever dragonmist you had getting in here. I don't think you have enough strength left to kill me. But talk, if that's why you're here. Ziraari will listen."

Caught off guard, Shade asked the first question that occurred to him. "Why did your men attack me?"

"Because I told them to."

Shade raised one eyebrow. "Forgive me, Prince. I was hoping for a little more detail."

Ziraari uncrossed his arms. Shade tensed, but instead of reaching for the sword, the prince picked up a nearby goblet of wine and took a sip. "We hear the sorcerers lost at the Wytchforest. Weak and desperate now. Why waste lives helping them?"

So much for honor. "There's no way you could have heard about our defeat this quickly."

Ziraari grinned again. "I didn't need to hear anything. I knew you'd lose. And even if you didn't, you'd be weak after all that fighting. My dear brother Karhaati"—he stopped to spit on the floor—"said I should help you fight the Sylvs. I decided not to. Is that clear enough?"

All too clear. Shade changed tactics. "Forgive me for being blunt, Prince Ziraari, but your brother sent you here to die. We both know that." Shade waited, but Ziraari's face betrayed nothing. "He wanted to get rid of a rival. You chose not to waste your strength and risk your life by helping us. That was a wise move. Attacking us was not."

Ziraari took another sip of wine, set down the goblet, and crossed his arms again. "Dhargots like a challenge. And they gave us one."

"Who are you talking about?"

Ziraari frowned. "Those others. The four. Three men and the pretty woman with short black hair. Never met a Shel'ai with dark hair before." He laughed. "The woman wouldn't talk, but the men did. That's how we knew, too."

Shade clenched his fist; tendrils of wytchfire sputtered between his fingers. Before the final battle at Shaffrilon, a Shel'ai woman named Zeia, one of Fadarah's oldest allies, had deserted. Three other Shel'ai had gone with her. Rather than kill them for their defiance, Fadarah had simply let them go. In all the chaos, Shade had forgotten them. *Four Shel'ai might have made the difference at Shaffrilon.* "Where are they?"

Ziraari drew back a step. "Three are dead. Cost me eighteen men to put them down, but by the Dragongod, it was worth it! Such a sight—"

"And the fourth?"

"The woman. My new pet. Two arrows in her pretty white skin, and still, she spurted fire when we threw her in the hole." He smiled with cold admiration. "I've never bedded a Shel'ai before. But we'll let her starve a little first. Ziraari doesn't want his cock burned off." When Shade said nothing, Ziraari frowned. "Aren't they why you come?"

Shade steadied his nerves. "I'm going to do something I usually don't do, Prince. I'm going to tell you the truth. I'm here because Fadarah is dying. A so-called Isle Knight cut him open at Shaffrilon. We need your help to get him back to our stronghold near the Wintersea."

Ziraari blinked. "We should play dice sometime, Sorcerer. If you survive, that is."

Shade caught his meaning but doubted that Ziraari would send half his army to scour the Wintersea when he was already in the middle of a war. "I speak the truth so that you'll know you can trust what I am about to say next." He paused for effect. "Karhaati wants you dead."

"He does?" Ziraari feigned shock then laughed. "You tell me what I already know."

"Call it a reminder, then. Karhaati is first in line to replace the Red Emperor when he dies, and from everything I hear, your youngest brother, Saanji, is no threat to anyone. You have ten thousand men with you, but they're all footmen. I saw hardly any horses and no elephants—"

"Damn Noshans poisoned my elephants. Unless it was Lochurites. Can't say. But both will burn."

Shade smiled coldly, heartened by the prince's display of emotion. "As I recall, Karhaati has a whole herd of armored elephants. Cavalry and chariots besides. Plus half a dozen conquered cities that he can bleed for wealth and slaves. And he has twice as many footmen as you do. If it comes to a fight, you'll lose."

Ziraari bristled but said nothing.

"You need all the help you can get. See us safely back to the Wintersea, and I'll kill Karhaati for you."

Ziraari studied Shade. "Ziraari has seen magic. He knows what it can do. It can't do that."

Shade smirked. "Magic got me into your tent, and I haven't even slept for two days."

The Dhargot picked up his goblet again. He seemed to be pondering this. Shade pressed his advantage. "Once Karhaati is dead, his army will flock to your banner. Even Saanji's men—"

Ziraari spat on the floor again. "Saanji's men are soft! Like him, they reject the Way of Ears. Like him, they deserve to die."

"Then you can kill him, too. And your father, once you get back to Dhargoth." Shade decided to take a chance. Reaching out, he picked up Ziraari's sword and handed it to the prince, hilt first. The rubies sparkled in the lamplight. "But first, Karhaati has to die. We can help you kill him. Or you can call your guards and gain nothing. Your choice, my prince."

Ziraari eyed the sword then took it. He held it as though testing its balance. Shade braced himself, hoping he had the strength to defend himself.

Surely, even if Ziraari accepted his proposal, he would turn on him as soon as Shade had outlived his usefulness. *But that will take time. If we can make it back to Coldhaven, if we can marshal what little strength we have left—*

Ziraari looked up, grinning suddenly. He reversed his jeweled sword and tucked the blade under one arm. He extended his other hand. "Ziraari accepts your proposal. Help me kill my brother, and I'll see you safely back to the Wintersea. I swear it on the Dead God."

Just as you swore to help us fight the Sylvs? Shade took Ziraari's hand, grasping the man at the wrist. He felt the Dhargothi prince's pulse beneath his fingertips and fought the urge to boil it with fire. "Agreed. One more thing, though." He tightened his grip. "Zeia. The Shel'ai woman you stuck in a hole. I want her back. Alive."

"Why, so you can bed her yourself?"

"So I can kill her."

Ziraari looked confused. Finally, he laughed. He picked up his goblet again. He drank until wine stained his braided goatee. "So be it. The bitch is yours." He called in his guards. "Wake my generals. Tell them the Shel'ai are our allies again. No one is to harm them. Then give this one an escort, fifty of my best men. They are to do whatever he asks. Any man who does otherwise will be impaled, on my orders." With a sidelong glance at Shade, he added, "Don't bother trying to wake General Cafaari. He sleeps with the Dead God tonight." Suddenly stoic, he upended his goblet, letting the final few drips of red wine fall to the ground.

CHAPTER TWO
GHOSTS

BRIEL SHOOK HIS HEAD AS he surveyed the destruction. Dawn filtered through the dense wytchwoods and illuminated the shattered remnants of the World Gate. His right arm hung in a sling, but he clenched his fist. The Sylvs, dead and wounded alike, had been carted away, but there had been no time to dispose of the slain Olgrym. Their great gray bodies lay everywhere, poised to rot. He breathed through his mouth to avoid the smell.

He glanced up at the sky, barely visible through the soaring branches of the World Tree, and wished it would rain. But he knew that any darkness in the heavens came not from an impending storm but from the lingering smoke of battle. He glanced at the phalanx of men and women following him. Some were bodyguards, but most were administrators, plus a few junior officers who had somehow survived the fighting. All looked exhausted.

But not as tired as the men guarding those damn broken gates.

He turned to face the World Gate again. Though the gates themselves had been hacked and burned to pieces, a line of Sylvan swordsmen still stood where the gates had been, as motionless as forsaken statues. Archers stood watch from above, enough to shred an entire company of enemies. He wondered if they were enough.

Though Fadarah had been killed and the Shel'ai driven back, many Olgrym had survived. So had Doomsayer. Scouts reported that the Olgish chieftain was still close by, marshaling what remained of his forces. Given all that had happened, Briel doubted the Olgrym could conquer Shaffrilon without Fadarah's help.

But does Doomsayer know that?

"We need more fighters here," he called over his shoulder. "And before anybody tells me there aren't any, I suggest you go look. Our brothers and sisters will have died for nothing if Doomsayer sleeps in the king's palace tonight."

An uneasy murmur accompanied the sound of footsteps. By the time he turned around, half the administrators had disappeared. Briel could tell they were not used to taking his orders. He could not blame them. Briel had only been appointed captain of the Shal'tiar a few days ago—though he'd held the post long enough to realize there could not be more than a dozen Shal'tiar left alive. The surviving Wyldkin had already deserted, presumably to return to the Ash'bana Plains to see if they could salvage something of their home villages. Briel might have stopped them, but he had no desire to punish those who had already sacrificed defending Sylvos.

The rest of his fighters were hastily armed civilians, almost none of whom had even known Briel before the attack. They might have gladly followed Seravin, but the renowned Sylvan general had fallen in battle. Not only had he been stabbed by an Olgish blade as he tried to defend the World Gate, it was said that Doomsayer himself had laughingly cut off both of Seravin's hands before castrating him.

If Seravin survives the day, it'll be a miracle. Or a curse.

That left Briel in charge of the Sylvan armies—and the city, since they could no longer rely on the king. He tugged at the strap securing his broken arm, then with his good hand, he tapped his new signet ring against the pommel of his sword. He considered breaking down the door of the king's bedchamber and dragging him out, but he reminded himself that only the day before, the king had watched his only son burned alive. Even before that, the king's sanity had been unraveling. Did they really want Loslandril on the throne, anyway?

But who does that leave? Me?

Briel laughed before he could stop himself. Sobering his expression, he turned. He gestured to his bodyguards. "You, men, join those others at the gates. And someone see that these men at the gates get water and food. If any man survives the Olgrym and the Shel'ai only to die of thirst, I'll be very unhappy." He glanced back up the Path of Crowns. "I'm going back to the House of Healing to check on our wounded. If there's any other business that doesn't involve Doomsayer on our doorstep, it can wait."

He started back up the walkway without waiting for a reply.

The House of Healing looked nearly identical to the House of Questions, wherein for centuries, strategies had been planned and prisoners interrogated—a fact that Briel noticed for the first time as he ascended the steps and passed a line of pillars and statues.

Did they really carry all the wounded up these steps?

He shook his head and resisted the impulse to order them demolished and replaced by a more accessible ramp. Once inside the sprawling marble structure, he returned the salutes of two guards with a quick nod, then simply followed the screams.

He passed more statues of gods and goddesses—Tier'Gothma, Armahg, Maelmohr, and Dyoni—before he paused beside one devoted to Zet. Portrayed as a fierce, haughty warrior in draconian armor, his six wings angled gracefully from his back. Briel wondered if the sculptor had thought to leave gaps in the armor or if the wings were part of the armor itself. He scowled up at the statue.

I don't know if you ever even lived, but if so, it's a fine damn mess you left for us.

Composing himself, he pressed on. The wounded were being tended in a great, sprawling chamber that reeked of filth and decay. Briel pinched his nose. He marveled that it could be worse inside than it was at the gates. Then he saw the cause: the chamber had no windows near the ground. The only windows in the entire chamber were the ornate, arrow-thin slits high on the arched walls.

Pretty, but useless… like most everything else here.

He forced himself to breathe, but the stench made him swoon. Resisting the impulse to retch, he studied the Sylvan clerics—all of them devoted not to the gods but to the Light—who rushed to and fro, tending the wounded and the dying. The chamber had long since run out of beds, and hundreds lay on the cold stone floor, bloody and shivering.

Briel's revulsion turned to pity. Clearly, the clerics were horribly outmatched. Used to treating just the occasional injury or mild bout of sickness, they had been forced to handle at least a thousand men whose bodies had been beaten, burned, or cleaved within an inch of death. Briel realized he should have forced the Wyldkin to stay, if only for their skill at treating wounds.

Nearby, a young, exhausted cleric probed a screaming man's wound with steel calipers while two other clerics tried to hold the man down. Seeing at once what was wrong, Briel hurried over.

"He says there's something in the wound, Captain," the cleric said. He paused to wipe blood from his face, onto his sleeve. "Must be an arrowhead, but I can't find it."

Briel gave the wide-eyed patient a piteous look. "Can't be an arrowhead. Olgrym don't use arrows." He gently pushed the cleric aside and took his place. He gripped his own tunic with the hand of his broken arm so that the arm would stay in place as he leaned forward, probing the outside of a ghastly rend in the man's side. The man whimpered. "Gods, didn't you give him any blood-tea for the pain?"

The cleric held up his bloody hands helplessly. "We have run out, Captain. Almost no herbs left, either. And we barely have enough wine to clean the wounds."

Briel shook his head but said nothing. He pressed the man's flesh a moment longer then nodded. "There's nothing in there. He's just mad from fever. Don't use boiled wine on this one. Boil water, then let it cool—but not much. Don't sew him up, either. The wound's already infected. Cover it with clean linen and let it seep."

And watch him die before sundown.

The clerics nodded.

"I'll see if I can find you more herbs," Briel promised. As he stepped back, he nearly collided with several more clerics who were hauling out straw pallets piled with corpses.

Gods, if Silwren were here—

"If Silwren were here, she could have healed these people herself," said a voice behind him.

Briel turned. "Are you reading my mind, Locke?"

The burly, smartly armored Human with unruly red hair blinked in surprise. The Isle Knight moved one hand to the long dragonbone hilt of the curved sword hanging at his side. Briel wondered if Rowen was about to attack them. Then he realized what the gesture really meant.

Silwren was still with them, in a sense. Somehow, she'd fed herself into that sword. She awakened whatever ancient magic had been buried there, allowing Rowen to cut clean through Fadarah's armor and win the battle.

Too bad that sword can't heal as well as it burns.

Before Rowen could answer, Briel said, "I sent your damn messages, by the way. Atheion, Lyos, Sorocco, Ivairia, Stillhammer, Quesh, and the Lotus Isles. I even thought about sending a copy to Dhargoth! Honestly, though, I'll be surprised if even half of the birds make it there."

Rowen frowned. "You sent birds? I told you to send messengers."

"Have you seen what happened to my army, Knight? I can't spare the men. You're lucky I risked the damn birds."

"How will they even know their way? I thought your people hadn't communicated with the other kingdoms for centuries!"

"We haven't, but these are wytch-ravens. The Dragonkin bred them long ago. Each chick is born knowing all the routes of its brood. Trust me, Knight, our ravens know the way. But that won't help if a predator or some hungry fool with a bow shoots them down."

"Thank you," Rowen said finally. "The people need to be warned."

"That a Dragonkin named Chorlga has declared war on Ruun?" Briel laughed. "Even if the birds arrive, whoever reads the messages will think it's a joke."

"Some will. Some won't."

Briel shrugged. "I see you found your armor." As he spoke, he scowled at the two Sylvan warriors behind Rowen, assigned as much to act as Rowen's handlers as his bodyguards.

"In the king's wine cellar," Rowen answered.

Briel almost laughed but stopped when the gesture hurt the stitches in his cheek. "You picked a fine time to grow thirsty."

"I was fetching casks for your healers." Rowen looked around. When next he spoke, Briel strained to hear him over the surrounding cries. "Haven't your clerics ever tended the wounded before?"

"Not like this. The clerics we had at Que'ahl had plenty of experience, but the Olgrym killed most of them. We have enough healing lore to fill ten libraries, but nobody thought to stockpile herbs and medicines."

"Remind me to have a word with whoever was in charge of this city's defenses."

"Let's see. That would either be General Seravin, who will likely die within the hour, or the king and his son—one of whom is mad, the other burned to death by—" He stopped himself from speaking Silwren's name. "By your friend."

Rowen gave him a cold look. "I learned a few things on the Isles. Enough to clean and sew wounds, at least. Since there doesn't seem to be anybody to kill at the moment, at least let me do what I can to help here."

Briel hesitated then nodded. "I can't do much with a broken arm, but I'll join you. Maybe we can even do some good. But take that pretty armor off first, unless you want to see it soaked in blood."

By sundown, Briel felt as though he had spent the entire day fighting for his life. He glanced over at Rowen, saw the Human's face awash with sweat and splattered with Sylvan blood, and wondered if the man felt the same. With only one arm, Briel could not sew wounds, but he could still bring water and blankets to the wounded. Though he had never been one to whisper words of comfort, his presence alone seemed to hearten them. After a few hours, the cries seemed not so loud.

Is that because we made a difference or just because the worst ones died?

Rowen was tending a young woman with a savage cut above her breast, probably from an Olgish axe. Unlike the other wounded in the crowded temple, this woman gritted her teeth and said nothing. Her plain attire and the feathers in her hair told Briel that she was a Wyldkin. As he drew nearer, he heard Rowen whispering to her in Sylvan.

I forgot he could do that. Some spell wrought by one of his Dragonkin friends had taught him their language.

Rowen had rolled up his sleeves, but blood covered him up to the elbow. Briel wondered how many battles the young Human had seen. Rowen had been wounded, but all of those wounds seemed to have vanished when Knightswrath came to life. Briel shuddered, remembering violet fire pouring from the blade, engulfing Rowen's body. Rowen had screamed then—though in pain or panic, Briel did not know. Since then, though, Rowen had worn the sword without any ill effect. He had even drawn it, holding it in the sun after Fadarah fell, without any flames appearing along the blade.

Maybe the damn sword's gone to sleep again. Silwren had poured her power, her very life, into Knightswrath. He wondered again if it could heal, too.

Briel studied Rowen's expression—if the sword could heal, Rowen had no idea how to use it. In fact, Rowen had seemed in a trance when he'd fought Fadarah. For all they knew, Rowen was nothing more than the pawn of a living piece of steel. And that made him as dangerous as that Dragonkin, Chorlga. They should kill him—or at least take the sword.

But what if Chorlga comes back? What if Fadarah's not really dead?

Briel considered the second matter first. He'd seen Rowen use a burning sword to cut a swath in Fadarah's body almost the length of a man's arm. Fadarah's disciples had carried him off, probably to try and heal him, but the Shel'ai were not Dragonkin. Their magic was impressive but not limitless. If Fadarah had not died right away, he would soon enough.

"Let's hope so." Rowen straightened, covered the Wyldkin woman with a blanket, said goodbye in Sylvan, and started to walk away.

Briel followed. The two guards assigned to watch over Rowen fell in behind them. Briel ordered them to wait. Racing after Rowen, he caught him by the arm and jerked him to a halt.

"You *can* read minds! That sword—"

Rowen twisted free with a look so icy that Briel drew back a step and reached for his sword, glad he'd learned to fight with his left as well as his right hand.

"I… don't know," Rowen said at last. "I can't control it. It just happens." He rubbed his eyes—still *green* eyes, Briel noted.

Green, not purple. He's still Human. For now.

Rowen shook his head, and Briel wondered if he'd just heard his thoughts again. "The sword did something to me when… when it burned me. It didn't make me into a Shel'ai. Not quite. That much is obvious. But Knightswrath's part of me now." He glanced down at the sword, and Briel could not tell whether his expression was longing or revulsion. "I can feel Silwren in there, sometimes. Don't ask me to explain it, because I can't. But I have to be careful—almost the way Silwren had to be careful." He smiled weakly. "She was always afraid to use the power because she said it would overwhelm her. I think I understand now."

Briel stared at him. *Gods, he's gone as mad as the king,* he thought before he could stop himself. "What are you going to do?"

Rowen straightened. "I have to finish this. I don't think Fadarah poses any harm now, but I have to hunt down the others—especially Shade. And I have to find that Dragonkin, the one called Chorlga. I have to kill him, if I can. And I have to do it all before… whatever this is… burns me from the inside out." He looked up sharply.

Briel gasped. For a moment, he thought the pupils of Rowen's eyes had gone white, though he convinced himself it was just a trick of light from the surrounding luminstones.

"Can I count on your help?" Rowen asked.

Briel rested his good hand on the hilt of his sword. "What do you need?"

"I need you to let me leave. I need you to let me take Knightswrath and go after Chorlga." He hesitated. "And if I have to fight the Dhargots along the way, I need you to honor the Oath of Kin and give me an army."

Briel almost laughed, despite the stitches in his cheek. "You want to borrow my army, Locke? There it is." He pointed to the sea of injured bodies beyond them. "Even if I didn't have to protect Sylvos—which I do—I'd be lucky if I could muster two hundred swords right now. Last I heard, the Dhargots have tens of thousands. If it's help you need, go and ask the Isle Knights."

Rowen smirked. "Half the Isle Knights probably want me dead. And the other half couldn't care less what the Dhargots do to the Free Cities... or the Wytchforest, for that matter."

Briel caught his meaning. "If the Dhargots come here, we'll fight them as best we can. But I don't think they will. Neither do you."

"No," Rowen admitted. "I think they'll stick to the Free Cities for now. I think they'll pillage two thirds of the continent before the Isle Knights get involved. And by then, it'll be too late. And Chorlga... wherever he is, *what*ever he is... will sit back and laugh." He paused. "I think I came here for nothing."

The Isle Knight stood, exhausted and blood smeared, then went to reclaim his armor. Briel watched him go, glad that Rowen had not pressed him for an answer. After all, he was probably right.

I should let him leave, then. And he can take that damn sword with him.

But Sylvos was not yet safe. Doomsayer was still out there. Briel imagined the howls of protest when the people heard he'd sent away their greatest ally. He wondered if those would match the cries of protest if he let Rowen stay: a Human, an Isle Knight at that, tarnished by magic.

Briel thought back to Fâyu Jinn's tomb. Just days ago, King Loslandril and the late Prince Quivalen had made a bargain with Chorlga and tried to kill Silwren in exchange for the Dragonkin sparing the city. Silwren had been stabbed. Quivalen, mad, had struck her with some kind of wicked magical blade. She'd fallen, yet something, maybe Fâyu Jinn's ghost, had saved her.

The silent, towering figure in ancient armor had appeared out of nowhere to heal her, then vanished. It had all happened so quickly. Even at the time, Briel had scarcely believed his own eyes. Then the madness had increased tenfold.

Briel shuddered, thinking again of Rowen stumbling down the Path of Crowns after Silwren threw herself onto Knightswrath, after they watched her melt into the blade and set it on fire. Ragged, burning, he'd reminded Briel of the stories about the Nightmare. Was that really the man he was supposed to trust?

Apparently, Fâyu Jinn—or his ghost, at least—does.

Briel had gone back later and opened Fâyu Jinn's sarcophagus, eager but fearful to see what was inside. He'd found the armor that had appeared to have temporarily reanimated itself: the armor of an ancient Knight of the Lotus.

But it was smaller, just the size of an average man. With trembling hands, Briel had removed the Shao facemask, expecting to find a thousand-year-old skeleton staring back at him—or perhaps the open, laughing eyes of Fâyu Jinn himself. But the armor was empty.

Does that mean that on top of everything else, we have the ghost of some ancient Human hero wandering around our city?

CHAPTER THREE

THE LAST HOUSECARL

J ALIST DID NOT KNOW WHETHER to rejoice or curse the fact that the storms had finally stopped. He was tired of running through rain and mud, cold and wretched, as he fled his pursuers. However, his pursuers did not sleep or rest, and he was alive only because the mud slowed them down considerably. But now, the dark clouds had cleared, and the sun shone through the haze.

Jalist stopped to catch his breath. Ignoring the aching in his legs, he glanced southeast. Sure enough, the creatures, though built more for murder than pursuit, still followed him. Surging over a hill less than a half mile away, the broad glistening column resembled hundreds of footmen in full armor, their weapons perpetually drawn. Jalist forced himself to move.

For the better part of a week, thunderheads had raged over Stillhammer, unleashing deluge after deluge on the ravaged land. There was something unnatural about the storms, though Jalist had no notion whether they were evidence of the gods mourning the abject destruction of the Dwarrish homeland or just some byproduct of whatever foul magic had unleashed the Jolym.

He had no time to consider this. For the unliving warriors—voiceless and wrought entirely of metal—had also proved to be eerily skilled trackers. Jalist had thought first to lose them by circling around the mountain, counting on the rain to wash away his tracks. But the Jolym had not been fooled. Once, trusting that he was safe, he'd lain down to risk a few much-needed hours of sleep.

His instincts awakened him in the middle of the night to find a Jol hovering over him, blades welded to its fists. Like the one he'd fought days before, it had a sardonic grin carved into its face, as though it were wearing a dancer's mask wrought of iron. Jalist had already learned that the things were hollow—no mind to reason with, no flesh to injure. But he'd also discovered that they could be killed, if that was the word for it, by stabbing them through their dark, empty eyes.

Jalist had managed to do so to the one that had awakened him, but before it fell in a wrenching crash of metal, the Jol's hands—a hook and a hatchet—had cut him in three places. Jalist had managed to clean and bandage the wounds before the rest of the host appeared.

Since then, the Jolym had chased him over hills and plain, through villages that were home now to nothing but rotting corpses. Jalist did his best to avoid both looking at and smelling the remains of his kin. Still, from time to time, he wept.

"I should try to get to Tarator again." Jalist touched his weapons. Though he preferred axes and maces, which allowed him to make best use of his strength, such weapons were useless against Jolym.

Maybe that's why the Housecarls never stood a chance.

He'd armed himself with a brace of stilettos, a spear, and a shortsword he'd found in an abandoned house. The shortsword, probably a dead man's family heirloom, looked as though it had been forged for a woman. While Dwarrish blades were usually wide and heavy, this one was light and thin, practically a rapier, and it had already saved his life once.

Based on the destruction he'd seen, Jalist was certain now that the halls of Tarator had not been spared. Still, he longed to see the Dwarrish capital for himself, to see if any others had survived. Dwarrish tradition would not have permitted King Fedwyr to flee the enemy, so Jalist had no doubt that the old monarch lay among the fallen. Still, a few of the king's Housecarls might have been elsewhere when Stillhammer was invaded. Perhaps they'd even fled Tarator altogether, driven not to save their own skins but to protect someone else.

"Leander..."

The thought of the prince quickened Jalist's blood, bringing fresh tears to his eyes. He had yet to encounter even a single Dwarrish survivor. But the way to Tarator had been blocked by countless Jolym, hinting that they had already been there. Surely, his former lover could not have survived such a thorough slaughter.

Jalist took a drink from his canteen, examined his wounds, and turned southeast again. The Jolym were gaining. Using his spear as a walking stick, he pressed on.

By sundown, both the Stillhammer Mountains and the Red Steppes were miles behind him. The Simurgh Plains stretched before him, spotted with snow. Tugging at a cloak he'd taken off a corpse days earlier, Jalist marveled that the land could look so different. Within weeks, blizzards would replace the thunderstorms that had washed over Stillhammer. Jalist imagined snow falling on those quiet villages, burying the dead. He shuddered.

I have to keep going. There are villages a ways north of here. I'll get a horse and warn whoever else is there to run like hell. Maybe somebody can even get a message to Lyos or the Lotus Isles. But would anyone believe it? Jalist laughed, and a fresh rumbling in his stomach accompanied the sound.

Jolym had not been seen since the Shattering War. People in these parts had already suffered the Throng, the Nightmare, and the Dhargots. Would they believe Jalist's warning or wait until they saw the Jolym for themselves?

"They can damn well believe whatever they want. If they're foolish enough to stay behind, maybe they'll make it easier for me to get away." He remembered an old joke he'd heard as a child: "One does not have to be fast enough to outrun a greatwolf, just everyone else the greatwolf is chasing." He did not laugh, though. He wondered if anyone had already used that strategy to escape the devastation at Stillhammer.

Within an hour, he had reached a fishing village nestled against a modest river. Though he could remember the name of neither the village nor the river, he recalled passing through there years earlier with Rowen and Kayden Locke. He especially remembered a well-built, soft-eyed lad who ran the sawmill.

But silence hung thick between the empty cottages and modest shops. Jalist looked around and, to his relief, found no bodies. In fact, he saw nothing but a few wild dogs that, thankfully, kept their distance. The village had been abandoned in a hurry. Jalist doubted the people could have already heard about the Jolym so far north. He thought of the Dhargots and wondered if they'd progressed even farther east than he'd thought.

He went down to the river and found a little boat abandoned in the reeds. "Well, it's no horse, but it beats walking." He searched the village again, salvaged a skin of wine and dried fruits from an empty tavern, and returned to the boat. He looked south. By the light of Armahg's Eye, he saw a broad, glistening arm of stars writhing across the plains in his direction, moving low against the ground. He stared, momentarily awed by the strange sight. Then he shook himself.

No, not stars—unliving, metal men who want to slice me into little pieces. But something tells me the bastards swim even worse than I do.

Jalist took a long swig of wine. Even though he knew they could not possibly see him, he raised one fist and made a rude gesture in the Jolym's direction. Then he climbed into the boat, grabbed the oars, and pushed off.

Though Jalist could not imagine anybody was close enough to hear him, he was careful not to lift the oars out of the water once he began paddling. He began sweating fiercely beneath his cloak, but he knew better than to slip it off and breathe in the cold night air. The last thing he needed was to get sick while he was already fleeing for his life.

He wondered where he should go next. He wanted to hurry west so that he could find Rowen Locke and warn him what he'd seen, but Rowen was on the opposite end of the continent. Jalist would need a horse and supplies to reach him. Like many sellswords, he'd hidden small caches of coins and weapons in various hiding places around the Simurgh Plains, but all were too far away.

Besides, even if he evaded the Jolym then bought or stole a horse, riding straight west was suicide. Since he'd parted ways with Rowen, the Dhargots had spread across more than half of the Simurgh Plains, conquering Free Cities left and right. The coming winter might have slowed the Dhargots' conquest, but to reach the Wytchforest, Jalist would still have to pass thousands of them. If he were lucky, they would only rob him. More likely, they would torture or kill him purely for sport.

He glanced northeast, wondering how far away the Lotus Isles were. As far as he knew, the Dhargots had not yet declared war on the Isle Knights. The Dhargots were bloodthirsty, but they weren't stupid. If Jalist were under the Knights' protection, the Dhargots might think twice about harassing him. Besides, the Knights would surely be interested to learn that an army of nearly unkillable creations had quietly decimated a nearby kingdom. If Jalist could convince the Knights that he was telling the truth, perhaps they would help him search for Rowen Locke.

After all, Rowen's a Knight! Then Jalist shook his head. *A Knight that half the other Knights want dead.* He thought of Crovis Ammerhel, the haughty Knight of the Lotus who wanted Knightswrath for himself. Jalist had met the man only once, outside the gates of Lyos, but that meeting had been enough to confirm all that Rowen had said about the man.

Jalist was still rowing when he thought of the last time he'd helped Rowen reach the Wytchforest; they'd tried to avoid the Dhargots by veering south, near Atheion, the City-on-the-Sea. Repeating that would be suicidal, given how they'd left the city. But south of Atheion lay the Southern Basin, home to the realm of Quesh, where nomadic tribes raised famously fleet red horses called bloodmares. The Queshi had always maintained passable trade relations with the Dwarrs. They might offer shelter to survivors of the Jolym massacre.

That's where I'll find Leander… if he's still alive.

Jalist grinned. If he could buy or steal a bloodmare, he could get to the Wytchforest by following the southern coast. The horse's speed might even make up for the time he would lose finding a ship to carry him down the eastern coast, past Stillhammer and the endless desert of Dendain. That would also save him from having to worry about Dhargots, Lochurite berserkers, Isle Knights, and any of a dozen other enemies.

But that still leaves the Jolym.

He looked over his shoulder. What he saw made him swear under his breath. Countless glints of steel swarmed along the shoreline. Jalist wondered if the Jolym would swim after him. Instead, their entire host seemed to have wheeled eastward, continuing their pursuit along dry land. He could not see them clearly in the darkness, but they spread out in the distance like a huge sea of steel. What he had first calculated to be a few hundred now seemed to number close to a thousand.

Gods, why are they still following me? He paddled faster.

Years before, he'd helped the Locke brothers escort a merchant to the Wintersea. The merchant had been half mad and poor, but the trip had given them an excuse to see a new part of Ruun. Rowen had even hoped they might see the Dragonward hugging the frozen shoreline; though, if it existed, it was as invisible as the legends claimed. But one day, near a spot of coast where the water was unfrozen, they'd seen something else: a great, terrible fish with fins and many teeth pursuing a much smaller fish, following it with dogged tenacity, ignoring closer prey that it might have caught more easily.

Jalist's hands white-knuckled his oar. He had the awful feeling that *he* was that little fish and the Jolym intended to pursue him with the bigger fish's same mad, hungry devotion. Cursing, he thrust the oar back into the water and pushed as hard as he could.

By the time the sun rose over the eastern hills, staining the grasslands like blood, Jalist had the sinking suspicion that he'd been wrong. The Jolym had either given up or had simply happened to be marching in his direction all along. He might have cheered, but something gnawed at him. Climbing a hill, he studied them in the distance. They were still a few miles behind him, but they had divided into two large steely masses. The larger half appeared to be marching northeast, turning unmistakably toward the Burnished Way.

"Guess I won't have to convince the Isle Knights." He studied the remaining force. There couldn't have been more than two dozen. *If those others are attacking the Isle Knights, where are these going?* He decided it made no difference. He had a plan.

Descending the hill, he hurried westward. Three hours later, he watched from his hiding place in a copse of trees, heart racing, as the Jolym shambled past. He breathed a sigh of relief when they were gone. It would be easier to reach the coast now. From there, he could head south, skirting Stillhammer and the desert, and head into Quesh as he'd intended.

Jalist continued to watch the smaller force of Jolym as they marched north, until they were out of sight. He had a good idea where they were going. He imagined what the Jolym would do once they reached Lyos.

That's Rowen's city. He just risked his hide saving them from the Throng. Now, the Jolym will tear it to pieces.

He'd been able to count the Jolym as they passed. Of the eighteen, most appeared to have been wrought entirely of iron, though three were blinding bronze. All the Jolym had blades in place of hands. Their dark eye sockets reminded him of cold charcoal.

Jalist swore. Under other circumstances, he might have laughed at the thought of eighteen warriors doing much damage to a well-fortified city, but he'd already seen what the Jolym could do. Besides, he doubted anyone in Lyos knew the Jolym's weakness, which he'd discovered by accident.

I don't have time for this. I have to find Rowen. And Leander.

He rubbed his eyes. "And I'd appreciate a gods-damned nap and some breakfast!" But he realized he would get neither. Turning north, he set out at as fast a pace as he could manage.

CHAPTER FOUR
RIPPLES

C HORLGA SLUMPED AGAINST THE WEATHERED stone of Namundvar's Well. He shook from exhaustion, his eyes clenched tight. Still, he grinned. It had taken hours, but it was over. Even though he had not yet beheld the fruits of his victory, he'd done it. Even the mighty Nekiel had never dared to attempt such a feat.

Of course, I had help.

He almost laughed. Opening his eyes, he slowly pushed himself up and looked around. For a moment, he wished he were somewhere else—outside under the open sky or, better yet, under the cooling shade of wytchwood trees—rather than deep in the dank vaults of Cadavash, surrounded by dead dragonpriests. By the flickering glow of a hundred candelabra, he saw them littering the cold chamber floor all around him.

Young and old, male and female alike, all the dragonpriests lay on their backs, eyes wide and mouths agape in expressions of ghastly euphoria. Though damp with sweat, their green robes showed no sign of injury. But Chorlga could sense the lingering psychic shadow of their last moments, their final screams of pain and triumph.

He returned his attention to the task at hand: determining the whereabouts of the Dragonkin he'd just resurrected. Chorlga had hoped the dead man would simply materialize in Cadavash, right next to him. On more than one occasion, Chorlga had seen the freshly dead brought back to life by Dragonkin magic as a reward for valorous service.

But this was different. There had been no body. The Nightmare had been dead for months. In order to keep his mind malleable, it had been necessary to resurrect him as he had been—powerful but mad. That added an element of unpredictability to his resurrection. He might very well emerge anywhere, belched out by the Light. Chorlga had always been warned against resurrecting anyone who had been dead for too long, lest they leave too much of themselves behind. The Nightmare might be even more unpredictable than before.

Chorlga hoped he would not have to search the length and breadth of Ruun to find the Nightmare. Then again, the search would give him time to regain his strength and prepare himself for what was to come.

Chorlga swept his gaze over the chamber again. Though it appeared that all the dead were dragonpriests, he had to be sure. He had no idea what the Dragonkin looked like now. He hoped he would be able to sense him, but if the man were unconscious, that could be difficult. Slowly, carefully, Chorlga checked every one of the more than two hundred corpses in the chamber. But all were green cloaked, wide eyed, and lifeless.

Chorlga smiled. He'd absorbed many of these bone-worshippers when he reached Cadavash, building his strength, just as his kind had once drained the life force of dragons. Once he'd shown those who remained what he intended to do, they had sacrificed themselves without hesitation. Their willingness lent extra potency to their sacrifice, granting him even more power than he could have seized otherwise.

Still, their fanaticism unnerved him. Even at the height of the Dragonkin Empire, the Dragonkins' subjects had never worshipped them with even half as much fervor as these priests showed for dead dragons. Their madness had nearly overwhelmed him. Also, there had been the visions.

What happened to drive them to that kind of madness?

Chorlga rubbed his eyes. The visions still swirled through his mind: sensory fragments, brief images, and raw jolts of sound. He did not know if they were the result of his briefly augmented powers or just some kind of prophetic warning sent to him by the Light. Of course, he would have to sort through them, but that could wait until he'd recuperated.

Leaving the chamber that contained Namundvar's Well, Chorlga made his way to a set of stairs that led directly up to the surface. The stairs had been concealed behind a false wall, and the only footprints in the thick dust were his own.

Last night, he'd descended into Cadavash in the traditional manner, with a legion of sacrificial dragonpriests behind him. But he had no desire to traverse those same reeking, subterranean streets lined by self-mutilating worshippers and countless shrines devoted to dragonbone. He reckoned at least a thousand people were waiting up there, anxious for his return. With his heightened senses, Chorlga could feel their roiling need to serve him. They would kill or die for him. He was their emissary of dragons. They would wait hours, days, even weeks for his return. As far as Chorlga was concerned, they could wait forever—or until he needed another sacrifice.

For now, I have to find my Nightmare.

Chorlga started up the stairs then stopped and glanced back at Namundvar's Well. He felt something stir: a faint tingling in his senses that filled him with dread and guilt. He shook himself free of it. Gathering his strength, he ascended the long dark staircase as quickly as he could.

Long before he had a body, he felt the thick silence hanging over the corpse-filled chamber. It seemed to him that he existed everywhere in the chamber at once, that he had no flesh and thus no senses, yet he sensed everything. The fingers of light topping the candelabra flickered and gradually died, one by one, returning the room to darkness. The only sound was the occasional, especially loud lamentation from the dragon-worshippers filtering through the stone floors of the chambers above. The darkness thickened until it became like stone.

Then, something sparked to life.

Faint at first, a pale glow drifted up from the stone mouth of what appeared to be just an ancient, ordinary well. The glow intensified. Gradually, the chamber gave itself back to the light. Then he felt his body take shape.

Just a shadow at first, slowly the shadow took on substance, shaping him into a small man crumpled facedown next to the stone well. He stirred then lifted his head. Slowly, he pushed himself to his knees. The hood of his cloak fell. White light streaming from the well illuminated a face of twisted features, as though the small man's body were busy suffering every malady at once. Violet eyes blinked. And with the opening of his eyes, he collapsed entirely into his own body.

The pain was too great for him to scream. Slowly, mercifully, it subsided. With great effort, he pushed himself onto his feet.

"Chorlga—" He choked on his own speech, as though using it for the first time. "All these years we fought the Sylvs, the Humans, each other. Turns out we should have been fighting *you*. Only we didn't even know you existed." He shook his head. "Clever. So bloody clever, aren't you? But you didn't know, when you brought *him* back, that you'd bring *me* back, too."

As the small man smiled, he felt his face tense and strain like a cracking sunburn. "But you should have. I died with Iventine. We melted into the Light together, like two ripples of water."

The small man winced abruptly and fell against the mouth of the well. He clutched his chest as though his heart had burst. His breath came and went in wet, ragged gasps as though he were rediscovering how to breathe. "Gods, it hurts to live this long. I can't even imagine how it must be for *you*."

Eventually, the small man straightened, even as the glow streaming from the mouth of the well began to dim. His gaze passed over the corpses of the dragonpriests. He shook his head.

"So much life wasted on madness. So much time. Now, I'm here. And I can feel the Light slipping away from me the longer I stay. I can feel myself forgetting." He paused. "Silwren is gone. Fadarah will be dead, too, before long. I can feel them all slipping away." He eyed the dark stairwell in the distance. "And I'm still talking to myself. I guess some things don't change."

He turned and peered into the well. He stared for a long time. Finally, nodding to himself, he took a step. He almost fell but caught himself and took another, then another. Carefully, he picked his way through the tangle of corpses toward the stairs he knew Chorlga had taken.

The light streaming from Namundvar's Well continued to dim with every step he took. By the time El'rash'lin reached the stairs, the chamber had been plunged back into cold, blinding darkness. Even so, pressing his hands to the rough stone walls on either side of him, El'rash'lin climbed.

CHAPTER FIVE

COLUMNS

ONE HUNDRED KNIGHTS RODE ACROSS the Simurgh Plains, silent save for the jingle of armor and harnesses and the occasional rustle as the wind ruffled their cloaks and azure-blue tabards. Though the thin crust of snow slowed their pace, the Knights maintained their neat formation and steely composure.

Nevertheless, Aeko Shingawa could see their frustration in their terse scowls and the way they held their reins a bit more taut than necessary. She could hardly blame them. They should be back at Saikaido Temple, sipping tea or lotus wine in front of a fire, not slogging through cold, war-torn lands on what most of them regarded as a fool's errand.

But it isn't. Rowen needs our help... if he's still alive.

From her position at the head of the column, she looked over her shoulder again, wondering how many of the Knights would betray her before their mission was done. Any other time, that would have been unthinkable. Isle Knights were known for nothing if not their dutiful sense of honor. But times had changed. Aeko had done what she could to select trustworthy Knights, but for every Knight who genuinely respected her or Grand Marshal Bokuden, two favored Crovis Ammerhel. And Crovis wanted what Rowen had—Knightswrath.

But by the Light, he's not going to get it.

Aeko scrutinized her Knights. At least a fourth were women. Some carried long-bladed spears, but most only carried curved, long-handled swords and knives. None carried a shield, since the kingsteel glint of their armor made it clear that they had little to fear even from crossbow bolts.

All the Knights wore tabards bearing the sigil of a snow-white crane balancing on one leg. A handful wore the additional sigil of a white golden-horned stag. Those men rode ahead of the others, a bit haughty in the saddle. Like the lesser Knights behind them, the Knights of the Crane, nearly all of the Knights of the Stag had the dark eyes, olive skin, and braided, uncut hair common to natives of the Lotus Isles.

A few had the paler skin of mainlanders, but most of these had been admitted into the Order by virtue of their pedigree—their lineage could be traced all the way back to Fâyu Jinn's first roster of Isle Knights who had served during the Shattering War. Though thousands of mainlanders sought to enter the Knighthood and paid a large sum to be trained in the Knights' lore and the ancient Shao fighting styles, fewer than one percent of these ever actually became Knights.

We have to safeguard our precious ethnic purity, don't we?

Aeko shook her head, fighting back a derisive smile. She wished she had the ability to glean their thoughts at a glance, the way Shel'ai did. But she could only see what was obvious. With her, at the head of the host, rode just a half dozen Knights with a third symbol on their tabards: a white nine-petaled blossom with a golden center. She was the first female Knight of the Lotus in the history of the Order.

As far as the histories have been chronicled, that is.

In the past, the Order had not hesitated to amend—or outright burn—certain texts they deemed too controversial or dangerous. They had all but eradicated written traces of Fel-Nâya, Knightswrath, the tragically obtained sword that Fâyu Jinn had used to win the Shattering War.

Few Knights below the rank of Stag even knew about it beyond fairytales and rumor. The Council's official excuse for the secrecy was concern that a thousand starry-eyed Knights of the Crane might tear across the countryside, looking for a fabled sword that probably did not even exist. Aeko saw their point. Still, if anyone could remake the Order into what it was supposed to be, the way Fâyu Jinn had intended it to be, that was Rowen Locke. She glanced at the man riding next to her.

If I can keep Crovis from killing him.

Sir Crovis Ammerhel had done an admirable job of concealing his disdain. Grand Marshal Bokuden had promoted Aeko and given her formal command of the expedition—an unmistakable slight directed at Crovis—but Crovis knew better than to be too obvious with his scorn. Instead, he asserted himself in small ways. He rode just a little too closely and spoke just a little too cordially to be believable.

And, of course, he insisted on leaving the squires behind.

Aeko was more popular with the idealistic squires and younger Knights of the Crane. Normally, the Knights were accompanied by at least as many squires, giving Aeko an additional advantage. But Crovis had uncovered an obscure passage in the ponderous annals of the Codex Viticus that said an offending Knight could be arrested *only* by fellow Knights. He'd interpreted it to mean that Knights alone could go in search of Rowen. To her disappointment, her fellow Knights had agreed with him. The law was the law.

It won't matter, though. Once the Knights see Rowen Locke wearing the Sword of Fâyu Jinn, maybe marching at the head of a Sylvan legion of reinforcements, they'll fall all over themselves swearing allegiance.

She shifted uncomfortably in her armor. *At least, I hope so.*

The Knight of the Lotus took a deep breath to clear her mind and returned her attention to the task at hand. The column was making good time, already well away from the city of Lyos and halfway to Nosh. But the way was not nearly as safe as it had once been.

She spied a curl of smoke on the northern horizon. "The Bloody Prince must be preparing to winter at Cassica. Let's hope the bastard stays there."

Crovis's reply said he'd missed her meaning. "Have no fear, Lady Shingawa. The painted men wouldn't dare attack us."

Aeko answered with a smile. "Dhargots aren't known for being timid. You remember what Sir Royce said."

Crovis frowned at the mention of the Lancer captain they'd encountered at Lyos. "I wouldn't put much stock in the military prowess of an Ivairian."

Still, the Lancers had shed and spilled more blood fighting the Dhargots than the Knights had. "Either way, according to the last report, the Dhargots outnumber us by hundreds to one."

Crovis shrugged. "Skill counts more than numbers. Besides, even the Dhargots would never be so daft as to incur the wrath of the Lotus Isles when they're already in the middle of a war."

Aeko shivered as a sudden gust of wind blew a smattering of snowflakes between them. Crovis had said the same about Fadarah's army—right before the Shel'ai laid siege to Lyos. "I am privileged to have your expertise on this campaign—if *campaign* is the right word."

Crovis reached back and smoothed his dark braid with sun-weathered fingers. "As fine a synonym for *fools' errand* as any, I suppose."

Aeko decided to let that go. She eyed the horizon again, still half fearing that she might see the ghastly banners of the Bloody Prince thundering down on them. To her relief, the hours wore on without incident. By sundown, hungry and tired with frayed nerves, she called a halt.

Immediately, the Knights went to work, glumly going about tasks that would have otherwise been delegated to the squires. Some set up tents while others tended horses. Still others dug a trench all around the camp, while still more Knights fortified the trench with sharpened stakes. By the time they were finished, the tents had been erected, fires built, and a meager meal of rice and vegetables. The Knights ate in silence, still armored, swords close at hand. There was lotus wine, but even the most aggravated Knights knew better than to get drunk amid the possibility of battle.

Aeko made her way through the camp, letting all the Knights see her. She was careful to avoid appearing too friendly, lest they think she was desperate for their approval. She even scolded a Knight of the Crane for staring too long into his campfire, as that could hamper his night vision in the event of an attack. She had considered banning campfires altogether, but she knew the Dhargots were likely aware of their presence already. She stationed more sentries than usual and even sent a handful of Knights to patrol a half mile beyond the camp.

Not that a bit of advance notice will mean much difference if the Bloody Prince decides to march in force.

She had nearly completed her second walk through the camp when she spotted Crovis stalking toward her, his face taut. She interpreted his expression and hurried to meet him, one hand straying for her sword hilt.

"Lady Shingawa, I have been looking for you—"

"What's wrong?"

"A lone Dhargothi ambassador just arrived at the perimeter. He has requested the honor of addressing the leader of this company."

Aeko caught the subtle rebuke. "You say he came alone?"

Crovis nodded. "No bodyguards. Just one haughty bastard in silk."

For one rare moment, Aeko almost liked her rival. "Lead the way, Sir Ammerhel. Best not keep the haughty bastard waiting."

To Aeko's surprise, Crovis had already shown the ambassador to her tent. A newly minted Knight of the Crane who had been tasked with acting as her servant had given the man wine and a chair but otherwise loomed over him with arms crossed.

Aeko sized up the Dhargot. He was middle aged and short but thickly built. Like nearly all the Dhargothi men she had ever seen, he had a shaved head, painted eyes, and a braided goatee. He was armed with a matching dagger and shortsword, both inlaid with black pearls in the pommels. He wore scale armor and black silk, plus a ghastly necklace of human ears: trophies from enemies he'd killed.

Aeko counted six ears and smirked to conceal her revulsion. Rumor had it that Karhaati, the Bloody Prince, wore forty-seven ears—though if that had been true, Aeko figured he'd added a few pairs since then. She cleared her throat.

The Dhargothi ambassador turned, looked at her, and rose slowly, draining his cup. When the cup was empty, he passed it without looking to the Knight standing behind him. "Are you the one I've been kept waiting for?"

Aeko bowed slightly, wondering how much of the contempt in the man's speech came from his accent. "I am Aeko Shingawa, Knight of the Lotus and Knight-Captain of this host. Whom do I have the pleasure of addressing?"

The ambassador did not answer for so long that Aeko wondered if he meant to ignore her. Then he simply said, "Vaanti."

Aeko forced a smile. "And I trust that you were sent by Prince Karhaati."

The Dhargot took his time nodding. "The Bloody Prince sent me."

After a long silence, Aeko said, "And his message?"

"Just this: you are in our lands without permission. We Dhargots have no quarrel with the Isles. Leave at once, and the Bloody Prince will forgive your insult without bloodshed or demand for reparations."

Aeko could smell the stink of the man's breath, only thinly veiled by the sweet smell of lotus wine. She wondered if the man had deliberately chewed on an onion before coming to the camp. "Tell the prince I appreciate his generosity. No offense was intended. This is not an invasion. We are merely on a training exercise and did not know the Dhargothi Empire had extended its boundaries all the way to the heart of the Simurgh Plains. It seems I shall have to be better about consulting maps before I leave my keep."

Vaanti sneered, though she could not tell if it was in derision or grudging appreciation. "The Bloody Prince claims whatever lands he wishes. If you object, meet him on the field."

Aeko tapped her sword hilt. *Someday, perhaps, when I have more men with me.* "As I said, we're on a training mission, nothing more." She intended to leave it at that, but her eyes fell on Vaanti's ghastly necklace again. She wondered if any of those ears came from women. She lowered her voice. "Cassica is not a protectorate of the Lotus Isles. Until its people request our help, Karhaati has nothing to fear from us."

Vaanti looked surprised. Then he laughed. "Cassica's a pen for dogs! We took it in accordance with the Way of Ears, which has guided my people for two centuries. If you want it, come take it. The Bloody Prince would welcome the fight."

Aeko held up her hand. "We didn't come here for a fight. I told you—"

Out of the corner of her eye, Aeko saw a flash of steel. Before she could stop him, Crovis strode forward and pressed the edge of his adamune to the Dhargot's throat. Vaanti's eyes widened. He tried to back up but collided with the Knight of the Crane standing behind him.

Crovis said, "Pray that your beloved prince never meets an Isle Knight on the field, little man, or else the Red Emperor will have one less son to pay him homage."

Aeko hissed Crovis's name, but he did not answer. She eyed the other Knights, some of whom looked back at her with uncertainty, and wondered if she should have Crovis seized. She decided against it.

Meanwhile, all the fight had gone out of Vaanti's expression. The edge of Crovis's sword had already drawn a thin trickle of blood, though given the steadiness of Crovis's hands, Aeko figured that was deliberate.

She took a step forward and fixed Vaanti in her most withering stare. "On the Isles, threatening someone in their own home is considered extremely rude. I believe that's the lesson Sir Ammerhel was trying to demonstrate."

With the sword still pressed to his throat, Vaanti tried his best not to swallow. "I didn't threaten—"

"Maybe we misunderstood. If so, I hope you'll accept our apology and convey our peaceful intentions to your prince."

Crovis pressed his sword against Vaanti's throat for emphasis. A fresh trickle of blood ran down his neck.

The Dhargot said, "I will. Of course I will!"

"Good." Aeko touched Crovis's arm. To her relief, he stepped back, made a show of wiping his blade on his sleeve, then sheathed his sword with the faintest of smiles.

Aeko gestured to the Knight standing behind the Dhargot. "Sir Wei, give the ambassador another bottle of wine and show him to his horse."

As the visibly shaken Dhargot was being led out of the tent, Aeko noticed that the pearl-inlaid dagger was missing from his belt.

Crovis twirled it between his fingers then offered it to her with a slight bow. "Care for a souvenir, Knight-Captain?"

Only two other Knights remained in the tent, but Aeko dismissed them with a look. "I would prefer that my second-in-command not assert his ego by trying to start a war."

Crovis blinked then laughed. "I beg your pardon, Lady Shingawa, but it seems I'm more familiar with Dhargots than you are. That was no show of bravado. Their kind hate courtesy. Had he returned to the Bloody Prince with nothing but gifts and reassurances, there would be bloodshed within hours. This way, Karhaati will think we're bold. He'll respect us. With luck, he'll use his assault on the Free Cities as an excuse to give us a wide berth."

Aeko saw his point, but she knew better than to concede too quickly. "You nearly killed his ambassador."

Crovis shook his head. "It's written in their laws, what they call the Way of Ears. If an enemy's messenger threatens you, you send him back bloodied. But you send him back *alive*." He offered her the dagger again.

Aeko took it. "I believe you. Still, a word of warning would have been appreciated."

Crovis bowed. "Next time we are accosted by a foreign dignitary, I will bear that in mind."

Aeko pretended to examine the edge of the dagger, then she twirled it between her fingers—faster and more deftly than Crovis had—and handed it back. "Keep it. I've never had much fondness for foreign steel."

If Crovis caught the rebuke, he gave no indication. After reclaiming the dagger, he left the tent. Aeko heard a chorus of laughter from the other Knights of the Lotus waiting outside. Before the tent flap closed, she saw Crovis idly pass the dagger to one of them, who gave her a sidelong glance, grinned, and slid it into his belt.

Vaanti pressed a silk cloth to his throat as he rode away from the camp. The pain from the shallow cuts had passed. Anger had replaced it. Vaanti swore oath after oath to the Dragongod that one day, he would face that man again and kill him. Though he had never fought an Isle Knight, he doubted the stories of their fighting prowess were true. Besides, even if they were, Vaanti had confidence in his own abilities.

He touched his necklace, fingering the first pair of dried ears he'd taken as a trophy. Despite his mood, he smiled. Those ears had belonged to a Dwarrish sellsword, the biggest man Vaanti had ever seen. He touched the second pair, tracing their dried swirls with cold affection. Those had come from an Iron

Sister at Hesod. He wished he'd had the chance to savor her, but the speed of her sword had convinced him to end the fight quickly.

He did not touch the final pair of ears, though his smile broadened when he remembered the look of terror and agony on his dying father's face. The man had savaged him all throughout his childhood—as was customary in the raising of warriors—but in the end, Vaanti had taken his revenge.

As I'll have my revenge on that Knight—and that pretty bitch who gives him orders.

He laughed and took a long swig from the bottle of lotus wine he was supposed to deliver to his prince. He'd opened the bottle the moment he was beyond the Knights' camp. After all, it would take him hours to reach Cassica, and the snow had just begun. The wine would keep him warm, though it was much too sweet for his liking.

Vaanti glanced up at the stars as he rode. Spotting Armahg's Eye, he shook his fist and spat on the snowy ground. Then he took another drink. He thought of all the other people he wanted to kill. He decided to add Prince Saanji to the list.

He'd happened to encounter the youngest of Karhaati's brothers right before leaving Cassica. Fat, not a single pair of ears around his neck, Prince Saanji had ridden through the gates at the same time as Vaanti—not to see him off but to break up a squad of Dhargothi warriors who had just begun their nightly celebrations by savaging some wives and daughters in full view of their impaled husbands.

Vaanti shook his head with disgust. Prince Saanji had no respect for the traditions and terror that had made the Dhargothi Empire what it was. Everyone knew that if Saanji had his way, the glorious empire would abandon the practices that kept their enemies at bay. It would fall practically overnight.

Vaanti took another drink of wine, but the sweetness overwhelmed him, and he spat it out. He liked how the wine looked like blood on the snow. Tipping the bottle, he poured out a little more, laughed, then returned the bottle to his lips. He forced himself to swallow.

"The Bloody Prince should have killed him already," he muttered. Of course, he knew why Saanji was still alive. Karhaati was the most powerful of the three princes, but he still had his brother, Ziraari, to deal with—not to mention the Red Emperor himself. Saanji's impalement would come, as it would for all those Earless who rejected the true Dhargothi way, but for now, they could still be useful.

Especially if that damn Lancer keeps winning battles.

Vaanti shook his head. For weeks, Karhaati's forces had enjoyed regular, bloody incursions into Ivairia, burning villages and raiding monasteries, killing and pleasuring without hindrance. Though Ivairia had little value compared to the Free Cities, rumor had it that the Ivairian king had ordered his Lancers not to fight back, to withdraw farther north so that they could protect him.

Lately, though, a company of Lancers had been defying their own king, boldly attacking Karhaati's larger forces at every turn. And they were winning. No one knew who was leading them, but Vaanti resolved that if he ever met the man, his impalement would be preceded by the slow removal of his skin.

Vaanti smiled. He guzzled the last of the bottle's saccharine contents then threw it against a tree and watched it shatter. His horse jerked, but Vaanti raked its flanks with his spurs, urging it to a full gallop. He was tired of snow and tired of riding. He wanted to get back to Cassica as quickly as possible, even if he had to ride his horse to death.

The night air tore at his face, but Vaanti laughed. Drawing his sword, he whirled it over his head. He imagined he was riding down on some helpless Ivairian village, as frightening as Fohl himself, a whole army of Dhargothi brothers behind him. Then he reined in.

Before him, on the snowy plains, lay a body, facedown in the snow.

He had not seen it during his ride south from Cassica, though the way the man's tattered white cloak melted into the snow, it would have been easy to miss. Vaanti dismounted his horse, wobbled unsteadily, then trudged ahead to investigate. Sheathing his sword, he reached for his daggers. He cursed when he realized one was missing. He wondered if he'd lost it in the ride. He drew the other.

Drawing closer, he saw splotches of blood all over the man's cloak, partially obscured by the snow. Vaanti rolled him over, then he leapt back.

The man looked young, his face contorted with pain, but it was his eyes that shook Vaanti to the bone: violet eyes with white pupils. Vaanti swore and signed himself. He looked at the man's tattered cloak again. What he had first mistaken for bloodstains were, in fact, wolves sewn in red thread.

"A Shel'ai…"

Though the man already appeared to be dead, Vaanti considered stabbing him just to make sure. He considered the possibility that the Shel'ai was merely asleep and might wake up long enough before dying to burn Vaanti to cinders. Vaanti took another step back.

But aren't the Shel'ai the Bloody Prince's allies now?

He could not remember. He rubbed his eyes and wished he had not consumed so much wine. Surrounded by darkness, he wondered what to do. Eventually, he made up his mind to ride back to Cassica and pretend that nothing had happened. But before he could take a step, the white-cloaked man blinked. His body jerked.

Vaanti jumped. He told himself it might just be a death spasm, but then the Shel'ai turned, lifted his head, and looked at him. He spoke.

Vaanti could not understand the man's speech, but it terrified him. Screaming, he threw his dagger. Whether the result of poor aim or some kind of devilry wrought by the Shel'ai, he missed. As he turned back toward his horse, he saw the Shel'ai sitting up. It seemed, strangely, that he was crying for help. Then Vaanti spotted a second man holding his horse by the reins.

This man wore a white cloak, too, minus the red wolves. He did not appear to be armed. The man smiled at him.

Vaanti drew his sword. "Get away from my horse!"

"Get away from mine," the man answered.

Vaanti frowned, puzzled. Then he heard a sound and whirled back around. The Shel'ai was on his feet, though doubled over, as though in pain. Violet eyes found Vaanti's again. The Shel'ai spoke a second time, sounding even more frantic, as if pleading for his life.

Vaanti readied his sword. "Stay away from me," he warned.

As though in answer, the Shel'ai screamed. Violet flames burst from his body. Instead of falling, he straightened. Then, before Vaanti's eyes, he seemed to grow.

Legs thickened like tree trunks. Hands sprouted claws the size of daggers. Pale skin took on a metallic sheen then darkened, abruptly covered in scales. Violet eyes turned yellow. An unevenly horned head tipped to one side, studying him, and screamed again.

"Gods!" Vaanti threw down his sword and fell to his knees. "Please, someone, help me..."

Someone touched his shoulder. Vaanti twisted, looked up, and saw violet eyes staring back at him. It was the man who had been holding his horse's reins.

The man pointed at the monstrosity before them. "Do you know what that is?"

Vaanti shook his head.

The other man grinned. "But you've heard of it, haven't you? Think hard." He grasped Vaanti's chin and turned it, forcing him to look.

Vaanti shut his eyes, weeping. He nodded.

The man laughed. "Good. A thing of beauty, is it not?" He touched the side of Vaanti's head. A strange jolt forced Vaanti's eyes open. "I hope you'll forgive me, but I'm afraid I must conduct a little test now. Please hold still."

The man stepped away, but Vaanti found that he still could not move. The monstrosity lumbered toward him. Fire spurted between gaps in its scales. Its deafening cry spoke of rage and anguish.

Unable to close his eyes, Vaanti tried once again to plead for his life. But the monstrosity opened its maw, and a sea of flame poured out. The last thing Vaanti heard was the sound of applause.

CHAPTER SIX

ALLIANCES AND BETRAYALS

BY THE GODS, HOW IS *he still alive?*
Shade shook his head as he studied Fadarah's ghastly wound. With the help of the Dhargots, the Shel'ai had carried the stricken Sorcerer-General into a tent. Dismissing their newfound bodyguards, Shade and the other Shel'ai stripped off Fadarah's armor and urged still more healing energies into his body. Then, exhausted, they collapsed for a few hours of rest. They had not expected Fadarah to be alive when they awoke. But he was.

Three days after sustaining a wound that would have killed most men within seconds, Fadarah continued to draw rasping, shallow breaths. His muscular body looked shrunken, the skin taut and ashen. Despite all their attempts to clean the wound, it had festered. A sickening smell filled the tent, so strong that it took all of Shade's willpower to keep from retching.

Some of the others had not been so lucky. Sensing that they had reached the limits of what their magic could accomplish, Shade decided to spare them the smell and sent them away. Besides, he could not bear to let them see Fadarah like this. Shade kept vigil alone, resolving that he would call the others back in only when the time came.

Though Fadarah had not regained consciousness, his eyes sometimes opened of their own accord. In those moments, the effect was so disconcerting that Shade would gently shut them again. He was just attempting to do so when his hand brushed Fadarah's cheek, and he felt a glimmer of consciousness. Startled, Shade pressed his hand to Fadarah's forehead, ignoring the instinct to recoil when the feel of the Sorcerer-General's skin reminded him of cold, wet stone. He sent his mind into Fadarah's, searching for some burgeoning sign of life. He found it.

Shade knelt beside Fadarah's bed, held his master's hand, and waited. After what felt like an eternity, Fadarah blinked. Slowly, he turned his head.

"Don't talk," Shade said. He communicated through mindspeak since he knew Fadarah would find it less taxing. *"We're safe. We're in a Dhargothi camp, a few miles northeast of the Ash'bana Plains. Ziraari's camp. I've made a deal with him. He'll see us safely back to Coldhaven in exchange for me killing Karhaati."* He forced a smile. Aloud, he added, "What's one more dead Dhargot?"

He sensed Fadarah's disapproval a moment before the Sorcerer-General shook his head. His voice was weak, barely a whisper. "Don't... trust..."

"I have no intention of trusting any Dhargot," Shade insisted. He suddenly remembered Brahasti, the sadistic Dhargothi general Shade had wanted to kill on more than one occasion. *"We've lost Sylvos. The Olgrym are scattered, too wild to control now. All we can do is fortify Coldhaven and try to keep our people safe."*

"That's what we should have done all along." Fadarah's pale face started to smile. *"El'rash'lin was right—"*

"You couldn't have known that. We tried minding our own business before, but the Sylvs hunted us. So did the Humans, the Dwarrs... everyone. You did what you thought was necessary."

Fadarah fell silent. "Silwren... dead..." Tears glistened in the big man's eyes.

Shade felt them spring to his own eyes, too, but blinked them away. *"She must have given herself to Knightswrath. I drove her to it. This is my fault, not yours. Because of me, the woman I love is dead!"*

Fadarah shook his head. *"No. I did this. My pride did this, my rage. So many sins I never dreamt I'd commit..."*

Shade considered summoning the others, but he heard a weakness in his master's voice that had nothing to do with his dying. He squeezed Fadarah's hand. "All you did, Father, you did for your people. You set your love, your strength, against the curse of our own birth."

Fadarah stared up at him then laughed. The effort shook his body and brought blood to his lips, which Shade dabbed away with his sleeve. Even as his body shook, Fadarah answered with his mind. *"My son, you have no idea what I've done. No idea what I've kept from you."*

"Father, whatever you did—"

"Brahasti," Fadarah croaked. "You have to stop... Brahasti—" He coughed. Awful pain twisted his body. Shade held him down until the spasm passed.

The mention of the Dhargothi general rekindled Shade's anger. "Stop

Brahasti from what? Father, he's gone. Don't you remember? After Karhaati took Cassica, you sent Brahasti north. He's supposed to wait there until spring then help Karhaati take Lyos. Even if I don't kill him, Karhaati will, sooner or later. Brahasti's nothing. He can't hurt us."

Fadarah tried to answer, coughed, then seized Shade's arm, pulling him closer. Shade resisted the impulse to recoil. *"Not us. Not us, my son."* Fadarah shook his head. Fresh tears ran from his eyes. *"You must stop him. You have to stop what I have started."*

Shade shook his head. "I don't understand."

Before Fadarah could explain, a surge of agony prevented the Sorcerer-General from speaking even telepathically. But Shade saw the desperation in his master's eyes. He pressed his hand to Fadarah's forehead and sent his mind into his master's. Fadarah did not resist. Shade sensed his need to confess, tinged with unendurable guilt.

Then Shade saw why. He pulled his hand away, aghast. For a long time, he could not speak, or even think. He just stood there in the silence, trembling. Then he stepped forward, pressed his hand to Fadarah's face, and unleashed a wash of wytchfire that burned his master's face to ash.

Fadarah never screamed.

Zeia shivered within her prison: a deep shaft dug in the earth, just a little wider than her shoulders, too narrow for her to sit down, and too deep for sunlight to penetrate. For days, snow had fallen through gaps between the boards that crowned the pit, enhancing her misery. She'd tried countless times to claw her way out, but the efforts only left her fingers raw and bloody. She wanted to try again, but she could not feel her legs anymore.

She could no longer summon wytchfire. Magic that had once coursed through her blood like quicksilver now moved slowly, like sludge, more a hindrance than anything. All the while, the Dhargots taunted her from above, detailing the many exotic, carnal punishments they intended to inflict upon her. They gave her nothing to eat. She'd had nothing to drink but snow. What little magic she had left, she'd used to staunch the flow of blood from her wounds. She heard nothing but the taunts and felt nothing but her own hunger and the needful, childlike buzz of her own magic, demanding rest and food she could not give.

But when they drag me out of here, I will find my strength. Somehow, I will conjure enough wytchfire to kill one or two of them and force the rest to kill me. She told herself it would be her final act of vengeance. Really, though, she had no desire to endure the torments the Dhargots had in mind.

She tried to meditate, hoping to prepare herself for what was to come, but the awful buzzing in her head mingled with the rumbling in her stomach and scattered all attempts at concentration. Fighting back tears of frustration, she shivered and prayed that the end would come soon. Still, when someone pulled the boards away, her heart leapt in panic.

Taking a deep breath, she let it go and forced herself to look up. She blinked. Instead of sunlight, she saw stars. She'd thought they would start on her in the morning, when they were well rested. She fought another surge of panic. When they lowered a rope ladder into the shaft, she considered refusing so that they would have to climb down and get her. But pride won out. Scooping up a handful of snow, she did her best to wash the blood and grime from her face. Then, with trembling limbs, she grasped the rope ladder and started to climb.

She'd managed no more than a few rungs before she realized she did not have the strength to climb all the way to the top. But her captors started hauling the rope ladder up on their own. Zeia clung pitifully, resisting the urge to let go and fall back to the bottom. She expected taunts but heard none. She offered none of her own, either, deciding to save what meager strength she had left for the battle.

But the moment she felt the night air on her face, strong hands grabbed her and hauled her up, and she knew she had no fight left in her. One of her captors hauled her out and lowered her to the ground, facedown. She could not see them, but she imagined leering warriors forming a ring around her, armed with that one weapon given to all men by nature.

No, I can't submit like this. Not now, not ever. If I can breathe, I can fight!

She unleashed a wild scream, rolled over, and tried to claw the face of her nearest attacker. But the man caught her wrists. He said something she could not understand, though the words seemed strangely familiar. Gathering her strength, she kicked. She struck something hard. Her captor grunted, and his grip slacked. With renewed strength, she fought harder, driving her knees into the shape looming over her.

Then, somehow, she was free. Twisting away, she tried to run, but her legs failed her. She fell hard. Snow pressed against her cheek. The world seemed to swallow her, blanketing her in darkness, but she fought through it and tried crawling away. A hand gripped her throat.

Zeia could not see her attacker, but she grabbed his arm and tried in vain to break free. She thought her attacker would strangle her. Instead, the hand gripping her throat abruptly let go and touched her forehead. A stunning jolt of power left her unable to move.

That was magic! No Dhargot did that...

She tried to push through her fogged senses. The figure before her removed his dark-plumed helmet. Violet eyes met hers. Her attacker spoke again. This time, she recognized the words as Sylvan. She did not answer.

Shade straightened. He stared at her then gestured, and she was free. But she did not run. She sneered up at him. "I'd rather you were a Dhargot."

"Even my magic has limits." Though Shade's reply was curt, he spoke it in a whisper. He drew a sword from his belt and pointed the blade at her as he put his helmet back on. "Stand up, if you can."

Zeia winced. Unwilling to die on her back, she summoned her strength and slowly pushed herself to her knees then her feet. She wobbled. Before she could fall, Shade caught her. He leaned close. She considered clawing his face, but he pressed the edge of his sword to her throat.

"Listen carefully," he whispered. "I already killed three men to get you out of there. I'd appreciate it if you didn't bring the whole damn camp down on us." He nodded toward two slain Dhargots lying in the snow. Both looked bloody and slashed, not burned. One lay on his back, his throat slit, staring wide eyed up at the sky.

Why didn't he just burn them with wytchfire?

For the first time, she realized that Shade was wearing the uniform of a Dhargothi officer. She looked past him and saw other Dhargothi warriors leaning on their spears, watching them with confusion. She opened her mouth to ask a question, but Shade whispered, "Later," and shoved her. A moment later, his voice rang in her mind.

"They don't know who I am. They think I was fighting the others for the right to be the first to rape you. If you want to survive, it's best they don't realize the truth until we're long gone."

Despite her exhaustion, Zeia found the strength to answer in kind. *"You're... rescuing me?"*

"Not at all," Shade answered. *"I fully expect you to be dead in a day. Me, too, probably. But for now, I need help."*

Zeia laughed coldly. She might have twisted around to face him, but Shade grabbed her by the arm. She felt him prod her with the flat of his blade. "Why in the gods' names would I help you?"

"Because of *this.*" Shade touched the back of her head. Zeia jerked and almost stopped, but Shade pushed her onward. She stumbled, trying to sort through all the images that Shade had just injected into her mind. "Don't talk," Shade warned. "Remember, you're still my prisoner. Keep your head down. The fewer who see you're a Shel'ai, the better."

Zeia nodded dumbly. As she pressed through the snow in her bare feet, she struggled even harder to understand what was happening. When the other Shel'ai discovered Fadarah's corpse, when they found him dead by wytchfire, they would almost certainly turn on Shade—regardless of what Fadarah had done. But the others were still his friends. Shade did not want to see them harmed. If Shade had used wytchfire to kill the guards, Ziraari would have blamed—and killed—the others as soon as he found out. She felt a grudging respect for Shade's actions.

The thought of what Fadarah had done filled her with even greater revulsion than she'd felt when she'd deserted him in the first place. She could scarcely believe it. But memories imparted by magic could not be forged. Her fists clenched and her stomach twisted.

As though she'd been there herself, she saw the Dhargothi general, Brahasti, proposing his ghastly plan before Fadarah and Shade: to take Sylvan women captive and have them forcefully impregnated until, given adequate time and chance, they birthed new Shel'ai whom Brahasti could raise to be Dhargothi servants. She saw Fadarah condemn the plan for Shade's benefit then, once Shade was gone, grant Brahasti his secret approval.

Zeia shook her head. Even Sylvs didn't deserve that. *"Let me rest. Get me food. And I'll help you send Brahasti to hell."*

A pair of Dhargothi soldiers sauntered by. They saw Shade's officer's uniform and saluted. Then their eyes fell on Zeia. She narrowed her eyes and looked down, hoping they would not notice her tapered ears. Luckily, they seemed more interested in her clothing, which was so torn that it was no longer decent. Shade gave her another token shove.

"You just deal with his bodyguards. Brahasti's mine." His wrath roiled in her mind, but she kept walking.

They had nearly reached the perimeter of the Dhargothi camp when someone behind them shouted. Word must have spread that some bold warrior had borrowed Ziraari's favorite prize for his own pleasure. Perhaps even Ziraari had heard. She hoped not, since she did not have the strength to fight, let alone run.

Shade led her to a pair of horses, already saddled and waiting. A young

Dhargot held the reins, obviously ordered to mind the horses until Shade's return. The Dhargot's eyes widened when he saw Zeia.

"Why—"

Shade whipped his sword across the young warrior's neck before he could finish. Dropping the blade, he caught the dying man then dragged him behind some trees and deposited his body in the snow. Zeia looked around. It was still the middle of the night. Half the sentries were asleep. No one had even noticed.

She eyed the bloody sword lying in the snow. She started to reach for it, but Shade gestured, and it sailed clear of her grasp and into his.

"Kill me later, if you can. But Brahasti dies first." He tossed her the dead man's cloak.

Concealing her gratitude, she threw the garment over her shivering shoulders and fixed the spear-and-dragon clasp beneath her chin.

Shade sheathed his sword and helped her mount her horse. "There's food and wine in the saddlebags. If we want to get away before they realize you're gone, we ride until dawn."

The prospect filled her with dread, but she nodded.

"And don't fall off your horse," Shade warned. "Fall, and I leave you behind. If you're that weak, you're no use to me anyway."

Zeia fixed a derisive expression to her face. "I won't fall, you bastard. I can promise you that." She grasped the reins, hoping that was a promise she could keep. Then something else occurred to her. "Who was the third?"

Shade frowned. "What?"

"You said you killed three men to get me out. That was *before* you killed that boy holding your horse. But there were only two men guarding me. Who was the third?"

For a long time, Shade was silent. Finally, he said, "Ziraari isn't quite as potent as he thinks."

It was Zeia's turn to be struck dumb. "You killed Ziraari…"

Shade kept his gaze straight ahead. "Once he discovered I'd left, our alliance would have fallen to dust anyway. This way, his army will be leaderless. They won't be able to organize in time to pursue us."

"But the Shel'ai you left behind… they'll be blamed—"

"I'll warn them through mindspeak when we're well away," Shade said. "I doubt they'll mind one more dead Dhargot. If they want, they can join us at Coldhaven."

"But when they find out what you did to Fadarah—"

62

"If I have to fight them, I will," Shade snapped. "Honestly, I don't expect to live that long."

"On that, at least, we agree."

Zeia was tempted to thank Shade for killing Ziraari but decided against it. *It's not like he did it for me, anyway.*

They rode in silence for a while. Then Shade reined in so suddenly that Zeia tensed, thinking they were about to be attacked.

Shade said, "I almost forgot…"

"What?"

A cold smile touched his lips. "Just a token of our new alliance. Given what Ziraari planned on doing to you, I took his favorite weapon as a souvenir." He withdrew a small pouch and tossed it to her.

Zeia caught the wet pouch. She looked inside then wiped her hands on her cloak. "You'll forgive me if I don't keep your gift."

"Do what you will. The point's been made." Shade flicked the reins.

"So it has." Zeia carefully closed the pouch and tossed it over her shoulder. It landed in the snow with a sickening thud.

CHAPTER SEVEN

THE CAPTIVE PROTECTOR

ROWEN TRIED TO IGNORE THE stares as he ascended the Path of Crowns. Morning light streamed through the broad, towering boughs of the World Tree, shining on the ancient white-and-emerald city. Most of the horrors of battle had been removed, and the walkway was crowded with the living again. Sylvan faces pressed in on all sides. Some eyed him with revulsion, others with reverence.

It's Silwren they should be revering, not me.

Rowen tried to quicken his pace, but he could only move so fast, surrounded as he was by a squad of Sylvan warriors acting as his bodyguards. Though the warriors seemed none too happy with the duty, they had carried out their assignment faithfully.

Rowen smiled to himself. Only a few months ago, soldiers of the Red Watch had been safely conducting him through Lyos, much as the Sylvs were conducting him through Shaffrilon. Wherever he went, he needed someone to protect him.

He wondered who would protect him once he left the Wytchforest, now that Silwren was dead and Jalist was gone. He tapped Knightswrath's hilt. He tried to remind himself that Silwren was still with him, somehow. He had only to draw the sword to feel something of her, buried deep within the sword's magic. But the prospect of drawing the sword terrified him.

The sword's terrible power seemed to be slumbering, but he still remembered the terrible visions the sword had given him, the firestorm that had nearly driven him mad. Though he'd forced himself to draw the blade a few times since then—and it appeared each time to be nothing more than a curve of finely wrought kingsteel—he still felt what slept within. It might wake on its own, but it would also wake if he called it. Something urged him to do so, even as another part of him longed to ungird the weapon and cast it as far away as he could.

Is this how Silwren felt when she was alive? So much power! Intoxicating but awful at the same time.

He shuddered. Pushing the thought from his mind, he distracted himself by trying to discern the speech of the Sylvs around him. Thanks to El'rash'lin, he had a passable knowledge of the Sylvan tongue. Listening to the heated whispers all around him, though, he almost wished he didn't.

He wondered where they were taking him. He had asked, but none of his escorts would answer. Rowen had heard a rumor that General Seravin, terribly wounded and mutilated by Doomsayer himself, was miraculously still alive. Perhaps the general had regained consciousness and wanted to see him.

Rowen shook his head. He'd caught a glimpse of the general in the House of Healing, his many bandages soaked in blood. He doubted the general could have regained consciousness yet, if he ever would. Rowen doubted they were taking him to see the king. From what little he could glean, King Loslandril had locked himself in the palace after his son's death and refused all visitors. He had not even bothered to tour his own city in the wake of the devastating battle. Many had already begun to speculate that Loslandril had gone mad—if he was still alive.

Given that Silwren had turned the king's son into a candlewick, Rowen understood. Still, the prince had deserved it. "Are you taking me to see Briel?" Though he spoke in Sylvan, he was not surprised when the bodyguards ignored his question. But a moment later, he spied their apparent destination: a squat structure called the House of Questions.

"Another interrogation? Probably shouldn't have left me armed, then."

Unsmiling, the bodyguards led him inside, past more guards, to Captain Briel's office. The Sylvan captain's arm was still bandaged, his cheek swollen and marked with stitches. The former injury was the result of a confrontation with Silwren. The latter was self-inflicted, as a sign of penance when Briel surrendered to Rowen.

But if he surrendered, why am I the prisoner?

Briel looked up from a stack of papers. He dismissed the bodyguards with a wave and rose to his feet. Without offering to shake Rowen's hand, he gestured to an empty chair and a full goblet of wine. "Sit. Drink."

"Not thirsty."

"I'd rather you were drunk when I told you what I have to say."

Rowen forced a smile. "Is this your attempt to poison me? I'm not sure I *can* be poisoned anymore." He gave Knightswrath's hilt a meaningful tap.

Briel's expression darkened. "No poison, then. Sit, Human. For the moment, at least, I promise no one's going to kill you."

"No one's going to *try* to kill me, you mean," Rowen amended, though his bravado sounded foolish even to his own ears. He sat. He picked up the goblet but did not drink.

Briel sat, too. "For once, this isn't about you. I have... a problem. It's an old problem for my people, I suppose, but a new one for me. Another Shel'ai has been born."

Rowen tensed. "Where? When?"

"Just last night, right here in the capital." Briel tapped the blade of his sword. His fingernail rang against the metal. "The parents wanted to kill it. More than half my people probably agree. Only there happen to be rumors of some kind of half-Dragonkin wytch teaming up with a crazed Isle Knight to save this city from certain doom, so I guess the parents thought they'd check with me first." He removed his hand from his sword, picked up his own goblet, and took a drink. "So what do you think I should do?"

"What do you mean?"

"I *mean*, there's been something of a tradition for as far back as I can remember. Whenever a Sylvan child is born with purple eyes, he faces two possible fates. One is a quick death. The other is a slow one." Though Briel did not blink, he white-knuckled his goblet.

Rowen resisted the impulse to leap out of his chair and draw Knightswrath. He forced a smile. "I'd suggest neither."

"I thought as much." Briel set down his goblet and leaned back in his chair. "So the infant isn't to be poisoned, stabbed, or left on the plains to starve. I presume you don't want it raised in neglect until it's old enough to be banished, either."

Rowen stared into the contents of his own goblet.

"That puts me in an odd position," Briel continued. "If I did as Loslandril wanted—as that Dragonkin, Chorlga, apparently *forced* him to do—I'd have the support of more than half of the city. But I'd be perpetuating the same cruelty that bred this conflict in the first place." He stared at Rowen as though awaiting an answer.

Rowen took a long drink of wine then carefully set down the goblet. Without standing, he drew Knightswrath and laid it carefully on the table in front of him. He gave Briel a hard look. "You'd also be giving me yet another reason to cut your fucking head off."

Briel started to smile then stopped himself. "I figured I'd given you plenty by now." He refilled Rowen's goblet then refilled his own. "Don't forget, Human, I turned against my king for you."

"I'd like to think you did it to save your city."

"Hard to say." Briel drank. "Let's speak plain, then. Shel'ai are going to continue to be born to Sylvs. Sylvs will continue to hate them. Even if I nail edicts to every wall and door and tree throughout Sylvos, even if I spend the rest of my life personally reminding every Sylv that Silwren saved them every bit as much as Fadarah endangered them, nothing will change."

Rowen considered the change he'd already witnessed in the Wytchforest, but before he could argue, Briel continued.

"Listen, Knight. If you want to be the naïve champion of the weak and the innocent, if you want to put a stop to the madness that got us here in the first place, I don't need threats. I don't need your Codex Lotius, with its poetry. I need a place close by—a safe, *real* place—where I can send these unwanted children. And I need whichever unlucky bastard is going to raise them to swear on every god he holds dear that they will *not* be raised to seek revenge on the rest of us."

Rowen caught his meaning. "Me?" He almost laughed. "I'm not a gods-damned wet nurse!"

"No, you're not a wet nurse," Briel conceded. "You're a Knight whose Order wants him dead. You're a Human who merrily rushes off to fight in wars that don't concern him. You're probably the dumbest bastard I've ever met. But you're also the luckiest. And gods save me, I trust you." He sipped from his goblet. "Take a drink and forget I said that last part."

Rowen obeyed. "Briel, where in the Light do you think I'm going to take this infant? In case it's escaped your notice, I still have a war to fight."

"What war? Fadarah's dead. The Olgrym are weakened. They'll be beaten soon. It's just a matter of time."

Rowen rose to his feet. "But Chorlga's still out there. And the Dhargots—"

"Humans fighting Humans," Briel interrupted with disgust. "Plus one mad Dragonkin who's probably scared of you—or will be, once he sees what you're carrying." The Sylvan captain gestured at Knightswrath. "Stay in Sylvos. Help us hunt down the Olgrym. Cut down Doomsayer the way you cut down Fadarah, and even Loslandril will call you a hero. You can protect the Shel'ai, too, if that's what you want. Fact is, no matter how many Sylvs hate you, you'll still be safer *here* than you will be out there."

Rowen stood in silence. Then he reached down and picked up Knightswrath. Briel tensed, but Rowen only sheathed the blade. "I can't. You know I can't."

"Fohl's hells, you can't." Briel stood, too. "I have less than half my army left, Human. I have a mad king who's starving himself and a comatose general who already had his cock and his hands cut off by an Olg who's twice my size. And if that weren't enough, I still have about a thousand more Olgrym raiding and raping throughout the kingdom." Briel shook his head. "I need help. I need generals, archers, swordsmen, healers, horses, and a good night's rest. Instead, the gods have given me one mad Isle Knight with a burning sword. Maybe you're as dangerous to us as you are to that already-hefty list of enemies you're carrying around with you. But right now, you're all I've got."

The Sylvan captain sat back down. He took a deep, calming breath.

"Kill me if you have to, but it won't change a thing. You're staying here, Locke. Set one foot beyond the Moon Gate without my permission or try to leave Shaffrilon by any of the bridges connecting the capital to the other trees, and my men will shred you with arrows."

Rowen fixed him with a stern expression. "For a man who complains about having too small an army, you seem to be in an awful hurry to get a lot of them killed."

Briel shrugged. "If you take Knightswrath, it won't matter how many—or how few—of my men you kill in your escape. We're lost either way."

"Fine. You want the damn sword? Keep it." Rowen drew Knightswrath and cast it onto the table, shattering the carafe of wine. A red stain spread across the table, soaking like blood into Briel's troop reports. The door flew open, and Sylvan guards rushed in. Briel dismissed them with a single, hard gesture. When they were gone, he looked from Rowen to Knightswrath.

The Sylvan captain hesitated then reached for the adamune's dragonbone hilt. He'd hardly touched it when he recoiled, hissing through clenched teeth. He pressed his good hand to his chest, swearing in heated whispers. Then he opened his hand, showing Rowen his blistered fingers. "I'm running out of places you can injure, Human."

Rowen blinked. "I didn't know—"

"Get out," Briel said. Despite his maimed hand, he picked up his own sword. "And take that damn demon-blade with you!"

Rowen scooped up Knightswrath, felt just a tingle of warmth from its hilt, and sheathed it. He stalked out of Briel's office. Immediately, his so-called bodyguards fell in silently behind him. Despite his dark mood, Rowen noticed that there were a great deal more of them than before.

Zeia tugged at her cloak, alarmed by the growing midday chill. "Did Fadarah really think those children would serve him?"

Shade looked up wearily from his own horse. "What?"

"The Shel'ai children born of rape. The ones Brahasti wants to make. Did Fadarah really think they'd serve him, after the kind of nightmare they were born in?" Her choice of words reminded her of the Nightmare, and she suppressed a shudder.

Shade was quiet for a moment. "I think he meant to wait until enough Shel'ai children had been born, then he'd sweep in with hands burning, kill Brahasti and their captors, and 'rescue' them. After something like that, they'd be every bit as devoted to him as we were."

Though Shade had shared some of the memories he'd gleaned from Fadarah's mind, that part of the plan had been absent. Was Shade merely making it up in effort to redeem Fadarah's memory? That seemed odd, given that Shade himself had been the one to kill him. She asked a different question. "El'rash'lin used to say that only one in a thousand Sylvan children is born a Shel'ai."

"Your point?"

"That's a lot of time and trouble to go through. I have no doubt Brahasti could find men willing to do the deed and Sylvan captives to bear the abuse, but still, it would take years. And what about the thousands of other children born without the dragonmist?"

Shade turned and scowled at her. He tapped the hilt of his shortsword.

She caught his meaning. "No wonder you killed Fadarah."

"He was already dying. That Isle Knight—"

"He *probably* would have died," Zeia corrected, "but you turning his skull into a pile of ashes made it certain."

Shade reined in his horse. "Forgive me, Sister. I've spent half the past couple days regretting my decision to haul you out of that pit and the other half running for my life, so my senses aren't what they should be. Were you just now *asking* me to kill you or only making conversation?"

Zeia reined in as well. Though she had recovered a measure of her strength since her rescue, she was no match for Shade. "Doesn't it bother you that we're about to risk our necks to save Sylvs… quite possibly the same Sylvan captives we were fighting only a couple of weeks ago?"

Shade shook his head and urged his horse onward. "Even in war, there are rules."

Zeia bit back a smirk. She remembered how she and a few others had made that same argument when Fadarah decided to forcefully transform imprisoned Isle Knights into near-mindless assassins, only to have Shade accuse them of being weak willed and naïve.

Has Shade finally found his conscience?

She considered how little time had passed since Shade killed his last opponent and decided it unlikely. "So what do we do with the Sylvs once we've dealt with Brahasti and his scum?" She half expected Shade to suggest they kill them.

He shrugged. "*That* war is over. We lost. The prisoners can do what they like. If they can make it back to the forest, so be it."

"You really think a pack of beaten, half-starved women without weapons will have no trouble passing through a snowy land rife with murderous Humans?" Zeia almost laughed.

"Are you suggesting we do nothing?"

Zeia urged her horse until she was riding a little ahead of Shade's. "I suggest we do the smart thing and head north, back to Coldhaven. Or have you forgotten all the other Shel'ai children who need protecting?"

"I've forgotten nothing. We'll make for Coldhaven once Brahasti's dead and I've ground his ashes under my boot."

If we survive… "Then what? What about the Dhargots? Do you really think they'll let you be after this?"

Shade shrugged. "I killed a prince whose brothers already wanted him dead. Besides, I never told Ziraari where Coldhaven is."

Zeia glanced back at Shade in time to see him wince, as though he'd just realized an error. She wondered if he had told Ziraari more than he'd intended and if that wasn't the real reason he'd killed the prince. The thought that Shade might have endangered the last few Shel'ai left enraged her, but she concealed this and made sure she'd walled off her mind, lest he try to read her thoughts. "Perhaps we should take the children elsewhere."

"Which children… the Shel'ai or the Sylvs?"

She realized he must have been joking. "We could try Stillhammer again—"

"Last time we were there, their king killed four of us and wounded six more, just for planting turnips in land nobody wanted." Shade laughed coldly. "The Dwarrs are no better than the Sylvs we left behind."

"Humans, then," Zeia suggested. "Not Dhargots, I know… and not the Isle Knights or any of the Free Cities after what we've done… but maybe we could head south. We never tried going to Quesh before. Maybe *they* would welcome us—or at least leave us alone."

But Shade was already shaking his head. "Too many enemies between here and there. One or two of us might make it that far, but not with children in tow."

"Sorocco, then." Zeia thought of the dark-skinned sea merchants. Though rumored to be a superstitious people, they were so far removed from the rest of Ruun that they might not share the preconceived notions of the Shel'ai. Thinking of the Soroccans gave her an idea. "Or better yet, get a ship of our own and sail off somewhere?"

Shade looked at her and scoffed. "Beyond the Dragonward? The Dhargots must have injured you more than I thought."

"Why not? The old Dragonkin are long gone… maybe even dead by now. Besides, we don't need protecting from *them*, anyway. We need protection from the rest of Ruun!"

She expected Shade to mock her, but his expression turned thoughtful. "Silwren suggested that once," he said quietly.

Zeia thought she saw a pang of nostalgia, even guilt, in his expression.

"It'd never work, though. I don't know any more about the sea than you do."

"Then we'll hire someone who does. The Soroccans, even the Isle Knights—"

"And go where? Sure, some say there are other continents out there, but we don't know how far or how safe they'd be even if we reached them in one piece. For all we know, we might inadvertently sail to the same damn place the Dragonkin went after the Shattering War."

But Zeia was not about to give up. "So what if we did? The Dragonkin wielded magic, just as we do. They might greet us as allies."

Shade's familiar look of derision returned. "Have you forgotten your fairytales, Sister? We were cattle to the Dragonkin. You know that as well as I do. Those of us they didn't kill, they kept as slaves. We'd be better off dealing with King Loslandril."

"But that was centuries ago. The Dragonkin might have forgotten. Or maybe they changed. *We* certainly have."

Shade reined in his horse again. "Have we? I wonder." Without waiting for her answer, he rode on.

Fuming, Zeia followed. She played over the idea in her mind. Even if Shade vetoed her plan, the other Shel'ai might be persuaded. El'rash'lin's way of peace had only seen them hunted down, driven from realm to realm as they searched for safety. Fadarah's way had gotten most of them killed and earned them new enemies. In time, their little fortress on the Wintersea would be discovered. If they wanted to avoid extinction, leaving Ruun behind might be their last, desperate option.

But for that, they would need Shade's help. He was the strongest Shel'ai left. But the only way he *might* be persuaded to agree to her plan was if she first helped him succeed in his. She would have to help him kill Brahasti.

And I hope he doesn't change his mind and try to kill me before this is all over.

Shaking her head, she fixed her thoughts on Brahasti. The thought of finally slaying that sadistic Dhargot pleased her. Besides, she knew they had little to fear. Brahasti might have Dhargothi bodyguards and maybe sellswords, but by the time she and Shade reached him, they would have recovered their full strength. Brahasti's bodyguards wouldn't stand a chance.

Zeia continued riding north as the snowfall thickened around her.

CHAPTER EIGHT

LYOS

EPHEUS LEANED ON THE BATTLEMENTS of Lyos and lamented his new position as captain of the Red Watch. Though he had inherited the position more than a month before, after his predecessor was slain during the city's pitched battle against Fadarah's forces, Epheus still chafed at the tedium of daily reports and the politics of his meetings with the king, the various priesthoods, and, of course, the Isle Knights.

Last week, he'd met with the most venerated clerics in Lyos, entertaining their frantic hopes that he might do something about all the people flocking to Cadavash to join that fanatical sect of dragon-worshippers. Epheus had listened then as calmly as he could, explained that he could do nothing. Worshippers of Zet and his dragons had been around for centuries. Epheus's predecessor had complained about them, too. Thankfully, the devotees of the Dragongod seemed interested in harming only themselves, so Epheus was not about to get in their way. Besides, he had other concerns.

Dignitaries from the Lotus Isles had been visiting Lyos so often since the attack that Epheus could hardly distinguish one from the other or remember when one left and another arrived. Officially, their mission was to assist in the reconstruction of the city and reassure King Typherius that the Lotus Isles had not forgotten their favorite protectorate, especially with dark rumors of the Dhargots drawing near. But Epheus knew the truth: the dignitaries had come to oversee the collection of taxes.

Many Isle Knights had died in the battle. Lyos had paid a higher price, but the Order still expected the city to compensate the Isles for those heroic deaths with every coin they could spare—and plenty they could not. For that reason, Epheus—who did not have his predecessor's tact—frequently had to remind himself that it would be inappropriate to have those dignitaries hung by their ankles from the city walls.

The captain thought of Aeko Shingawa. She was different from the other Knights. Epheus sensed that she sympathized with the city's plight—unlike Crovis Ammerhel. Epheus clenched his fist, remembering how Crovis—then leader of Lyos's defenses—had taken most of his Knights and abandoned the city as it was being attacked from within, just so that he could claim credit for arresting a mass of men beyond who were already surrendering.

Thanks to Aeko, Silwren, Rowen, and the late Captain Ferocles, the city was saved. But that didn't prevent Epheus from imagining the pleasure he would derive from visiting his anger on Sir Crovis Ammerhel and every Knight and dignitary like him.

Epheus shook his head as he felt his stomach rumble, as it often did when he got too worked up. To distract himself, he thought of Aeko, wondering where she had gone. Supposedly, she and the other Knights were looking for Rowen Locke, though whether they intended to help or arrest him depended on which rumor one believed.

His stomach rumbled again. Epheus groaned, rubbing his chest as a nauseating tremor rose up through his throat. He leaned over the walls and spat. When he straightened, he noticed some of the men of the Red Watch staring at him. He forced himself to smile. "Too damn much of the quartermaster's cheap ale!"

The men laughed and returned to their duties. Epheus watched them work. The Red Watch oversaw trading in all of Lyos. As a sergeant, Epheus had hated the duty. He hated it even more now that he was captain. But it was still a crucial job.

Despite the light snow dusting twin columns of wagons and carts, King's Bend was as crowded as ever with travelers, traders, and, despite the sense of kinship felt by the people of Lyos after they repelled the Throng, thieves. Though gangs from the Dark Quarter had been crucial in the defense of Lyos, those gangs had hardly joined the priesthood afterward. Elements from the slums still lent their own special flavor to Lyosi trade, seeding the crowds with pickpockets, brawlers, unlicensed flesh traders, and drunks. Epheus appreciated that at least the gangs had all but eradicated flesh trade involving children, but keeping the gangs' less honorable practices in check was still a full-time job. So the captain was none too pleased when commotion reached his ears.

He waved over the battlements, catching the attention of a squad of Red

Watch milling below. He pointed in the direction of a distant scream. They nodded, formed ranks, and started pushing through the crowd, even as new screams joined in the chorus.

Epheus groaned. "Must be a damn gang fight." He strained to see, but the commotion seemed to originate at the base of Pallantine Hill, where King's Bend began. That put it close to the slums. He was tempted to just let the gangs of the Dark Quarter resolve the squabble, but crowds of screaming citizens began rushing up King's Bend, flooding into the city, obscuring the path of the men he'd just sent to inspect the source.

He turned to his junior officer. "This sounds bad. Get another squad up here." The officer started to go, but Epheus grabbed his arm. The screams increased. "Make it two." He shoved the officer on his way and turned back to the battlements.

Epheus was familiar with the occasional bit of knife work wrought by the less savory elements of Lyos, but that usually involved just one or two opponents. Whatever was going on at the base of the hill was no simple knife fight.

Epheus's pulse quickened. He'd spoken to King Typherius about the Dhargots only last evening. All reports insisted that they were wintering at Cassica, far from Lyos. They had raided the surrounding villages and farmlands but kept their distance from the city. *Surely, they would not send a company to slaughter Lyosi civilians when such an action would result in said company being annihilated by the Red Watch. Then again, when was the last time in the last year that one of our many illustrious enemies did something that made sense?*

Epheus sighed and drew his sword. "Let's get down there and knock some heads before this gets out of hand." Guardsmen followed. Epheus considered heading down King's Bend on foot, but the growing commotion convinced him to make for the stables. Mounting his horse, he ordered the guardsmen nearest him to do the same. Then, a dozen in number, they started off.

Though she made sure her appearance spoke to the contrary, Igrid still felt uncomfortable in the King's Market. It wasn't the roiling crowds or the handful of pickpockets moving among the populace—she probably knew their tricks better than they did. She wasn't afraid of being attacked, either. In the city proper, with the Red Watch close by and a pair of stilettos concealed in her sleeves, she was about as safe as one could be.

She knew it was important that she be seen. If she ever wanted to open a tavern or brothel of her own, she would need friends in Lyos. Thanks to the coin paid to her by Arnil Royce, she was well on her way, but she wasn't there yet. For that reason, she'd taken care to learn the names of the local noblemen and city officials and smile accordingly. Despite the chill in the air, present even in the warmer climate of Lyos, she'd chosen a clingy gown that showed off the curves afforded her by a dash of Dwarrish blood in her ancestry. She wore her long red curls past her shoulders—red hair was a prized rarity in these parts.

But as she moved through the tables and vendors, stopping sometimes to pretend to study an object for sale, she constantly had to stave off the urge to turn and run away.

What's wrong with me?

Discomfort turned to self-directed rage, but she concealed it by smiling and examining a golden, diamond-crusted broach. She held it up to the light and nodded, even though a quick look confirmed her suspicion that it was a fake.

"A fine piece from Syros, m'lady," the vendor said. "Just the thing for a beautiful creature such as yourself."

Igrid offered him a crooked smile. "Syros, eh? Last I heard, they'd just begun to recover from the thrashing the Nightmare gave them when the Dhargots swept in and burned everything that was left."

The vendor blinked then smiled. "All the more reason to buy such a rare piece, while you still can. The Syrosi jewelers may have gone to the gods—" He paused to glance reverently at the sky. "But their art remains."

Quick recovery. Igrid set the broach back down, bowed, and walked away. While pretending to study the vendors' wares, she studied the crowds, searching for someone she should flirt with, but a sinking feeling began to grow in the pit of her stomach, stronger than ever. She wondered if it was because she'd mentioned the Nightmare. Had that, in turn, reminded her of Rowen?

Speaking of red-headed fools wandering in circles...

Igrid swore, startling a merchant who happened to be walking beside her. He blushed at her attire. Bowing, he stepped back, believing he'd offended her somehow. Igrid forced a smile again. She stopped at a table and ran a fur-lined jacket between her fingers, even as she resisted the impulse to draw one of her stilettos, just so she could feel its reassuring heft.

Stop thinking about Rowen. The fool's probably dead by now, anyway—and his wytch with him.

The thought of Silwren rekindled Igrid's anger. The famous Shel'ai-turned-Dragonkin had magicked Igrid away from Rowen after Igrid had tried to steal Knightswrath—the wytch had probably also told Rowen what she'd tried to do. Igrid could not puzzle out why, but the thought of that dumb, trusting Isle Knight being disappointed in her was maddening.

Igrid shook her head, inadvertently answering the question of the street vendor who was trying to sell her the fur jacket she'd just been inspecting. She decided to seek out the quartermaster of the Red Watch. She'd been speaking with the man lately, and while Igrid strongly suspected the man's nightly interests precluded her gender, he might still be an ally in helping her gain access to Captain Epheus. Once she had that, she might try to gain the favor of King Typherius himself.

Of course, if I wanted to gain favor more quickly, I could just tell them I'm friends with their precious heroes!

Igrid grimaced. She'd said nothing to anyone in Lyos about her companionship with Rowen Locke and Silwren, the two figures who had helped save Lyos the last time it was threatened. Though she suspected that doing so might gain her all the favor and credit she needed to see her business plans come to fruition, the thought of feigning friendship with those two made her skin crawl.

Why is it that whenever I tell myself to stop thinking about something, that's the very thing I think about ten seconds later?

Forcing her thoughts to clear, she made her way toward the gray battlements looming in the distance. She suspected she would find the quartermaster at the nearby barracks, though she also toyed with the idea of strolling outside the city, to the lesser market along the road that ran from the base of Pallantine Hill to the walls of Lyos. Gang leaders from the Dark Quarter were known to frequent that road, and they, too, could be powerful allies.

Igrid was still contemplating this, nearing the gates of Lyos, when she heard the first scream. Reflexively, she unsheathed one of the stilettos from her sleeve. She crouched, ready to defend herself, but realized a split second later that the scream had originated well beyond the walls. Just as quickly as she'd drawn her blade, she replaced it.

Luckily, no one seemed to have noticed her. The Red Watch tensed, even as the citizens milling about the gates of Lyos looked bewildered. Confusion turned to fear when the scream was followed by another then another. Igrid considered hurrying back to her room at the inn. Surely, this was gang business, best left to Captain Epheus.

Nevertheless, when a squad of Red Watch mounted horses—led by

Captain Epheus himself, his face pinched with worry—Igrid touched the hilt of her stiletto and hurried to follow.

Jalist heard the screams and knew he was too late.

Cursing, he pressed on. Though for days he'd caught just a few scant minutes of rest when it was absolutely necessary, panic gave him fresh strength. He stumbled on, using his spear as a walking stick. Pallantine Hill rose in the distance. He'd lost sight of the Jolym when they dipped behind a lesser hill, but the chorus of battle cries told him they'd reached Lyos.

Tears of frustration ran from his eyes. He'd tried as hard as he could to get ahead of the Jolym, hoping to warn Lyos, but his advantage of speed had been replaced by bone-deep exhaustion. More cries were punctuated by the sound of trumpets.

As the Jolym neared Pallantine Hill, they'd been spotted. They might even have been mistaken for Isle Knights at first. Some Red Watch officer had probably gone down to meet them, flanked by a dozen or so men who weren't expecting trouble. Then the slaughter had started.

Jalist gripped his spear and managed a brief sprint before exhaustion overpowered him again. He fell, gasping for breath, then pushed himself back up and continued at a stumble. His vision clouded so that he nearly collided with the drovers before he spotted them.

Three young men gazed fearfully at Pallantine Hill. A small herd of sheep milled nearby. The Dwarr almost laughed at the expressions on their faces. He wondered what he looked like to them—wild, bloody, and sweating—then the glint of the Jolym beckoned from a distance.

One of the drovers had a horse. Little more than a pack mule, it stood just a little taller than the drover in front of it. Still, Jalist nearly wept with gratitude. He went straight at the man holding the reins. The man backed up, wide eyed, and reached for his knife. His friends raised quarterstaffs and blocked Jalist's path. The Dwarr considered trying to explain to them that he needed the horse to warn the city, but he doubted they would believe him.

Jalist drew a stiletto and threw it. The pommel struck one of the young men in the nose. He shrieked and backpedaled, dropping his quarterstaff. Blood welled between his fingers. Jalist charged before the others could react.

Gripping his spear, Jalist feigned a lunge at the drover's face. When the young man moved his quarterstaff to block, Jalist sank low and swept the man's legs out from under him. Rather than kill him, Jalist feigned another stab at the drover's face that sent him scurrying for cover. Jalist faced the final drover, who made the mistake of trying to mount his horse.

Jalist tossed aside his spear, seized the man by the back of the tunic, and hauled him down. He punched him twice—enough to drive the air from the young man's lungs but not enough to do serious damage—then dropped the lad onto the plains. He caught the pack horse's reins before the skittish beast could run away.

"Easy, poor girl. Or boy. Whatever you are."

He tried to haul himself into the saddle, stumbled when his weakened legs buckled, then gathered his strength and managed to mount the horse. "I know you aren't built for speed, but if you've got any, now's the time to use it."

He patted the pack horse's neck then called over his shoulder to the stunned drovers. "Come get your horse at the gates, if I don't get her killed trying to play the hero." Then Jalist drove his heels into the horse's flanks and raced toward Pallantine Hill.

CHAPTER NINE

A NEW TASK

Rowen Locke stood at the edge of the dais and looked down upon the tangled green depths of the Wytchforest. Though his bodyguards stood in the distance, he was otherwise alone. He was glad of that. After leaving Captain Briel, the ability to sense the thoughts and feelings of those around him had seemed to intensify until the Sylvs' loathing and mistrust overwhelmed him. Torn between casting Knightswrath into a well and seeking isolation, he chose the latter. Luckily, as quickly as it had manifested, the ability dimmed. Now, Rowen could read the thoughts of his captors only by gauging the respectful coldness in their blue eyes.

He faced the wytchwood trees, took a deep breath, and let it go. He couldn't smell smoke anymore, which surprised him, though he wondered if that was only due to his height, perhaps half a mile above the forest floor. He glanced over his shoulder. The palace of King Loslandril loomed in the distance, a splendid amalgamation of stone and wood, carved halfway into the stunning white broadness of the World Tree. Something in its simple but elegant design reminded him of Saikaido Temple, where he had trained to be an Isle Knight, though he knew the Sylvan palace was hundreds, even thousands of years older.

"Is your king still locked inside? If he's done foaming at the mouth? Perhaps he'd like to come out for a little chat."

His bodyguards did not answer, though the way more than one touched his sword hilt made it clear that Rowen would not be permitted anywhere near their king, let alone inside the palace. That suited Rowen fine. He still had half a mind to cut the Sylvan king in half, damn the consequences.

As for the palace, Rowen had seen its interior only briefly, after King Loslandril's guards had trundled him and hauled him through to the other side. There, a secret walkway led to the tomb of Fâyu Jinn, where the king had hoped to kill Silwren when she came to rescue Rowen. Silwren had indeed been mortally wounded before Rowen could fight his way free, but something had saved her—if only so that she could give her life to rekindle Knightswrath and give Rowen the power to save the Wytchforest.

That was Fâyu Jinn. It had to be.

Rowen had seen it himself, though he hardly dared believe his own memories of those mad, frantic events: a giant ghostly figure in the armor of a Knight of the Lotus appeared to heal Silwren after she'd been struck down by a cursed blade. Silwren, blazing with wytchfire, had thrown herself on Knightswrath then melted into the blade.

Rowen shuddered. He touched the sword's hilt and thought he felt a slight tremor of response. He withdrew his hand. The thought of Silwren filled him with aching loss of a friend and the overwhelming knowledge of her sacrifice, coupled with the knowledge that he had failed to save her.

He thought back to the first time he'd encountered her, in the depths of Cadavash. El'rash'lin had been there, too. Using the ancient magic of Namundvar's Well, El'rash'lin had given Rowen a glimpse into the divine, into the Light itself. The indescribable, selfless peace he'd felt there hadn't lasted. And Rowen wished he could trim the memory from his mind completely.

The thought amused him. El'rash'lin had given him something that countless priests and pilgrims would have killed for. And all he wanted to do was throw it away. Like the knowledge that Silwren had sacrificed herself for a higher cause, it seemed to broaden the ocean of doubt within him rather than comfort him.

His cold amusement vanished in a sudden rush of nausea. He rubbed his eyes. Thoughts of Silwren turned to thoughts of his brother, of Kayden's mad look of gratitude as he'd died on Rowen's sword. He thought, too, of the Nightmare sloughing up Pallantine Hill toward the city of Lyos, howling like a scalded bull with its skin on fire.

He tried to calm himself by thinking of Fadarah, remembering his confrontation with the infamous half-Olgish leader of the Shel'ai. He tried to reconjure the feeling of brutal satisfaction he'd felt when Knightswrath cleaved clean through the giant's armor, but the thought of Fadarah only heightened Rowen's nausea. He remembered the look of grief in Fadarah's violet eyes. At the time, Rowen had taken that as the despair of a man who realized his cause was lost. Now he wondered if that grief hadn't been caused by the sight of Knightswrath and the knowledge that the burning sword meant Silwren was dead.

Rowen sank to one knee, retching. Grasping at his stomach but meeting only armor, he retched until he wept. The forest far below blurred. He closed his eyes and remained kneeling until he caught his breath. He thought of all the other platforms beneath this one, which held homes, shops, and temples of the Sylvan capital. He glanced back at his bodyguards.

"My apologies if I just threw up on somebody's rooftop." He rose slowly, using Knightswrath's sheathed blade as a crutch. "Seems we Knights don't live up to the stories any more than you Sylvs do." He wiped his eyes then his mouth. "Gods, anybody have any wine with them?"

To his surprise, one of the bodyguards stepped forward and offered him a small silvery flask. Rowen nodded his thanks then took a drink. The flask contained only water, but Rowen rinsed out his mouth, spat over the side of the dais, then took another drink. He started to pass the flask back to its owner, but the Sylvan bodyguard shook his head and stepped back.

"My thanks," Rowen said.

"It wasn't a gift," a voice said. Rowen turned to see Briel leaning against a stone bench. "He just doesn't want anything a Human's touched. Am I right?"

The bodyguard faced his captain but did not answer. Briel waved him off and approached. Rowen felt a rush of embarrassment at the thought that Briel had seen him retching, but that turned to shame when he saw the Sylvan captain's bandaged hand. "I swear, Briel, I didn't know—"

"That your damn sword likes to cook any hand that isn't yours?" Briel smiled thinly. "No, I don't suppose you did. Besides, it seems to be a recent development, since I remember Captain Essidel once held that sword without getting his palm crisped." Briel stood at the very edge of the dais and peered over, unflinching.

Rowen resisted the impulse to push him over. "Don't your people believe in railings?"

"In the Shal'tiar, Sylvs are required to stand on the highest tree branch they can find then walk out and back blindfolded. It's a sign of guts and balance." Briel paused. "Not as high as this, though." He stepped away from the edge. "A dumb test if you ask me, since we spend most of our lives on the ground, fighting Olgrym." He waved at the bodyguards. "Leave us."

When they were gone, he gestured to the stone bench. Neither man sat.

"Something's happened," Briel said. "Several things, actually. None of them good."

"Is one of them you saying I'm still not allowed to leave this damn forest?"

Briel shook his head. "Actually, one of them is me sending you out of here tonight, right now, before sundown."

Rowen blinked.

"Seravin just died." Briel plucked the silver flask from Rowen's grasp, took a sip, then passed it back. "No big surprise, given how badly he was hurt, but still far from welcome news. Because it means, more than ever, that I'm in charge of the whole damn Sylvan nation."

Rowen wondered if Briel was joking, but the flicker of panic in the man's eyes proved otherwise.

"King Loslandril has ordered you put to death."

Rowen swallowed hard. He started to reach for Knightswrath but stopped himself. "When?"

"An hour ago. And this morning. And half a dozen times before that." Briel smiled thinly. "Obviously, the fact that you're still alive means my men are more comfortable taking orders from me than they are from a raving madman. But that could change. Seravin was a general. Popular, too. He could be a fool, but he was no mindless lapdog. Had he lived, I think he would have sided with you. He might have even deposed Loslandril without bloodshed. Now—"

"Doesn't the king have any other children? Nephews? A cousin?"

"Sylvan families aren't as large as Human broods. Loslandril had one son—and Silwren turned him into kindling." He added, "Don't bristle. I know the spineless bastard deserved it. Anyway, besides Quivalen, there *was* a nephew, living in the southern half of the forest, but the Olgrym killed him a week ago. There *might* be a distant aunt of royal blood, lost somewhere in the forest, but we can't find her. She's probably dead, too. And even if she isn't, she's old, even by Sylvan standards."

"So you're sending me away to save my life? Forgive me if I'm not convinced."

"I'm not doing it for you. What I said about needing you here still stands. But something else has happened." His voice took on a hard edge. "A scout came in, just a while after you left. For weeks now, we've been getting reports of Sylvan captives—*female* captives—being sent north. Instead of having their fun with them, the Olgrym are selling them to the Dhargots." He paused. "Do I have to explain how strange that is?"

Rowen shook his head.

"Sylvan women know better than to be taken captive by Olgrym. They'll slit their own throats before they let that happen. So at first, we thought the reports were just rumors. But they aren't. Apparently, for weeks, some of the Olgrym have been using some kind of poison on their arrows to sedate Sylvan captives. Only Olgrym don't use poison. Or arrows, for that matter. They consider them weak. So the only reason they'd do that..."

"Is if Fadarah ordered them," Rowen finished. "So while everything else was going on, Fadarah was also using Olgrym to collect Sylvan slaves for the Dhargots. Should I be surprised?"

"By *this*, yes." Briel lowered his voice. "Tell me, Human, when the Throng was tearing through the Free Cities, how did Fadarah get so many of the survivors to join him afterward?"

Rowen thought of Jalist, who had briefly served under Fadarah as a sellsword. "Partly by fear, but also by treating them decent, all things considered. They were fed and well paid. No mass executions. No rapes—"

Briel nodded. "Exactly. I'm not surprised that Fadarah tried to convince us that the Isle Knights were our enemies. I'm not even surprised that he formed an alliance with the Olgrym and the Dhargots. But there are some things even Fadarah wouldn't do."

Rowen thought of the Unseen. "I don't quite have as much faith in Fadarah's sense of morality as you." Something else occurred to him. "Wait, are you saying it *wasn't* Fadarah?"

"That it was Chorlga, collecting Sylvan captives?" Briel shrugged. "I don't know. Maybe Fadarah just got desperate. Gods know for all the harm he caused, the war hasn't exactly gone the way he must have hoped. Either way, all this makes me nervous." He lowered his voice further still, so that Rowen strained to hear. "There's something Captain Essidel and I used to talk about. It kept us up more nights than I can count. What Olgrym do to Sylvan women if they capture them... well, if you know anything about my people, you've heard the stories." Briel looked over the edge of the dais again. "But Fadarah himself was half Olgish. And a Shel'ai."

"I remember," Rowen said. "So?"

"Gods..." Briel rubbed his eyes in exasperation. "Besides Fadarah, have you ever seen a Shel'ai who wasn't a Sylv?"

Rowen said, "No."

"Even once?"

"No," Rowen repeated.

"But Fadarah's existence means it's possible. You need a Sylvan mother, but the father could be something else. A Sylv, a Human, even an Olg."

Rowen nodded slowly. "I suppose, but why—"Then he understood. "Gods!"

Briel answered with a grimacing smile. "I could be wrong. I *hope* I'm wrong. But the last thing this world needs is Chorlga, or someone like him, trying to breed Shel'ai slaves."

The foul Dragonkin was undoubtedly involved somehow, just as he seemed to be involved in nearly all the misery that had befallen the people of Ruun in recent years. "Chorlga... I still haven't even met him." *And I'm supposed to kill him.*

"Our king saw him, more than once, and it drove him from wisdom to madness." Briel flexed the fingers of his broken hand. "From what I can gather, it was Chorlga who encouraged much of the animosity between Sylv and Shel'ai. But you probably already guessed that. Whether or not Chorlga's responsible for these Sylvan women being taken captive, he's still out there, working his devilry. The way that Dragonkin turned us all against each other, I half expect to turn around and find him laughing at me."

"He's not here." Rowen touched Knightswrath's hilt. "Don't ask me how I know that, but I do."

"Do you think he knows about Silwren and Knightswrath?"

"That Silwren's... gone?" He shook his head. "I don't think so, or else he would have struck while we were vulnerable. I think he's cooking up... something else. Back to these captives. You know where they are?"

Briel nodded. "My scout found a Dhargothi compound a week's ride north of here, full of Sylvan captives. Women only. She said... she could hear what was going on inside." The captain shuddered. "I don't care whether Fadarah's involved. I don't care whether the Dhargots are trying to breed Shel'ai of their own or are just after what passes among Humans for pleasure. I want it stopped. And I want every man involved in this cut to ribbons."

Rowen flashed back to the Dark Quarter of Lyos, where certain brutes visited their own brand of violence not just on women but on children, too. An old loathing crept up within him. "What do you want me to do?"

"Do what I can't," Briel said. "There's still fighting in the forests. I still have to hunt down Doomsayer and his Olgrym, even if I have to chase them all the way back to Godsfall. I might be able to spare a single squad of men, but I have no officers left to lead them. Nobody familiar enough with the outer lands, anyway."

"Do you really think they'll follow me?"

"They will if I order it."

"And afterward?"

Briel hesitated. "I still need you here, Isle Knight. But I need this done more. Besides, come back a hero, and maybe you can keep King Loslandril from having me put to death."

Rowen saw a spark of fear in the Sylvan captain's eyes. His mistrust of the man turned once more to sympathy. Nevertheless, he heard himself say, "I won't promise I'll come back."

Briel looked surprised. "Gods, Locke, you have the brains of an urusk. But I guess I didn't really think you'd return and help us… which is why I think you actually might." He straightened. "You'll find your horse at the gates. The scout will ride with you, too, to show you the way. Her name's Kilisti. She's one of the last Shal'tiar I have left, tough as kingsteel but nothing you'll want to cuddle with." He smiled thinly. "I'm not giving you an army, you understand, but I scraped together a few volunteers."

"You assembled them before you even asked me?"

"I had a feeling you'd say yes. But if you want to stay and try your luck with King Loslandril after I'm dead, you're free to try. Hells, maybe I'll lead the rescue party myself. I suppose the danger's about equal." He cleared his throat. "My men won't love you. They don't even like you. But they won't betray you. I can promise that. And this: if they can, they'll get you there and back in one piece." Briel glanced down at Knightswrath. "Though I suspect they'll be relying on *you* for protection as much as the inverse. If you can bring all of them back unharmed, I'd appreciate it."

Rowen knew better than to promise that, either.

Briel hesitated, uneasy. "That's it, then. Good luck, Human." He turned to walk away.

"What about the child?"

Briel stopped. "The child?"

Rowen glanced at the bodyguards, some of whom were within earshot. He drew closer to Briel and lowered his voice, uncertain the news was common knowledge. "The Shel'ai girl you told me about."

Briel nodded. "Funny how things change in a day. But I'll keep her as safe as I can."

Rowen frowned. "That's not very reassuring."

"It'll have to do. Besides, what do you care? You don't even know her name."

"Then tell it to me."

Briel shrugged. "As far as I know, her parents didn't bother to give her one."

A surge of sadness hit Rowen. Blinking back tears, he cleared his throat. "Name her Sariel."

Frowning, Briel asked, "Do you know what that word means?"

Rowen nodded.

Briel stood in silence for a heartbeat then cleared his throat. "Why all this concern over one squalling infant you've never even seen?"

"I haven't seen those Sylvan women you're sending me to rescue, either."

"Fair point." Briel sighed. "Then how about this? So long as I'm alive, Sariel will be safe. But I don't expect to stay alive for long without your help. So see this done, and help both Sariel and me reach old age. Agreed?"

A hint of raw desperation in his eyes, Captain Briel waited for an answer. Rowen bit his lip. Finally, Briel sighed, turned, and walked away.

Rowen found Snowdark saddled just outside the bulwark that the Sylvs were using in place of the ruined World Gate. The spirited piebald palfrey perked up at the sight of him, straining against the Sylvan attendant holding the reins. Smiling, Rowen took the reins and patted the familiar horse's neck. He was sorry that he had not been able to visit her more often, let alone liberate her from the stables where the Sylvan horses seemed about as friendly toward her as the Sylvan people were toward Rowen.

"Enough of that," he promised. "We're going north again. Open plains. Probably running for our lives before long, so I hope you're well rested."

She had already been loaded with his few possessions, apparently taken from his room. These included an ancient scroll taken from the famous Scrollhouse of Atheion. To contain the scroll, the Sylvs had gifted him an ornate, waterproof container wrought of silver. Rowen opened the container to make sure the scroll was inside. He doubted the Sylvs would steal it—priceless though it was—but Silwren had risked so much to get it for him, to say nothing of what its lost histories could mean to the Knighthood.

If they're willing to believe a word of it, that is...

Rowen stowed the flask his bodyguard had given him, fit one foot into the stirrup, and hoisted himself into the saddle. Only then did he turn to face the Sylvs waiting for him. Though he'd spied them immediately, milling restlessly near his horse astride their own mounts, he had deliberately avoided the impulse to greet them. He was tired of exchanging words and looks with people who hated him, and a glance confirmed that these people were no different.

Five men, all dressed in brigandines and forest-green cloaks, were armed with longbows and curved swords. Four looked young, even by Sylvan standards, while the fifth had white hair and wore a patch over one eye. The older Sylv urged his horse closer to Rowen's. When he waved, Rowen saw that the Sylv was missing two fingers on his right hand. Judging from the bandages he wore, despite his calm expression, the loss had happened fairly recently.

"Greetings, Knight. I'm Sergeant Rhos'ari." He introduced the other Sylvan men, each of whom offered a curt nod. After introducing all the men, Rhos'ari pointed to a woman who had turned her horse away from them and was already waiting some distance down the road. The old Sylv's expression soured. "That's Kilisti. She says she can lead us north, to that Dhargothi compound. But we'll have to get around Godsfall and Quorim first." He seemed about to say more but stopped himself.

Rowen gave the woman a hard look. That she had not even waited for his arrival was a bad sign, but he could deal with her later. He glanced at the faces of the men he was to command. They were the first men he'd commanded since his brief stint as a gang leader in the Dark Quarter. He sighed. "Captain Briel tells me you all volunteered. I can't imagine you're happy about it. But I'm glad for the help. Thank you."

Iventine cleared his throat. "We aren't here for you, Human." He spat on the ground.

Rhos'ari broke in quickly. "I think what Iventine means, Knight, is that we'd all rather stay and help drive the Olgrym from our lands, but those are *our* people—our women—being held captive out there. If the Dhargots really are trying to breed more wytches, then saving those women is the most important thing we can do right now."

Rowen forced a smile. "I see Captain Briel isn't the only one who fears the Dhargots might be up to something worse than slave trading. So be it. We don't have to like each other to have common enemies."

Rhos'ari nodded a bit too quickly for Rowen's liking. "We'll follow your orders, Knight. Don't worry about that."

Rowen tapped Knightswrath's hilt, realizing he might very well summon its power and read the Sylvan sergeant's mind if he wanted to. Instead, he urged Snowdark away from the World Gate, half hoping the other Sylvs would refuse to follow.

He quickened Snowdark's pace until Kilisti was right in front of him. Though she was armed like the other Sylvs, she wore the dark fighting leathers of a Shal'tiar. Her armor was torn in several places and speckled with dried blood. Rowen cleared his throat. The woman did not slow.

Rowen swallowed his irritation and said, "You're the one called Kilisti. Tell me—"

The woman hissed for him to be quiet. Without turning her head, she said, "We're close to the capital, but there might still be Olgrym hiding in these forests. Keep your voice down unless you want a fight."

Rowen's face warmed. Though none of the other Sylvs made a sound, he did not have to turn around to feel their eyes on him. He wondered if the Shal'tiar fighter was testing him or merely offering sound advice in a curt manner. He decided to pretend it was the latter. Lowering his voice, he said, "We won't reach the Ash'bana Plains until morning—and that's if we ride all night."

"Your knowledge of *my* homeland's geography is impressive, Knight. Your point?"

Rowen felt his face heat further. "Just that we'll need to camp somewhere safe. Is there any place you'd recommend?"

"No camp. You said yourself, we'll reach the plains by sunrise."

"And beyond the plains is Godsfall. You may relish the idea of traveling through Olgrym country while tired, but I don't."

Rowen hoped his tone would get his point across, but Kilisti's quick response said otherwise. "Sylvs can go days without sleep. Nap in your saddle if you need to, Knight. We'll keep you safe."

Rowen heard someone chuckle behind him. He bit back a curse then grabbed Kilisti's arm. She jerked away as though touched by fire. Steel flashed. Snowdark reared even as Rowen swung up his hand and met Kilisti's blow with his vambrace. Sylvan steel sparked off kingsteel armor. Rowen grabbed Knightswrath's hilt but did not draw. He forced another smile.

"Is it common for Sylvs to attack their commanding officers?"

Rowen was mid-sentence when Kilisti turned her horse and faced him. Rowen managed to finish without pause, but the sight of the Sylvan woman's face made him wish he'd drawn Knightswrath after all. At least a half dozen scars crisscrossed her cheeks. The tip of her nose was gone, along with the tapered points of both her ears. But most striking of all were her eyes, which were not azure like other Sylvs', nor violet like those of a Shel'ai, but ice blue. Rowen had not seen eyes like that among any of the Sylvs, save Captain Essidel. Those eyes had lent the late Captain of the Shal'tiar a certain air of foreboding calm. In Kilisti, though, those eyes flashed with murder.

"You are *not* my commanding officer. Essidel was. Briel, after him. Not you."

Rowen heard the others surge forward to join them. To his relief, Sergeant Rhos'ari urged his horse between them. He said something in Sylvan to Kilisti that Rowen did not catch.

Kilisti gave Rhos'ari a scathing look, spat on the ground, then faced Rowen again. "Apologies, Knight. You startled me. That's all."

Unable to formulate an appropriate response, Rowen merely nodded.

Sergeant Rhos'ari spoke up again. "I heard your question, Knight. There aren't any villages left north of the capital. The Olgrym burned them all. Same with the Shal'tiar forts. Might be a Wyldkin village left somewhere—"

Rowen shook his head. "We'd have to go too far west to find it." He thought quickly. "Que'ahl is closest. We'll stop there."

Rhos'ari blinked. "I just told you, Knight, all the Shal'tiar forts were burned."

"I heard you. We can hide in the wreckage, if needs be. If I recall, Olgrym are superstitious. Lots of people died at Que'ahl—I know. I was there. The Olgrym won't go near it. We'll rest until sundown then travel north under cover of darkness." He watched the Sylvs exchange glances. "I'm not asking, damn you."

He guided Snowdark past them and continued on, hoping he was going in the right direction. He thought of Igrid. Something in Kilisti's demeanor reminded him of his first encounter with the Iron Sister. She'd been drunk, lamenting the destruction of Hesod by the Dhargots. Despite this, she'd nearly killed him when he'd made the mistake of getting too close. Despite his foul mood, the thought of Igrid made him smile.

CHAPTER TEN

THE HILL

Igrid was barely beyond the gates of Lyos when a man pushed past her, running back into the city. The man's face was ashen. He had one hand pressed to his shoulder. Blood welled between his fingers. A glance at his blood-speckled toga told her that he was no slumdweller, and the tempting coin purse still hanging from his belt told her that he had not been robbed. A moment later, two men of the Red Watch stumbled up King's Bend. One supported the other, who was missing an arm.

Igrid's pulse quickened, but she resisted drawing the stilettos from her sleeves. She helped up an old man who had fallen and was about to be trampled, then did the same for a young nobleman, plucking the coin purse from his belt before she pushed him toward the safety of the city gates. Then, pivoting, she picked up a crying child who could not keep pace with his mother, who was already holding two babies under her arms, and carried him through the gates herself. She sat him down then ran back out.

Somehow, in just those few scant moments, the chaos on King's Bend had doubled. Citizens streamed up the road by the dozens. Others raced toward the slums on the south side of the hill. Street vendors abandoned their wares while others tried to hastily load their goods into carts. Some of the carts had overturned, spilling contents that were either stolen or kicked aside in the rush. A few men fought.

Igrid turned, tempted once again to return inside—then she saw a glint of metal down the curving road, at the base of the hill. More screaming citizens ran past, knocking her out of the way and obscuring her view. She side-stepped off the road, hoping for a better look.

Far below, men in scarlet uniforms emblazed with the falcon of Lyos— some on foot, others on horseback—were locked in a pitched battle against a company of Isle Knights. Sunlight flashed off swords. Igrid's eyes widened in disbelief. Then she shook her head. No tabards, no sigils. Yet the attackers wore full armor.

Lancers, maybe?

She shook her head again. The Ivairians had no conflict with Lyos. Besides, if Arnil Royce had spoken the truth, the Lancers were busy fighting the Dhargots. Her eyes narrowed. The Red Watch was losing. One man fell, then another. Horses cried. Some bolted, tossing their riders. By now, most of the citizens on King's Bend had either fled back into the city or run to the Dark Quarter. More men of the Red Watch streamed toward the battle. A trumpet sounded. Below, the Red Watch was desperately calling for reinforcements.

A guardsman got behind an enemy and shoved his sword deep into a chink in his armor—an unmistakably mortal blow. But when the guardsman withdrew his blade, no blood darkened the steel. The armored figure did not even seem to notice the wound, though it turned and cut down the guardsman with strange, frightful nonchalance.

A shudder ran through Igrid's body. All the armored men wore steel or brass facemasks. That meant their voices would have had a distinctive, metallic reverberation. She listened closely but all the shouts, screams, and frantic orders that echoed in the afternoon air seemed to issue from the throats of the Red Watch.

Those are not men.

She turned back to the gates of Lyos. A young, frightened guardsman caught her eye. He beckoned to her. "Back into the city, miss! The king says shut the gate." As he spoke, a final squad of Red Watch rode out on horseback, looking determined but none too eager to join the fray.

The guardsman at the gate called out to her again. Igrid glanced at him then back at King's Bend. Most of the people were inside, though a few dozen still struggled up the road, hauling carts or wounded loved ones. Meanwhile, the Red Watch had all but lost. Despite their advantage of numbers and their horses, they couldn't hold the armored men at bay. The shining armor closed ranks and marched slowly, quietly, up King's Bend. Blood ran from their weapons. Some of their facemasks wore ghastly smiles. Men of the Red Watch began to panic. Some fled back up the road. Others fled the hill altogether, forsaking the struggling citizens they were sworn to protect.

Igrid touched her stiletto. She knew she could do nothing for the ones locked outside the gates, aside from urging everyone to make for the Dark

Quarter. *Time to save my own skin. Even Rowen couldn't blame me for that. Nothing I can do out here, anyway.*

But somehow, her feet disobeyed, carrying her away from the gates instead of through them. The guardsman called out to her again, pleading and frantic. Then she heard the city gates slam shut.

Fen-Shea emerged from his little house, holding a blackened mace with a long handle wrapped in snakeskin. He rubbed his eyes.

Though technically still a resident of the Dark Quarter, Fen-Shea had received special permission to have his house built a little higher on Pallantine Hill, where he had a better view of the slums. This was in recognition of his service at the Battle of Lyos, and hero or no, he was still the leader of the Bloody Asps—and gangmen were not welcome in Lyos.

He could see the source of the cries that had woken him from his midday slumber. "Either I've been smoking too much *fran-té,* or this damn city's under attack again." He glanced at the other members of his gang who milled about, many of them half naked, all stunned into silence.

Finally, one said, "Dhargots?"

Fen-Shea fingered his famous necklace of rodent skulls. "Don't think so. There'd be warning if it was."

"Then what?"

"Gods, Will, if I was smart enough to know that, I wouldn't be living *here,* now would I?" Fen-Shea pointed. "You two, go see what's happening." He turned south.

A crowd was rushing into the Dark Quarter, screaming and frantic. *Are they lost, suicidal, or did they just get locked out of their own city?*

Then Fen-Shea saw a group of frightened men and women, all half naked. He might have mistaken them for brothel workers who had been driven from their labors before they had time to dress, but the spiritual symbol of Dyoni—a nude, smirking hermaphrodite—hung around their necks. He spotted an old priest of Armahg in blue robes, too, looking almost as out of place as the others.

"Send some boys to make sure those clerics don't get harmed," he said to Will. "Last thing I need is the gods turning against me." Then he turned back toward the sounds of battle. He listened then shook his head. "Might need to run. Lem, you and Dirk find all the boys and get them armed. Warn the other gangs, too, I guess. Though if they ain't already bristling, they're probably too deaf to care about. Remind everybody I'm in charge here."

A fresh chorus of battle cries nearly drowned out his final statement.

Fen-Shea turned back toward the door of his house. A pretty young woman stood in the doorway, half naked, holding a squalling infant to her breast. "Cadney, get back inside!" he snapped. "No, wait." He listened a moment longer, clutching his mace. "Forget all that. Get Little Thass in the wagon and ride east. Go now. Don't pack a thing. I'll send some boys to keep you safe."

"Like hell you will." Cadney came out of the house and stood beside him. She was holding their baby with only one hand. Her other held a kitchen cleaver.

Fen-Shea smiled. "I'll be fine, girl. I'm just gonna watch your pretty back for a spell. Besides, you know I'm better at busting skulls when I don't have to worry about you two." He kissed her then kissed the crying baby's forehead. He gave her a gentle push.

He thought that she might argue, but then more screams reached their ears. The slum woman looked down at their baby then back at him. Her features hardened. She nodded. She rushed toward a wagon and the small stables that held their horse.

Fen-Shea forced himself to turn his back on her. He gestured to the last two members of the Bloody Asps standing within earshot. "Help her hitch up the wagon. And keep them safe, or even Fohl won't want you when I'm finished!"

The men nodded and hurried to obey.

Fen-Shea hefted his mace and faced the sounds of battle again. Metal glinted in the distance, where corpses littered the ground, most wearing the scarlet tabards of the Red Watch.

"Never thought a sight like that would make me sad." He glanced back at the slums. He saw hundreds of people running. He thought of the last time the Dark Quarter had been threatened. Then, they'd all banded together, led by Rowen Locke—and a Shel'ai wytch, of all things. But Fen-Shea did not think that would happen again.

"Pity," he sighed. "I liked this house."

He strode down into the slums, shouting for attention over the chaos. He hoped he still had time to organize some kind of defense before whatever had decimated the Red Watch did the same to them.

Jalist had hardly reached King's Bend, trying to find the nearest Red Watch officer, when a Jol turned and cut the horse out from under him. Jalist managed to leap clear before the rouncey fell, but a jagged cobblestone gashed his forehead. Wiping blood from his eyes, Jalist drew his sword, but the Jol had already moved on to a more tempting target: the very Red Watch officer Jalist had been trying to reach.

"Damn."

Then a second Jol swung hands that ended in scimitars. Jalist ducked, rolled away, and ducked again when a third Jol thrust for his neck. On reflex, Jalist struck back. His blade left a scratch in the Jol's grinning facemask, but the Jol did not slow. Jalist backpedaled, dove to avoid yet another attack, then ran.

Ahead of him, a guardsman tried to parry a Jol's blade, but the Jol's strength easily guided the blade through the man's tabard and chainmail. A second guardsman howled in rage and attacked the Jol from behind, swinging at its neck with both hands. The sword shattered. The guardsman gaped at the broken blade then flung the hilt at the Jol's face and reached for another weapon. The Jol swung first, ending the fight.

Jalist dove between the Jol's legs and ran clear before it could swing. He slashed its knees for good measure, though he knew the blow did no harm. He ran a few yards farther up King's Bend, angling toward a squad of Red Watch on horseback. A dozen strong, bloody and ragged, they hesitated, seemingly torn between reengaging the Jolym or fleeing for their lives. Jalist shouted to another officer. The man frowned at the sight of him.

"Their eyes," Jalist screamed. "Stab the bastards in their eyes!"

The officer stared, uncomprehending. "Back to the city, boys. Ride for your lives!" He spurred his horse toward Lyos without waiting for the others to follow. Some of the guardsmen hesitated, glancing back at their still-fighting comrades, but most thundered back up King's Bend as fast as their horses would carry them.

Jalist swore again as another Jol came at him. This one was wrought all of brass. Sunlight shown off its body, blinding him. Jalist shielded his eyes, stepped back, then turned and ran. He made it halfway up King's Bend before his strength failed. He slumped, exhausted, against an abandoned turnip cart. Gasping for air, he glanced over one shoulder.

He'd managed to outrun the Jolym, but they had not stopped. As the last of the Red Watch fled, the Jolym shambled steadily up the road in neat, deathly quiet formation. Jalist tried to catch another Red Watch officer by arm as he ran past.

"The eyes! Listen to me—"

The panicked officer shoved him away then blindly swung his sword for good measure. Jalist managed to block the blow with his own weapon, but before he could speak, the frightened officer was running again.

Jalist looked toward the city. Perhaps fifty survivors—some guardsmen, plus a handful of citizens—massed before the closed gates of Lyos, screaming to be let in. The battlements swarmed with archers. He felt a surge of hope. The Jolym were not within bow range yet but would be soon enough. Surely with so many arrows raining down on them, chance would guide a few to the Jolym's only weak spot.

A ragged smile formed on his lips. Then his smile vanished. The Jolym had drawn to a halt, just out of range. They stared up the road, quiet and motionless, blood running off their weapons. The only sound came from the wounded and dying men the Jolym had left in their wake and those trying to beg their way back into the city.

Jalist braced one hand against the turnip cart and pushed himself up. With great effort, he staggered the rest of the way up King's Bend. He reflected on the last time he'd been to Lyos. Then, as now, he'd been on the wrong side of the walls—though at the time, he'd been leading a revolt in Fadarah's Throng, just as it was about to attack the city. But that hadn't stopped the defenders of Lyos from arresting him afterward. He wondered how they would greet him now, if they recognized him.

He scanned the panicked crowds for a familiar face, hoping to find at least a veteran officer calm enough to listen. The gates of Lyos finally swung open, and the survivors began to surge inside. Then he saw *her*.

Igrid leaned against a wagon, accompanied by an old man wearing the priestly red robes of Maelmohr. Blood matted her red hair. For a moment, he was torn between helping the cleric drag her inside and finishing her off with his own sword.

The priest looked up at his approach. He flinched when he saw Jalist then smiled with relief. "I've never been so happy to see a Dwarr in all my life. Please, son, help me carry this poor woman—"

"I'll carry her, Father. Don't worry. Get inside. I'll be right behind you."

The cleric glanced back at the motionless Jolym and nodded. He stood and made for Lyos without looking back.

Jalist knelt in front of Igrid. "Hello, Iron Sister."

Igrid looked up, dizzily blinking her green eyes. Then with astonishing quickness, she plucked a stiletto from one sleeve and thrust it at Jalist's face.

Stunned, the Dwarr leaned back and caught her wrist. He plucked the knife from her grasp and tossed it away. He grabbed her other wrist then eyed the wound at the top of her head, half hidden by her red curls. "Girl, you're lucky that Jol didn't split your brains. Can you stand, or do I have to toss you over my shoulder like a sack of potatoes?"

"I can stand," Igrid hissed through clenched teeth. "But I wouldn't have to, if that blasted wytch would make herself useful, for once."

Jalist blinked in confusion.

"What, is she out of wytchfire? Tell her to melt those damn things down." Igrid looked around.

Jalist finally understood. "Silwren isn't here. Neither is Rowen. I'm alone."

Igrid stared at him for a moment. "Sack of potatoes it is, then."

But before Jalist could gather her up in his arms, the gates slammed shut once more. Jalist straightened, shouting up at the battlements, but a great crash drowned him out. Fireballs and jagged rocks arced over the city walls. Momentarily forgetting their danger, Jalist whirled after the siege missiles.

Some flew wild, but more than a few stones struck the Jolym, eliciting a sound like the ringing of a bell. Meanwhile, clay pots filled with burning pitch shattered at the Jolym's feet, spreading fire. But the Jolym did not cry out. Those hammered down by rocks sat up and rose to their feet without pause. Despite great dents in their brass and steel bodies, they looked unfazed.

"The eyes, you fools! That's their only weakness!" Jalist shouted up at the battlements, only to be drowned out by the blaring of trumpets. He guessed that meant the Red Watch was calling in their reserves. Jalist turned back to Igrid. To his surprise, she'd managed to stand, though she leaned heavily on the cart.

"We'll have to seek refuge in the Dark Quarter." *Gods, there's something I never thought I'd say.* "Just so you know, I'm better at carrying people when they don't stab me in the back."

Jalist waited until Igrid nodded. Then he wrapped one strong arm around her waist and hoisted her over his shoulder. Though she was light, his muscles protested, already shaking with weariness. Jalist spotted a few more wounded guardsmen stumbling up King's Bend, dumbly staggering toward the gates. "No, make for the slums," he shouted. He started down, fighting to keep his balance.

CHAPTER ELEVEN

BONES AND DUST

CHORLGA STOOD ON A HILL half a mile outside Lyos, watching the slaughter. Despite the distance, he had no trouble witnessing it, for he could see through each Jol's eyes as if they were his own. Three hundred Jolym marched into the crowds with icy nonchalance, hacking and cleaving everything in their path.

Chorlga watched stoically as an officer led a second force of defenders down the road and into battle. He felt a pang of respect for the man's courage. He was tempted to have his Jolym spare the man—he might need officers of quality in his new empire—but decided against it.

Though the new company of defenders outnumbered the Jolym three to one, they fared no better than their comrades. Crossbows shuddered. Swords snapped. The Jolym shrugged off every blow and surged up Pallantine Hill, unhindered. Despite heavy losses, the Lyosi officer led his riders against the Jolym in one reckless, hopeless charge after another. Finally, the Jolym cut him down. The defenders' courage faltered. Those who remained fled back up the hill and sealed the city gates.

Chorlga had proven his point. With a mere thought, he ordered his Jolym to cease their attack. They stood in tight formation outside the gates, just beyond bow range, lest a lucky arrow strike one of them in the eye. This still left them within range of siege weapons, though. Catapults, trebuchets, and ballistas hurled all manner of stones, spears, and burning pitch at the Jolym— without effect.

Chorlga saw what he knew must be the city's ruler standing at the battlements, his face ashen. Chorlga would wait a few more minutes for panic to spread, then he would present himself before the Lyosi king and demand the city's surrender. If they refused, Chorlga would blow open their gates and send in his Jolym.

"But I won't kill everyone. As Nekiel was so fond of saying, there's no sense in crowning yourself king of a cemetery." He turned to the cloaked, ruined man kneeling beside him. "Don't you agree?"

The Nightmare did not answer.

"Perhaps I should have sent you to burn the Lotus Isles. You aren't proving to be much of a traveling companion."

He thought of the next phase of his plan, as far as the Nightmare was concerned. Once Chorlga had secured the loyalty of Lyos and his Jolym had destroyed Fâyu Jinn's detestable Knighthood—a lost cause, since their rigid code precluded surrender—they would head west. With the Shel'ai all but obliterated and Silwren surely dead, the war Fadarah had started, secretly prodded along by Chorlga, still raged from one coast of Ruun to the other. The chaos sewn by that war would make it easier for Chorlga to finally take control. But to do that, he would have to contend with the strongest remaining faction: the Dhargots. He could either destroy them or subjugate them. He favored the latter.

All Chorlga had to do was present himself before their blood-crazed princes and show them the Nightmare, and they would be his. If any hesitated, he could unleash the Nightmare long enough to destroy a few battalions.

Everything was finally falling into place. Chorlga faced Pallantine Hill again. A cold breeze mingled with the sound of screams kindled a memory ten centuries old. He'd once stood on a hill—perhaps this very one—and watched Nekiel's forces raze a previous incarnation of Lyos, as repayment for some slight that Chorlga could no longer remember. He'd pleaded with Nekiel to show mercy—the city had housed a woman whom Chorlga fancied. Not even a Dragonkin, she was just a pretty slave girl who had caught his eye.

Chorlga shook off the memory. "Bones and dust," the Dragonkin snarled. "As we'll all be, soon enough."

It was not the Nightmare who had spoken. The young man was kneeling, blank faced, rocking himself. Beyond him stood an old man in a tattered cloak. His Sylvan features were marred by a patchwork of scars, warts, and sores. His lips were twisted into a permanent sad smile, as though they'd been torn apart then poorly resewn. But the man's eyes were violet, the pupils bone white.

Chorlga turned to the Nightmare as though he might ask him for confirmation, but the young man's expression remained unchanged. Finally, Chorlga summoned wytchfire that coursed the length of his arms. "I must learn to be more careful with my spells. I should have known I'd bring you back."

El'rash'lin stepped forward. He kept his gaze on Chorlga but squeezed the Nightmare's shoulder, as if in greeting, though the kneeling man did not respond. "There are a great many other things you've failed to foresee, Dragonkin. But that's to be expected when one drinks too often from a poison well."

Chorlga sneered. "You refer to Namundvar's Well as poison now? Interesting."

"All things can be poison, if they're misused. The same goes for the Light." El'rash'lin gave Chorlga a piteous look. "I know. *We* used the Well, thinking it would give us enough power to keep all the Shel'ai safe. Instead, it drove Iventine mad and nearly did the same to the rest of us." He glanced at the silent figure again, who was still rocking himself incessantly.

Chorlga laughed. "Of *course* it didn't work, you fool. You're a Shel'ai. I am a Dragonkin. My cup is deeper than yours."

El'rash'lin gave Chorlga a sad smile. "But you've still drunk too much." El'rash'lin gathered his tattered cloak and sat down, cross-legged, on the plains. He gestured for Chorlga to do the same. When the Dragonkin did not, El'rash'lin said, "The Well didn't just corrupt my good looks or muck up poor Iventine's mind. It showed us something we aren't supposed to see." He paused. "You know what I'm talking about."

Chorlga's fists clenched. Wytchfire leaked between his fingers. "Did you come here to talk metaphysics or to fight?"

"I admit, neither sounds appealing." El'rash'lin sighed. "There is a reason why the Light does not reveal itself to us, the same way it did to the dragons. That feeling of peace and calm, of unity with something higher... then *losing* that... is more than our kind can handle."

"*Our* kind?"

El'rash'lin continued without acknowledging Chorlga's response. "Namundvar's Well wasn't built to satisfy your thirst for power. It wasn't made to look without. It was made to look *within*. That's the mistake we Shel'ai made." He paused. "*My* mistake. In that, I suppose I am not so different from my Dragonkin forebears."

The Nightmare whimpered suddenly, startling them, though his expression remained unchanged. El'rash'lin gave the kneeling man a piteous look then faced Chorlga. The look did not disappear.

"If we're not careful, we end up mistaking peace for power, then pursuing power at the expense of everything else. That's what happened to *you*, isn't it?"

When Chorlga did not answer, El'rash'lin took a step toward him. "I cannot even begin to fathom how lonely you've been. So many centuries, trapped on this continent with people you view as little more than animals—"

"You *are* animals!" Plumes of wytchfire writhed between Chorlga's fingers again. "Do you think the Dragonkin ruled without help? For every Human, Sylv, and Dwarr who fought us, six more were willing to betray their own kind, just to earn our favor. I've seen fathers offer up daughters. I've seen children stab parents in their sleep. Is *this* the world you're trying to protect?" Chorlga continued before El'rash'lin could answer. "At least under Dragonkin rule, there was order. No one died of starvation. No plagues. Even our slaves received a measure of justice."

El'rash'lin's twisted lips formed a sneer of their own. "Please tell me more about Dragonkin justice."

Chorlga took a deep breath and let it go. "We both know you aren't strong enough to oppose me. I haven't killed you yet because I sense a secret you've walled up in your mind. Are you going to tell me, or should I reduce that to ash when I do the same to your bones?"

El'rash'lin did not speak. Then, in a voice suddenly heavy with grief, he said, "Silwren is dead. Only it was not the Sylvan king who killed her." El'rash'lin's grief became derision. "Before she died, she rekindled Knightswrath. She entrusted the blade to an Isle Knight, one of an order descended from Fâyu Jinn himself. She died so that he might have the power to destroy you... just as Nâya sacrificed herself, all those centuries ago." El'rash'lin rose to his feet. "And you didn't foresee any of this... did you, Dragonkin?"

El'rash'lin took a step forward. Chorlga stepped back.

"You didn't think Silwren would find Knightswrath in time or that she wouldn't have the courage to act. That there weren't any Isle Knights left who could use it, anyway. But you were wrong. The Light chose someone. And he's coming for you. If I were you, I'd run."

Chorlga stared, speechless. Sensing his agitation, the Nightmare had risen like some faithful hound, wytchfire burning all around him. But Chorlga did not give the order to attack. He probed El'rash'lin's mind. The Shel'ai-turned-Dragonkin had unwalled his thoughts. Chorlga saw that he was not lying. He shook his head in disbelief.

"This cannot be... I was *in* Sylvos. If the Sword had been there, I would have sensed it. If Silwren had done this—"

"You *should* have sensed it, with all your power. All the control you *think* you have. But you didn't, did you?" El'rash'lin shook his head. "When you brought Iventine back from the dead, when you drained those poor fey bastards to increase your power. You saw glimpses of what Silwren had done, but you ignored the visions. And what will you do now? Burn cities and frighten children? Is that what you've spent the better part of ten centuries planning? Is *this* the lofty empire you hoped to design, Dragonkin?"

As though in answer, a fresh chorus of battle cries echoed across the Simurgh Plains. Instead of panic, these rang out with defiance. Puzzled, Chorlga faced Pallantine Hill. He looked once more through the eyes of a Jol. Puzzlement became disbelief. Another host of defenders was charging his creations, originating not from the gates of Lyos but from the slums far below. What was more, the host was armed with bows and spears. As Chorlga stared, the wretched slum dwellers took aim and loosed a cloud of arrows—aiming for the eyes.

Chorlga winced as one Jol after another fell. He was about to order the rest to charge the slum dwellers when the Jol he was temporarily inhabiting was struck down. A raw jolt sent Chorlga reeling. He quickly regained his senses, but rather than see through yet another Jol's eyes, he issued a mental command. All the remaining Jolym quietly turned their backs on the arrows and began to march away.

Back on the hill again, fully returned to his own body, Chorlga faced El'rash'lin. Though the latter did not speak, his twisted lips had lifted to form a broader, mocking smile. Chorlga tensed. Wytchfire pulsed from his hands.

"I will cast myself into the Dragonward before I cede this land back to the dogs."

He brought his hands up. His fingers uncoiled. He expected El'rash'lin to defend himself; the old man simply stared back as wytchfire flowed over his body, burning his shadow into the plains.

Chorlga stood there, his breath ragged. Then he faced the Nightmare. The young man had stopped rocking and was staring at the scorched grass where El'rash'lin had been. Then he started rocking again.

"Follow," Chorlga called out. He started down the hill, his fingers still clenched into fists.

The small company made its way through the ravaged Wytchforest, where corpses of Sylvs and Olgrym still scattered the forest floor. Fighting the impulse to pinch his nose, Rowen employed an old trick he'd learned as a sellsword. He breathed deep, forcing himself to take in the smell of the surrounding rot without retching, so that it would clog his senses and he would forget it was there more quickly.

"Gods, I thought they'd gathered all the bodies by now."

"Just the ones near the capital," Rhos'ari answered. "Too many kin to bury, too many Olgrym to burn."

"And we still have a kingdom to defend," Iventine added coldly.

Rowen resisted the urge to reply.

Rhos'ari called out to him, "Wait a moment, Knight."

Rowen reined in and turned to see Rhos'ari unslinging his bow. The others did the same—all save Kilisti, who drew her shortsword. Rowen marveled that Rhos'ari was able to draw a bow despite the missing fingers on his right hand. Indeed, he held the bow awkwardly and winced, but his arms were steady. Rowen was close enough to Rhos'ari to see a burgundy smear of a poison called quickdeath on the arrow's tip. It was the strongest, fastest poison the Sylvs had, though like all poisons, even quickdeath had trouble bringing down an Olg.

Before Rowen could ask what they were doing, Rhos'ari took aim and loosed an arrow into the corpse of a nearby Olg. The arrow met its target with a sickening thud. The corpse did not stir. The other Sylvan warriors loosed arrows of their own, each choosing a separate target. Rowen finally understood. He'd seen the trick before: a man lay on a battlefield, surrounded by the slain, pretending to be one of them. Then he attacked whoever ventured near. Rowen remembered how a variation on this strategy had nearly gotten him killed by a cruel, one-eyed sellsword named Dagath. He drew Knightswrath.

"Everything smells dead here." Still, he scrutinized the fallen Olgrym for movement. As he did so, he felt a pang of sorrow. Their hulking forms looked obscene, almost surreal in contrast to the sleepy beauty of the surrounding trees. Their ash-gray skin, pulled taut over muscular bodies, was crusted with dried blood, bristling with arrows. A few stared up at the leafy canopy with wide, fey eyes.

Rowen thought back to the Olgrym's night charge on the Shal'tiar fort of Que'ahl, when all the Olgrym had howled like rabid beasts and some even lit their own bodies on fire. The Shal'tiar and their Wyldkin allies had succeeded in defending Que'ahl that night, albeit at great cost, but the Olgrym's pent-up fury had been enough to wash over the Wytchforest.

He was still contemplating this when, to his left, Rhos'ari took aim at another Olg. This one kneeled against a tree about thirty feet away. Though it was covered in dried blood, no arrows protruded from its body—it wasn't moving. But when Rhos'ari's arrow struck its shoulder, the Olg howled and straightened. One bloody arm retrieved a spear from the forest floor.

Rhos'ari reached for another arrow. "Damn." Despite his age, he moved with lightning speed, nocking his arrow as the Olg charged. He fired. Two other Sylvs fired, too. Three poisoned arrows punched fresh holes in the Olg's chest. Still, he did not slow. One great arm flexed, hauling back the spear, then snapped forward.

Rowen's heart leapt into his throat as he moved Snowdark into the Olg's path. The spear struck him full in the chest, driving him from the saddle. Rowen grunted as the earth hammered the breath from his lungs. Dimly, he heard the snap of another bowstring, then another. Snowdark screamed. A Sylv screamed—in rage first, then panic. Rowen fumbled for his sword, realized he was still holding it, and pushed himself up into a sitting position.

One of the Sylvan warriors dangled between the Olg's fists. The Olg had crushed his skull with his bare hands, despite the fresh arrows in his chest and arms. Rhos'ari and another Sylv named Faeli flanked the Olg on horseback, swords drawn. The Olg howled again. He drew a blade from the dead Sylv's belt, turned, and cut Rhos'ari's horse out from under him.

Rowen swore and pushed himself to his feet, using Knightswrath as a crutch. He spotted Snowdark in the distance, unharmed. He took a step toward the battle, but a jag of pain swept through his chest, driving him to one knee. Rowen swore again, leaning heavily on Knightswrath. His kingsteel breastplate had kept the Olg's spear from hurtling clean through his body, but the force had still broken his ribs. If he kept moving, he might pierce a lung. He looked up.

The wounded Olg was on his knees. Kilisti stood behind, coolly dragging her shortsword from the back of the Olg's neck. The Olg toppled face first onto the forest floor, atop the corpse of Rhos'ari's horse. Rowen spotted movement behind Kilisti. He tried to shout a warning but coughed blood.

A second Olg charged out from the trees. This one did not howl. Instead, he pounced to the attack, an axe in each hand. But Faeli was already in motion. The Sylv wheeled his horse around, and the beast reared up. Flailing hooves caught the Olg in the face. Somehow, the Olg swung anyway. Faeli leapt clear of the saddle before his horse could fall. The Olg swung again, missing Faeli's head by a hair's breadth. Wide-eyed, Faeli fumbled for a weapon, trying to crawl out of the Olg's reach.

I have to help...

Rowen took another step. A fresh jolt of pain swept over him. He fought the wild impulse to tear away his armor and tried to keep going, but staying on his feet took all his resolve. Knightswrath wavered in his grasp.

Rhos'ari was still struggling to rise. The other two Sylvan warriors dismounted and drew their swords then hesitated. But Kilisti was a blur of motion. She leapt past Faeli, feigned a lunge at the Olg's face, then danced back. The two circled each other. Rowen watched, dismayed. The Olg towered over her. Blood from Faeli's horse ran from the Olg's axes.

But Kilisti's ice-blue eyes did not blink. She ducked beneath the Olg's first swing then another. Then she leapt sideways and slashed the Olg's thigh. Instead of falling, the Olg answered with a sound like laughter and followed her, still swinging. Kilisti dodged one blow, ducked beneath a second, then rolled to escape a third. The Olg kicked her in the ribs as she did so. Rowen winced, imagining her pain so vividly that he forgot his own. He hefted Knightswrath, lowering his eyes to its kingsteel blade. He willed it to life.

He feared for a moment that it would not work. After all, his attack against Fadarah had been instinct. But the adamune turned searing hot in his grasp, so suddenly that he almost dropped it. Violet flames blossomed from Knightswrath's blade. Heat raced up his arm, into his chest. The pain in his ribs disappeared, replaced by a dizzying warmth. Rowen laughed without knowing why. Then, with a wild shout, he broke into a run.

The Olg faced Rowen, eyes wide. Dimly, Rowen was aware of the Olg's towering height, bulging muscles, and bloody axes. Then he swung. The Olg swung one axe to counter. Knightswrath cleaved through steel as easily as air, then kept going.

The Olg howled in pain and looked down to see his own chest burning.

Rowen stepped forward and stuck Knightswrath in the Olg's chest again. Wytchfire poured and pulsed from the blade. The Olg shuddered. Then flames leaked from his eyes, his nostrils, and his open mouth. But before he could howl, his entire body collapsed into ash.

Rowen stood over the scorched grass, shaking with exhilaration. Ashes blew in his face. Knightswrath's burning blade pulsed, brightened, then dimmed. He stared at it, laughed with giddy warmth, and sheathed it.

Only then did he see the others staring at him, horrified.

CHAPTER TWELVE
EARLESS

SAANJI SHIFTED UNCOMFORTABLY AS HE paced the battlements of Cassica, tugging at his robe. Built for a warrior, the garment did not fit him properly. Too large in the chest and arms, it hugged his gut, making him look like a ripe tomato. But Saanji still preferred that to armor.

Sweet gods, how am I still alive?

He'd been asking himself that question for days. He'd marched his disgraced force to Cassica two weeks ago, per his brother's orders, fully expecting Karhaati to kill him as soon as he arrived. That was, after all, the Dhargothi way. Karhaati was strong; Saanji was not. But the days had turned into weeks, and instead of having him impaled or strangling him in front of the men for a bit of sport, Karhaati had simply ignored him. For the Bloody Prince, that was practically a loving gesture.

Saanji contemplated this as he strolled along the walls of the conquered city, followed by half a dozen bodyguards. He tapped the hilt of his shortsword, still unaccustomed to the weight on his belt. Though Saanji trusted his bodyguards to protect him from any would-be assassins hiding among the conquered people of Cassica, he did not think they would protect him from his brother.

Saanji paused, glanced over the walls, and wondered how his own men were faring. He'd received no further reports since that great fire blazed up to the south, accompanied by a sinister cry. Karhaati had ordered Saanji's men north, to camp a mile from the city, almost as soon as they'd reached Cassica, insisting it was necessary to protect his border from Lancers.

But Saanji knew that was a half truth. Karhaati had ordered Saanji's men away because they disgusted him, just as they disgusted the rest of the Dhargots in Cassica. Like Saanji himself, the so-called Earless had rejected the usual Dhargothi ways. Another time, they would have been killed for that. Yet Saanji's men—some, the noted veterans of past wars; others, the cowardly sons of noblemen—were important enough that, for now, Karhaati preferred to let them live on in humiliation. But that didn't explain why Karhaati hadn't improved his standing by wringing the life out of the Tomato Prince.

Saanji reminded himself that Karhaati might not even be his greatest threat, given what he'd witnessed on the walls the other night. He'd seen the flames with his own eyes. That had been no mere wildfire or the doing of the Shel'ai, since they were all still fighting in the Wytchforest. It could mean one thing: the Nightmare had returned.

But who is that demon fighting for? Fadarah's in the south—if he's even still alive. Why would the Nightmare be here?

Saanji wondered if it had something to do with their father. The emperor had made a deal with Fadarah, sure, but he'd ordered Karhaati and his other sons to break it should the Shel'ai display any sign of weakness. Perhaps the emperor had a secret plan of his own, to rid himself of all three sons before one could try to wrest the crown off his aging head. He might have expected the Red Emperor to be that cruel, but not that clever.

Saanji heard footsteps. He tensed. Then he turned, saw who was coming, and forced himself to relax, if only to avoid giving Karhaati another excuse to kill him. "Good afternoon, Brother." He nodded. His bodyguards moved aside at Karhaati's approach—a little too quickly for Saanji's liking—and bowed.

Ignoring them, Karhaati stood before Saanji. Not for the first time, Saanji marveled at how different they were. Though not as large as his other brother, Ziraari, Karhaati was almost as tall, with muscles that strained beneath his scale armor. An impressive necklace of dried ears hung around his neck. Unlike Saanji's shortsword, which he'd simply snatched at random from the armory, Karhaati's had a dragon-shaped pommel with rubies for eyes. Karhaati's eyes were darkly painted and beamed coldly, so that Saanji felt as though he were being scrutinized by a wolf.

Karhaati smiled. "Well met, brother." Karhaati embraced him.

Surprised, Saanji returned the gesture, only slightly heartened by the fact that Karhaati did not have a knife in his hands.

"I was just napping when I dreamt of a field choked with dead men. A great victory had just been won for our father." Karhaati paused. "*You* won that victory."

Looking past his brother, Saanji thought he saw some of the bodyguards snicker. He could not blame them. "Tell me, in your dream, did our dear father's heart swell with pride or burst from surprise?"

Karhaati tensed. Saanji wondered if his brother would strike him. Karhaati waved his hand, dismissing Saanji's bodyguards as well as his own. The two squads fell back to a discreet distance, mingling until the two forces were indistinguishable. Karhaati squeezed Saanji's shoulder. "You should not speak so, especially in front of the men. You are a prince in the Dhargothi Empire. You should conduct yourself accordingly."

Saanji feigned a look of shame. "You are right, dear brother. I ask your forgiveness."

"Better you beg the Dead God for courage. You will need it soon."

Saanji had been about to make another joke—one acknowledging the absurdity of praying to any god with *dead* in his title—but Karhaati's final statement gave him pause. "What do you mean?"

"Those Lancers attacked our supply lines again last night. Somehow, they slipped right past your men." A faint, mocking smile touched Karhaati's lips. "Royce is proving to be more of a nuisance than I can ignore. I'd go after him myself, but those Isle Knights are still out there somewhere, trying to evade capture after they killed my emissary. And I have Lyos to worry about. And... there have been strange reports of late."

Saanji wondered if his brother was referring to the Nightmare.

"So I'm sending you." He smiled as Saanji felt the blood drain from his body. "What's the matter, brother? You're out of wine, and Cassican women smell like dogs. I thought you'd be thrilled to leave here and have a bit of fun."

"Chasing after a bunch of mad Lancers isn't my idea of fun."

"Not chasing. *Hunting*. Royce has only two hundred men with him. You'll have five thousand. They might as well be rabbits."

Rabbits with twelve-foot claws. "Maybe you could find some other ill-suited task for me to perform. Cleaning the stalls for your war elephants, perhaps?"

Karhaati tapped his sword hilt for emphasis. "I think not. Ride north, take command of your force, and hunt Royce down. Chase him into Ivairia. Chase him to the Wintersea, if you have to. But I want an example made of him—or his corpse, if you can't take him alive." Karhaati paused. "I don't think I need to tell you what the men say behind your back. This will be your chance to change their opinion of you."

Saanji nodded contemplatively. "You might be right. Can't waste my whole life with wine and whores, can I?" He started to walk away, but Karhaati grabbed him. All pretense of kindness evaporated from the Bloody Prince's expression. He leaned in so close that Saanji could smell the faint musk of decay wafting off Karhaati's gruesome necklace.

"Enough of your playacting, brother. You're a Dhargot, not some book-loving fop from Atheion. Understand?" His hand squeezed around Saanji's upper arm, almost completely encircling it.

Saanji looked past Karhaati's shoulder and saw the bodyguards grinning in the distance. He forced an obliging smile. "As you say, brother."

But Karhaati did not let him go. "I'm sending you to kill an enemy. Succeed, and you'll find me a kinder ally than Ziraari. I swear it on the Dead God." He seized Saanji's face, pinching his jaw so hard that Saanji's eyes watered. "Fail, and you'd better hope Royce opens your fat belly with his kingsteel longsword. Or else I'll do something far, far worse." He paused. "If you doubt me, dig up Maryssa's bones."

Saanji's fear turned to rage. He fingered the small opal ring on the little finger of his left hand. He wanted to curse his brother for daring to speak his lover's name, but he could not speak. Karhaati held his face a moment longer, squeezing harder and harder until Saanji thought his jaw would shatter. Then Karhaati smiled and let go. He embraced Saanji again, as though nothing had happened.

"Good luck, my brother. If the Dead God wills it, we'll embrace again."

"Thank you," Saanji managed. He felt the dragon head on Karhaati's sword hilt pressing into his gut. He started to reach for it. He imagined drawing that sword and pushing it into his brother's neck, turning it until Karhaati's eyes went dark. But then he changed his mind.

Karhaati stepped back. His painted eyes fixed on Saanji, giving Saanji the awful feeling that his brother knew exactly what he'd nearly done. Something flickered in Karhaati's eyes. Saanji thought it looked like disappointment. Then the Bloody Prince shook his head and walked away.

Chorlga shuddered. The cold stone chamber lay before him, dark and empty. He could sense that he was alone. Still, this place frightened him as it never had before. A wave of his hand summoned a sphere of light that floated up to the ceiling and hung there, but its ghostly light only made things worse. Fanatics from the surface of Cadavash had clearly been to the chamber. Though they'd hauled away the dead dragonpriests and burned incense in their wake, they'd left stains on the stone floor.

Chorlga stepped carefully around them and made his way to Namundvar's

Well. He was glad that he'd ordered the Nightmare to remain above. Chorlga had a feeling that he would need all his energy and focus for what he was about to do.

He knelt slowly, afraid to look inside, even though he knew that it would only be so much dark, dry stone until he used his magic to activate it. El'rash'lin's words rang in his mind: *You should have sensed it, with all your power. All the control you think you have...*

With his right fist, Chorlga struck the ancient stone structure, ignoring the jolt of pain when the rough stone bloodied his knuckles. How many times since the Shattering War had he ignited the Well's magic? How many times had he drawn power from the Light to increase his own? Through the Well, he'd peered into Fadarah's mind. He'd learned of Brahasti's secret plan to breed Shel'ai. He'd even subjected himself to the tortured thoughts of the Nightmare. After all that, after enduring so much, how could he have committed such blunders?

"Maybe El'rash'lin was lying," he muttered. The Dragonkin had often speculated that if one believed their own lie with enough fervor, it might appear true to anyone reading his mind. With fresh hope, he closed his eyes and held one hand over the well's dark mouth.

He imagined that bottomless void filling slowly with mist, water, then finally, light. All his senses began to tingle. His pulse quickened. He felt a familiar knotting in his chest: a curious amalgamation of terror, calm, joy, and dread. Raw knowledge washed over him, filling him and erasing everything he knew. A swirling, contradictory rush of emotions surged up within him. He wept—in pleasure or sorrow, he could not tell—but he kept his eyes shut. He held fast to a single piece of information—his own name—and repeated it like a mantra.

He felt the Light's displeasure, but he clung to this strategy as he always had, repeating his own name until the void withdrew and his memories and identity returned. Keeping his eyes shut, he floated on the Light like a raft on the ocean. He dipped his hands in the water and drank.

Namundvar's Well wasn't made to satisfy your thirst for power. It wasn't made to look without. It was made to look within.

Chorlga laughed. He leaned over the raft and faced his own reflection. "I am no quivering priest, no weeping beggar clutching his bowl. Do you hear me? I am a Dragonkin, the right hand of Nekiel. I am a god."

His reflection rippled and disappeared. The waters dimmed. The ocean went dark. Chorlga felt another surge of panic, but he fought through it.

"Show me," he called out to the dark waters. "Show me all that you have kept hidden. Show me Knightswrath. Show me who carries it."

The Light resisted. Never had he made such direct demands of it. He sensed the danger: if he lost focus, the Light would rend him to pieces.

"But I will *not* lose focus," Chorlga whispered. "I beat you. You cannot refuse me. Not here, not now."

Whether they struggled for a thousand years or only for a moment, Chorlga could not tell. But the ocean brightened again, as though some unquenchable fire raged far beneath the water. Gradually, something took shape. He gazed down upon a great forest that stretched in all directions, as though propagated somehow by a gigantic, even greater tree blossoming at its heart. But then the forest gave way to broad, sweeping grasslands. To the north, he saw a land of barren, blasted rock.

"Godsfall? He's gone to Godsfall?" Chorlga found that hard to believe. He'd expected to find Knightswrath housed in Shaffrilon or perhaps to see an Isle Knight carrying it east, back toward the Lotus Isles. But he reminded himself that the Olgrym had just been laying siege to the Sylvan capital. Perhaps the Isle Knight, having thwarted them and driven them from the forest, was pursuing them to their own homeland, hoping to vanquish them.

Chorlga willed the image to sharpen. He had the sudden feeling that he was falling from a great height, plummeting toward the rocky realm. But he controlled his fear and kept his focus. A moment before it seemed he would be dashed to pieces, his descent slowed. A new image formed beneath him. Chorlga stared. Then he laughed.

His control began to slip. He'd been in the well too long—far longer than he ever had before. He was weakening. But it made no difference. Chorlga imagined floating on the ocean again. He lay on the raft and closed his eyes. He repeated his own name, over and over. Slowly, he opened his eyes—his *real* eyes—and found himself kneeling beside Namundvar's Well again.

Chorlga stared into the dimming light then took a breath. His lungs ached. Raw pain wracked his chest as though he'd never breathed before. But Chorlga was used to the feeling. He calmed his senses and waited until the feeling passed. He took another breath. Finally, when he could, he laughed again.

He pictured the Isle Knight as he'd seen him a moment before. He'd expected some proud, armored hero riding at the front of a great, gleaming legion, burning sword in hand. He'd expected someone like Fâyu Jinn, the fearsome mortal who'd forged a vengeful army out of warring slave-tribes, who had made even Nekiel quake with fear. Instead, the Light had shown him a ragged, dirty sellsword hiding in the rubble, hunted by friends and enemies alike. The man was roiling with doubts and self-loathing, both terrified of and intoxicated by his newfound power, as likely to destroy himself as an enemy.

Chorlga stood. Straightening to full height, he cast a derisive look into the well's dark mouth. "I've led armies of a hundred thousand men, all chanting my name. I've watched nations burn. I've spat in the face of the gods. And *that* is the champion you send against me?"

He spat into the well then strode away, leaving the sphere of light he'd summoned earlier to burn itself out, slowly returning the chamber to grave-like darkness.

CHAPTER THIRTEEN

SHADOWS IN THE RUINS

BLINKING UP AT THE STARS, Rowen fumbled in the darkness for his sword. His hand closed on Knightswrath's hilt. The dragonbone felt so cold that he jumped.

"Easy, Knight. Don't worry. We didn't steal your precious bit of devilry."

Rowen realized that he was lying in a ruined temple, surrounded by broken statues. Stars shown through a shattered ceiling. He was still wearing his armor. He sat up, groaning with soreness. He turned and saw Kilisti sitting on a toppled statue across from him. A drawn shortsword lay across her knees.

"Where are the others?"

"Outside, keeping watch." Kilisti stood. Rowen tensed, but she sheathed her sword. "Nice armor you've got there. I thought that Olg's spear would sail right through you."

Rowen examined his breastplate. The kingsteel was dented, his tabard torn, but he did not think his ribs were broken anymore. He glanced down at Knightswrath. Its blade gleamed in the soft blue light of a single luminstone at Kilisti's feet. Rowen sheathed his own sword and stood.

Kilisti's scarred face gave him a long, unfathomable look. Then she tossed him a wineskin. "You scared the wild piss out of the boys, you know. Faeli wanted to kill you while you were passed out. Even Rhos'ari looked like he was giving it some serious thought."

Rowen took a long drink. "And you?"

Kilisti shrugged. "Briel said take you north. Shal'tiar follow orders."

"I guess I'll have to settle for that." Rowen tossed the wineskin back. "What happened to the Olgrym?"

"You mean the two dead ones, or the three we killed carrying you to Que'ahl?"

Rowen tensed. "Three?"

Kilisti nodded. "Luckily, we had more warning this time. Brought them down with arrows. Young Cathas took a scrape but nothing serious."

Rowen nodded, relieved. He looked around again. "We're in Que'ahl?"

"That's what I said, isn't it?"

"Just surprised you didn't leave me in the forest to die. Anybody else hurt?"

Kilisti shook her head. She took a drink from the wineskin. "Want to tell me what happened?"

Rowen had no idea how to answer her question. "I will if you will."

Kilisti moved one hand as though about to cover her face then stopped herself. "Not much to tell. I was scouting. Got careless. An Olg caught me, started cutting me up, got so wrapped up in his fun, he didn't see Captain Essidel coming up behind him." She returned the wineskin to her pack. "Now you."

Rowen shuddered at the coldness in her voice.

"Don't know. I willed the sword to life, it started on fire, and I swung the damn thing. What more do you want to know?"

"What it did to *you*, for starters." Kilisti tapped her sword hilt. "I've seen men laugh like that, when the bloodlust takes hold. Only you don't seem the type. So if that thing you're carrying can change you like that, that makes you dangerous to this mission... and to me."

Rowen ignored the not-so-subtle threat. "This *thing* is also what let me kill Fadarah, drive off the Shel'ai and the Olgrym, and save your entire city."

"So I hear." Kilisti drummed her fingers on her sword hilt as though deciding what to do next. "I don't know a damn thing about magic, besides that it can't be trusted. That means *you* can't be trusted. Only I saw that compound where we're going, swarming with armed men. More than just the six of us can handle, no matter how quiet we creep in."

Rowen looked down at Kilisti's luminstone. He had seen such enchanted stones in abundance at Shaffrilon. He had seen a few at Atheion, too, probably obtained by trade or theft many ages before. But he had not seen any of them at Que'ahl. He remembered hearing something about how they were forbidden beyond the forest and wondered if Kilisti had stolen it. Then his thoughts turned to more important matters.

We've only just set out, and I've already lost a man. "The one who died—"

"Seth'el."

Rowen repeated the name to himself. "Did you bury him?"

"Didn't have time. Besides, your horse got skittish. All the noise she made, we didn't dare stay in one place too long."

Rowen hesitated. He wondered if he should apologize. Glancing at Kilisti, he had the feeling she'd take it as an insult. He massaged a crick in his neck.

"There's more," Kilisti said. "We're being followed."

Gods, of course we are. "How many?"

"Can't tell. They're keeping their distance—strange, for Olgrym. We tried to lose them. Rhos'ari and Aerios even tried leading them off our trail, but the bastards are persistent. A dozen at least, though. Couldn't tell which clan. But whoever's leading them, he's smarter than the usual skull busters we deal with."

"A smart Olg. Just what we need."

Kilisti's sour look said that for once, they were of the same mind. "Looks like they won't come near Que'ahl, like you said. That might be all it is. But you can believe they'll be after us again, once we start out." She added, "Faeli thinks we should send someone back to the capital for reinforcements."

"That would take too long. Besides, I doubt Briel has any to give us. We'll have to try and outrun them. But we only have five horses left, if memory serves."

"Might be enough, so long as we don't stop for tea and sweet rolls."

With great effort, Rowen kept himself from smiling. "If we hug the Dead Shores, we'll have to pass right through Godsfall. That's suicide. But if we avoid Godsfall, we'll have to go around Quorim, which belongs to the Dhargots now." Rowen pictured a map in his mind. "So we go east around Godsfall, then west along the Dead Shores, then east after we pass Quorim—"

"Or straight north," Kilisti interrupted. "It'll take us right between Hesod and Quorim, but we have a better chance of avoiding the Olgrym."

"But not the Dhargots." Rowen cursed. "Either way, sooner or later, we're bound to run into someone."

"Well, it's that, or you go chop at them with your burning sword while the rest of us go on without you."

Rowen gave her a hard look, unable to tell if she was joking. "We should go. We've been here long enough. Tell the men—"

Kilisti left the shattered temple before he could finish.

Rowen watched her go. "I think that one will try and kill me, before this is over," he muttered. His voice echoed in the temple, sending a shiver down his spine. The last time he'd been in Que'ahl, he'd been fighting Olgrym, but at least he'd had Jalist and Silwren with him.

He wondered where the Dwarr was. It was a long, dangerous road, but he hoped that Jalist had made it back to Stillhammer, into the arms of his lover. He deserved that.

Rowen picked up Kilisti's luminstone and studied its blue glow. When he covered it with both hands, it darkened. The stone looked like nothing more than a plain stone, noteworthy only for its perfect roundness and silk-smooth texture. He considered giving it back to Kilisti then decided that if she wanted it, she could ask for it. Sliding the stone into his pocket, he thought of Igrid. He wasn't sure what she deserved, but wherever she was, he hoped she was safe.

The Sylvs turned collectively as Rowen left the temple. Their azure eyes scrutinized him in the ghostly darkness of the burned-out fortress. Rhos'ari gave him a slight nod, but no one spoke. Aside from the jingle of the horses' harnesses, there was no sound.

I should say something, thank them for carrying me here or at least express my condolences for Seth'el...

Rowen went to Snowdark. Faeli handed him the reins without comment. Rowen hoisted himself into the saddle, and the others mounted. Cathas, his left thigh wrapped in a red-stained bandaged, shared a horse with Kilisti. All the Sylvs stared at him, their expressions cold in the moonlight.

Finally, Sergeant Rhos'ari cleared his throat. "Ride on, Knight. We'll follow you."

Rowen nodded, hesitant. Then he pointed Snowdark north and guided her through the darkened ruins.

Jalist drained his wine glass, wiped his beard, then refilled his cup. He took a drink as he scrutinized the figure lying on the bed before him. "You know, if it was so important, you'd think somebody would have written down how to kill those bastards."

When his companion did not answer, Jalist said, "Or maybe they did. Books don't last forever. Or maybe they just figured with the Dragonkin gone, there wasn't any point. But that gets me wondering where the Jolym came from. No Dragonkin left to make them."

"What about Rowen's wytch?"

"I suppose you could call her a Dragonkin, based on what she could do. But she didn't do this. And the others... El'rash'lin, the Nightmare... they're all dead."

"Maybe it was the gods." Igrid's voice dripped with sarcasm.

"Maybe," Jalist grunted. "Gods, it wasn't enough that I had to survive all that foolishness with the Locke brothers, tromping all over Ruun from Quesh to the Wintersea. Now I've got to go and keep living through battles that should have ended with my skull split open." He took another drink. "We Dwarr have a saying." He frowned. "Must not be very important since I can't remember exactly how it goes, but here's the gist of it: whatever Lady Luck gives you, you'll have to pay it back before the end." He took another drink. "Which goddess is paired with luck, anyway? Dyoni, right?"

Igrid groaned, though Jalist could not tell if her distress had to do with the tightness of the bandages wrapped around her head or with his late-night attempt at conversation. "Dyoni's a *man*, you fop."

"Is he?" Jalist took another drink. "Doesn't matter. Only one *my* people pray to is Maelmohr... though I have to say, the Firegod hasn't been too great about answering prayers lately." He stared into his cup.

Igrid leaned on one elbow. Though the sheet slid off her bosom, she made no move to cover herself. "Go somewhere else, Dwarr. I'm not going to die—at least, not tonight—and I don't need a damn bodyguard."

Jalist smirked. A young cleric of Tier'Gothma paused on his rounds and stared at Igrid, wide eyed, from across the great chamber that had been converted into a hospital. Jalist seized the sheet and covered Igrid, wondering if she was immodest or had already guessed that his tastes precluded her gender. "I'm not your bodyguard, Iron Sister. More like your jailor."

Igrid reached for the nearest weapon—a candleholder—but Jalist held up his hands. "Peace, you humorless wench! I just mean, I plan on keeping track of you until Locke shows up."

Igrid tapped her fingernail on the candleholder. "And... when will that be?"

"Whenever he's done fighting the Sylvs' war for them, I suppose. But he'll pass through here on his way back to the Lotus Isles. He has to."

"Him and that crazed, platinum-haired wytch of his." Igrid tugged at her bandages.

Jalist stared into his cup again. "He doesn't know I'm here. Last he heard, I was on my way to Stillhammer."

"Then why aren't you there now?"

Jalist blinked. He thought of all he'd seen. It seemed impossible that Igrid didn't know. *Then again, why would she?* He had not told her, and any Dwarrs lucky enough to have escaped the Jolym would not have come so far north, into Human lands. The only Dwarrs in such parts were either wanderers or outcasts. Jalist had spotted a few from a distance, in Lyos after the battle, and had resisted the impulse to inform them of what had happened to their homeland.

Let them find out on their own.

Jalist looked up. He realized that Igrid was still waiting for an answer. He forced a smile. "I'll talk about that once, to the king or one of his captains, but that's it. Get your answers from them." He stood. "Sleep well, Iron Sister."

He left before she could reply.

Outside the temple, Jalist paused between matching statues of Tier'Gothma and breathed in the night air. Lyos was finally quiet. Two temple guards nodded to him. Jalist returned their gesture with a shake of his wineskin. He knew he should be enjoying his newfound fame, but the thought of his homeland had drained all the joy from him.

After Jalist had insisted that he was friends with Rowen Locke, which Igrid, dazed as she was, managed to vouch for, the gangs had taken his advice and managed to drive the Jolym off Pallantine Hill. Three Jolym had even been struck down. The heavy shells they'd left behind—armor wrought of steel and brass, each piece joined by intricate straps and hinges—were lashed to mules and dragged into the city for inspection. After collecting their dead, what remained of the Red Watch had ridden down into the Dark Quarter and demanded that the gang leader, Fen-Shea, tell them how he'd driven off the Jolym.

Fen-Shea had directed them to Jalist. Half hero, half prisoner, the Dwarr had been taken to the palace of King Typherius to await questioning. But after waiting until sundown, Jalist decided he'd had enough. He'd slipped out of the palace so that he could check on the wounded, but he had no doubt that by then, word of his whereabouts had reached the king.

Well, they can give me a medal, or they can clap me in irons. Doesn't make a damn bit of difference anymore. He raised his wineskin to the sky. *I saved your damn city, Locke. You're welcome.* He tipped the wineskin and drank until wine ran down his chin, then he threw the empty wineskin on the temple stairs. An acolyte quietly hurried over and picked it up. Jalist sat on the temple stairs and put his head in his hands. He was still sitting like that when he heard boots marching in unison. Nevertheless, he did not look up until someone cleared his throat. Jalist frowned, shielding his face from the glare of their torches.

"Gods, are you trying to see me or burn me blind?"

Two men seized him by the arms and dragged him to his feet, but a voice rang out, ordering them to let him go. Jalist was sorry when they did, because he fell back into a sitting position on the temple steps. He tried unsuccessfully to stand. Finally, he bowed his head. "Your Majesty."

King Typherius came forward, his expression stoic. In place of kingly robes, he wore an extravagant doublet over gleaming ringmail, along with a gilded bastard sword. The king crossed his arms. "My scouts report that whatever tore my army in half has retreated west, toward Cadavash." He paused. "Meanwhile, my officers told me about the letter you made them send."

Jalist needed a moment to realize what the king was talking about. When he finally remembered, he nodded. "A warning. The Isles needed to be warned. The other, bigger force was heading their way. Might already be too late."

"So I hear."

Jalist rubbed his eyes. "You sent them, right? The messenger birds... you sent all the ones you could, right?"

"We did," the king said. "I sent emissaries on my fastest horses, too. If the Isle Knights don't know yet how to destroy those... abominations, they will by morning."

"If their keeps haven't already been torn down by then."

"Birds and emissaries will get there faster than my army, if that's what you're thinking."

The severity in the king's voice made Jalist try again to stand up. This time, he succeeded. With the king standing at the bottom of the stairwell and Jalist three steps above him, they were almost the same height. "No, Sire." The Dwarr reminded himself that, Rowen Locke notwithstanding, there was no love lost between Lyos and the Lotus Isles.

"Now," the king said, "I'm told you know what those abominations were. I intended to speak with you at the palace, once I was done conferring with my captains and comforting widows, but you wandered off. So we'll talk here."

Jalist had a look at the king's captains. They followed him with such urgency that at first, he'd mistaken them for bodyguards. All looked young and untried, some barely old enough to shave. Jalist wondered how that could be, then he remembered that the Jolym had sent most of the veterans of the Red Watch to the funeral pyres.

"Well?" The king gave him a piercing look.

Jalist looked away. "I don't know what they are any more than you do."

"But I'm told you called them Jolym when my captains asked what they were."

Jalist shrugged. "That's what they look like to me."

"No Jolym have been seen since the days of the Dragonkin. I'm told they have a few husks on display in Atheion, but most people don't think they were ever more than an old wives' tale told about living men in armor."

Jalist felt his anger rising. "Tell that to what's left of the Red Watch."

The king scowled. "Jolym or not, how about you tell me how you knew how to kill them?"

Jalist snickered coldly. "The first time I met one, it nearly cut me to pieces. I got lucky. Nothing else worked, so I tried sticking it in the eyes after I got it down on the ground."

Behind the king, his bodyguards exchanged looks and whispers of disbelief. Jalist could guess why. Each Jol stood at least six feet tall, most seven. They were hollow, but their thick armor made them twice the weight of the stoutest warrior. During his first battle against them, Jalist had managed to hoist one off its feet and dump it on the ground, then stab it through the eyes before it could get back up.

The king gave his men a scolding glance. "Continue," he told Jalist.

He hesitated. Grief stung his eyes. He had no wish to proceed, but he had no choice. "Those things... Jolym, if you believe the fairytales... they ravaged my homeland, not one week ago."

The king blinked. "My father traded with King Fedwyr Thegn a long time ago—even met him once, before he became king. He always said it's good the Dwarrs aren't our enemies, because Stillhammer is impenetrable... especially the fortress at Tarator."

Jalist wished he had another wineskin. "Had you asked a week ago, I would have told you the same."

"Where is your king now?"

Jalist thought of Leander. The night air chilled Jalist's damp face. The Dwarr wiped his eyes and cleared his throat. "Dead, probably. So are all his Housecarls." *And his son...*

The king shifted uneasily. "And... a few hundred of these things, these Jolym, did that?"

"Closer to a thousand, maybe more. The rest veered east, for the Isles. Didn't I tell you that?" Jalist took a deep breath and let it go. "Sire, I need a drink and a bed. I've told you all I know."

The king raised one eyebrow at Jalist's bravado. "I doubt it, Dwarr. You said you're Rowen Locke's friend. The last time I saw Rowen Locke, he had a certain kingsteel heirloom that the other Isle Knights very much wanted to take from him." The king took a step forward and uncrossed his arms. He touched Jalist's shoulder. "Where's Locke now?"

"The Wytchforest."

The king hesitated. "And... Silwren?"

Jalist shrugged. "With him, waist deep in Olg blood, I suppose."

The king looked about to say more, then apparently thought better of it. He stepped back and gestured to one of his officers. "Get this man a room at the palace." He faced Jalist. "We'll talk again tomorrow." Then king turned to go then stopped. "You saved my city. Why ever you did it... thank you, Dwarr." He bowed.

Jalist returned the gesture, almost toppling off the temple steps. Once the king was gone, two men of the Red Watch seized him—more gently, this time—and guided him back to the palace. After that, Jalist was vaguely aware of one servant helping him out of his leather armor while another offered him food and a bath. Instead, Jalist pushed past them to the bed. He lay down, and for the first time in as long as he could remember, he slept.

CHAPTER FOURTEEN

THE LONG NIGHT

SAANJI SAT AT THE HEAD of a long oak table surrounded by chairs. Various officers, who had been forced into his army as punishment, filled the chairs. They had been summoned from their slumber near midnight. Saanji shivered, though he was not sure whether the cause was the contents of the letter or the cold wind whipping through the flap of his tent. The wind stirred the flap again, revealing the darkness beyond.

Gods, what am I doing? Why didn't I think about this until morning, at least?

Saanji shook his head. To dwell any longer on what he planned to do would only sap what little courage he had managed to rouse. Still, the stares and growing anxiety from his officers unnerved him. He could not remember the last time he'd spoken to them without being drunk. He looked down, pretending to read the letter once again, then back up. "What's our latest report on Royce?"

The captains shifted uncomfortably. Saanji could have obtained the information earlier, had he made a point of frequenting such meetings, without dragging them all out of bed.

Finally, one captain answered, "Little has changed, my prince. Sir Royce is somewhere in the Ivairian foothills, but his force is small and quick and familiar with these lands. So far, they've eluded us."

"What kind of losses have we had?"

"None, my prince," another captain continued. "Royce seems to prefer to skirt us and go on harassing your brother's supply lines."

The first captain picked up where the second had left off. "Sire, we might still trap them in the foothills and wipe them all out in one battle. If we just marched in force and—"

Saanji shook his head. "I think not... for reasons that will become clear in just a moment." He took a deep breath to steady himself. "This might come as a shock to some of you, but it seems my dear brother, Ziraari, has contracted an incurable case of death."

Eyes widened. Men exchanged quick looks. A few touched their sword hilts. No one spoke.

After a moment, Saanji continued. "If this letter is to be believed, he forged an alliance with Shade, Fadarah's right hand." He held up his hand as everyone started talking at once. "Yes, I know how that sounds. Shade and the other Shel'ai turned on him, somehow ghosted past the guards, and killed Ziraari in his sleep." He added, "Apparently, my dear brother was found with... parts of him missing."

Despite the terror knotting his gut, Saanji fought the impulse to smile.

His officers, on the other hand, looked as if they were torn between fainting and bolting. Saanji understood. One asked, "Did... Prince Karhaati send the letter himself?"

Saanji laughed. "Gods, no. I'm sure he would have preferred I know nothing. Only one of Ziraari's captains appears to have sent letters not just to me and my dear living brother but our loving father back in Dhargoth." He pretended to study the parchment. "Apparently, Ziraari actually expired some time ago, but his captains were afraid to send word because they feared they'd be punished for letting the killers get away." He looked up. "We're lucky. I don't have to tell you what would have happened had Karhaati received this letter while we were still in Cassica."

His captains exchanged looks. Once again, no one spoke.

"As it is," Saanji continued, "I'm sure an emissary will arrive in a day or two, kindly demanding that I return to Cassica. There might even be a letter telling me that Karhaati had to ride off to battle, and he needs me to take command of the city. Something about rebellion and needing my soft hand to sway the populace." He smiled thinly. "But the moment I set foot in Cassica, Karhaati will have me stripped naked and impaled on a stake. I can only assume he will do the same to my captains since—let's be honest—none of you are exactly crucial to his campaign."

His captains exchanged glances again. Saanji had spoken with open contempt for his brothers before, but never so strongly. Saanji studied their faces. Then, looking down, he saw that his hands were shaking. He dropped the parchment on the table and rose to his feet.

"None of Ziraari's generals are foolish enough to try and take his place. Some will go back to Dhargoth to rejoin my father. But most will flock to

Karhaati. By the end of the month, he'll have half again as many men, horses, chariots, and war elephants as he does now. And I don't have to remind you that Karhaati already outnumbers us four to one."

A captain said, "Prince Karhaati sent us to protect his northern flank against Arnil Royce and his Lancers. Perhaps if we could capture or even kill Royce—"

"My dear brother will reward our courage and welcome us back into his good graces?" Saanji smirked. "He kept me alive in case he needed me against Ziraari. Now, Ziraari's dead. Time to finish pruning the family tree."

An officer cleared his throat. "Maybe we should go back to Dhargoth. With Prince Karhaati getting this strong, the emperor might be worried. Could be he'll welcome us back on our own terms."

"Not bloody likely," someone muttered. Grumbles of agreement followed.

"Then what do we do?" someone asked.

Saanji said, "Let me tell you a little story about my brother. That might help you decide." His heart leapt into his throat at the thought of what he was about to do, but he pressed on anyway. "When I was a boy, I fell in love with my cousin. Her name was Maryssa." He gripped the edge of the table until his knuckles whitened, trying to steady his hands. "I know what you're thinking. Women don't mean much where we're from. I doubt any of you can name your own mothers any more than I could name mine. But Maryssa..." Saanji choked. He looked down, afraid to meet his captains' gaze. "She wasn't especially beautiful, I suppose, but I was fat and weak, and she was kind. So while my brothers were following our dear father's example and proving their manhood by raping all the slaves, I sat with Maryssa and talked." Saanji smiled despite the lump in his throat. "We read books on what Dhargoth was like just after the Shattering War, before famines and in-fighting convinced our ancestors that the Way of Ears was a good idea, and nobody gave enough of a damn to stop them."

Saanji felt unsteady. He wished he were drunk. "One day, Karhaati found us together..." Saanji started to shake again and realized he could not continue. He took a deep breath, let it go, then looked up. He smiled faintly at the lack of expression on his captains' faces. Saanji knew that stoicism well, for he'd practiced it in the mirror many times, training himself not to retch when their father made them watch an interrogation or stroll beneath ghastly rows of men who had been impaled for some dereliction of duty.

"I wanted revenge. One day, I took a little bottle of poison from the armory. I brushed it onto a caltrop and slipped the damn thing into his boot while he was asleep, way down at the bottom. Only I lost my nerve. I took it out. Gods, if I hadn't…" He trailed off, realizing he was losing his way.

"Let's try this." He straightened. "You're all here for the same reason I am… namely, because no one's killed you yet."

The remark brought scattered smirks.

"You haven't distinguished yourself by plundering the islands, kidnapping women from the Free Cities, or sticking a knife in the gut of somebody who gave you a sour look. They call you Earless because you wear no trophies around your neck. They think you're weak. I think they're wrong. I think the problem is just that you haven't been given the chance to kill the right person."

The captains bristled. No one answered, but Saanji could see that he was getting through to them. He pressed on with renewed hope. Piece by piece, he told them his plan. Though he'd been formulating it for weeks and fine-tuning it for days, it still sounded absurd when he said it aloud.

When he was done, his captains sat in stunned silence. Saanji saw at once that some would refuse. Those, he knew, might have to be put to death before they could escape the camp and get word to his brother. But the rest looked intrigued, if nothing else.

Well, that's a start.

As the captains began to argue some of the finer points, Saanji toyed with the opal ring—a woman's ring—on the little finger of his left hand. Maryssa had given it to him a moment before she'd flung herself off the parapets—choosing death over giving birth to Karhaati's child. Saanji shuddered. He was glad the captains were no longer watching him. He seized a pitcher of wine and filled his goblet until it overflowed.

Brahasti el Tarq paced the outskirts of his compound, eyeing the slave pit in particular. Despite the late hour, he could not sleep. But it was not the screams that kept him awake. He was used to the screams. After all, he had made more than a few captives scream himself. It was the silence he found disconcerting.

For weeks, the Sylvan women held captive in the pit had fought off Brahasti's men with admirable resolve. Some of them had been forest dwellers, but most were Wyldkin, already accustomed to a hard life spent fighting Olgrym. A few had even been killed when they came close to fighting their way free with bare hands. Ever since Chorlga's visit, though, things had been different. The Dragonkin had given Brahasti a recipe for an ancient, noxious elixir, with orders that the women be forced to drink it on a daily basis. Chorlga claimed it would greatly increase the women's fertility, as well as the chance that they would give birth to Shel'ai.

Brahasti had been skeptical. The elixir's exotic ingredients, ranging from snowthistle, queensroot, and frogleaf to the bone marrow of an urusk, included ingredients like felberries, which Brahasti knew were poisonous. Yet Chorlga had been true to his word. Unfortunately, the foul elixir had had another effect that Chorlga had not mentioned: it had sapped the women's will, dulled their wits, and left them like walking dead.

Brahasti sighed with disappointment. The women's eyes resembled wet stones. They made almost no sound—not when Brahasti's men descended into the pits for a bit of fun, not even when they noticed their bellies beginning to swell. Brahasti wondered if any of the women still had the presence of mind to realize that they were pregnant. He decided it did not matter. Nearly all thirty of the Sylvan females were with child—which was good, since the sport had gone out of it.

Brahasti was starting to wonder if there was even any sense in guarding the pit anymore. Days before, a careless warrior had dropped a knife within easy reach of a Sylvan girl while climbing out of the pit. The girl might have easily snatched it up and stabbed him in the back—she surely would have weeks earlier—but the girl simply rocked herself, oblivious to the weapon at her feet. Brahasti did not expect that any of the women could have escaped even if his men weren't there, thanks to the Jolym.

He lifted his gaze from the pit to its tireless sentries. He shuddered. Two Jolym stood at opposite edges of the pit. A third guarded the only gateway into the compound. Before the elixir had taken effect, he'd seen a Jol move with surprising quickness to seize a Sylvan girl who had been about to climb to freedom. Another time, as a test, Brahasti had ordered one of them to tear a man in half for disobeying an order. Without speaking and without the slightest hesitation, it seized the condemned man, displaying strength that rivaled an Olg's.

If Karhaati ever calls me back to the front, I have to take these three with me. Even the Bloody Prince wouldn't be able to threaten me then.

Brahasti shook his head. *Why go back to the front at all?* He'd loaned his strategic brilliance to Prince Karhaati, just as he'd loaned it to Fadarah before that, and that had gotten him very little. Chorlga was another matter: he was the first true Dragonkin that Brahasti had ever seen, maybe the last one left alive. Based on what Brahasti had witnessed already, Chorlga's power easily surpassed that of any of the Shel'ai, including Fadarah.

Brahasti faced one of the Jol. Moonlight reflected off its armored chest. He scrutinized it for the slightest movement but saw none. It still looked like a propped-up suit of armor.

Chorlga gave them life. And he has a whole army of these things to the east!

Brahasti smiled. Chorlga was the true power on Ruun, the worthy master he had been waiting for. He appreciated Brahasti's talents in a way that none of his previous masters—the Red Emperor, the Sorcerer-General, the Bloody Prince—had managed to do. All Brahasti had to do now was be himself, and the rewards and recognition he so richly deserved would rain down on him.

Careful, the Dhargot warned himself. *Fadarah got overconfident. Look what happened to him.*

Brahasti decided to check on things at the gate of his compound. He headed away from the slave pit, ignored the lazy salute of a couple sellswords who stood up from their campfire at his approach, and waved to Dagath. The one-eyed sellsword was just coming into the compound, a pitcher of wine in hand.

Brahasti frowned. "Drinking on duty again?"

"No, General. It's Farl's watch. See for yourself." Dagath gestured vaguely at the gate.

Brahasti tensed. He was willing to be lax with Dagath because the man got results, but boredom was making the sellsword captain too impudent. "Farl's watch just started. You sound like you've been drinking since sundown." He paused. "Remember what the Jolym did to Pate? Drink on duty again, and I'll have them do the same to you."

Dagath winced. He lifted the patch off his eye and scratched the dead, scarred socket. "Won't happen again." He took a step then stopped so suddenly that he almost lost his balance. "Will that be all, General?"

"Almost." Brahasti nodded back toward the slave pit. "Pick me out a girl. Whichever one has the most fight left in her. I'll take her in my room when I'm done inspecting the grounds."

When Dagath was gone, Brahasti turned on his heel and walked out the gates. Two more sellswords stood watch. Both reeked of *fran-té*, but they stood and saluted as he passed. Brahasti decided to deal with them later. He crossed over the dry moat and stopped in the shadow of a wooden watchtower. A grubby sellsword descended a ladder in time to meet him.

"G'evening, General."

Brahasti considered backhanding the man for forgetting to salute, then he noticed the shortsword hanging from the man's belt. He drew it and examined it, appreciating its simple but fine craftsmanship. "Isn't this Dagath's?"

"Was." Farl grinned. "I won it in a dice game."

"You beat Dagath in a dice game, and he didn't gut you in your sleep?"

Farl blushed. "I told him I'd give him a chance to win it back tomorrow. Wasn't Dagath's, anyway. He says he stole it off some dumb squire he met on the road."

This caught Brahasti off guard. "A squire?"

Farl nodded. "Like, from the Lotus Isles."

"Did Dagath kill him?"

"Didn't sound like. He got away somehow. Dagath thinks he killed his half brother or something. Swears he'll catch up and get revenge someday." Farl chuckled softly.

"Where was this?"

Farl shrugged. "East of here, I think he said. South of Lyos, near the Burnished Way."

Brahasti glanced at the shortsword again, noting its fine balance and bright, waisted blade. It was unmistakably Ivairian. Brahasti remembered the letter he'd received weeks ago from Prince Ziraari. The letter claimed that a cousin of the Dhargothi princes had gone missing. There were rumors that he'd died in a duel with an Isle Knight of Ivairian descent.

Could be a coincidence. Either way, it never hurt to have powerful friends. Capturing the Ivairian and sending him to Prince Ziraari as a token of friendship might go a long way to helping him establish his position. *Or else I could send him to Karhaati as a peace offering. Depends on which prince seems stronger once the snows melt, I suppose.*

Brahasti flipped the sword, caught it by the hilt, and slid it into his belt. He walked out to where the third Jol stood. It looked so dark in the absence of torchlight that Brahasti might have mistaken it for a ghastly tree.

"Too bad I can't send one of *you* to look for this Isle Knight," Brahasti muttered. "Gods know how I'd ever find him, anyway."

Shade almost could not believe his eyes, let alone his luck.

As they lay on the dew-damp plains, surveying the compound, a single figure stepped off the bridge and joined the armored Olg keeping watch beyond. Rays of moonlight fell upon coldly handsome, familiar features.

"That's Brahasti," he told Zeia through mindspeak. *"If we kill him first, his men will be leaderless."*

Shade sensed Zeia's doubt before she replied. *"A scream is a scream. By the time we're done killing those three, the rest will be warned."*

He almost laughed. *"See? The little one is going back inside the compound. Are you telling me that two Shel'ai can't dispose of two guards without making noise?"*

"Two Human guards, yes." Zeia gave him a cold look. *"But Brahasti's friend appears to be an Olg in full armor. Or did you somehow fail to notice?"*

Shade hesitated. *"Wytchfire can burn through armor."*

"Yes… but not quickly. And whoever takes down that Olg will be a lot weaker for it."

Shade took a deep breath and let it go. Zeia was right. Still, when Brahasti turned and started back into the compound, it took all of Shade's willpower not to stand up and kill him right then.

Zeia touched his arm. *"We're not here for revenge. We're here to make amends for Fadarah's sins."*

"I haven't forgotten." Shade scowled at the necessary reminder. *"Muddle the Olg's senses so we can get past it. I'll do the same to the two guards on the other side. We won't start killing until we have to."* Slowly, quietly, he rose to his feet. *"Remember: if we're spotted, don't hesitate."*

Zeia stood, too. *"This isn't my first battle."* She undid her cloak and let it fall. Shade did likewise. They moved stealthily through the shadows. Crouching low, they approached the Olg from the side. When they were close enough, Zeia touched Shade's arm. Both Shel'ai sank to one knee.

Zeia closed her eyes, and Shade imagined her carefully extending her consciousness into the Olg's mind, confusing its sense of hearing so that its ears would not register the sound of their footsteps as they crept past it. Shade smirked. He had the harder job: muddling both the hearing and the eyesight of the two guards who were looking right in their direction.

Shade prepared himself, willing his mind through certain thought exercises designed to improve his focus. He was nearly ready when Zeia grabbed his arm. *"Something's wrong."*

Before Shade could answer, the Olg turned to face them. Both hands came up, each one holding a blade. Instead of shouting a challenge or howling a warning to the other guards, the Olg charged.

"So much for stealth," Shade muttered. One hand came up, already trailing wytchfire. He unleashed a blast that struck the Olg's chest with the force of a crossbow bolt. Instead of crashing to the ground, the Olg shuddered, righted himself, and kept charging. Moonlight glimmered off blackened armor.

"Tough bastard," Shade conceded. He took a step backward and unleashed a second blast. Zeia joined him. Twin streams of wytchfire rammed into the Olg's chest. Armor rang as though struck by a hammer.

The Olg stopped, as though he had just run headlong into a solid stone wall. Though the Olg still had not screamed, Shade imagined the force of their blows resounding through armor, shattering ribs like glass. He imagined the magical heat of their wytchfire seeping in, transforming the Olg's armor into an oven and broiling his organs. But still the Olg did not fall.

Armored legs carried it forward in great strides, devouring the final few feet that separated the combatants. Blades glistened. For the first time, Shade noticed that the Olg wore an eerily placid facemask wrought entirely of brass.

Shade shoved Zeia one direction then dove in the other. He bit back a scream as something cold and sharp kissed the back of his thigh. He sent out another blast of wytchfire, striking the Olg's knee.

The Olg's leg buckled but did not fold. Then the Olg swung both blades at the same time. One angled for Shade's face. The other stabbed down toward Zeia's back with uncanny precision as she rolled away.

Shade leapt backward, drew his sword, and unleashed another torrent of wytchfire. He targeted the blade in the Olg's other hand, turning it just enough so that it missed Zeia's back and sank into the earth. Then Shade swung his sword in a hard, fast arc. He meant to drive the Olg's remaining weapon out of the way and push his sword beneath the Olg's facemask. However, his sword turned off the Olg's, unable to force it down.

Shade stepped back again. Hearing shouts, he looked past the Olg and saw men running across the bridge, their swords drawn. He counted six, all Human. Rather than rush to the Olg's aid, they hung back and watched.

Bad choice, Shade thought. As the Olg swung at Zeia, she backpedaled, both of her hands spouting wytchfire. Shade side-stepped, spotted a dark gap in the Olg's armor, and thrust his sword into the back of the Olg's thigh. He pushed hard. "Now we're even," he muttered.

The Olg whirled with frightful speed. Unable to free his sword in time, Shade ducked then leapt sideways to avoid another swing. He cursed as his wounded leg gave out. He fell hard but managed to roll away. He brought both hands up, fingers splayed, and poured more wytchfire onto his enemy. "Die, damn you!"

He unleashed more and more flames, driving the Olg back. He maintained the deadly outpour until he felt the bottom drop out of his stomach. A dull, jarring pain swept through his brain—he was running out of strength. If he kept fighting with magic, he could die of exhaustion.

Shade pressed his hand to his wounded thigh. Wincing, he forced himself onto his feet. The armored Olg was still standing. Somehow, it had died on its feet, Shade's sword still jammed into the back of one leg. The Olg's cuirass glowed red hot.

Shade turned to face the rest of the guards. Zeia struck first, unleashing a blast of wytchfire that burned down one and scattered them like leaves. Then, glancing at Shade, she took notice of his wound. She started toward him. As she passed the Olg, one of the Olg's blades flew up. Zeia screamed. As she fell, she blasted the Olg one last time. The Olg's cuirass flared even brighter. Still, the Olg stepped forward and thrust a second blade next to the first.

For a moment, Shade could only stare. With frightful nonchalance, the Olg dragged both blades free, turned, and faced him. Moonlight shown off its grinning brass facemask. Dark, unblinking eyes regarded him in silence.

Zeia lifted her head. Blood ran from her lips. Through clenched teeth, she hissed, "Not an Olg..."

Shade nodded dumbly. His opponent charged, its blades dripping Zeia's blood into the dark grass. With no time to dive clear and shaking with exhaustion, Shade lifted both his hands. Wytchfire exploded from his fingertips, splashed over the brass facemask, and clawed at the eye holes.

The armored figure jerked then pitched forward. Shade pressed his hands against it, but its weight bore him down. He feared he would be crushed, but both blades stuck in the earth, one on each side of him, propping it up. Wincing, Shade crawled free.

"Not an Olg," he repeated. He crawled toward Zeia. She had managed to roll onto her side, both hands pressed just beneath her ribcage, but she could not sit up. Shade got behind her and positioned her head on his lap. He looked up.

Sellswords watched them from a distance. More had crossed the bridge. At least twenty milled near the watchtower. Brahasti was among them, a wolfish grin on his face.

Shade stared back. Forcing a defiant smile, he motioned for Brahasti to come closer. The general laughed. He said something that Shade could not hear. The sellswords laughed, too. Then Shade spotted two more huge figures crossing the bridge, their armor gleaming coldly. They took up position in front of Brahasti and the others. Some of the sellswords produced crossbows and loaded them but kept the armored figures between the Shel'ai and themselves.

Derision turned to panic. "Two more... Zeia, I can't..." Shade shook her. "Can you stand? We have to run."

Zeia did not answer.

Shade looked down at her. He blinked then gently lowered her head onto the ground. Gritting his teeth, he braced himself against the cold earth and tried to stand. He'd risen only halfway before he fell back down. He glanced up. The gleaming steel was almost on top of him. Shade clenched his eyes shut then opened them. With the last of his fading strength, he pushed himself to his feet and faced his attackers.

CHAPTER FIFTEEN

OUT OF THE WATER, OUT OF THE DARK

BOKUDEN WATCHED AS SUNRISE GILDED the grove of dogwood trees south of Saikaido Temple, burning away the mist known for centuries as the Dragon's Veil. He imagined the clearing where he'd faced off against his fellow squires so many years ago, sparring with wooden swords. He thought of the salmon pond where he used to sit as a boy, reading and rereading the ancient legends of Fâyu Jinn when he should have been studying the ponderous dogma of the Codex Viticus. He turned his attention back to the temple, scrutinizing the one thousand clean, white steps carved painstakingly into the bluff. He smiled faintly, remembering those mornings as a squire when he'd lamented those thousand steps and the Shao masters who'd made him climb them.

I can't climb them so well anymore, either. One wrinkled hand touched the hilt of his adamune then slid down to the scabbard, touching the long row of notches representing the men he'd slain in battle. *But I'm not dead yet.*

The Grand Marshal turned his gaze westward, out beyond the island, to the blue waters of the Burnished Way. Cranes and seagulls cavorted in the morning mist. There was no sign of the Jolym yet. But he knew they were coming.

"We're ready for them."

The officers standing nearby, all Knights of the Lotus, must have thought he was trying to reassure them. Several bowed in agreement. Others recited oaths in Shao. Bokuden smothered a grin, wondering if he looked as scared and unconvinced as they did.

The Grand Marshal directed his gaze back to Saikaido Temple's defenses.

Everything was in place. Beyond pit traps dug along the beach, hundreds of Isle Knights waited with spears. Higher along the shore, hundreds more stood armed with longbows. All had strict orders: aim for the eyes. Anything less was a waste of effort.

A reserve force of a thousand squires was prepared to make short work of any Jolym that fell into the pits. The squires were also set to attack any Jolym that avoided the pits and the Knights. They had been given coils of rope fitted to metal hooks. Once the Jolym had been caught, they would be tethered to horses and dragged on their backs round and round the island, until the Knights could finish them off.

Bokuden permitted himself a thin smile.

The Jolym had already annihilated two smaller islands and massacred an entire garrison of Isle Knights and squires that had been caught unaware. The Jolym had simply walked out of the sea by the hundreds, dripping in water, as quiet as death, and swept like a scythe through one Isle village after another. But no more. Word of the Jolym's weakness had reached them from Lyos— nearly as strange a message as the one Bokuden had received weeks earlier, supposedly from the Wytchforest, warning that a Dragonkin had returned to Ruun.

Bokuden had ignored the message about the Dragonkin at first, thinking it must be someone's idea of a jest—especially since it mentioned the name of Rowen Locke—but he'd reexamined it after receiving the message from Lyos. Then he'd tested the advice sent by the Lyosi by sending out a squad of his best archers. The archers reported that the Jolym dropped stone dead when shot through the eyes, though such a shot was profoundly difficult for even the most skilled of archers.

It would be even more difficult with the Jolym's entire force surging up the beach, but Isle Knights were trained to stay calm in battle, to control their passions, and aim true. Besides, numbers were on their side. Bokuden had called in the garrisons from every temple throughout the Isles. Practically the entire Knighthood was gathered before him. For every Jol that shambled up the beach, forty Knights and squires waited to kill it.

Everyone will want to be able to say afterward that they killed a Jol single-handed. Bokuden smiled again. *Let them. So long as the Isles are safe, they can be as vainglorious as they damn well please.*

He wondered if Aeko Shingawa would agree with that sentiment. He had already dispatched a messenger raven to give her word of what had happened, though he wondered if she would believe it. She and the other Knights might not have heard about the Jolym yet. In her place, Bokuden might very well have dismissed word of the Jolym as the ravings of a senile Knight.

Bokuden smiled. He wondered how the newly minted Knight of the Lotus was faring, especially in the presence of Crovis Ammerhel. Bokuden had to admit that he would have felt better if she were with him. Even Crovis— admittedly, as fearless as he was arrogant—would have been welcome. But finding Rowen Locke was more important, especially if Jolym were walking the earth for the first time in nearly a thousand years.

By the Light, where did these damn things come from?

He'd heard terrible stories of Shel'ai magic, but Fadarah and the rest were supposed to be in the west, fighting for control of the Wytchforest. Legend had it that the Dragonkin possessed the power to make Jolym… but thanks to the Dragonward, all of those ancient, cruel sorcerers had been exiled from Ruun.

The Grand Marshal shook his head, trying to clear his thoughts. He surveyed the rows of armored Knights and horses massed below. Then one of the younger Knights to his right cried out and pointed. Bokuden's heart leapt in his throat. He followed the Knight's gesture and saw a broad glint of steel, rising slowly from the misty water.

Cranes and seagulls scattered. Someone blew a horn, sounding the alarm. Another followed, then another. A great, restless murmur swept through the Knights' ranks. Well-trained war horses shifted and screamed; some even threw their riders, as though they could sense what was coming.

Bokuden clapped a shaking hand around his sword hilt. "Steady, men," he shouted down the temple steps. A few Knights turned to look back at him. Bokuden fixed a grizzled snarl to his face. He had intended to remain at the top of the steps with his officers so that he could monitor the battle and coordinate troop movements with horns and signal flags. Now, though, something called him down, urging him to join his Knights.

He hesitated then drew his sword. The curved blade gleamed wickedly in the rising sunlight. "All right, lads," he called out to his officers. "Why should these young Knights get all the fun?"

He started down the steps. A few of his officers laughed. All drew swords and fell in around him. Meanwhile, a few of the Knights on the temple steps turned around again and saw the Grand Marshal's approach. Someone began to chant Bokuden's name. Others took up the chant. By the time Bokuden had descended a hundred steps, the entire army had joined in the chant.

Bokuden grinned. For the first time in as long as he could remember, he did not feel old. All the aches and pains had disappeared. His sword felt lighter. His footsteps quickened. He raised his sword into the air and shouted his battle cry. Others took up the shout. Blood pounded in his ears. He wished he could launch himself into the air like a dragon, fly over his entire army and face the Jolym himself.

Then someone grabbed his arm. A Knight shouted in his ear, but Bokuden still could not hear him over the din. He pulled away with a rush of irritation, then his eyes followed the Knight's gesture.

The Jolym had stopped on the Burnished Way, spread out in a row, side by side, knee deep in the surf. For all their size and strength, they looked small, even pitiful from a distance.

"They're afraid," Bokuden cried. "See, lads? The iron bastards are afraid of us!"

Thousands upon thousands of Knights and squires erupted into a wild cheer. Many lost their composure and shouted taunts out at the sea, anxious to draw the Jolym into a fight. Others bashed their swords against their armor. The crashing sound spread across the ranks, from one end of the beach to the other.

Still, the Jolym did not move.

Bokuden bashed the flat of his sword against his cuirass, adding his own challenge to the din. As he did so, though, he wondered what they would do if the Jolym refused to fight. Marching his Knights around their own pit-traps and sending them into the surf to do battle would have been foolish. But he could not let the Jolym go, either.

No, once he'd destroyed the abominations before him, he would march westward and hunt down the others that had threatened Lyos as well. And if the Dhargots objected to his presence on the mainland, they could meet him on the battlefield, too.

By the Light, I may just take this army all the way to the Wytchforest!

Then, to his right, a Knight of the Lotus fell forward and tumbled down the temple steps before Bokuden could catch him. Bokuden thought the man had simply lost his footing. Then another Knight, on his left, fell. A third Knight staggered. Bokuden dropped his sword and grabbed the man. He was too heavy to hold up, but Bokuden managed to lower him to the steps. The man bore no wounds that Bokuden could see, but his eyes were wide and lifeless.

Bokuden retrieved his sword and spun around. Three Knights still stood with him. Confused, they turned, too. Then, one by one, they fell. Bokuden still heard thousands of Knights and squires shouting and chanting behind him, oblivious to what was happening. But for the moment, the Grand Marshal stood alone.

His eyes fixed on two cloaked, hooded figures descending the temple steps. One stumbled as though dazed, but the other strode with slow, chilling purpose. When only ten steps separated them, they stopped. The taller figure regarded Bokuden, then swept back his hood. Haughty, Sylvan features shown in the morning light.

Bokuden tightened his grip on his sword and stared into the other man's violet eyes. "Are you Fadarah?"

The other man sneered. "You mistake the stray dog for the hungry greatwolf." He took another step. "So *this* is Jinn's legacy." He looked around, smiling. "How kind of you to gather all your mighty Knights in one place." His mist-white pupils fixed on Bokuden, unblinking.

Bokuden did not answer. He thought of the message from the Wytchforest. *Chorlga…* Then he heard shouts of a different sort coming from the Knights behind him. They'd seen the danger their Grand Marshal was in. Dozens raced up the temple steps, swords drawn. But Bokuden knew they would never make it.

With his free hand, he touched the notches carved into his scabbard again. *"Singchai ushó fey,"* he said. He raised his sword and saluted.

The Dragonkin snickered. "Fine words, Human. Here is my response." He moved behind the man crouched next to him and touched his shoulder. The man jerked then straightened and threw off his cloak. Cold, mad eyes fixed on Bokuden. Wytchfire unfurled from the man's hands, his eyes, and even his nostrils.

Bokuden shouted with defiance and forced himself to charge up the steps. Steel glinted in his fist. His armor flashed. He made it halfway before the flames washed over him.

Chorlga surveyed the destruction before him. Burnt flesh and blackened steel littered the ground amid heaps of ash and piles of discarded weapons. The moaning had stopped. The wounded had either succumbed to their injuries or crawled to safety. All the cranes and seagulls had flown away. The only sounds came from the rolling surf and the labored breathing of the cloaked form lying at his feet.

I should be happy…

Chorlga scowled down at the Nightmare. Though he knew it was too late, he wondered if he should try to do more to help him. The Nightmare's wytchfire had burned up whole squads of men like dry leaves, shredding the great army that had tried to clamber up the temple steps and avenge their slain Grand Marshal.

But even the Nightmare was not inexhaustible. As the young man's strength waned, a few arrows had weathered the firestorm and made it through. The Nightmare had been struck three times. That, plus his near-fatal level of exhaustion, made Chorlga wondered how the young madman was still alive.

Perhaps I should drain him, devour what's left of his essence, the way my ancestors fed off dragons. He shook his head. There were laws—a Dragonkin did not absorb the energies of another Dragonkin. True, the Nightmare had been born a Shel'ai, but the line had to be drawn somewhere. Besides, he risked imbibing the Nightmare's madness along with his remaining power. He remembered the bitter taste left after he'd absorbed the life force of the dragonpriests at Cadavash.

Chorlga lifted his gaze to the ruined temple. His Jolym had just finished scouring the island, killing all they could and scattering the rest. Soon, he would send them west, back to Cadavash. Meanwhile, the Jolym he'd withdrawn from Lyos had been diverted south, toward Atheion. He had no intention of damaging the famous Scrollhouse, of course, but nothing else about the City-on-the-Sea interested him. He would destroy a good portion of it then give its citizens the option of servitude. He had no doubt they would take it. Dwarrs and Isle Knights might not surrender, but they were the exceptions to the rule—and easily disposed of.

Well, perhaps not easily.

Though Chorlga had intended to use the Nightmare as both weapon and shield, he'd underestimated the Isle Knights. So many arrows and spears had swept in, and so quickly, that his wytchfire could not burn away them all. Two arrows had struck Chorlga—one in the leg, the other in the chest. Though the wounds might not have been mortal, Chorlga had taken no chances. Stretching out his mind, he'd stolen back the life from half a dozen Jolym, instantly healing himself.

But that was too close. I must never underestimate my enemies again.

Chorlga looked down at the Nightmare. The young man's eyes were as wide as coins and wet with terror. Chorlga shuddered and looked away.

"Now I know why Fadarah never used you against the Sylvs," Chorlga told the prone figure. "Hard to control, harder still to focus. What is it the

Dwarrs say about a greatwolf in a pewter shop?" He watched smoke rise in great, gray plumes off the temple summit. "No matter."

He turned his back on the Nightmare and was about to walk away when he heard a moan. He turned back.

The Nightmare was looking at him. Though terrified, he looked almost sane. The young man tried to sit up. "Silwren," he gasped again. "Where... where is..."

Chorlga recovered from his surprise and knelt in front of the young man. He met the Nightmare's gaze. "Dead. You killed her," he lied.

The Nightmare's eyes widened. "No..." He shook his head. "Don't remember..." He looked around. "Father?"

Chorlga smothered a grin. "Fadarah's dead, too. So is El'rash'lin. All of them are dead. You killed them all." He paused. "Don't you remember?"

Aghast, the Nightmare trembled. Then, as though noticing them for the first time, he touched the arrows in his body. With damp eyes, he looked to Chorlga for help. One bloodied hand reached out. Chorlga pulled back, and the Nightmare whimpered. Chorlga stared a moment longer, then he took the Nightmare's hand.

"Are you afraid?"

The Nightmare did not answer.

Chorlga watched the Nightmare struggle for breath. He felt a curious stinging in his eyes. Finally, after what felt like an eternity, the Nightmare jerked and went still. Chorlga stared. Then, pulling his hand away, he stood and walked back toward the sea.

The old man woke in the dark. Cold from the stone beneath him seeped through the fabric of a tattered cloak that seemed as much a part of him as his skin. He blinked, wondering if he'd gone blind. His throat tightened. He could not remember how to breathe.

Then he took a breath. Raw pain filled him, twisting like fire through all his extremities. He wept. Groping in the dark, he felt a curved stone structure just in front of him. He slumped heavily against it.

Who am I?

For a moment, he did not move. Then he took another breath and let it go. It did not hurt as badly as his previous attempt. Slowly, he nodded. "El'rash'lin," he gasped. "My name... is El'rash'lin..."

He clawed the stone well in front of him. He tried to push himself up, but his strength failed him. Slumping back to the floor, he wept. "Silwren… Gods… please help me…"

The chamber echoed with the sound of El'rash'lin's labored breathing. Then a flash of light caught his eye. El'rash'lin turned and found himself staring into the stone well as the light grew in intensity. El'rash'lin stopped shaking. His breathing slowed.

Calmly, he tipped his head to listen. After a long time, he nodded. "I understand."

The light dimmed. El'rash'lin took another deep breath. He braced himself against the stone wall. With great effort, he pushed himself up. He waved his hand, and his palm exhaled a weak, fluttering sphere of light. The light illuminated an ancient stairwell across the chamber.

El'rash'lin stared at the stairwell obscured by shadow. The sight of it terrified him. He thought of all he had to do. Momentarily overwhelmed, he nearly wept again. Then he shook his head. He took a step, then another.

As he approached the stairwell, the flickering sphere moved with him. The shadows retreated. El'rash'lin reached the stairwell. "Gods, must I do this again? How many times?" Gasping, he paused, pressing his wrinkled hands against cold stone. Then he began to climb again.

CHAPTER SIXTEEN

NO FLAMES

WITH MODEST EFFORT, DOOMSAYER WRENCHED his mace from the skull of the Olg at his feet. Sunrise mingled with blood. Doomsayer lifted his shaggy head, turning slowly from side to side. The motion caused the rodent skulls braided in his hair to clatter, making the only sound besides the faint trickle of blood.

"Who else challenges for chieftain?"

Fifty Olgrym stood before him. Some wore mismatched armor and thick coats of ash on their palms. A few wore vests of crude fur sewn with shards of bone. But most—the Felmauls, the last of his clan—were naked, save for a crust of dried blood that had been painted onto their flesh, along with other, even more unsavory substances.

"Who else challenges?" he repeated. He raised his mace. Blood ran down its shaft and twisted down his wrist. Doomsayer swept his gaze over the warriors of his dwindling host, giving each man a chance to meet his gaze. All looked away. Despite his scowl, Doomsayer was glad. He had lost so many warriors that he did not relish the thought of killing still more of them just to prove a point.

"Now," he began slowly, "we go on like I said before. We hunt the man with the burning sword. We hunt his magic. We take it for ourselves."

Doubt flickered in his warriors' eyes. Many of them wanted to return to the Wytchforest and continue fighting the Sylvs. After all, both the Wyldkin and the Shal'tiar had been all but annihilated. The forest lay open for the first time in centuries. Doomsayer understood this. He had become chieftain of the strongest clan in part because his hatred for the Sylvs burned brighter than any other Olg's. But things had changed.

Doomsayer thought once again of that sea of violet flames, how the pitiful

Human with his burning sword had cut down the mighty Fadarah, and how the very air had seemed to crackle with power. How could he go back to petty skirmishes after that?

But there will be a price. All of our brothers still fighting in the Wytchforest will say we abandoned them. They'll turn on us. We will not be able to go back to Godsfall... unless we win.

A wild grin spread across the Olg's taut, gray face. The Shel'ai had proven to be weak allies. The invasion of the Wytchforest had failed. But he imagined rallying the Olgrym a second time—only this time, with terrible magic of his own. He saw himself wading into battle with flaming hands, screaming in pain and triumph as whole legions withered before him.

One of Doomsayer's warriors stepped forward. Doomsayer hefted his mace again, but the warrior bowed. "Great One, we serve your fury. But how will we catch this Human?"

Doomsayer considered this. At first, he had thought it a blessing from the gods when the Human was spotted outside Shaffrilon, virtually alone. Somehow, though, he'd managed to get clear of the forest before Doomsayer's warriors could encircle him. Now, the Human was riding north, pressing hard toward the borders of Dhargoth. Doomsayer could not fathom why, nor did he care. He knew only that if he did not catch this Human before the Dhargots did, he might very lose his prize to those small men who painted their eyes and rode elephants to prove their courage.

"We run," he said finally. "Horses are weak. Men are weak. We are not. We do not sleep. We do not eat. While *they* sleep, we draw closer." He pointed northeast with his mace. "We do not stop until we taste blood. Let all who fail be forgotten."

He waited until his warriors nodded. Then, squinting in the rising sun, he began to run. The earth trembled as his warriors fell in behind him.

Rowen and the Sylvan fighters rode quickly from the burnt-out fort of Que'ahl, pressing their horses as hard as they could. With one more rider than they had horses, they rotated frequently to distribute the burden. Rowen glanced over his shoulder many times, heartened by the absence of pursuers. Finally, early in the afternoon, he reined in Snowdark.

"Let the horses rest." Before anyone could argue, he turned to Rhos'ari. "Sergeant, I want you, Faeli, and Aerios to scout around on foot." He eyed a copse of trees in the distance. Though it looked too small to conceal a force of

Olgrym, he thought he'd seen a wisp of smoke rising from the trees. "Might be a sellsword or two camping there. If they're no threat, leave them alone." He pointed westward, toward the gray, rocky horizon. "Cathas, do me a favor and make sure a whole damn army of Olgrym don't come charging out of Godsfall while I'm not looking."

He dismounted and turned his back, signaling an end to the conversation.

Kilisti quietly took the reins of the other Sylvs' horses. Instead of arguing, as Rowen had expected, she went to work caring for the horses while he did the same for Snowdark. When he was finished, he assisted her, which she did not acknowledge. Cathas stood watch, steady despite his bandaged leg, as the others fit arrows to their bowstrings and went to examine the copse of trees.

When the horses had been tended, Rowen considered dining on some of the bland but adequate rations they carried in their saddlebags. He took out the scroll that Silwren had given him, but this was not the proper time or place for reading it.

Kilisti paused and looked over her horse brush. "Are you going to read that or just stare at it?"

"No need. I didn't have much to do while I was under house arrest in Shaffrilon, so I must have read the damn thing a thousand times."

"What's it about?"

"The founding of the Knighthood and the end of the Shattering War." He hesitated. "And Knightswrath. How and why they made it."

Kilisti paused then went back to brushing. "Nâya sacrificed herself so that Jinn would have a way to fight the Dragonkin." She glanced up and smirked. "Sylvs are better than Humans when it comes to remembering things that matter. Funny that we'd know more about your precious Order than you do."

Rowen bristled, though he had to admit that Kilisti was right. Isle Knights still told stories about Fâyu Jinn, but none of them mentioned Nâya, the Dragonkin he loved. Likewise, they made no mention of Knightswrath. Rowen had speculated that when the sword became tarnished—for its powers were tied to the honor of the Knighthood—the Knights had tried to erase all mention of it. He thought of the small silver dragon inlaid in the blade next to the sword's name. Once, he had taken that to be the mark of the sword's maker. He wondered now if that symbol represented Nâya. Then he thought of an insult of his own. "And strange, Sylv, how a people who remember Nâya's sacrifice still justify the killing of any infant born with white eyes."

Rowen wondered if he'd gone too far, but Kilisti kept brushing. "I had a sister," she said after a moment. "Her name was Shi'as. I found her in the forest when I was coming back from that Dhargothi compound. The Sorcerer-General had left that big sword of his in her corpse, left her there like she was nothing."

She spoke so flatly that it took Rowen a moment to register what she was saying.

"From what I hear, the Shel'ai captured some Knights from your Order," Kilisti continued. "Forced them to switch sides, to swear an oath they couldn't break. Your brother was one of them. They made you kill him."

Rowen considered throwing the scroll casing at Kilisti's face. Instead, he returned the scroll to his saddlebag. "Enough." He turned his back on her and stroked Snowdark's neck. The horse pricked up her ears, sensing his building rage. Rowen saw Cathas watching, too, his expression taut.

"I guess that means I owe you for killing Fadarah," Kilisti said from behind him, "though really, I'd rather you'd left him for me."

"He would have killed you in a second."

"You think so?"

Rowen turned. He looked her up and down. "Yes."

"Well, I don't have a burning sword to help me... but given how that thing muddled your brains, I'm not sure that's a bad thing."

Rowen touched Knightswrath's hilt. "I've had enough of your goading, Sylv. What say you take a walk?"

With deliberate slowness, Kilisti stowed the horse brush in a saddlebag, patted the final horse's neck, then sidestepped and crossed her arms. "Or what, Knight? You'll deny my rations? Or you'll tell Captain Briel that I took time out of the war to hurt your feelings?"

Rowen forced a cold smile. Releasing Snowdark's reins, he stalked toward Kilisti until he stood right in front of her, his face hovering inches above hers. He flexed one gauntleted fist and considered striking her. He was being tested, and that would have been the appropriate response for an insubordinate soldier. But Rowen chafed at the idea of striking a woman.

Meanwhile, Kilisti uncrossed her arms but did not blink or waver. A mocking smile spread across her scarred face. "What's the matter, Knight? Lost your nerve?"

Rowen remembered how Igrid had goaded him similarly. He took a deep breath and released it. Then he answered Kilisti's smile with one of his own. "If it pleases you to mock me, Sylv, go right ahead. I'm past willing to duel with allies over insults to my honor."

"Oh, are we allies now?"

"Your king doesn't think so," Rowen admitted. "Neither do half your people, probably. But I don't care about that. I'm riding north to stop the Dhargots. If you want to help, I'm sure we'll find plenty of men you'll enjoy killing more than me."

Kilisti started to laugh. "We'll see," she muttered, and turned away. Rowen stepped back. He saw that Cathas had been coming to separate them then seemed to have thought better of it. Rowen returned to Snowdark. He pretended to rummage through his saddlebags so that he could give his hands time to stop shaking.

A few moments later, he heard Cathas swearing in Sylvan. Rowen turned, hand on his sword. Rhos'ari, Aerios, and Faeli were returning from their scouting mission, their expressions taut. All had their swords drawn. Aerios was leading a horse, while the others escorted a prisoner. The man was Human, with a dirty face and torn leather armor. But the braided goatee and smeared paint around his eyes were unmistakable. Despite his predicament, the Dhargot was grinning.

Rowen met them halfway.

"A deserter," Rhos'ari said. "Says he's on the way to Quorim. He was alone." He handed Rowen the Dhargot's weapons: a shortsword and a dagger, both with matching horse heads carved into the hilts. Rowen noted the necklace hanging around the Dhargot's neck. He counted three pairs of ears strung to the necklace. One pair looked small, like a child's.

Before Rowen could speak, the Dhargot gave a low whistle. "A red-haired Isle Knight, traveling in strange company. Not a common sight on the Simurgh Plains." His grin broadened. "You must be the one who killed Jaanti. My prince was looking for you."

For a moment, Rowen was speechless. "Who is your prince?"

"Ziraari." The Dhargot turned and spat on the ground. "Dead now. Shel'ai killed him."

Kilisti took a step forward, a drawn shortsword in hand. "What are you doing here?"

The Dhargot looked at her. His eyes widened at the sight of her scarred face. "Being prettier than you, it seems."

Faeli kicked the back of the Dhargot's leg, driving the man to his knees. The man grunted but did not stop grinning. Faeli tapped the tip of his sword against the Dhargot's cheek. "Answer her."

"Gladly," the Dhargot said. "Running for my life! Most of Ziraari's men are flocking to Karhaati, getting ready to fight Lyos or Ivairia... whichever he picks first." He made a curious sign and spat on the ground again.

Rowen committed the names to memory. He'd never heard them before, but he knew enough about Dhargots to remember stories about the assassinations and rivalries common among their princes and officers. "And why aren't you with them?"

The Dhargot puffed up his chest. "Braanti is first archer on an elephant. That's a rank of honor. But Karhaati will give Ziraari's beasts to his own men. I won't start on foot again, least of all there."

Kilisti snickered. "Too afraid to fight on equal ground?"

The Dhargot gave her a cold look. "Braanti serves the Dragongod. Braanti loves fighting. But Braanti is no fool. Men have seen the Nightmare in that direction. Only fools fight where demons live."

Rowen frowned. "You should pay less heed to drunken rumors. The Nightmare is dead."

"The princes said that, too. Then, one night, we hear it scream, see it set the plains on fire. Fire shows for miles."

Rowen thought back to the Battle of Lyos, when El'rash'lin and the Nightmare had destroyed each other. There had been no bodies, but Silwren had sworn she'd felt El'rash'lin die. Later, at Rowen's insistence, she'd entered a trance, trying to feel the Nightmare's presence. She'd emerged from the trance certain that the Nightmare was dead, too.

Could she have been wrong? Or is he describing Chorlga? Rowen gave the Dhargot a hard look. *Or is he simply lying?*

Rowen tapped Knightswrath's hilt. A Shel'ai would have been able to pry into the Dhargot's mind and know whether or not he was telling the truth. Rowen was no Shel'ai, but there was still a way. His pulse quickened as he remembered the rush of intoxication he'd felt when he called upon the sword's power to kill that Olg. He willed the adamune to let him know whether or not the Dhargot was telling the truth. He did not know if it would work with the blade still sheathed. But a moment later, he jerked as memories that were not his own tumbled into his mind. His vision blurred, as though he were momentarily seeing the world through two pairs of eyes at once.

He reeled, almost losing his balance. One of the Sylvs caught him, but Rowen pulled away. As quickly as it had begun, it was over. Rowen found everyone staring at him.

The Dhargot looked somewhere between bemused and frightened. "Maybe you're as mad as the Nightmare. Maybe I should have gone to Karhaati after all."

Ignoring the Dhargot, Rowen turned to Rhos'ari. "He's telling the truth… or thinks he is, at least. Let him go."

The Sylvan sergeant's eyes widened. "But, Knight—"

Faeli grabbed the Dhargot's long hair and jerked his head back. "No way we're setting him free."

Rowen scowled. He faced Faeli and gave an appropriate answer in Sylvan.

Taking his cue, Rhos'ari interjected in Sylvan, too. "Knight, I think Faeli means to say that the Dhargots are our enemies. They allied with Fadarah for a time. They have taken our people captive. They have threatened *your* people, too. You came to Sylvos to secure an alliance *against* them. Besides, we need his horse. Why—"

Rowen waved him off. He gave Braanti a hard look. Thanks to Knightswrath's magic, he knew what kind of man he was dealing with. Still, he'd been disarmed. They could not afford to haul a prisoner with him, and the Codex Viticus strictly forbade the execution of prisoners.

He's no threat to us. If I let him go, he'll be back in Dhargoth in a few days. But what will he do after that?

Rowen eyed Braanti's necklace of ears. "Let him go," he repeated in Sylvan. He gave Faeli a hard look. Finally, the Sylv cursed and stepped back, shaking his head. Rowen held up Braanti's weapons. Then he took three steps away and dropped them on the grass.

The Sylvs exchanged looks. Braanti knelt a moment longer then scooped up his weapons. He sheathed his dagger but kept his sword in hand. "My thanks, Knight. I hope you die well."

"I hope I do, too," Rowen said. "Are you ready?"

The Dhargot blinked, confused.

Rowen drew Knightswrath and leapt forward. The Dhargot's eyes widened. He managed to block Rowen's first swing then his second. The Dhargot backpedaled, trying to draw his dagger with his free hand. Rowen slowed, giving him time. Then he charged. They locked swords. Rowen held then twisted sideways. He kicked the Dhargot's knee, cut the dagger out of his hand, then sliced the head off his shoulders. Braanti fell before he could make a sound.

Rowen took a few deep breaths to calm himself, then stooped and wiped his sword clean on the Dhargot's corpse. The smell of fresh blood filled his nostrils. A familiar pang of guilt swept through him. As he stood, he muttered a prayer in Shao. He saluted with his blade before sheathing it. When he turned, the Sylvs were regarding him coolly.

Kilisti said, "No flames this time?"

"Didn't think I'd need them."

Kilisti snickered. "How honorable. But would you have done that if you didn't think you could take him?"

Rowen wondered the same thing as he headed back toward Snowdark. "Let's get out of here. Faeli, take the Dhargot's horse. He may have been trash, but his people know how to train horses. She'll obey. Just guide her easy with your heels at first."

Faeli answered with a gruff, begrudging nod.

Sergeant Rhos'ari cleared his throat. "Should we bury the Dhargot?"

Rowen shook his head. "If anybody's following us, let him serve as a warning. If not, he can feed the crows."

CHAPTER SEVENTEEN

ALLIANCES AND DISTRACTIONS

J ALIST HOPED THE LONG WALK from the tavern to the palace would help clear his head. But in the three days since the Jolym's attack, the streets of Lyos had not calmed. Citizens still roiled with panic, and what remained of the Red Watch had to patrol the city streets just to maintain order. Jalist remembered Rowen saying that in the wake of Silwren's appearance in the Dark Quarter, mingling with the approach of Fadarah's Throng, the Lyosi—normally so proper, even haughty—had actually rioted.

"That's what comes from too many years of soft living," he muttered. He lifted a wineskin to his lips. When he slowed to drink, one of the guards shoved him, causing him to spill on his tunic. He growled a Dwarrish insult to the man's parentage.

"Keep moving, sir," pleaded the officer tasked with bringing him back to the palace. The young man looked as nervous around Jalist as he did around the crowds. Jalist felt sympathy for the boy as he wiped his tunic.

"What's the hurry? Last I heard, I wasn't under arrest. If the king wants to talk, he can wait."

The officer ordered the three men of the Red Watch he was commanding—none older than he—to walk ahead and clear a path through the streets. Jalist watched them, shaking his head. A moment later, a pickpocket pretended to collide with the officer then plucked a jeweled dagger from his belt, all whilst furiously bowing and muttering apologies. Despite his drunkenness, Jalist intercepted the pickpocket, retrieved the dagger, and sent the man on with a shove. He returned the dagger to the officer, who accepted it with wide eyes.

"I don't suppose I can stop and change first." Jalist inspected his tunic as he took another drink. "I know the wine matches the color, but I like to look my best when I chat with royalty."

The officer reached out and snatched Jalist's wineskin. He threw it on the ground, grabbed Jalist's arm, and pushed him onward. Jalist resisted the impulse to break the young officer's arm. "Easy, lad. I'm not your enemy. In fact, I seem to remember something about *killing* a few of your enemies—if killing Jolym can be called killing, since I'm not sure the bastards count as alive."

Jalist allowed himself to be prodded along but took the jeweled dagger from the officer's belt as payment for the wineskin. "Any notion what your king wants to talk to me about?"

The officer scowled, though Jalist could not tell whether it was in answer to his question or a passing flesh trader who appeared to know him and called him sweetly by name. "Probably this morning's council meaning, which you missed."

"I knew I was forgetting something." Jalist rubbed his eyes then perked up at the sight of another tavern, with a gigantic terrace and a multitude of young, pretty servers wearing bright sarongs. A sign proclaimed the tavern's name, but all he could make out was the name of the god, Dyoni; the rest of the sign was obscured by a soft-eyed young man who caught Jalist's eye and smiled.

"Listen, lad, if the meeting's over anyway, how about—"

Before he could finish, the officer shouted at his men, chastising them for being too rough as they tried to clear a path through the streets. A moment later, the officer himself almost backhanded a merchant who strode up to offer an angry protest. Jalist changed tactics. He strode well ahead of the officer and his men so that they had to struggle to keep up. By the time they reached the palace, the poor officer had gone from anxious to livid. But the sight of at least fifty clerics to the various gods and goddesses descending the temple steps prevented him from berating Jalist.

"The king wanted to see you while he was still meeting with the clerics," the officer said, aghast. "Best you go in before things get any worse."

Jalist inspected his wine-stained tunic again but did not argue.

The officer turned him over to a pair of palace guards, who led him in. Neither spoke. Both seemed as tense as the clerics that Jalist had passed on the steps. The Dwarr had the odd feeling that he was being led to his own execution. But when they reached the great hall, the king stood and greeted Jalist with a terse smile.

"Lord Hewn, how good of you to finally join us." He dismissed the palace guards then gestured for Jalist to join him at a great oak council table. The table was empty except for a buxom, red-haired woman in a low-cut dress. She'd risen when the king had, but the look she gave Jalist was anything but friendly.

Jalist looked around, surprised by how dark and empty the great hall appeared. In the distance, he could make out the shapes of gigantic statues of gods and goddesses, all cloaked in shadows. He thought he saw a flicker of movement near the statues but dismissed it, settling his gaze on Igrid. "I see you removed the bandages from your skull. I trust that was against the clerics' warnings, though to be fair, it's hard to seduce royalty when you have your head wrapped up in gauze."

Blushing, Igrid glanced at the king then opened her mouth to offer an icy retort.

The king stopped her. "Lady Igrid is here at my invitation. I should add that, unlike you, she arrived on time."

"Good for her." Jalist took the empty chair to the king's left, belatedly reminding himself not to sit down until the king had sat first. Then he seized the gilded cup in front of him and filled it from a nearby pitcher. He look a long drink. The wine tasted sour but strong, better than what he'd been drinking at the tavern. He took a second drink, started to set the cup down, then thought better of it. After draining the rest, he refilled it.

King Typherius's smile thinned. "Slow down, Dwarr. I want you sober for this conversation."

"Then I'm afraid you're a few hours late, *sire*," Jalist answered then took another drink.

Igrid snorted with disgust.

Jalist raised his cup, smiled at her, then faced the king again. "What can I do for you, m'lord?"

"First things first," the king said. His voice took on an edge. "Allow me to fill you in on what you missed from this morning's meeting. I was discussing strategy with my captains—"

"Was it a productive conversation?" Even though his cup was still half full, Jalist refilled it.

"No, not really. Between my father's murder last year, Captain Ferocles dying in the Battle of Lyos, and Captain Epheus and most of the veterans dying in... whatever men decide to call what happened last week, I'm suddenly the most experienced commander at the table." The young king grinned sardonically. "Not an enviable position."

Jalist stared into his cup. "No, Sire, I wouldn't imagine it is."

"Did you see the clerics when you were coming in?"

Jalist nodded. "For scions of the gods, most of them didn't look too happy."

"That's because half of them still think magic comes from Fohl the Undergod, and what I'm about to do will damn all our souls to his numerous hells. But I'm getting ahead of myself." The king handed Jalist a tiny rolled-up bit of parchment. "This arrived by raven a few weeks ago... supposedly from the Wytchforest. I thought it was a joke at first."

Jalist studied the script, realized the writing was too small, and pushed it aside. "What does it say?"

"That a Dragonkin named Chorlga has declared war on Ruun. The warning comes from Rowen Locke." Jalist's eyes widened, but before he could answer, the king asked, "Have you heard what happened on the Isles?"

Jalist started to take a drink but stopped himself. He nodded again.

The king glanced at Igrid then turned back to Jalist. "Well, in case you haven't heard it all, I'll give you the short version. Grand Marshal Bokuden is dead. The flower of the Knighthood was massed at Saikaido when the Nightmare appeared. Those Knights who weren't burnt up like scarecrows in a wildfire were mowed down by the Jolym or driven into the sea." He leaned back in his chair. "By your expression, I'm guessing you know what that means."

Jalist shook his head. "Sire, my expression is that of a man who's only drunk about half as much as he needs to. Don't read more into it than that."

The king hesitated. "I've heard... what happened at Stillhammer. What you must have seen..."

Jalist gave the king a look so icy that the monarch paled. Forcing a smile, Jalist said, "Thank you, Sire. I appreciate your kind words. Now, if we could get to why you summoned me here..." He hiccupped.

"Did you hear what I said about the Nightmare?"

Jalist started to refill his cup. "The Nightmare's dead. We all saw it."

"So we did." The king took the pitcher from Jalist and filled his own cup. "Only the descriptions are exactly the same. Also, a few of the Knights who got away say they saw someone else with the Nightmare. Someone who looked like a Shel'ai but couldn't have been, considering what he did." The king raised his cup but drank more slowly than Jalist had.

Jalist shrugged. "One of Fadarah's henchmen. Shade, probably."

"They're all fighting in the west," the king said. "There are rumors of some kind of Shel'ai stronghold in the north, somewhere on the Wintersea, but I don't think that's where the Nightmare came from. And I don't think that's where this... other one came from, either."

Jalist rubbed his eyes. Suddenly, he had a headache. "There were others. Other Shel'ai-turned-Dragonkin. Initiates, they called them. Silwren was one. So was El'rash'lin. And the Nightmare. But there were more. When I was with the Throng, they kept them in a separate tent."

Typherius nodded. "I heard. Only they all died. Silwren said she killed them, by accident, when she woke. El'rash'lin and the Nightmare died outside Lyos." The king paused. "There is something you should know, Dwarr. Before my father was killed, he was negotiating a trade alliance with your people. I continued the talks after his death. Both our peoples would have benefited. In another year or two, Lyos might even have been strong enough to shrug off the Isle Knights' control. So, when I heard that the kingdom of the Dwarrs had been ravaged, I thought the Isle Knights might be responsible."

Jalist thought of Rowen Locke and wondered what he would have said to that, especially after so many Isle Knights had died fighting for Lyos.

"But the Isle Knights can't be responsible for the Jolym—or the Nightmare, for that matter," the king continued. "That means someone else wanted to prevent an alliance between our kingdoms."

Jalist rubbed his eyes again. He was having a hard time understanding what the king was saying. "So the Nightmare came back from the dead. Plus, there's a Dragonkin and an army of Jolym on the loose, tearing up the countryside, and they don't want any of us joining together. Is *that* what you're saying?"

The king exchanged glances with Igrid. "I'm not sure I believe in the Dragonward. Everybody who's been up north says they can't see a damn thing. My father thought it was real, though. He said the Dragonkin had been driven away. They could never pass through that barrier and set foot on Ruun again. So either the Dragonward doesn't exist anymore... or it never existed... or—"

"There's been a Dragonkin hiding in Ruun all this time," Igrid finished. "That's a little hard to believe."

Jalist noted that, although her voice had taken on a hard edge, Igrid finished by giving the young king a coy look. If the king noticed, though, he gave no indication. Jalist looked around the great hall and spotted four old men standing by the far wall, their arms crossed. He'd mistaken them for servants, but now he thought they must be stewards or advisers of some kind, though the king had ordered them to remain quiet and keep their distance.

Their disapproval was obvious. *Are they mad about Igrid's presence here or mine... or both?* Jalist lifted his cup and nodded to them before he took a drink.

The king said, "My scouts tell me that some of the Jolym marched back to Cadavash. The ones we drove off, that is. But the rest are still thrashing the Isles. When they're done with the Knights, they'll come here."

"I guess they will." Jalist faced Igrid. "Well, Iron Sister, best gather all your coins and your pretty dresses and sleeve knives and move on. That's what I'm going to do. Anybody dumb enough to stay here deserves what they get."

"Does that include me, Dwarr?" Before Jalist could answer, the king continued. "This city has suffered ten generations of extortion from the Isle Knights. Still, we didn't run from Fadarah. We haven't run from the Dhargots. We aren't running now, either."

"Fine. Well said, m'lord." Jalist raised his cup again. "To a noble death!"

"Don't mock me in my own hall, Dwarr."

Jalist blinked. "Apologies, Sire. But if you brought me here to buy my counsel, I'll offer it to you for free: get out. The Knights may have robbed you blind, but they were still your protectors. Now, they're gone. The Jolym will come back. So will... whatever else is out there. And if nothing else, the Dhargots are still massed at Cassica. You have too many enemies, and you're out of friends. Either run or pick the lesser of evils and surrender."

Igrid gave him a look of disapproval. The stewards at the other end of the hall shook their heads in disgust. Jalist reached for the pitcher, but the king grabbed it first and moved it out of reach.

"You're wrong, Dwarr. I have one friend left. And *you* are going to find her for me."

Jalist set his cup down. "I'm what?"

"I need Silwren. She's the only one I know of who might be able to help us. But she's in the Wytchforest with your friend, Rowen Locke. So I'm sending you to find her." He glanced at Igrid. "I'm sending *both* of you. Lady Igrid has already agreed."

Jalist gave Igrid a hard look. The former Iron Sister's expression was so dreadfully earnest that Jalist almost laughed. He wondered how much the king had offered her. "With respect, Sire, you should send someone else. Your new Captain of the Guard—"

"I *am* sending my new Captain of the Guard," the king interrupted. "I'm sending you."

Jalist was speechless. *No wonder everybody looks so peeved.* "I appreciate the offer, Sire, but I spoke in haste. The Captain of the Guard generally doesn't leave his city on a fool's errand on the eve of battle."

"No," the king conceded, "but I'm out of ambassadors, and these are strange times. Besides, by making you my captain, I'm giving you a reason to come back… unless you want to be strangled for desertion." The king drained his own cup, refilled it, then did the same for Jalist's.

Jalist touched the jeweled dagger in his belt as he studied the king. "Sire, I'm a sellsword. I fought *with* the Throng, for a time. The nobles of Lyos—"

"Will do as I command, since they're too terrified to leave their mansions without pissing themselves," Typherius finished. He cast a sidelong glance at the old men across the room.

"But the clerics—"

"Mostly disapprove, which might concern me, if I could spare the energy to care." The king snickered. "Some were open to the idea, but the clerics of Maelmohr in particular seem to think that Dwarrs are a lesser race, some form of demon, what with their gray skin and dark eyes. Ironic, since if memory serves, the Firegod is the one *your* race worships."

"Worship might be too strong a word for it." Jalist drank. "Sire—"

"Five hundred cranáfi now, another thousand when you bring Silwren back," Typherius interrupted. "You and Lady Igrid can divide that between you, however you like. Somehow, I'll find fifty men to act as your bodyguards. And when you come back, you have my word that each month, I'll pay you twice what I paid the last two captains."

"You mean, the last two men who got themselves killed?"

Typherius started to smile then snapped his fingers. Half a dozen palace guards melted out from behind the shadowed statues, stone faced, all holding crossbows. Jalist could tell by the look on Igrid's face that she was as surprised as he was.

The king cleared his throat. "And since I'm feeling about as desperate as I am blunt, if you say *no* one more time, or if either of you betray me, I'll pay Fen-Shea whatever I've got left in the treasury to peel off your skin and bury you in a salt pile." He took a long drink, set his cup down, and fixed his gaze on Jalist. "That clear enough, Dwarr?"

Jalist forced himself to stop gripping the hilt of the jeweled dagger. "One death is as good as another these days, I suppose. Only there's no sense pinning all your hopes on me. You've got to know I don't have a prayer of making it past all those Dhargots swarming on the Simurgh Plains. And unless the

Olgrym have been beaten, I doubt Locke will come back with me, anyway. He's still trying to keep that sword of his out of the Knights' hands."

Typherius shook his head. "Dwarr, right now, I couldn't care less about one Isle Knight and his symbolic sword. I'm sending you after Silwren, not Locke. I need Silwren because she can turn armies into ash. If Locke wants to stay in the Wytchforest, let him."

Poor Locke. The more he tries, the less anyone gives a damn. "Fine, I'll go." Jalist glanced at Igrid. "But I'll go alone. I'll have a better chance of slipping through that way."

Igrid opened her mouth to protest, but the king spoke first. "No. Leave most of the soldiers, if you like, but I'm still sending two men to keep an eye on you. And this woman goes with you, too. She may be pretty, and I know she knows Locke and Silwren, but she's cut a few too many purse strings for my liking." The king stood up. "My quartermaster is expecting you. He'll pay you and give you horses and whatever else you need. I don't think I have to explain what will happen if you're both still here at sundown."

Igrid managed to look so believably hurt and offended that Jalist laughed. But the king stood and walked away. His stewards hurried to follow. The crossbowmen congregated around the council table. Jalist stood up and toasted them. "Nicely done." He set down his cup and started to walk away.

Igrid followed. She grabbed his arm a moment later. Her green eyes flashed with rage. One hand held the king's cup. She threw the remainder of its contents into Jalist's face. Then, casting a sidelong glance at the crossbowmen following just a few paces behind them, she whispered, "You idiot, he would have paid us *twice* that."

Jalist wiped his face with his sleeve. "The good king can promise us all the coins in Ruun. That doesn't mean either of us will live long enough to collect them." He smirked. "Besides, Iron Sister, he's paying me. Not you."

Igrid's right hand blurred, plucking a stiletto seemingly out of thin air. She pressed it to Jalist's throat. The crossbowmen tensed, but Jalist waved them back.

Igrid leaned so close that Jalist could smell her perfume. "Dwarr, you can sleep with fleas and live off paupers' root, if it pleases you. But by the time this war's over, I mean to be a rich woman. Don't get in the way of that again." The stiletto disappeared. She smiled sweetly. "I'll meet you at the front gates in half an hour." She turned and walked ahead of him.

Jalist followed more slowly. "Fine woman," he grumbled. As he left the palace, blinking in the sun's glare, he remembered the tavern he'd seen earlier.

He considered stopping off there first, but the crossbowmen seemed to have other ideas.

Aeko Shingawa reined in her horse and paused to stare at the broad, snow-flecked Noshan Valley. Somewhere to the south lay Atheion, the famed City-on-the-Sea. Though she had never been there, she'd heard stories about enormous skiffs of some magical design that pre-dated the Shattering War, on which the city's marvelous stone buildings floated on water.

She wondered if she should lead her Isle Knights south. The Simurgh Plains were still swarming with Dhargots, and Rowen could have passed through Atheion on his way to the Wytchforest. But Noshans were not known for their hospitality, and she doubted their king would be terribly excited to have one hundred foreign Knights riding toward his capital.

Then again, an angry king might be preferable to dealing with the Nightmare.

Glancing over her shoulder, she half expected to see the demon hurtling out of the northern sky, but she saw only blue clouds lording over distant, rolling hills. She wanted to believe that what she'd heard days ago had not been the same demon that had single-handedly torn through half the Free Cities and very nearly destroyed all of them at Lyos. But she trusted her own ears.

Crovis Ammerhel rode down the column of Knights and joined her. "What will it be, Captain? Do we regroup at Atheion or continue west in search of Locke?"

Aeko sensed the disdain behind Crovis's cordiality. She had not forgotten that while her intention was to find Rowen Locke and protect him, Crovis was only interested in Knightswrath. That alone tempted her to lead the expedition toward Atheion, if only to give Rowen more time to get away, but Aeko reminded herself about the message they'd received.

Dispatched by raven to find them on the plains, the message told of Jolym assaulting both Lyos and the Lotus Isles. Aeko might have thought the message some kind of jest had she not recognized Bokuden's signature at the bottom. If the Jolym had indeed emerged from some dark fairytale, just as the Nightmare appeared to have sloughed back from Fohl's hells to torment them, time was of the essence.

Aeko shook her head. "We ride west. But send a man south to warn the Noshan king of..." She hesitated. "Of every damned crazy thing that's happened." She thought of the message she'd sent back to Bokuden, using his own raven, to warn him about the Nightmare. She hoped he received it before the demon had a chance to act.

Crovis cleared his throat, visibly displeased. "Captain, why warn the Noshan king? What is he to us?"

"An ally, maybe, if we need one."

Looking unconvinced, Crovis sighed. "As you say, Captain."

Beyond a group of nearby Knights, who were eavesdropping, Aeko spotted a telltale glint of armor on the horizon. Her eyes narrowed.

Crovis followed her gaze, and the derision melted from his eyes. He snapped his fingers. "Sir Wei, your spyglass."

While the young Knight rummaged in his saddlebag, another Knight raised one gauntleted hand to shield his eyes from the sunlight.

"Dhargots?" he asked.

Aeko shook her head. Dhargots preferred scale or leather armor covered in black silk. Besides, they usually rode in chariots or on the backs of horses or elephants. The force in the distance looked more like a broad column of men in full-plate armor. They might have been Lancers, though she couldn't imagine why they would be on foot so far south. She turned to Crovis, who was raising a spyglass to one eye. "Any banners?"

Crovis squinted then lowered the spyglass, shaking his head. "No tabards, either."

Aeko's pulse quickened. "What kind of armor?"

Crovis pressed the spyglass to his eye again. "Full plate. Looks like steel, some brass. No horses. All have their weapons drawn."

Aeko caught his meaning. Crovis handed her the spyglass then cursed when his horse turned skittish, as though smelling something foul in the air. Other Knights' horses did the same. Aeko steadied her own mount then lifted the spyglass. A moment later, she lowered it. "Damn."

Crovis angled his horse closer and lowered his voice. "I confess, I was hoping our dear Grand Marshal had simply lost his mind." He drew his sword. Facing the column, he called out, "In Jinn's name, stand ready!"

The Isle Knights reacted at once. Some drew swords while others produced bows. A few wielding polearms moved ahead of the others, forming a defensive perimeter.

Crovis faced Aeko again. "Fight or run?"

She could tell by the look on Crovis's face which option he favored. "I think they're after Atheion, not us."

"Does that mean the captain would prefer to run? Or attempt a parley, perhaps?"

Aeko gave Crovis a withering look. "I count about twenty."

Crovis nodded. "Not much of a challenge, I know, but it might offer the men some sport."

Even from this distance, it was obvious that each Jolym stood well over six feet tall. While the Knights outnumbered them four to one, legends spoke of the Jolym mowing down armies ten times their size. If Bokuden was right, each Jol could only be slain by a strike through the eyeholes of its facemask. But even for fighters as well trained as Isle Knights, that was easier said than done. The curved blades of adamunes and Isle polearms were better suited for quick, devastating slashes than precise thrusts. Bows and arrows were their best bet, and all Knights were trained to fire from horseback, Queshi-style, but they were unaccustomed to aiming solely at an enemy's eyes.

The column of Knights bristled, anxious to charge. But that tactic would only get them killed, and they had no time to erect a palisade. Aeko turned back to Crovis.

"The demands of honor are clear. Locke is our priority, but we can't leave Atheion to these… things."

Though Aeko doubted that Crovis cared anything for the Noshans, the prospect of battle made him smile. "As you say, Captain. I suggest we divide our forces. I'll lead a frontal assault while you lead a flanking maneuver." He turned to wheel his horse, but Aeko grabbed his arm.

"Not here. Not now. We'll ride for Atheion and fortify there."

Crovis's expression darkened. "Captain, sending a messenger to the Noshan king is one thing. Riding into his city with a hundred armed men is another. If he doesn't believe us, we might end up fighting the same people we're trying to protect."

Maybe, but it's what Rowen would do. "Then I suggest you send our fastest rider on ahead. He can announce us." She glanced at the steely column of Jolym on the horizon. Already, it looked significantly closer. "Choose your rider while I scribble a message for the Noshan king."

Crovis glanced at the Jolym then turned back to Aeko. "No need, Captain. I choose myself. If I'm not waiting for you outside the city by the time you get there, the Noshans have killed me." He bowed. Then, wheeling southward, he spurred his horse to full gallop.

Aeko noted the look of approval on the faces of the other Knights. She sighed. *Well played, Ammerhel.* Then she waved for the Knights' attention.

She ordered them to sheathe their weapons, form ranks, and follow her. They obeyed with obvious reluctance. She wondered how Bokuden had lived so long, suffering such foolishness.

Some Knight of the Lotus I am! If my own men don't rebel against me, sooner or later, Crovis will challenge me on some matter of honor and cut me to ribbons.

As she turned her horse southward, Aeko half hoped that Crovis would be unsuccessful in his appeal to the Noshan king.

CHAPTER EIGHTEEN

REUNIONS

R OWEN LOCKE FROWNED AT THE faint plume of dust on the horizon. While similar plumes of smoke to the northwest corresponded to the city of Quorim, which Rowen had every intention of avoiding, these dust plumes came from the south. He shuddered. It had just begun to snow. "Looks like our pursuit hasn't given up after all." He glanced at Rhos'ari. "I don't suppose you brought a Soroccan spyglass, did you?"

Faeli answered before the Sylvan sergeant could respond. "Sylvs do not pollute themselves with objects from other cultures."

But you'll accept the horse of an enemy and help from an Isle Knight. Rowen wished his friend, Hráthbam, were there. He had a feeling that the Soroccan merchant would have enjoyed lecturing the Sylv on the advancements of culture.

Sergeant Rhos'ari shielded his eyes from the sun. "Looks to be a whole war party. I've heard of Olgrym running themselves half to death, but we're too far ahead for them to catch up."

Kilisti, seated on a nearby boulder, glanced up from sharpening her shortsword. A gust of wind stirred her hair away from her scarred face and missing nose. "Don't count on it."

"I could try to lead them away again," Aerios offered. "If they get closer, I mean."

Rhos'ari examined his maimed hand, wrapping clean bandages over the stubs of his severed fingers. "Don't bother. If they get too close, we'll take the horses to full gallop."

"They won't," Faeli said. He caught a falling snowflake on the edge of his knife then handed Rhos'ari an open wineskin. The sergeant poured wine over his hand without wincing, then took a drink. Rowen thought of how

Knightswrath had healed his wounds before. He wondered if it could do the same for Rhos'ari—not to mention Cathas, who was changing the dressing on his thigh. But the thought of igniting Knightswrath's powers frightened him. He decided not to mention it.

Cathas looked up from his wound. "Might be easier to trick them now. From this distance, they might think one or two horses are all of us."

"Fohl's hells," Kilisti muttered. She pocketed her sharpening stone, stood up, and nodded at the dust plume. "They're hunting us, fey as mad dogs. They won't stop. Either we lose the horses and travel on foot so the Olgrym can't track us, or else we ride the horses until they burst."

Rowen glanced at Snowdark. He patted the horse's neck. Though he'd fought Olgrym before, he had no doubt that Kilisti's battle experience exceeded his own. Still, with the Olgrym so far behind—and on foot—he didn't see how they could possibly catch up. Then again, he did not relish the idea of covering the rest of the way to the Dhargothi compound on foot, especially if they needed to flee from the Dhargots in a hurry.

Jinn's name, even if we free these captives, how are we supposed to get them safely back to the Wytchforest?

He faced Aerios again. "All right, try to lead them away. Take Faeli with you. If they don't follow, circle back and join us. If they *do* follow, ride east or south, as far and as fast as you can." Ignoring Faeli's scowl and Kilisti's look of disgust, he touched Aerios's shoulder. "Don't get close enough to fight. Just loose a few burning arrows and ride like the hells are behind you... because if this works, they will be. Understood?"

The two young Sylvs exchanged looks. Aerios nodded. To Rowen's surprise, Faeli did not protest. "Faeli, take Cathas's horse. You'll do better with a Sylvan mount if you have to be quick."

Faeli stopped to exchange hushed, terse words with Rhos'ari then cast an icy look in Rowen's direction before mounting his new horse. Aerios readied his own mount. The two Sylvs checked their bows.

Rhos'ari came closer to Rowen. "Knight, let me go with them. Or send me in their place. I'm the better rider."

Rowen cast a meaningful look at Rhos'ari's freshly bandaged hand then shook his head. He faced Faeli and Aerios again. "Don't get careless. A few arrows, then ride. They'll either follow, or they won't."

"Understood, Knight," Faeli grumbled. "Try not to die while we're gone." He turned his horse southward and started off. Aerios followed. Rowen watched them go then returned to Snowdark.

"The horses have rested enough. Let's cover some more ground before sunset."

Rhos'ari and Cathas mounted without comment, but Kilisti cast Rowen a cold look. "Even if we get away from the Olgrym, Knight, we're going to have a hard time slaughtering all the Dhargots in that compound with just four swords."

Rowen shook his head. "Faeli and Aerios will be fine. And this was always going to come down to crawling and throat-slitting, anyway." *Though that, too, would be easier if half my men weren't already wounded.* He glanced in the direction of the Olgrym again. He hoped he'd made the right decision.

"We don't stop until dark." He flicked the reins.

Rowen finally called for a halt at twilight, though earlier than he'd hoped. The flanks of their horses ran with sweat and shuddered from cold. The snowfall had swallowed the green plains before them. Rowen had sent Kilisti to scout the way ahead. At first, he'd feared they would have to camp in a blizzard, but she rode back and reported a small copse of trees in the distance.

"Not much for shelter, but it's better than nothing." Her teeth chattered as she spoke.

Rowen reminded himself that even the Shal'tiar had little experience with true winter, living as close as they did to the eternal summer of the Wytchforest.

"Dry rations," he said. "No fire."

Cathas cast a worried look at the preponderance of wolf tracks woven between the trees. "Are you sure?"

A frigid gust almost changed Rowen's mind, but he shook his head. "Even without the Olgrym chasing us, these are bad lands for travelers, probably worse after Syros fell. Best we don't draw attention to ourselves. Besides, wolves will keep away when they smell how many we are."

Kilisti gave him a dour look. "What about bears and greatwolves?"

Rowen said, "I'll take first watch." He dragged off Snowdark's saddle and hauled it to the edge of the camp, intending to use it as a chair. The horses seemed only slightly less displeased than their riders with their new surroundings. The boughs of the trees afforded them a little protection from the falling snow. They wrapped themselves in all the cloaks they could find, but Rowen realized the Sylvs had not packed clothes adequate for the wilderness.

Even Kilisti, who had been in these lands, had not realized how cold they were about to become.

Rowen thought back to the winters in Lyos, where he'd spent his childhood. As loathsome as the Dark Quarter had been, at least the winters had been mild. He could have said the same for the Lotus Isles. And the Wytchforest seemed immune to cold. But the rest of the Simurgh Plains was another story. The lands bordering Dhargoth threatened to become impassible before long, nearly as frigid as Stillhammer.

Though Rowen had never been to Stillhammer, he'd heard that its harsh winters were prefaced by heavy thunderstorms. A hearty folk, the Dwarrs suffered the winters without complaint. But Jalist had been living in the wilderness for many years, even before Rowen had met him. Rowen smiled, imagining the endless stream of curses that Jalist would have muttered as he tried to keep warm. Rowen hoped his Dwarr friend had found his lover and was hunched near a roaring fire, sipping mead in some Dwarrish great hall. As much as Rowen could have used Jalist's help, this was not the Dwarr's fight. He deserved some happiness.

He glanced back at the shivering Sylvs. "Sleep sitting up," Rowen advised them. "At least parts of you will stay dry."

Rhos'ari and Cathas obeyed, but Kilisti cursed and got up. She came to join him, carrying a sheathed shortsword.

Rowen laid Knightswrath across his knees, still in its scabbard. "Not going to try and stab me again, are you?"

"Not just yet." Kilisti's azure eyes scanned the snowy darkness. When next she spoke, she'd lowered her voice. "If Faeli doesn't come back, watch yourself with Rhos'ari. I think they're... friends."

Rowen nodded slowly. He scrutinized Kilisti's ravaged face in the dark. "You think we should have kept moving."

"Doesn't matter. This was never going to end well, anyway." Kilisti sighed. "One man dead, two maimed before we even left the forest. In the old days, Captain Essidel would have sent a whole company of Shal'tiar to free the captives and hang all the rapists by their entrails. Instead, Briel gives me a maimed sergeant and his lover, a few recruits, and one crazed Knight who's probably as dangerous to us as he is to his enemies."

Rowen gestured. "Then go. Walk away. I won't stop you."

Kilisti snickered. "We Shal'tiar have a code, Knight. They took some of our own. We either take them back, or we die trying." She shrugged. "Always figured I'd die fighting Olgrym, under trees instead of cold stars. But death is death, I suppose."

She shivered. Rowen wondered if it was from cold or fear. He started to peel off his cloak and offer it to her. She stopped him with a withering look. But before she could speak, something else caught her attention.

She turned eastward, her features taut. A gesture warned Rhos'ari and Cathas, who quietly rose to their feet and reached for their bows. Meanwhile, Kilisti drew her sword between her fingers to muffle the sound. Rowen had risen, too, but he saw nothing beyond their camp except dark, snowy trees. As quietly as he could, he whispered, "How many?"

Kilisti held up a single finger and pointed. A moment later, Rowen saw a single cloaked figure stumble toward them, moving heavily through the snow. Rowen hoped that it was either Aerios or Faeli coming to rejoin them, with the other following a little farther behind. Then he recognized the stranger's stooped, weary gait as that of an old man.

"Must be a merchant who survived a raid," Rowen offered. "I'll go talk to him. Watch for bandits coming up behind us."

Kilisti nodded. She sheathed her shortsword, picked up her bow, and took up position behind a tree. Cathas and Rhos'ari did likewise. Rowen girded his sword and strode out of the clearing to greet the stranger.

He expected the old man to cry out in surprise at the sight of him. Instead, the old man bowed. As he straightened, two gnarled hands came up and lowered his tattered hood. The old man stood in silence, hands folded in front of him like a cleric.

Rowen blinked in disbelief. Then he drew his sword. "A trick…"

The old man smiled with twisted lips. "No trick, Knight of the Crane. And no kindness, either."

Rowen remembered Kilisti and the others, still watching from behind trees. He held up his hand. "Don't fire," he called over his shoulder, even as he wondered what use arrows would be against El'rash'lin, anyway.

"Arrows kill me the same way they kill you. The difference is I have some small choice in the matter." El'rash'lin took a step forward. He smiled again. "You must learn to guard your mind, Knight. You never know who might be listening."

Rowen glanced back and saw the Sylvs moving slowly out from cover, arrows still fit to their bowstrings. Rhos'ari swore. Kilisti spat on the snow and raised her bow.

"I said, don't fire," Rowen repeated, stepping into their path. "Don't you know who this is?"

"He's a Shel'ai," Kilisti answered, "which means I'll be using his blood to paint my arrows. Step aside." When Rowen did not move, she sidestepped.

Rowen followed, blocking her again. "He *was* a Shel'ai. Then he became a Dragonkin." Rowen paused. "This is El'rash'lin." To his surprise, Kilisti's expression did not change, as though she did not recognize the name. "He turned against Fadarah," Rowen said. "He saved us at Lyos. He's not your enemy."

Kilisti's arrow did not waver. "The eyes say otherwise."

"He's my friend," Rowen said. "Lower your bow, or I'll cut it out of your hands." He gripped Knightswrath and loosened it in its scabbard, ready to draw it the rest of the way. He noted the hilt's warmth and wondered if the sword was responding to El'rash'lin's presence.

Kilisti raised one eyebrow. "You're fast, Knight, but you're not *that* fast." Nevertheless, she took a step backward. She glanced at Rhos'ari and Cathas, who had already lowered their bows but still held them at the ready. Slowly, she followed suit.

Rowen was not about to turn his back on her, though. "All of you, go back to the camp." He waited until the Sylvs had obeyed, then faced El'rash'lin again.

The old man's twisted lips smiled again. "What strange allies these times have given us."

"I thought you were dead."

"I was. Twice."

Rowen frowned. "Care to explain that?"

"I'd rather not, though I don't think it's up to me." El'rash'lin winced, as though in great pain. He started to fall but waved off Rowen's help and regained his composure. "This... hurts, Knight. More than you can understand. But I have to tell you..."

Something in his tone made Rowen shudder. "Tell me what?"

He looked up, and it stopped snowing. Rowen wondered if that was El'rash'lin's doing or just coincidence. Finally, El'rash'lin said, "Iventine lives again."

Rowen blinked. "The Nightmare?"

"If you wish to call him that." El'rash'lin gave Rowen a cold look. "This is Chorlga's doing. That's why I live, too. But that part was an accident." He paused. "I can't explain. I can only ask you to believe me."

Rowen took a deep breath. El'rash'lin exhaled, too—an impossible thing for a ghost—and Rowen watched the fog of their exhales mingle then dissipate into the winter air. "I believe you," he said at last.

"I'm afraid there's more." El'rash'lin winced again then regained his composure. "Chorlga knows that Silwren is gone. He knows about you... and Knightswrath. He knows because I told him."

Rowen tried to ignore the fresh shiver that ran down his spine. "I didn't have many advantages, old man, but surprise was one of them. Now that's gone."

El'rash'lin smiled slightly. "It couldn't be helped. Chorlga was about to destroy Lyos. Telling him about you was the only way to unsettle him, to distract him long enough that he forgot. But I was too late to stop what he did to the Isles."

Rowen's fear became cold dread. He thought of Aeko, the squires he'd trained with, and the magnificent temple where he'd studied the Shao arts. "What happened?"

"I'll tell you in a moment. I'll tell you everything. But first, Knight, you have to understand: my sanity is like a rope bridge that's been doused in oil. The ropes are on fire. If I don't cross before it breaks, I'll be as dangerous to you... to everyone... as Chorlga. I'll be as mindless as Iventine. I have to—"

Rowen caught the old man as he slumped and almost fell in the snow.

El'rash'lin offered a weak smile. "It seems, Human, that you're fated to spend a great deal of time keeping overpowered Shel'ai from destroying themselves... and those around them." Using Rowen's shoulder as a crutch, he lifted himself. "Is that how you envisioned your Knighthood?"

"Not really," Rowen admitted.

El'rash'lin clung to Rowen's arm, but he managed to stand to full height. "There's something else."

"I figured as much."

El'rash'lin managed to stand on his own. "I know where you're going. I know why. I can't explain, but I need you to go south instead."

Rowen heard Kilisti scoff. Without having to turn around, he could imagine the expression on the faces of the other Sylvs. He shook his head. "We came to free those captives. We can't leave until—"

"I'll free them myself. Don't ask me to explain, but I have to do it alone. You'll have to trust me on this."

Rowen gestured southward, into the darkness. "We have a pack of Olgrym chasing us. If we can't lose them, we'll have to—"

"Head south," El'rash'lin said firmly, all trace of humor gone. "Sooner or later, you'll have to face the Olgrym yourself. I can't deal with them *and* save the captives. And I need to do the latter alone."

"What's waiting for me there?"

"The Free Cities need you. Besides, Chorlga won't anticipate that. He'll expect you to go straight to the Lotus Isles. The longer you can avoid him, the better."

Rowen rested one hand on Knightswrath. "I don't mean to avoid him. I mean to kill him."

El'rash'lin smiled faintly. "Not yet, Human. You aren't ready. If we had months in which I could train you, perhaps. But we don't. Again, I can only ask you to trust me."

Rowen glanced back at the other Sylvs. He lowered his voice. "They came to free those captives, not fight Chorlga. They won't follow me to the Free Cities. And even if they did, what am I supposed to do when I meet the Dhargots? It may have escaped your notice, Shel'ai, but I don't have an army waiting for me anywhere... not a friendly one, anyway."

"There's a host of Isle Knights at Atheion."

Rowen blinked. "Aeko?"

"And Crovis, I'm afraid."

Rowen considered this. "Atheion's far. I'd have to sneak past Hesod first. But—"

El'rash'lin held up his hand. "I leave the rest of this to you. Goodbye, Knight." He turned to go.

Alarmed, Rowen reached for the Shel'ai's sleeve. Somehow, the cloth passed through his fingers. "Wait! I need help, old man. You have to help me with Knightswrath. You have to tell me about Chorlga!"

El'rash'lin answered with a sad smile. "I'm sorry, Knight. I will do everything I can to help you. But I do not think we will meet again. Goodbye."

And then, he was gone.

CHAPTER NINETEEN
HANDS

EL'RASH'LIN STOOD ALONE, RACKED WITH guilt, as he watched Rowen and the others ride away. The Sylvs had argued with him for hours, but finally, Rowen had won out. Despite his rage at El'rash'lin's sudden departure, he'd agreed to abide by El'rash'lin's wishes. Rowen wouldn't attack the Dhargothi compound. That meant the Sylvs either had to attack it without him—and Knightswrath, which meant certain death—or abandon the mission and turn south. El'rash'lin sensed the Sylvs' rage, though he was reasonably sure they would not try to stab Rowen in his sleep.

I'm sorry, Rowen. I should have told you everything. But if you'd known Shade was there, you would have killed him. And we'll need him before this is done.

El'rash'lin shook his head. Then he stumbled on through the snowy darkness, alone. He told himself that it could not be helped. But he wished he could at least have spared the strength to drive off the Olgrym or teleport Rowen safely across the Simurgh Plains. But that would have left him too weak for what lay ahead. Rowen would have to rely on Knightswrath.

If he can survive it...

El'rash'lin tried to clear his thoughts, trusting Rowen to the Light. He glanced up at the stars. He thought of Iventine as he'd been: a quiet, trusting boy to whom El'rash'lin had taught the constellations while Fadarah was busy teaching the others how to fight. Where had that boy gone? How had El'rash'lin stood by and permitted Fadarah to transform him into a mindless killer?

But I will give him rest, El'rash'lin swore. *I did it once. I can do it again.*

He traveled on through the night until a dark structure took shape on a distant hill. As he drew closer, the shape became a small, high-walled compound fitted with watchtowers and surrounded by a deep, dry moat.

El'rash'lin did not have to search the moat to know that the snow concealed countless traps and caltrops.

A single bridge spanned the moat. In front of the bridge stood two huge, imposing men in full armor. Both of their arms ended in long, naked swords. Snow fell all around them and piled about their ankles.

El'rash'lin slowed at the sight of them. The Jolym had not seen him yet. Such creatures could not be confused by magic, but if he searched, he might find another way inside the compound. He quickened his pace. It had been a long time since he'd been in a battle, and the thought of wrecking Chorlga's creations made him smile.

He lowered his hood and walked out of the night, straight toward the bridge. A guard in the watchtower spotted him and called out a challenge. El'rash'lin ignored it. As he drew closer, the Jolym stirred to life, blocking his path, looking down at him with their dark eyes and dull facemasks. Four sword blades rose, gleaming in the starlight. El'rash'lin lifted his hands. Wytchfire sprang from his fingertips. The Jolym jerked backward, their facemasks burning. Then they crashed to the snowy ground and did not move again.

El'rash'lin felt a rush of exhilaration, even as a buzzing in his mind threatened to erase his identity. He repeated his own name to himself, over and over, as he started forward. He walked between the fallen Jolym, feeling small compared to their great size. He looked up at the watchtower. He waved one hand, causing a crossbow bolt to burst into flames and burn to ash before it reached him. Before the crossbowman could fire again, El'rash'lin burned the tower down around him. He felt a surge of pity for the dying man when he heard his screams, but El'rash'lin reminded himself what the men had been doing.

He burned down two more guards as they were sprinting toward him with swords drawn. He burned down a third as he stood, dazed, his eyes wide with fright. Then, with vengeful slowness, El'rash'lin crossed the bridge and entered the compound, wytchfire trailing off his fingertips.

Shade blinked in the darkness, roused by the cries that echoed through the walls of his cell. He tried to sit up, momentarily forgetting the chains that pinned him—naked—to the cold stone floor. A flash of light caught his attention. He blinked, tensing, then realized it was just a torch passing by the bars in the window of his cell. Another torch followed, then another. More shouting echoed through the corridor.

Shade did not bother calling out to them, though he wondered what had happened. For days, he'd been chained in the dark, weak from his wounds, pinned to the floor with his arms outstretched so that he could not hurl wytchfire at his interrogators. But after he used his mind to strangle a guard with the chin strap of his own helmet, his captors had switched to asking questions from the corridor, beyond the locked door.

The men—sellswords, by the look of them—had wanted to know why Shade was here. They'd asked if Fadarah had sent him or if he was in league with one of the Dhargothi princes. But Shade sensed that the questions themselves were pointless. They were simply testing him. The sellswords wanted to ascertain the best way to keep a Shel'ai captive without getting killed in the process. Once the Sylvan captives began to give birth, the sellswords would have a whole generation of Shel'ai to deal with.

Shade ignored their questions, demanding that the sellswords tell him what had happened to Zeia. The captain of the sellswords—a cruel man with only one eye—informed Shade that Brahasti himself had been raping Zeia for days.

Shade relaxed. He knew just by the tremor of fear in the sellsword's voice that he was lying. Shade wanted to force his mind into the sellswords' so that he could truly ascertain whether Zeia had died from her wounds—as he thought she must have—but he was too weak for that. Instead, he spent his days wondering how Brahasti had obtained Jolym guards. There had been no hint of the Jolym in Fadarah's mind, meaning it must have happened recently. And as far as Shade knew, only the Dragonkin could make Jolym. And the only Dragonkin he knew of—Silwren, El'rash'lin, Iventine, and the other Initiates—were all dead.

Unless there's another Dragonkin in Ruun... a real Dragonkin!

That seemed impossible. Then, once only, Brahasti himself had come to gloat. Careful to remain in the hallway and address Shade through the door, he bitterly mocked the Shel'ai, reminding him of all his past threats, detailing the many punishments he had in store for Shade—unless he decided to sell him to the Dhargots, which might be the worse fate. Brahasti had asked about Fadarah, too.

Shade, determined not to reveal how much he knew, said as little as possible. But when Brahasti spoke of a mysterious benefactor and indicated that it was he who had entrusted the Jolym to him, the impossible became a certainty.

More screams outside his cell caught Shade's attention. The screams sounded closer. He saw the flash of more torches and heard the clatter of steel falling to the floor. He wondered if Zeia had gotten free somehow. His pulse quickened. They were not exactly allies, but he thought surely she would not leave him here to die. Besides, she would need his help to get away.

"Zeia!" Though he meant to shout, his parched throat offered only a whisper. He strained against his chains, wishing again that he had the magical strength and focus needed to spring the locks. He feared she would pass by, unable to hear him.

Then the door opened. More flames illuminated the cell. Violet flames burned quietly from the palm of a cloaked figure he could not see. "Zeia," he whispered again, suddenly conscious of his own nudity.

The figure gestured. Shade expected his manacles to spring open. To his surprise, they shattered. Shade tried to move his arms. Nothing happened. He flexed his fingers and willed his blood to quicken, trying to awaken limbs that had not moved for days. A little of the feeling returned. He managed to move his arms to his sides, brace his elbows, and sit up.

Zeia knelt beside him. She pressed a waterskin into his hands. Shade's limbs shook, unable to lift it. Zeia helped him raise the spout to his mouth. Water ran down his chin, so cold against his bare chest that he shivered. Still, he drank. The taste of cold water made him weep with relief.

He tried to face Zeia, but her wytchfire blinded him. Then it dimmed. Instead of Zeia, Shade faced an old man with twisted, ghastly features. The old man smiled.

"I greet you, Kith'el. And by the Light, I forgive you."

Shade's eyes widened. He answered by weakly lifting one hand and hurling a violet gout of wytchfire into El'rash'lin's face. El'rash'lin raised one hand, absorbed the flames with his palm, then shook his head. "Enough of that, young one, or I'll leave you here." With surprising strength, he hauled Shade to his feet. He took off his own tattered cloak and wrapped it around Shade's shoulders. "While you're busy not thanking me, you should be grateful that I steered Rowen Locke away, or else you'd probably be cinders by now. After what you did to his brother, he might not be as forgiving as I am."

"This can't be real," Shade gasped. "You're just a shade..."

"To some," El'rash'lin answered with a twisted smile. "For Chorlga, a nightmare."

Before Shade could say he did not understand, El'rash'lin led him into a hallway littered with ash and fallen swords.

Brahasti woke to the sound of his bedroom door being thrown open. He sat up, using one hand to shield his face from the glare of a torch while his other hand fumbled for the hilt of his sword. Then he remembered that he'd locked it in the trunk at the foot of his bed, just in case his female captive regained enough will to try to stab him in his sleep. He got out of bed without dressing and looked about for a weapon. He relaxed when the intruder moved his torch to one side and revealed himself. Dagath wore mismatched armor, and the hand holding the torch also had an oak-and-iron shield strapped to the forearm.

Brahasti scowled. "Dagath, what in Fohl's name couldn't wait until morning?" As he reached for the fine silk robe draped over his chair, he glanced at the Sylvan woman lying on his bed. Though awake and nude, she lay blank faced, blinking at the ceiling.

The Dhargot sighed at the sight of her. Though the prettiest of the remaining Sylvan captives, with the lean body of a fighter and hair of interwoven auburn and platinum, like the rest, she'd been left so emptied by Chorlga's elixir that she didn't even seem to notice what was happening to her. Brahasti might have killed her for disappointing him, but a faint swell to her belly convinced him she had value in other areas.

Dagath said, "Sorry, General. An attack at the gates. The watchtower's burning!"

Brahasti listened. For the first time, he heard shouts and screams of panic elsewhere in the compound. His irritation turned to bemusement. He'd recently ignored a summons from Prince Karhaati, but that had been only a few days ago. Brahasti had not expected even one as brash as the Bloody Prince to respond so quickly. He wondered how many men Karhaati had sent to fetch him—or kill him. It hardly mattered. Thanks to the Jolym, they would not be enough.

Brahasti took the key from around his neck, opened the chest at the foot of his bed, and removed the Ivairian shortsword he'd taken from Farl. Dagath's eyes flickered with recognition at the sight of the waisted blade, but Brahasti ignored him and started girding the weapon over his robe. "I want prisoners. The Jolym will tear any attackers apart, so once the battle's nearly won, I'll order them back. Have your crossbowmen aim for the legs of whoever is left."

Dagath shook his head. For the first time, Brahasti realized the big man was shaking. "Not Karhaati. The gates, the watchtower, everything is burning... the flames... they're *purple!*"

Brahasti froze midway through girding his sword. He listened again—

173

more screams. Brahasti swallowed a sudden lump of fear and finished girding his sword. "Is it Fadarah?" Remembering that Dagath probably didn't know what Fadarah looked like, he added, "Big man, black armor, blue tattoos. Half Sylv, half Olg. Probably very angry."

"No idea. Didn't see who or how many. I just ran here as soon as I got my armor on."

Brahasti swore. He sat down on the edge of the bed and tugged his boots on. It *had* to be Fadarah. But Brahasti still had his Jolym and a small host of sellswords. The latter might be panicking now, but once Brahasti entered the courtyard and took command, that would change.

Brahasti rose. "Send more men to guard the pits."

"I did. Pretty sure that was them screaming just now."

Brahasti smiled in grudging admiration. "Seems I underestimated Fadarah's fury. Very well. Assemble all your men in the courtyard, armed with crossbows. We'll—"

A fresh chorus of screams interrupted him. Men fled by his door, ignoring Dagath's shouts. The sellsword captain moved out into the hallway, shield held before him. He threw down his torch and brandished a broadsword. "He's coming this way," he called back to Brahasti.

The Dhargot hesitated then rushed out into the hallway, careful to keep Dagath in front of him. Beyond the captain, another sellsword turned the corner at the far end of the hall. A moment later, the man screamed and fell as wytchfire flowed over him.

Brahasti said, "Out the other way. We'll circle around to the courtyard." He glanced back at the Sylvan woman and decided to leave her there.

Shade shuddered as night air touched him, cooling the blood splashed across his face. Though El'rash'lin had seemed intent on doing all the fighting himself, a terrible strain showed beneath his twisted features, and Shade could feel both the old man's exhaustion and his fraying sanity. When Shade had extended his mind into El'rash'lin's in order to determine if the old man really had come back from the dead, he'd promptly recoiled. What he felt in El'rash'lin's mind reminded him too much of the Nightmare.

So Shade had scooped up a fallen sword, gritted his teeth, and charged the nearest guard. Luckily, he was able to summon enough wytchfire that he did not have to rely solely on his weakened sword arm. As the fatally burned sellsword lurched and fell against a stone wall, dead before he could cry out,

Shade followed. Rage blinded his senses, and he swung his sword with both hands, slashing until his sword shattered against the stone wall. He stared at the hilt, then cast it down and picked up another.

"Does your heart still quicken at the sight of blood?"

Shade blinked. He took it for a jest until he saw the seriousness of El'rash'lin's expression. He chose not to answer.

They searched all the basement cells, but Zeia was in none of them. El'rash'lin insisted that she was still alive, though Shade had no notion how the man knew this. In one room, they found a Sylvan woman lying conscious in a bed—nude, blank faced, and visibly pregnant. She offered no acknowledgment when El'rash'lin covered her with a sheet.

"What's been done to her?"

El'rash'lin closed her eyes with almost grandfatherly affection. He pressed one hand over her eyes and the other to her stomach. He nodded. Then he pressed one hand to each side of her face. Wytchfire flared from her fingertips. Shade thought that El'rash'lin was killing her in an act of mercy, but the flames vanished as quickly as they'd appeared. The woman blinked. El'rash'lin withdrew his hands.

"Come," he said. "When she regains her senses, she will not think us allies."

They left the room and stalked through the rest of the compound one room at a time, scouring the place with wytchfire, killing everyone who either stood against them or was too slow to run away. Finally, they emerged into the courtyard.

To one side, the gates and one whole curtain wall blazed with wytchfire. Men had given up trying to extinguish the blaze. Empty buckets lay on their sides, abandoned in the snow. El'rash'lin turned his back on the flames. Despite his size and apparent frailty, his violet eyes kindled with such wrath and focus that Shade finally understood why Fadarah had once held this man in such high esteem.

Before them lay a broad, dark pit. Shade guessed the pit contained Zeia and the Sylvan captives, though to his amazement, none made a sound. On the other side of the pit stood Brahasti. Shade cursed at the sight of him. The Dhargothi general wore a nightgown, despite the sword girded about his waist. He sat in a chair, surrounded by guards. Shade counted at least ten, all holding crossbows.

"Too many," Shade said in a low voice. "I can't ward off all the bolts if they fire. Better we draw them back downstairs, make them fight us one at a time. Maybe I can—"

El'rash'lin lifted his hands. His fingertips exhaled no wytchfire, but a moment later, all the men's crossbows burst into flames. Screaming with surprise, they cast them away. A few discharged, sending bolts thudding harmlessly into the snow. Some of the men drew their swords, but most fell back and sank to their knees, pleading for mercy.

Shade stared at El'rash'lin in awe. Like whatever he had done to the Sylvan woman, this use of magic was totally foreign to him—and complicated, it appeared. El'rash'lin winced, and Shade had no need to delve into his mind to see that he was rapidly losing control.

Shade stepped in front of El'rash'lin and strode forward. At the edge of the pit, he managed a flicker of wytchfire around his hands. The rest of the guards threw down their swords. With the only way out of the compound blocked by flames, they joined the other crude Humans in their pleas for mercy—all but two.

Brahasti was on his feet now. He blinked at the crossbows as they burned to ash in the snow. Far from afraid, he looked merely startled. Then he smirked. Next to him stood the huge man with a patch over one eye. He was crouching low behind a shield.

Shade wanted to kill them right away but doubted he had the strength. He turned and saw ladders stacked in the snow. He called to the guards who had just surrendered. "Lower those into the pit. Let the women out."

The men hesitated then obeyed. Brahasti and the one-eyed man watched quietly. The one-eyed man spat on the snow and clattered his sword against the edge of his shield in challenge. Shade ignored it.

Shade kept his eyes on Brahasti. "Climb out," he called down into the pit. He glanced back at El'rash'lin. In mindspeak, he asked, *"If they know we're Shel'ai, will they listen?"*

"That's the only thing they can do," El'rash'lin answered. Even telepathically, his voice echoed with sadness. He started forward, circling the far side of the pit.

Sure enough, a moment later, Shade heard one ladder creak, then another. One by one, Sylvan women emerged from the pit. Though snow had obviously fallen within, soaking through their meager, tattered clothing, none of the women shuddered. A few blinked in the glare from the burning wall in the distance, but none screamed or pointed at their tormentors and demanded justice. They stood like a cluster of sadly painted statues. Shade counted twenty-nine of them. Most had swollen bellies.

"Gods…"

He shook himself. Zeia was not among them. He glanced into the pit: a figure lay curled in the snow. He called out to her. She did not stir. He addressed her in mindspeak. Though she did not answer, Zeia slowly lifted her head. Shade saw blood on her clothes. She had her arms pressed against her stomach.

Shade addressed El'rash'lin. *"I've found Zeia. She's hurt but alive. She can't climb out on her own. I'll get her out."*

"Wait," El'rash'lin said, but Shade ignored him.

He pointed at the surrendered guards again. "Two of you go down there and bring her up… *gently*, or I'll teach you a new definition for pain."

The guards exchanged glances. They seemed even more hesitant than they'd been to release the Sylvan captives, but a moment later, they descended into the pit. Shade watched as best he could, still glancing up frequently, lest Brahasti and the one-eyed sellsword try to fly while he was distracted. Neither had moved, though like the surrendered guards, both looked fearful now.

The one-eyed sellsword was growing desperate. He berated the other guards, ordering them to retrieve their weapons and fight. When no one obeyed, he edged away from Brahasti and stood with the guards. He kicked one and struck another with the pommel of his sword. Still, no one joined him.

Shade considered stopping him anyway, then movement caught his eye. It was the Sylvan woman they had found below. She stumbled into the courtyard, wide eyed, still wrapped in a sheet that was knotted above her breasts. In one hand, a sword glinted with vengeful coldness. Azure eyes met Shade's violet ones.

Shade said, *"I won't hurt you."* The woman's eyes widened when Shade's voice rang out in her mind. *"I won't hurt you,"* Shade repeated. *"The war's over. I came to set you free."*

The woman turned. Shade followed her gaze to Brahasti. Too late, he read her intent. The pregnant woman gave an animal-like howl and charged. The one-eyed man might have blocked her, but he stepped back, apparently deciding not to interfere. Brahasti barely had time to draw his own sword before the woman was upon him.

Shade watched the two fight. Though smaller, the woman fought like a Wyldkin. Her sword blurred, faster than Brahasti's. The Dhargot backpedaled.

He called out for the one-eyed sellsword to help him. The sellsword gave Shade a questioning look. Shade shook his head.

The Wyldkin woman drove Brahasti steadily backward. Despite her fury, her attack had focus. She blocked each of Brahasti's desperate swings then opened a bright red slash on the Dhargot's forearm. With surprising deftness, Brahasti switched his sword to his other hand, then switched it back when the Wyldkin pressed her advantage too quickly.

The woman threw her head back, but the tip of Brahasti's blade still cut her, jaw to forehead. She did not scream. Their shortswords clashed again. They struggled in swordlock. Brahasti grabbed the woman's throat with his free hand. He squeezed.

The woman's eyes widened. She tried in vain to break Brahasti's grip. Shade lifted one hand. He wondered if he could burn Brahasti without hitting the woman, too.

But before he could act, the woman kicked Brahasti's knee, drove her own knee into his groin, then kneed him again. Brahasti's grip went slack. The woman twisted free, still holding Brahasti's hand, and bit his finger. Brahasti howled. He managed to swing his sword, but the woman ducked and slashed his groin. Brahasti fell to his knees. His torn robe slipped, revealing one bone-pale shoulder. Brahasti glanced at the woman. Then, facing Shade, he pleaded for his life.

I should kill him myself, Shade thought. *I promised I would.* He shook his head again.

The woman loomed over Brahasti. She gave the Dhargot an icy look. She no longer seemed aware that there was anyone else in the courtyard besides Brahasti. She stood naked in the snow, blood running from the terrible gash in the side of her face. But she breathed easily as she slowly pushed her sword into Brahasti's throat, twisted it, then dragged it free.

"Brahasti el Tarq..." Shade turned and spat on the snow. He heard a crunch in the snow that meant someone was coming to stand next to him. He tensed, but it was only El'rash'lin, whom Shade had all but forgotten. Rather than watch the battle, the old man fixed his eyes on the pit.

Shade remembered Zeia. The guards were helping her out, pushing her up one rung at a time. Shade frowned. Instead of using her hands to climb, Zeia still had her arms folded tightly against her stomach. Her head drooped indignantly against the ladder. If not for the slow, awkward lifting of her feet, he would have thought her unconscious.

"Let me help you, Sister." Shade moved to the edge of the pit, smiled, and held out his hand. Zeia looked up weakly, her face frightfully pale. She did not reach for him, so Shade caught her under the arms and hauled her the rest of the way out. He lowered her onto the snow. She quietly doubled over. Her jaw clenched, as though she were trying not to scream.

"They never bandaged her wounds," Shade called back to El'rash'lin. "Gods, it's a wonder she's still alive." He leaned closer to Zeia. "They probably cut your stomach. That's why it hurts so much. But don't worry. You'll be all right now."

He sent the two guards back to join the rest. Shade saw them eyeing the still-burning gates, as though they meant to make a run for it. He snickered at the thought. Then he watched the one-eyed sellsword move quietly over to Brahasti's corpse and retrieve the dead general's shortsword.

"I don't care that they've surrendered," Shade said to El'rash'lin. "We're not letting them go. None of them."

"Look to Zeia," El'rash'lin said. His voice sounded weary, resigned.

Shade cast a warning look at the Wyldkin woman, who had gone to help the still-blank-faced Sylvan women who had climbed out of the pit, then turned his attention back to Zeia. Blood had frozen in her clothes, making them nearly as rigid as the rest of her. He tried to inspect her stomach, but she would not move her arms. He seized her wrists so that he might pry them apart. Then he gasped and let go.

"Gods…" He whirled to face El'rash'lin. "Did you know?"

El'rash'lin answered with a slight, sad nod.

Shade faced Zeia again. He stared. He had been in error before. Brahasti's men had bandaged Zeia's wounds after all, though she'd bled so much that the wraps were barely visible. But most of the blood had not come from the deep gash to her side. Her hands had been cut off.

Shade trembled. He leaned in and kissed Zeia's forehead. "I'm so sorry…" He straightened and faced El'rash'lin. "Help her."

El'rash'lin said nothing as he approached and knelt beside Zeia. Shade stepped away. He faced the prisoners. All were kneeling again—all save the one-eyed sellsword, who abruptly turned and sprinted for the gate. Shade tried to burn him down, but the sellsword caught the wytchfire on his shield. Shade burned away the shield, but the man kept running, howling, his arm on fire. Then he leapt through the burning gate.

Shade did not know if he'd made it through. He turned to face the remaining guards. They were still kneeling. He took a step toward them. "Which one of you cut off her hands?"

For a while, nobody answered. Then one trembling guard lifted his hand and pointed after the one-eyed sellsword. "Not us! It was him…"

Shade glanced at the flames, then at Brahasti's corpse, then at Zeia trembling in the snow. His gaze fell on the wretched Sylvan women, all but one of whom remained as still as statues.

He faced the guards again. "No matter." His hands came up, unleashing death.

CHAPTER TWENTY

THE BLOODY PRINCE

KARHAATI SAT ASTRIDE HIS BLOODMARE on the snowy fields outside Cassica, listening to the lingering cries of the dying. He wondered whether he should curse or celebrate his recent shift in fortune. Thanks to Ziraari's death, nearly all the Dhargots garrisoned in the south had marched north to swear fealty to him. Karhaati's host had already swelled by five thousand footmen, two hundred cavalry, and half a dozen armored elephants, but more streamed in every day. Karhaati had never commanded such power.

But strange rumors had reached him, telling of an attack on Lyos that had decimated most of its famed Red Watch. Equally strange were the stories of a massive invasion of the Lotus Isles and pitched battles that had somehow crippled the mighty Knighthood. That might be cause to celebrate, too, but what was this new force that had so easily dispatched Karhaati's strongest enemies?

And then, of course, there was Saanji.

Karhaati spat on the snow at the thought of his last surviving brother. Then he lifted his head to grimly survey what his men had appropriately dubbed the Field of Shame. In the wake of Saanji's betrayal, Karhaati had culled from his ranks every coward, every weakling, and the men too wounded to serve the Dhargothi Empire. This did not only strengthen his army; it also served as a warning.

By now, most of the screams and pleading had stopped, though the greased, bloody stakes stretched on for half a mile, creaking in the winter wind. *Saanji will be here, too. And so will Brahasti, if he doesn't obey.*

Karhaati had reluctantly swallowed his pride and requested that Brahasti rejoin him on the front. Of course, the request had been voiced as a command, laced with threats, but he knew that Brahasti would see it for what it was. The thought of asking for Brahasti's help filled Karhaati with shame, but he had no choice—Brahasti's tactical brilliance was second to none. Brahasti had helped Ziraari break the Iron Sisters after a long stalemate. He had won Cassica almost without a fight. Surely, with superior numbers, he could take care of Saanji.

But Karhaati knew that was easier said than done. In an act of surprising defiance and resolve, Saanji and his misfit host had formed an alliance with the very men they'd been assigned to hunt down. Now, aided by two hundred lightning-fast Lancers, despite being outnumbered and forced to fight in the snow, Saanji's renegade Dhargots had wreaked havoc on Karhaati's supply lines, killed hundreds of his scouts and foragers, and even infiltrated his camp long enough to poison four of his prized elephants.

But those acts had not gone unanswered. After Saanji fled into the northern foothills, Karhaati had sent thousands of vengeful troops into Ivairia. They torched one village after another, took countless slaves, and left impaled victims like a ghastly forest in their wake. He'd even demolished a small stronghold, disemboweling the Ivairian lord and his entire family, despite their protests that they'd had nothing to do with Royce's Lancers.

Karhaati hoped this bloody act would drive a wedge into the alliance. He'd hoped that, at the very least, it would compel Arnil Royce and his Lancers to return to Ivairia in order to safeguard their homeland. It had created the opposite effect. More and more Lancers had ridden south. Karhaati estimated that, in addition to Saanji's four thousand renegades, Arnil Royce had close to a thousand Lancers and twice as many footmen.

But that won't save him if I take my entire army into Ivairia. Karhaati wondered if he should. That would mean postponing his attack on Lyos and braving the even harsher winters of the north, but there would be benefits, too. The island nation of Sorocco was rich and easily accessible from Ivairia's coast. Karhaati had no navy, but once Saanji and the Lancers were dealt with, come spring, he could build one.

Or else Karhaati could abandon the north entirely and march south, for Atheion. The City-on-the-Sea was a tempting target, too. Ziraari had been poised to invade it before; now that he was gone and his army had joined Karhaati's, sacking wealthy Atheion made sense.

Karhaati cursed. Power and plunder, he understood. But when it came to complicated military campaigns, with all their convoluted tactical elements, one direction seemed as good to him as another. *Maybe I'll leave it up to Brahasti... provided I don't have to have him impaled for violating orders.*

Karhaati's bloodmare reared up so suddenly that he nearly fell from the saddle. He tugged at the reins and raked the beast's flanks with his spurs. He managed to regain control of his war horse, but then a commotion drew his attention. He glanced over his shoulder to find his bodyguards—all mounted—in a similar predicament. Some had already been thrown from their saddles and lay on the ground, struggling to rise. One had even been trampled to death by his own horse.

By the Dead God, what's happening?

Though his bodyguards' destriers were accustomed to the smells of blood, rot, and filth that perfumed the Field of Shame, they might still have been spooked by the smell of a wolf or the sight of a snake. Not so for Karhaati's bloodmare, though. That unnerved him. He looked about, scanning the ghastly forest of dead men for a threat. A moment later, he found it.

A column of footmen approached from the south. Sun glinted off full armor, but Karhaati saw no banners. Karhaati frowned. He withdrew a Soroccan spyglass from his saddlebag. His frown deepened when he lowered the spyglass a moment later. He snapped his fingers. The captain of his bodyguards rode forward. The man had been thrown from his horse and had just climbed back into the saddle despite blood running from his forehead.

"I see a hundred fools where they aren't supposed to be."

"Yes, my prince. Shall we get you inside and call the archers?"

Karhaati resisted the urge to strike the man. "I want three hundred cavalrymen outside the city gates, on the double. I'll lead the charges myself. Meanwhile, have the watch captain send fifty chariots to cut off the trespassers' escape."

The bodyguard saluted and rode away at once.

Karhaati scrutinized the distant column of footmen. It writhed across the plains like a metallic serpent, seemingly unhindered by the snow. Though he could not fathom what a hundred heavily armored men were doing on foot, let alone where they'd come from, it made no difference. They were on his lands.

Karhaati rode down to the gates to await his men. Dimly, he realized that his orders—which the captain of his bodyguards had not questioned—were a mistake. The snows would definitely slow his cavalry, but they would do worse to the chariots. The wheels would get stuck almost as soon as they were outside the gates. His charioteers would be lucky to make it onto the battlefield in time to witness the fighting, let alone cut off the trespassers' escape.

The Bloody Prince considered amending his orders, then decided against it. He could not appear flawed before a Dhargothi host. That would only embolden all his would-be assassins. Better he claim that he'd given the order to test the charioteers' loyalty or to amuse himself as he watched them struggle in the snow.

Karhaati drew his sword and fixed his gaze on the steely serpent glinting in the distance. One hand idly touched the ears hung around his neck. He wondered how many he would add before the end of the day. Grinning, he savored the familiar, reliable heft of his sword and braced for battle.

Jalist tugged at his hood, wishing he'd been able to leave Lyos a day or two later. A fierce chill had set in almost as soon as they passed through the gates and rode onto the Simurgh Plains. Jalist's lungs burned, and the skin on his face felt as taut as a wind-blown flag. But delaying his departure had not been an option. The king of Lyos was adamant that Jalist set out at once on his fool's errand to find Silwren, and his so-called bodyguards seemed more concerned with getting him out of the city than with actually protecting him.

Jalist glanced over his shoulder at Vardan and Braggo. They rode just behind him, stone quiet, their faces wrapped against the cold. Over chainmail surcoats and the scarlet tabards of the Red Watch, the men wore heavy cloaks that covered their weapons: matching crossbows and longswords, which they carried with the ease of men who knew how to use them. They'd hardly spoken since leaving Lyos, offering not so much as a curse when the winter wind clawed at the four riders. But Jalist did not mind the quiet.

Though Braggo was tall and lean, obviously a full-blooded Human, Vardan looked to have some Dwarrish blood somewhere in his ancestry. He was shorter and stockier, with arms almost as thickly muscled as Jalist's. His eyes were so brown that they were almost black, and his skin had a faint gray tinge. Both men were middle-aged. Jalist was surprised that the king had sent two of his last surviving veterans to shepherd him on his way, but he reminded himself that if the Jolym or a Dragonkin—or both—returned to attack Lyos, a couple of extra swords would make no difference.

Jalist glanced down at his new tabard, faded scarlet and patched in places. Its sigil was still unmistakable—the falcon of Lyos. *What would Rowen say if he saw me like this?*

Turning westward again, he surveyed the snowy, rolling hills that dominated the horizon. *Maelmohr's cock, how am I supposed to find Silwren in all this?* Distant wisps of smoke, too big to come from villages, told him that the Dhargots were already everywhere.

He looked over his shoulder again, glancing past the two men of the Red Watch, to where Igrid brought up the rear. He wondered if she was thinking the same thing. She was certainly dressed for the part. Before leaving Lyos, the Iron Sister had exchanged wispy gowns for a brigandine, matching greaves, tassets, and vambraces, a helmet with a noseguard, a pair of shortswords, and most surprising of all, a Queshi composite bow.

Jalist concealed a smile. As a sellsword, he was familiar with Queshi bows. Explosively powerful, their elegant, curving design was ideal for firing on horseback. But they were made of laminated wood and bone in a process that took an entire year to complete. A good Queshi bow cost as much as a war horse. Jalist wondered if Igrid had stolen the composite bow from the armory or taken it off a wall in the palace one afternoon when no one was looking.

The Dwarr rubbed his temple. "Gods, I need a drink!"

"I think you've drunk enough lately, Dwarr."

Jalist turned to scowl at Igrid, concealing his surprise that she'd managed to ride up beside him without him noticing. "Not by half, Iron Sister. These days, I don't drink, my hands shake. That's dangerous when you're swinging a big damn axe."

Igrid scowled back at him, even as the cold winds died down a little. "I wish you'd stop calling me that."

Jalist shrugged. "I'll stop calling you Iron Sister when you stop calling me Dwarr."

"I wasn't *born* an Iron Sister, you dunce. Gods, I was only in Hesod for a year."

Jalist did not miss the spark of grief and anger in her voice. He wondered if she was remembering how that year had ended: with the brutal siege of Hesod, which had culminated in the killing or brutalizing of nearly all her fellow swordswomen. Igrid had escaped that by disguising herself as a priestess and running south, into the valley of Nosh, where she'd chanced upon Rowen, Jalist, and Silwren.

I'm not sure this one's ever stopped running. He felt a pang of sympathy for Igrid, even as he made sure his coin purse was tucked well out of her reach. "How's your skull?"

"Thick as ever," Igrid answered with a smirk that instantly reminded Jalist of Rowen. "Sore, I guess, but nearly mended. Those Lyosi clerics can work wonders if you pay them enough."

"I won't ask where you found the coin for that." Jalist chuckled. "So tell me about that Ivairian captain of yours."

Igrid shifted uncomfortably, obviously caught off guard. "What about him?"

"You said you met him south of here, near the Red Steppes. That must have put you close to Stillhammer."

"I never saw your homeland, if that's what you mean."

"I never said you did." Jalist gestured with his thumb back to Vardan. "That one says there's rumors of a Lancer lord riding around in the snow with no more sense than we have, nipping the Dhargots wherever he can. Just wondered if it's the same man."

Igrid just said, "Probably."

"You think the Lancers will form some kind of alliance with Lyos?"

Igrid shrugged. "Royce might. But from what I hear, the Ivairian king is even more of a simpering idiot than you are."

"Seems to be a lot of that going around."

The winds quickened, and the snowfall intensified. Near sunset, Jalist was relieved beyond words when he spotted a village in the distance. He slowed his horse, reminding himself that caution was called for, but he saw no sign of Dhargothi occupation. "Surprised they left this place standing."

Braggo rode ahead to find an inn while the others lingered at the edge of the village. The tall man returned soon enough and informed them that the inn was deserted. Apparently, all the villagers had fled. But shelter was shelter, so Jalist declared that they would spend the night in the inn.

"I'll check the larders for food." He glanced at Igrid. "If you'd like to search the town for valuables, feel free."

Igrid answered with a withering look before following him into the inn. Braggo and Vardan led the horses toward the adjacent stables, loosening their swords as they went, just in case the village turned out to be less abandoned than it seemed. Jalist realized that now would be a good time to flee, but he did not relish the idea of navigating through snow and darkness on foot.

The squat inn, with its dirt-floor common room, three adjoining rooms, and a small kitchen, looked to have been picked clean before the villagers fled. Jalist and Igrid quietly split up and searched, but found nothing but broken chairs, a child's ragdoll, and a cast-iron pot that must have been too heavy to carry.

Jalist lamented the lack of wine but shrugged. "Dry rations, it is. At least the walls will keep the winds out."

"At this point, I'd settle for a slab of charred urusk meat and a bowl of paupers' root."

Jalist spotted a small pile of dried wood and set about starting a fire in the hearth. Twilight had darkened the inn, but soon, a fire drove back the shadows.

"A far cry from Lyos," Igrid muttered, watching a fat spider wriggle along the bare, dusty bar. She took a sip from her waterskin and looked around. "Gods, whoever heard of an inn without music? Empty towns make my skin crawl."

Jalist had sat down on one of the few surviving chairs, but he leaned forward on his long axe. "Saw plenty like this in Stillhammer." He looked away from her and pretended to study the fire.

"Did you... know anyone there?"

"Of course."

"Did anyone get away?"

Gods, is she trying to make conversation now? Jalist gripped his axe. "Don't know. Didn't see another living soul the whole time I was there, unless you count the Jolym."

"Not really." Igrid walked over and passed him the waterskin. "Somebody must have made it out. Even the Jolym couldn't wipe out an entire kingdom. Gods, there must have been ten thousand Dwarr there!"

"Ten thousand in Tarator alone."

Igrid whistled. "You said the whole Jolym force was only about—what? A hundred? No matter how tough they are, there's no way—"

"Probably had a lot more than a hundred, starting out." Jalist jabbed the fire with the shaft of his long axe. "I didn't see any dead Jolym, but they could have hid them. Can't believe my people wouldn't have made an account of themselves."

"I didn't say they didn't."

Jalist scowled at her then shrugged. "If anybody got away, they didn't go north, or we'd have seen them."

"South, then?"

"Dendain is south. I doubt they'd run into the damn desert."

"I meant west of there, into Quesh."

"Where the Queshi would probably riddle them with arrows for trespassing." Jalist started to lift the waterskin then changed his mind and passed it back. "When this war's over, maybe I'll go look for them."

Igrid answered with a crooked smile. "You don't really think either of us will survive this war, do you?"

Before Jalist could answer, the inn door opened. Vardan and Braggo returned, uncomplaining, despite their pale skin and the snow in their hair and beards. Jalist waved them toward the fire. "See anything out there?"

Vardan shook his head.

Braggo said, "A couple stray dogs. Poor things looked hungry." He pulled off his gloves and held his hands over the fire. "Might take them some food once I've thawed out a bit."

"No point in that," Vardan snapped. "They don't learn to fend for themselves, they'll be dead inside a month, anyway."

Braggo glared at him but said nothing.

"We'll leave at first light," Jalist said. He pointed. "That room has two beds... well, two pallets of straw. But it's all yours."

Vardan cracked his neck then flexed and unflexed his fingers over the fire. "I'll sleep out here on the floor so I can watch the door."

"Don't be stupid," Jalist said. "We can bar the door. Get some rest."

Vardan looked angry then smiled. "Begging your pardon, Captain, but I'll sleep better if I know my ears aren't going to end up tied around a Dhargot's neck."

"Same here," Braggo said. He nibbled a slab of dried, heavily peppered meat then accepted Igrid's waterskin with a gruff nod of thanks. When he was finished with it, he passed it to Vardan.

Vardan drank, then asked, "Do we keep straight west or veer south? Nosh might be safer."

"But out of the way," Braggo countered.

"And we didn't exactly leave Nosh on friendly terms last time we were there." Jalist cast a sidelong glance at Igrid. "We need to find Silwren fast. The quickest way to the Wytchforest is straight west, past Hesod."

Igrid tensed at the mention of her former home, but Braggo was already protesting. "Begging your pardon, Captain, but the Dhargots are bound to spot us."

"They'll see us, but they won't stop us. We're going to run into the Dhargots sooner or later, so we might as well do it now."

Igrid cocked her head. "Just what in the fey hells are you talking about, Dwarr?"

"Uniforms," Jalist answered. "We find some Dhargots... officers, preferably... and take their uniforms. We pretend we're escorting a prisoner back to Dhargoth." He gave Igrid a pointed look.

Igrid's green eyes flashed with rage. "No."

Braggo and Vardan exchanged looks. "Might work," Braggo mused.

"Or they might think we're deserters and shove our asses down on sharpened stakes," Vardan growled. "I'd rather join a dragon cult."

"Whoever heard of deserters escorting a prisoner?" Jalist countered. "Besides, I can write. I'll scribble some orders from a general giving us safe passage back to Dhargoth. If we *are* challenged, that'll take care of it."

"Like hells it will!" Igrid backed away, touching her sword. "Look in a mirror, Dwarr. You look about as Dhargothi as I do."

"True. But Dhargots hire sellswords sometimes." *I should know. I've worked for them before.* He glanced at Vardan and Braggo. "As for these two, paint their eyes and dress them in black scale armor, and nobody will be the wiser."

But Igrid was already shaking her head. "I told you, no. Go stand in the fire, Dwarr. I won't go along with this."

"We'd need ears," Braggo mused. "Enough for a few necklaces."

Jalist smirked. "Well, if we're bothering Dhargots for uniforms, we might as well take their ears, too."

"Perfect," Vardan grunted. "Now, we just need to find a squad of Dhargots small and dumb enough that the four of us can kill them without dying in the process."

Braggo looked doubtful. "Captain, maybe Nosh *is* a better idea. If the Noshans come after us, we can press the horses and outrun them."

Jalist thought about the Lochurite berserkers they'd fought while passing through the valley. A bizarre clan of barbarians that roamed Nosh, the Lochurites—men, women, even children—imbibed mysterious drugs that gave them great strength and ferocity but also drove them mad. He had no desire to encounter them again.

But heading to the Wytchforest by way of Nosh would take us by Quesh... Jalist thought of Leander—maybe he could still find Dwarrish refugees in the south. With great effort, he pushed the thought from his mind.

"My way is faster and safer. The Dhargots have other things to worry about. They won't pull a hair for a few bored soldiers escorting a prisoner."

Igrid took a step toward him, a dangerous glint in her eyes. "Easy for you to say. You won't be the one in chains."

"More like rope. I don't have any chains, unless you brought some with you." Jalist laughed. No one joined him.

"Tell me," Igrid said, "how long did you spend coming up with this brilliant plan of yours?"

"About as long as we've been talking about it," Jalist confessed. "Doesn't make it a bad one. Anyway, once we're past Hesod, we turn south and ride for the Wytchforest like Fohl himself is chasing us."

"Straight through Godsfall," Vardan mused. "Now you want us to risk the Olgrym, too?"

"The Olgrym are who Silwren is fighting," Jalist countered. "We find them, we find her."

Igrid threw up her hands in exasperation. "Even if we find the wytch, what makes you think she'll *stop* fighting the Olgrym to help us instead?"

"That was always going to be the last stone in our path. But Locke will talk her into it. If Lyos is in danger, he'll come."

No one spoke. Jalist sensed that he had nearly convinced the two men, but he suspected that Igrid would only go along at swordpoint. But that was a concern for another day. "Rest," he said. "We'll leave at first light. I'm sure we can argue more about it then." Without saying more, he turned and headed for one of the empty rooms to sleep.

"Locke, my friend, you better still be alive," Jalist muttered as he lay down, still armored, his long axe resting on the straw beside him.

CHAPTER TWENTY-ONE

QUESTIONS AND LOYALTIES

S HADE WOKE IN A BED, staring up at a roof. He thought for a moment that he was dreaming. Then he turned and found El'rash'lin sitting in a chair, smiling faintly. The old man's twisted features looked even more ghastly for the dark circles under his eyes.

"Good morning, Kith'el. I must say, you have a remarkable knack for staying alive."

Shade closed his eyes, testing the magic inside him. He felt it roil through his blood. He opened his eyes again and considered attacking El'rash'lin, then reminded himself that even at full strength, he was no match for a Dragonkin. "Where are we?"

"A town, east of Brahasti's compound. I can't tell you the name because everyone was gone when we got here. Looks like the Dhargots passed through." He added, "You almost killed yourself, burning those guards."

"Where's Zeia?"

"Still asleep. I induced it. She'll stay that way, for the time being. The Light knows she needs the rest."

Shade got out of bed and found a fresh change of clothes on a nearby table next to a washbasin. He started to dress.

El'rash'lin said, "If you need to use the chamber pot, I'll step out."

Shade could not tell if he was joking. "Am I your prisoner?"

"I'd prefer to think of you as my ally."

Shade spotted a sheathed longsword lying nearby. He wondered if El'rash'lin had left that for him or if it had simply been left behind by the room's last occupant. He touched the cold, wire-wrapped hilt. "I have questions."

"I figured as much."

"But first, have you restored Zeia's hands?"

El'rash'lin shook his head.

Shade frowned. While restoring severed limbs was well beyond the limits of Shel'ai magic, he imagined such feats were simple for Dragonkin. "Can you?"

"I can," El'rash'lin said, "but I won't."

"Why not?"

"I'll explain that later."

"You'll explain that now."

El'rash'lin smiled. "No, Kith'el, I won't. For now, just trust that Zeia is not in pain. I saved her life and stopped the bleeding."

"But without her hands—"

"She can't summon wytchfire," El'rash'lin interrupted. "Is that what you were about to say?"

"In part."

"No need. For now, she's safe. We all are."

Shade's eyes narrowed. "You don't sound too sure of that." When El'rash'lin did not answer, Shade asked, "What about the Sylvs?"

"I restored their will. Their minds are their own again."

Shade turned back to the washbasin and splashed cold water on his face. He stared at his reflection. "I couldn't care less about their minds. I'm more concerned with what's in their bellies."

"The ones who aren't pregnant have left," El'rash'lin said. "I tried to talk them out of it, but they chose to take their chances in the wild. They might have tried to kill me, but Keswen stopped them."

Shade turned.

El'rash'lin said, "That's the one who killed Brahasti."

Shade answered with a noncommittal grunt and continued buckling the sword around his waist.

"All the Sylvan women who are pregnant are carrying Shel'ai babies."

Shade froze, mid-buckle. "How is that possible?"

"Chorlga's devilry. But I don't suppose you know who Chorlga is yet, do you?"

"I can guess. A Dragonkin. A *true* Dragonkin. He made Jolym and took over Brahasti's... breeding program."

El'rash'lin nodded slowly. "He's done a lot more than that. He's been moving in the shadows for centuries. We didn't even know he was there. But all the while, ever since the Shattering War, he's been stoking the fires of hatred against the Shel'ai."

Shade thought of all the Shel'ai he'd seen murdered, including Rhas'ero, the old man who had adopted and raised him. "I doubt the races needed much help." He sensed that El'rash'lin was about to argue with him and decided to change the subject. "Why did they stay?"

"The pregnant Sylvs?" When Shade nodded, El'rash'lin said, "I think because they knew they would not be welcomed back in Sylvos. They knew they'd be hated by their own people. One even drowned herself." The old man's voice was filled with grief.

So they finally understand. Shade almost laughed. "Where will they go?"

"I'm taking them to Coldhaven."

Shade's smile vanished. "No, you're not."

"Do you know a better place for them?"

"For the Shel'ai babies they'll have, no. But I don't relish the idea of letting Sylvs see where we've been hiding. What if they run back to Sylvos and tell their king?"

"They won't betray us."

"Even if they don't, Coldhaven isn't safe anymore."

"It never was. But I agree that we'll need a new place, somewhere Chorlga can't reach."

Shade hesitated. "Zeia talked about getting a boat on Sorocco and leaving Ruun altogether."

The idea sounded absurd when he said it out loud, but El'rash'lin nodded. "Fadarah and I argued about that many times. He said it was cowardice to flee a land we should we ruling." He smiled slightly. "I should have argued harder. If I had, thousands might still be alive."

Shade sensed the old man's despair but had no desire to comfort him. "So we gather all the Shel'ai who are left... plus these Sylvan women, if we must... and flee. We find some island off the coast and hope the Dragonward is real enough to keep Chorlga from following us. Is *that* your plan?"

"The Dragonward is real. We'll have to trust in that if Rowen Locke loses."

He will. "Will you stay and help him?"

El'rash'lin shook his head. "The Isle Knight needs me... but I can't stay."

"Why not?"

"Because I'm not the only Dragonkin that Chorlga brought back from the dead. In fact, my resurrection was an accident. Chorlga only intended to bring back one other."

Shade frowned. Then his eyes widened. "The Nightmare…"

El'rash'lin nodded. "While one of us lives, the other cannot stay dead. We will keep coming back to life until the spell is broken."

Shade was quiet for a time. "If we could yoke his strength again, like before…"

"You can't," El'rash'lin snapped. "Have you learned nothing?"

Shade ignored the question. "Where is he?"

"He's here on Ruun somewhere. His madness affects his resurrection so that every time he comes back to life, he appears somewhere else. Chorlga will have to find him." El'rash'lin calmed himself. "Chorlga can see through the eyes of his Jolym, so he knows I'm alive. He'll surmise the same about Iventine. Once he finds him, with Iventine's power added to the strength of the Jolym and the Dhargots, Chorlga will be too powerful."

"Powerful enough to kill all the enemies we leave behind."

"So everyone on Ruun is your enemy now?"

"Near enough." Shade saw a pair of boots. He sat down on the edge of the bed and pulled them on. "We should get moving. If this Dragonkin knows about you—"

"He won't come himself. He's much too busy thrashing every kingdom south of here."

Shade tested the fit of his new boots. They were a little loose but adequate. "If you're so worried about the people of Ruun, stay and help them. I don't particularly want you with us, anyway."

"I'm not staying on Ruun," El'rash'lin said, "but I'm not sailing beyond it, either. There's only one way I can help Rowen Locke, and that's by eliminating Iventine. To do that, I have to eliminate myself."

Shade tapped the pommel of his new sword. "I'd be happy to assist you."

El'rash'lin smiled thinly. "It wouldn't work. I wouldn't die for good. But I think I know of a different way…"

"The Dragonward," Shade said finally. "You're going to throw yourself into it."

El'rash'lin did not answer.

A pitcher of wine was sitting on the end table. Shade filled a cup and drank. "If you want me to try and talk you out of this, you're going to have a long wait."

El'rash'lin turned to the window and watched a slant of setting sunlight move along the floor. "The Isle Knight needs help," he said at last. "I can't send him you. So I have to send him Zeia."

Shade lowered his cup. "You're sending him a Shel'ai with no hands?"

"I've already spoken with her. She knows what's at stake. She's agreed to stay behind."

Shade raised one eyebrow. "I find that hard to believe. Up until a few weeks ago, she was fighting *with* Fadarah against the Sylvs and everyone else."

"So were you. Then you turned Fadarah's skull to ash."

Gods, how did he know that? Shade drained his cup and said nothing.

"We Shel'ai have lost this war. But another, bigger war rages in its place. We each must do our part." El'rash'lin paused. "Silwren understood that."

Shade considered throwing his cup at El'rash'lin. "Don't talk to me about Silwren."

El'rash'lin nodded. "Then I'll talk to you about Zeia. She's staying because there are still Shel'ai in Ruun. They will keep being born in Sylvos, to Sylvan parents, one birth in a thousand. And there are others in hiding, ones Fadarah and I never found. If Locke survives the war, he'll do what he can. But they will still need a Shel'ai protector. Just as you will safeguard all those who sail beyond Ruun, Zeia will protect all those left behind."

Shade thought of the Shel'ai he'd left in Ziraari's camp. After freeing Zeia, he'd warned them through mindspeak to flee, as well, lest they be blamed for Ziraari's murder. But by then, they'd discovered that Shade had killed Fadarah. "There may be Shel'ai in Coldhaven who want me dead."

"Oh, I'm quite certain there will be. But I'll be with you."

"They probably want *you* dead, too."

"Then we'll have to rely on Zeia to talk them out of it."

"I thought you were sending her to help the Isle Knight."

"I am. But she'll have to go to Coldhaven first… not just to keep us alive but to give her time to train."

Shade scoffed. "Train for what? You honestly think a lone Shel'ai woman who can't even defend herself will be able to travel all the way back from the Wintersea to… wherever that Isle Knight is? The first Dhargot, Olg, or Human bandit she comes across will make her wish she was dead."

El'rash'lin offered a frustrating, knowing smile. "Even without her hands, Zeia can defend herself."

"I doubt it." Shade remembered her pale, stricken face and the blood-soaked rags around the stumps of her wrists. "Wytchfire is our strongest form of attack. She can't summon it without her hands—which *you* won't restore."

"She still has her mind."

"Yes," Shade conceded. "She'll be able to read thoughts, maybe move small objects or confuse some dull-witted enemy, if she concentrates hard enough. That's still less useful than a squad of trained swordsmen."

El'rash'lin shook his head. "For centuries, no Shel'ai has bothered to develop other magical forms of attack, relying instead on their wytchfire. Now, without her hands, Zeia will have to correct this. That will make her unpredictable."

"Unpredictable, but still weak," Shade countered. "It would've been better if Brahasti had just killed her. Restore her hands or put her out of her misery." He refilled his glass, took a drink, and glanced up. "Don't look at me like I'm a monster, old man. I saved her life."

"You only saved her so she'd help you free the Sylvs."

"Exactly." Shade raised his glass. "So she'd help me free *enemies* who were being treated unjustly. How monstrous of me."

El'rash'lin rose from his chair. "I must check on Zeia. Feel free to wander around the compound, but if I were you, I'd stay well away from the Sylvs. They have as much cause to hate you as you have to hate them." He started for the door.

Shade looked down at the contents of his glass. He thought of the Sylvan women, imagined how they must be feeling given all they'd endured, and decided not to argue.

Chorlga stood alone in Cadavash, having ordered the rest of his disciples to wait for him on the surface. The eerie depths of the dragon graveyard lay before him, a dizzying mass of temples and excavated tunnels. For centuries, Chorlga had preferred the silence of the deeper, secret chamber that housed Namundvar's Well. He'd visited it in secret, using it to tap into the Light and add to his own considerable magic.

No more.

Chorlga understood that the Well had a will of its own—the will of the Light. Though Chorlga had conquered that will countless times, something had changed recently. Somehow, the Well had learned how to defy him. He could no longer use it to draw power from the Light or use it for divination.

Still, days ago, through the eyes of his Jolym, Chorlga had seen El'rash'lin. The sight of the twisted old man had forced Chorlga to admit that somehow, he'd misjudged the nuances of that resurrection spell even more horribly than he'd first thought. If El'rash'lin was alive, so was the Nightmare. But the Well would not help Chorlga find either of them, let alone the Isle Knight who carried Knightswrath.

Chorlga had considered teleporting himself to Brahasti's compound, capturing El'rash'lin, and studying him to better understand what had gone wrong with the resurrection spell—or, at the very least, in order to prevent the old man from interfering any further with his conquests. But even for a Dragonkin, teleportation was difficult. Without access to Namundvar's Well, recovering his full strength could take days.

Of course, that left the Nightmare. He'd tried to locate the Nightmare on his own, but somehow, the madman remained hidden. That, too, should have been impossible, meaning either that Chorlga had made still more mistakes in the resurrection spell—mistakes of which he was still unaware—or else the gods themselves must be interfering.

The latter prospect made him shudder. Never in all the bloody ages of Dragonkin rule had the gods done such a thing. Then again, he might have brought it upon himself. The gods were children of the Light, and Chorlga had directly defied the Light countless times.

Chorlga shook his head, trying to wash the doubts from his mind by focusing on what lay before him: the bones of a dragon. While most of the excavations at Cadavash had encountered just a few fragments of dragonbone, occasionally parts of a skull, or a webbing of wing bones, the skeleton before him was entirely intact. And it was huge.

"Godsbane..." Despite his growing anxiety, Chorlga smiled as he spoke the name. Discovered centuries ago, its awful visage had supposedly been the impetus for the founding of the dragonpriests' order. They thought the discovery of the dragon's skeleton was a message from the gods. Chorlga could not blame them. The dragonpriests had suspended the massive skeleton from the chamber ceiling, using gigantic chains of brass and iron. Each link of the chain was as thick as a man's wrist. Enough metal to arm and shield an entire army had gone into the making of those chains. Nevertheless, the dragonbones creaked as though they might fall free from their own weight at any second.

Though the great dragon had died countless millennia before Chorlga's time, he'd heard tales of it all his life. Born in an age before the gods had pacified the dragons out of jealousy and fear, Godsbane had been the terror of the skies. Supposedly, even Zet had feared her.

For centuries, the dragonpriests had starved and mutilated their own bodies to show their affection for the dragons whose bones they'd uncovered. Though Chorlga had drained the life force of hundreds of them, more arrived every day. It was possible that their life force would be enough to sustain him without the well. But the risk would be great—greater, even, than all he'd risked with the Nightmare.

But if I stop, I have only what I have now…

He eyed his surroundings—stone, darkness, and corpses—and shook his head. This was not enough. There had to be more. He had to try. The gods left him no choice.

"No choice…"

Godsbane's massive skeleton creaked and swayed on its chains as though in answer.

Rowen knelt in the ruins, warmed his hands over the fire, and tried to ignore the looks from the Sylvan captives. Despite El'rash'lin's insistence that Rowen must go south, the sorcerer had strangely directed the women toward Rowen's camp shortly after their rescue. Now, they sat around the fire, regarding him— some suspicious, some murderous, all pained. He could only imagine what they had gone through. But they were far from the Wytchforest, surrounded by enemies. He did not have the heart to tell them that in all likelihood, their torments were far from over.

Kilisti joined him a moment later, standing before the fire. Several Sylvan women looked away at the sight of Kilisti's mutilated features, but she paid them no mind. She offered Rowen a wineskin. Rowen shook his head.

"Are they still arguing?" Rowen asked, even though he could hear for himself.

He spoke in Sylvan, hoping that might endear him to the Sylvan captives, but Kilisti answered in Common. "Rhos'ari thinks they should head southeast toward Hesod to avoid the Olgrym, then turn southwest for Sylvos."

"Hesod belongs to the Dhargots now. It's no safer than Quorim."

"That's what I said. But Faeli says the Dhargots are a safer bet than the Olgrym."

Rowen glanced at the far end of the ruins, where Rhos'ari and the other Sylvan fighters were locked in a heated debate over which route to take to the Wytchforest. Cathas had pointed out that they had gained six more fighters, as all the Sylvan women had arrived well armed. What's more, the women, who had been captured by Olgrym but chiefly tormented by Dhargots, were pressing for the quickest route back to the Wytchforest.

To everyone's amazement, Faeli had come back—but he'd come back alone. Aerios had fallen after they'd run out of arrows, and Aerios's horse had lost its footing. Faeli had nearly died, too, when the Olgrym came close to surrounding him time and time again. They'd gotten so close that Faeli could identify their leader as Doomsayer himself. Finally, he'd managed to escape.

Or else he was let go so he could lead the Olgrym back to us.

"There's no route that's worth a damn," Kilisti said. "Either the Olgrym hack us to pieces, or the Dhargots make those women slaves."

That's if they don't kill us now because of this damn fire. Though Rowen had initially forbade a fire, some of the women were so close to freezing to death that he had to reconsider. He had to admit, too, that he preferred facing death while he was still warm. He ran his hands through his unkempt red hair, shaking out the snowflakes. "Dhargoth isn't formally at war with the Lotus Isles. Not yet, anyway. They might think twice about kidnapping Sylvs if I'm with them."

Kilisti snickered. "I think you think a bit too highly of yourself, Knight. And anyway, it sounds like you have your own problems to worry about."

Rowen glanced at the Sylvan women. A glint in their eyes reminded him of trapped animals. He thought again of what they must have endured in captivity, and shuddered. "I promised Captain Briel I'd get these women safely back to Sylvos. That's what I intend to do."

Kilisti eyed him with curiosity. "Don't think I've ever met a Human who called it that."

"What?"

"Sylvos. Only Sylvs call it that. And Shel'ai, I suppose. Everyone else just calls it the Wytchforest."

Rowen considered telling the woman about how El'rash'lin had magically infused some of his memories into Rowen's mind, then he reminded himself that Kilisti detested anything associated with magic. "Must be El'rash'lin's influence."

Kilisti nodded slowly. She looked skeptical. "Strange old man. Dead, but not dead. Half one thing, half something else."

I wonder if the same couldn't be said about me. Rowen glanced down at Knightswrath. "He's a friend, and one of the bravest men I've ever known."

"You don't sound too sure of that."

Rowen glared at her. "Easy, Sylv. I'm not forgetting that he started out fighting on the same side as Fadarah. So did Silwren. But people make mistakes. The gods know I have."

"And you're about to make another."

"Meaning?"

"Meaning you're not going back to Sylvos." Kilisti knelt and drew her shortsword.

Rowen tensed but forced himself to relax when she simply began to sharpen the blade. "I wasn't aware you could tell the future."

Kilisti shrugged. "Don't need magic to see what's on your face. What that old Shel'ai said spooked you. All this business with Dragonkin aside, from what I could understand, you've got friends in the east. Maybe they're dead; maybe they're not. But you're leaving to find out."

Leaving for where? Rowen chewed the inside of his lip. "If all of you came with me, I could get you shelter in Lyos. You'd be safe there until the war's over."

"Safe in a Human city on the other side of the continent, surrounded by metal-skinned demons?" Kilisti laughed. "I think not. Rhos'ari and Faeli will give up soon. This bunch will head straight south and take their chances with the Olgrym."

Rowen eyed the other Sylvan women. He saw a few nod almost imperceptibly, touching their weapons. They were ready to fight. They *wanted* to fight. Some had probably even fought Olgrym before. Still, they had no chance.

Rowen faced Kilisti again. "Sounds like you're not going with them."

"I'm not. I'm going with you."

Rowen blinked, speechless.

"Don't take it personal. I haven't fallen in love with you, Knight. I'm just not stupid. Only way any of these poor bastards get home is if you lead the Olgrym away."

Rowen looked into the fire. "We've already tried that."

"*We* tried it." Kilisti gestured at the Sylvan fighters. "*You* didn't."

"What's the difference?"

"I know Olgrym, Knight. They love and fear magic. That's why they're chasing us. They're after *you*. So give them what they want."

Rowen kicked an ember with his foot. "Are you suggesting I surrender to Doomsayer or just tie up Knightswrath with a ribbon and leave it in the snow for him?"

Kilisti shook her head. "I'm saying the Knight with the burning sword should stand on a hill tonight and wave the damn thing against the dark sky until every Olg for a hundred miles comes running."

Rowen laughed. "Well, that's certainly *one* course of action."

"It's the *only* course of action." Kilisti stopped sharpening and looked up from her blade. "Tell me I'm wrong."

Rowen said nothing for a moment, then he answered, "If getting myself killed is the only way to save everyone else, why are *you* staying?"

"Because I lied earlier. Truth is, I've fallen hopelessly in love with you." Kilisti snickered. "Or maybe it's just because I want to kill every Olg and Dhargot I can before I die, and staying close to you seems like a good way to do it." She rose to her feet and slid her sword blade back into its well-oiled scabbard. "Shall we, lover?"

Rowen's heart leapt at the thought of using Knightswrath, though he could not tell whether it was excitement or panic. He glanced at the setting sun, imagined how bright the violet flames would appear against the dark sky, and rose to his feet. "Fine. Let's get this over with."

CHAPTER TWENTY-TWO

THE TOMATO PRINCE

SAANJI READ THE MESSAGE A second time then a third. He looked up. "Royce, is this one of your men's idea of a joke?" He passed the message to one of his own officers seated beside him.

Arnil Royce answered with a mirthless smile. "I might have thought so, Prince, if it weren't for the reports we've received of the Jolym."

Saanji glanced at the tiny scrap of paper. *What's an Isle Knight doing in the Wytchforest?* "That doesn't say anything about Jolym."

"But it *does* say something about a Dragonkin. A raven brought that message to my king, and he threw it away, thinking it was one of his children playing around. Luckily, his steward saw it and sent it to me. And speaking of disconcerting scraps of paper, here's another."

Royce pushed a larger piece of parchment toward Saanji, whose eyes widened when he read it. "At the risk of repeating myself…"

"Not a joke," Royce promised. He gestured to another of the Lancers seated around the council table.

The man, a white-haired veteran with a stoic expression despite the bloody bandages wrapped around his arm and forehead, answered for him. "I saw it myself, m'lord. Your brother's entire army marches southwest, toward Hesod. Footmen, cavalry, elephants—everything but the chariots, which they appear to have left behind. At the head of their army march several hundred of those same men seen returning from the Lotus Isles—giant men covered in steel and brass. Alive, but not."

Jolym, Saanji thought in disbelief. *Gods, what fey times are we living in?*

The Lancers whispered to each other, but when Arnil Royce stood, all fell silent. Saanji concealed a grin. Royce hardly seemed like an impressive figure—medium height, plain faced, he had a receding hairline—but his men worshipped him. Saanji had a feeling that not all their admiration had to do with Royce's tactical expertise and brilliant swordsmanship.

I wonder if my men will ever look on me that way. Saanji almost laughed at the sheer impossibility.

Arnil Royce sighed, resting one hand on the pommel of his kingsteel longsword. "Cassica has been abandoned. Likewise, the threat has been removed from Ivairia's border. Furthermore, scouts report that the Dhargots occupying Syros are marching south, too. No word yet on what's happening in Quorim, but for now, it seems we've won." The statement prompted no cheers. Indeed, the Lancer-Captain's voice sounded flat and joyless.

"This makes no sense," Saanji protested. "It's the middle of winter. My brother had Cassica ground under his boot. Same with Syros. We're nowhere near breaking him. Why would he retreat?"

"Perhaps his reputation as a warrior was undeserved," someone suggested halfheartedly.

"We could have broken his will," said another.

Saanji scoffed. "On both counts, gentlemen, I assure you that I know my own brother better than that."

The wounded, white-haired Lancer offered, "Consolidating his forces to try and usurp your father, perhaps?"

Saanji said, "With Ziraari dead and me out of reach, I might believe that. But he'd be better off massing at Syros or Quorim, right on my father's border. Why in the gods' names would he take his army back to Hesod?"

Arnil Royce sat back down but cleared his throat, drawing everyone's attention. "And more importantly, why are the Jolym marching with him?"

No one answered for a time.

"Last night, we... interrogated a Dhargot prisoner," the Lancer-Captain told Saanji. "He claims the Bloody Prince has struck an alliance with a Dragonkin. Were we living in different times, I might have called him a madman. But these days, I don't have that luxury."

"Speaking of luxuries..." Saanji held out his cup. One of Royce's squires refilled it.

Royce drummed his gloved fingers on the table. "Your brother doesn't strike me as the kind of man who would let himself be another man's pawn."

"Agreed. Which is why I suggest we all get good and drunk before the world ends."

Royce's eyes narrowed. "Meaning?"

"Meaning anyone that my brother agrees to serve is guaranteed to be someone you don't want to know."

The Lancers exchanged looks. Finally, Royce said, "When my king hears that the Dhargots have withdrawn... no disrespect to our new allies"—he nodded toward Saanji and the two Earless officers seated beside him, causing Saanji to lift his glass and drink in response—"I'm sure he'll celebrate. He'll pretend he sent me in the first place and recall his Lancers home. Given the circumstances, I will have a hard time refusing."

Another Lancer cleared his throat. "Begging your pardon, Captain Royce, but why should you refuse? If the Dhargots have withdrawn, *why* they've withdrawn doesn't matter. Ivairia is safe again. Our slain have been avenged. We've even liberated some of the Free Cities, which might help us improve trade. What happens to the rest of Ruun hardly concerns us."

"Especially since all these troubles are probably their own doing," another added.

Some of the Lancers nodded.

Saanji noticed that most of his own officers nodded, too. He felt the bottom drop out of his gut. He drained his cup as fast as he could, but the gnawing feeling remained.

Turning the opal ring on his finger, he glanced at Royce. Despite the Lancer's taciturn nature, Saanji had gotten to know him well over the past few weeks. The Ivairian never looked afraid. At most, when facing insurmountable odds or reading news of some disaster, he looked merely troubled. *He looks pretty damn troubled now, Gods save us.*

Royce stood again. Everyone fell silent. "I don't pretend to understand the mind of a man like Prince Karhaati. I don't pretend to understand what motivates a Dragonkin, either. But I trust my instincts, and my instincts say that Prince Saanji is right."

Saanji had the misfortune of spilling wine on his tunic just as Royce's statement caused many to turn and look at him. Saanji blushed and tried to hide the wet spot with his goblet.

"We've had word of a second force of Jolym marching into Nosh and laying siege to the city of Atheion," Royce continued. "I don't think the Bloody Prince is going to relieve this force, since the reports say Atheion is about to fall, anyway. That means Karhaati—or this Dragonkin, the one they call Chorlga—is after something else. We must find out what."

Saanji scrutinized the expressions of the other Lancers. A few, particularly those who had been with Royce since the beginning, nodded in agreement.

But the majority, who had been late joining in the fight and had likely viewed Royce as a renegade until a few weeks ago, looked uncertain. Saanji guessed that they couldn't wait to declare the war over and toast to their victory, however uneasy. If Royce continued fighting the Dhargots, how many of his Lancers would abandon him, forcing him to defy his king yet again?

"Gentlemen, I have a proposal." Everyone turned to face him. Too late, Saanji realized that he'd voiced what he'd only intended to mull over in his mind. Thinking quickly, he said, "I suggest we march for Cassica. We can winter there and see what kind of devilry greets us come spring."

One of the Lancers said, "The Cassicans might not appreciate that."

"As far as they know, we're their liberators," Saanji countered. "Besides, don't forget that I lived in Cassica for a time. I may be a Dhargot, but I was far kinder to them than my brother was."

"But still a Dhargot," another Lancer mumbled.

"In my defense, I had little say in the matter." Saanji held out his cup to be refilled again. "And while we're on the subject, I'm also a Dhargot who's sick to death of sleeping in the snow. Some of you Lancers might agree with me on this. At least Cassica has walls and firewood."

"But what if King Hightower orders us to return?" a Lancer protested.

"Then his messenger can find you in Cassica. It's a big city, hard to miss." Saanji hiccupped halfway through his sentence.

Some of the Lancers bristled at the jest, but Royce smirked. Still on his feet, he pounded the table with his fist to get everyone's attention. "I'm sure I don't have to remind my own countrymen that Ivairia's mountain roads can be treacherous, even in the warmest of seasons. All talk of enemies aside, it would simply be prudent to winter in Cassica until the northern roads are more passable. Agreed?"

His stern tone made it clear that the matter was not open for discussion. Royce dismissed the council a moment later. Saanji's officers followed, though Saanji stayed where he was. Royce dismissed his squires, filled his goblet using a pitcher of wine on a small serving table at the other end of the tent, then sat back down.

"You shouldn't drink so damn much, Dhargot."

Saanji shrugged. "What was it that philosopher said about the tremors of a bad childhood?"

The Lancer shrugged. "Gods if I know. I was a lousy student of philosophy."

"I was a lousy student at everything." Saanji drained his cup, held it out, then remembered that Royce had dismissed his squires. He set his cup down, unwilling to fetch the pitcher himself.

"Is this the hour when you start feeling sorry for yourself?"

Saanji laughed. "I only get one hour? Most unfair." He tipped his cup and leaned back in his chair, letting the last few drops fall from his cup into his mouth.

"The men are getting along better than I would have expected," Royce said.

"I think your men just keep forgetting that mine are still Dhargots."

"I doubt that… though the fact that they don't decorate their necks with dead men's ears doesn't hurt."

Saanji took a deep breath, held it, and forced himself out of his chair. He stumbled, clutching his belly, and fell against the table. Then he pushed off and reeled across the tent. Once he'd refilled his goblet, though, he managed to return to his chair without spilling a drop. "You know, before some fool started the Way of Ears, we Dhargots weren't much different from anyone else."

Royce raised one eyebrow. "Given what I've seen, I find that hard to believe."

"Believe what you want, Lancer. Seems to me that a few generations of plagues and famine will turn any kingdom into a den of monsters."

"Ivairia's had its share of plagues. We don't impale men on sharpened stakes or drag children's guts out."

Saanji raised his goblet. "Bloody good for Ivairia!" He took a drink. "Maybe you just never had the kind of plagues that Dhargoth has."

"I hope we never do." Royce gave him a critical look. "By the way, did you forget our agreement?"

"What agreement?"

"The one we made a week ago, after that close battle in the foothills."

"You're going to have to be more specific, I'm afraid."

Royce's eyes narrowed. "You said you'd quit drinking and let me train you."

"Was I drunk when I agreed to that?"

"Most definitely."

"Well, there's your answer." Saanji raised his glass. "Trust me, Lancer, trying to teach me swordplay is a lost cause. My father and brothers tried for years."

"Something tells me I'm a better teacher."

"Well, gods know you couldn't be a worse one." Saanji laughed. "Seriously, Lancer, thank you, but save your breath. My weapon of choice is a fork. I piss the bed more nights than I don't. The most violent thing I've ever done is hurl an empty pitcher at a portrait of my father, and even *that* had me shaking like a leaf in a storm." He patted his great, round stomach. "Besides, do you really think I've got the build to be a fighter?"

Royce shrugged. "You've got the will and the hate. And I think, somewhere down in there, the courage."

Saanji laughed. "Don't mock me, Lancer. You know what my own men call me."

"Would these be the same men who risked impalement to follow you?"

"People make mistakes."

Royce stood up so abruptly that Saanji wondered if the Lancer would strike him. Instead, Royce drew his kingsteel longsword and cast it on the table. "Know how I got that, Dhargot?"

Saanji shrugged. "An expensive gift from your king?"

Royce shook his head. "Isle Knights guard their precious kingsteel more jealously than a father guards his virgin daughter. You might be able to buy a sword made out of it, but even a king would have a hard time affording it. No king's that generous." He snickered. "No, I bought this damn thing *myself*, with coin I earned from tournaments, which I won by knocking bigger, stronger men on their armored asses."

"Well done." Saanji toasted him.

Royce shook his head. "I'm not bragging." He held out his arms. "Look at me, Dhargot. Half the Lancers in Ivairia are twice my size. I'm not even the fastest. But I've won most every fight I've ever been in. How do you suppose that is?"

Saanji shrugged. "Honestly, Lancer, I couldn't care less."

Royce lowered his arms. Shaking his head with disappointment, he sat back down. "So what do you think your brother is up to?"

"Murder and glory, same as always."

"And this Dragonkin?"

"Probably the same kind of monster as my dear brother, just with tapered ears and burning hands." Saanji drained his goblet and wiped his mouth on his sleeve.

"Then he's either a monster who made it past the Dragonward, or else he's been hiding here since the Shattering War."

"Or he's a Shel'ai who transformed himself, like the others," Saanji offered.

"None of those options sound very appealing."

"If options were appealing, they wouldn't be options." Saanji wasn't exactly sure what he meant by that, but he liked the sound of it. His stomach grumbled. He looked around the council table for something to eat, but all he saw were maps and reports. He wished that Royce had not dismissed his squires. Saanji disliked the bland Ivairian food, but his own cook had been killed, and boiled potatoes and soldiers' mash were better than nothing.

Saanji blinked, realizing that Royce was talking to him. "What?"

Royce's face flushed with irritation. "I said, there's something else I have to tell you. Something I didn't report to the council."

Saanji's stomach grumbled again, punctuated by a twist of nausea. He gripped the edge of the table. "This might have to wait."

Royce ignored his protest. "Chorlga is looking for someone."

Saanji laughed. He turned the opal ring on his finger. "Aren't we all?"

Royce did not laugh. "The Isle Knight who wrote the letter. The Dhargots are supposed to form a massive line running north and south of Hesod, despite the snow, and cast nets to catch him. The Dhargots don't know the Knight's name, but they have a description." Royce trailed off.

Saanji frowned. "But *you* know who he is," he guessed.

"I might. I met someone awhile back, when the Dhargots chased me all the way down to the Red Steppes. An Iron Sister."

"Gods..." Saanji winced. He remembered what his late brother, Ziraari, had done to the Iron Sisters at Hesod.

"She spoke of an Isle Knight, traveling west in the company of a Shel'ai... rather, a Shel'ai-turned-Dragonkin."

"Silwren?"

"Probably."

Saanji snickered. "No wonder you didn't mention this in council."

"Most of my men think magic is an abomination. When I was young, Shel'ai tried to settle in western Ivairia, in the foothills. The king drove them off. Many people blame them for the famines... even though famines are nothing new."

Saanji pondered this. "So Chorlga and my dear brother are looking for this Isle Knight, but *not* for Silwren?"

"Igrid said they were going to the Wytchforest to try to broker some kind of alliance with the Sylvs. Maybe the Sylvs have already killed her. Or maybe the Olgrym did."

"Well, there goes another potential ally." Saanji poured a little wine on the ground and laughed. Royce scowled at him so fiercely that Saanji hiccupped.

"Igrid said that this Knight, Rowen Locke, had a kingsteel sword with him. Not like mine, though. An ancient adamune, supposedly worn by Fâyu Jinn himself."

Saanji had been starting out of his chair, about to try his luck at refilling his goblet, but he sat back down. He sat a moment in silence, blinking at the table. "Knightswrath?"

"You've heard of it?"

"Just an old story I read as a child. Maryssa read it to me, actually." Saanji rubbed his eyes. "Supposedly, the man who founded Dhargoth was Jinn's friend. He named a city after him. He even patterned his sigil after Jinn... a lone warrior stabbing a dragon with a burning sword. Only it changed over time to a dragon impaled on a spear."

"So Chorlga's after the sword."

Saanji sat a moment longer then pushed himself up and stumbled across the tent. "Well, if he's after that Isle Knight, I doubt there's a damn thing *we* could do to help him. We're better off worrying about Cadavash and whatever they're brewing there."

Royce nervously tapped his fingernail on the blade of his longsword, still lying unsheathed on the table. "The Isle Knight probably doesn't need our help, anyway," he said at last. "A man that important has to have allies."

CHAPTER TWENTY-THREE

DOOMSAYER'S HOUR

ROWEN REINED IN SNOWDARK AND twisted in the saddle. At the sight of the gray, muscular tide surging through the snow, barely a hundred yards behind them, he winced. "Well, that worked a bit better than expected."

Kilisti had reined in, as well, her face pale. "They're gaining."

"At least there aren't as many."

"Only because half of them ran themselves to death."

Rowen touched the Sylvan shortbow that Faeli had given him before riding off with the others. Rowen was no expert archer, nothing like a Sylv, but an Olg was a hard target to miss. "We could try picking them off—"

"Still too many. Unless you want to take your sweet time aiming, even with the arrows poisoned, it'll take five or six to drop each one."

The Olgrym barreled through the snow in a wide, frightening row. Rowen shook his head in dreadful awe. Instead of the usual taunts and howling, the bestial figures seemed to be focusing all their energy on closing their pursuit. And it was working.

"Split up," Rowen said at last. "Ride south. I'll keep east. They'll follow me."

Kilisti scowled. "I don't like you, Knight, but I gave you my word."

"I don't remember you taking any oath."

"I took an oath to the Shal'tiar."

"I'm not in your damn Shal'tiar."

"Doesn't matter. Briel said help you. So I'm helping."

Rowen patted Snowdark's neck. Like Kilisti's horse, she could smell the Olgrym gaining on them, and her nostrils flared with panic. But even with the Olgrym this close, the horses needed a moment to rest. "Dying won't help me."

"I told you, I came along to kill an Olg or two."

"Then get away and kill one somewhere else."

Kilisti answered by spurring her horse eastward, pressing as fast as she could. Rowen swore. He considered turning south and leading the Olgrym away from her, but they had been riding almost nonstop for three days. Hesod had to be close, just beyond the distant hills and the sheen of a frozen river. It was a reckless plan, but the Dhargots were their only hope. Rowen had no intention of surrendering to them, but if he crossed the path of a patrol, the Dhargots would be forced to fight the Olgrym, whether they wanted to or not. That would buy them some time—provided the Dhargots didn't kill him and Kilisti first.

Rowen glanced back at the Olgrym again. They moved faster than he would have thought possible. The fog of their breath mingled with the snow kicked up by their boots. They were close enough that he could hear their laborious grunting. Some of the giant warriors wore armor made of bones. Rowen heard the bones rattle.

A knot of fear swelled in his throat. "*Singchai ushó fey*," he muttered. His voice broke. Cursing, he spurred his horse after Kilisti.

Doomsayer ran through the heavy snow, striving to ignore the ache in his bones. His legs felt as though they'd turned to sand—then to glass, which broke anew at every step. He had not slept or eaten in three days, driving on without pause through the heavy, drifting snow. Sometimes, he looked back to see what remained of his war band. Each time, the numbers dwindled. Fifty became forty, then thirty, then twenty. The weak ones collapsed, unmourned, unburied save by the falling snow.

Doomsayer felt as if his own heart might burst from exhaustion, but the chieftain prayed for the strength to continue. He thought of the burning sword, the raw exhilaration when he'd felt the air crackling with magic during his disastrous charge into the Sylvan capital. That battle had wrecked his army and hamstrung his grand ambitions to rule both Godsfall and the Wytchforest, but fate had given him a second chance.

The burning sword is near. I only have to slay one puny Knight and a Sylvan woman to get it.

He saw them atop a snowy hill in the distance, desperate and frightened, pausing for a useless moment's rest. Doomsayer laughed. Somehow, he quickened his strides, surging ahead of his warriors. He'd come too far and lost too much. Nothing as paltry as exhaustion would stand in his way.

If they'd had bows, his men might have shot them off their horses. But Doomsayer had no desire to end so glorious a chase in such a cowardly way. It was bad enough that he'd allowed his warriors to use bows to wound and capture Sylvan prisoners to trade with the Dhargots. This chase would end the way the gods intended.

Doomsayer called out to his warriors—just a wild howl to urge them on.

Preferring not to waste his breath on the weak, it was the first time he'd spoken to them in days, but it was enough. Drawing on some deep, inner well of strength, the Olgrym surged after him, keeping pace. The rattle of weapons and armor mingled with their grunts and ragged breaths. The snow started again, but the Olgrym drove through it without pause.

When Doomsayer lost sight of his prey behind a hill, he ran quicker still. Though he knew his prey could not hide their trail in the snow, he still wanted to keep them in his sight. He wanted to see them afraid and struggling. He remembered the greatwolves he'd hunted as a child—he'd run them down, mile after mile, until they slowed enough for him to hurl his spear clean through their sides. He remembered the delicious reek of their blood and their final, desperate thrashing.

So the Olgish chieftain could hardly believe his eyes when he crested the hill and spotted the Human and the Sylv stopped below, their horses reined in, surrounded by armed men. About thirty strong, all the men wore black silk and black scale armor. One carried a dark, familiar banner. Doomsayer slowed. These men were Dhargots, his allies. But they'd just claimed something that did not belong to them. He could not allow that.

For the first time in days, Doomsayer and his warriors stopped. One made the mistake of collapsing face first in the snow, thinking it was time to rest. Doomsayer answered by stomping the back of the warrior's neck. A dreadful crack brought a smile to his lips. Doomsayer took a long, deep, ragged breath and let it go. Then he reached past his shoulder and unslung the great mace of scorched iron from his back. He held it high.

His remaining warriors drew their own weapons—axes, clubs, and spears longer than a Human's height. Doomsayer howled. His warriors howled back. Their cries reverberated through the cold air. Below, men whirled to see what could have made such a sound. Doomsayer showed them. Waving his mace, he sprinted down the hill. He could already taste blood.

"Sweet gods…"

The Dhargothi officer stared past Rowen at the gigantic figures sprinting down the hill. Terror replaced an earlier expression of irritation at having to deal with fresh prisoners. He froze for a moment then began barking orders. One of the Dhargots raised a war horn to his lips and blew it, again and again. The rest of the men whirled their horses back toward the wretched city in the distance. They broke into a gallop.

"See, Knight? I told you," Kilisti said. "They aren't going to stand and fight."

Rowen spurred Snowdark after the fleeing Dhargots. "If we can get ahead of them, they won't have a choice."

Kilisti urged her exhausted horse after him. "We can't outrun them."

Rowen wondered whether she meant the Dhargots or the Olgrym. Intoning a quick prayer, asking the Light for forgiveness, he drew a dagger from his belt and threw it.

The blade struck a Dhargot in the back. Though the blade lacked the force to pierce the Dhargot's armor, the man reared up and turned. Seeing Rowen, he gave a defiant cry and lunged with his spear. Rowen wheeled Snowdark to the side, warded off the blow with his vambrace, and rode past the Dhargot before he could strike again.

Rowen hoped that Kilisti would grasp his intentions and join in. The snap of a bowstring confirmed that his trust in her had not been misplaced. Kilisti's arrow missed a Dhargot but struck a horse.

Rowen realized that the shot must have been intentional, for the horse collapsed in a gruesome tangle, taking its rider and another horse and rider with it. Kilisti loosed a second arrow just as quickly as the first. It struck yet another Dhargot in the back of the shoulder. He reined in too sharply, twisting in the saddle to try to glimpse his attacker, and collided with another rider who could not veer away in time.

Chaos swept through the Dhargothi ranks. Some of the riders continued on, thinking only of themselves, while others slowed to help their comrades. The officer shouted, but no one could hear him over a new, terrible chorus of Olgrym howls.

Rowen waved to Kilisti and tried to lead her right through the mass of Dhargots. But then the line shifted. Seeing the way blocked, Rowen tugged the reins so sharply that Snowdark reared, nearly dumping him from the saddle. Rowen tugged her to the left, thinking he might ride around, but Kilisti screamed. Rowen turned.

An unhorsed Dhargot had cut the horse out from under her. The Sylvan woman fell hard into the snow, and her bow flew wild. The Dhargot started toward her, spear in hand, but another unhorsed Dhargot grabbed his arm, pointing at the approaching Olgrym. The Dhargot ran.

That's what I should be doing.

Rowen whirled Snowdark around and galloped back to Kilisti. Three Dhargots started toward him—one on foot, two on horseback—but Rowen drew Knightswrath and held it high. Violet flames washed over the blade. The Dhargots' eyes widened. The one on foot froze then backpedaled until he fell over in the snow. The two on horseback yanked their horses about and galloped away, driving them so fast that one horse lost its footing and crashed to the ground.

Rowen glanced at the Olgrym. Their chieftain pointed a mace at him and howled again. His heart leapt into his throat. Nevertheless, he dismounted Snowdark and raced to Kilisti's side. He jammed Knightswrath's blade into the snow. The flames vanished.

Kilisti was pushing herself up. Rowen saw blood in the snow. A quick look at Kilisti's leg showed red bone jutting through her torn pants. Somehow, the woman did not even cry out as she pushed herself up onto her good leg.

Rowen turned back to the Olgrym again. He gauged the distance then made his decision. He gathered Kilisti in his arms, surprised by how light she was, and carried her to Snowdark. He hoisted her into the saddle. The Sylvan woman winced but instinctively gripped the reins. Then she blinked. "Wait—"

"Be good to my horse. I called her Snowdark, but my friend told me that was a stupid name. I guess you can name her whatever you want."

Before Kilisti could protest, Rowen turned Snowdark southward and gave the horse's piebald flank a hard slap. She leapt into motion. Rowen watched them go. He figured Kilisti would make it back to the Wytchforest. He hoped Snowdark would end up in Quesh. The Queshi were kind to horses. Rowen sighed then plucked Knightswrath from the snow. Flames washed over the blade again. Slowly, he turned.

Most of the Dhargots had scattered or ridden on, but a few, either mad or confused, remained in the Olgrym's path. The Olgrym cut them down without hesitation then barreled on through the snow, toward Rowen. The Knight of the Crane glanced over his shoulder, still half hoping he would see the rest of the Dhargots riding back to assist their fallen comrades. Instead, he saw broad, snowy plains painted by sundown and, a few miles beyond, a squat city shrouded in smoke.

Rowen stared eastward, imagining the faraway Lotus Isles. Then he turned back to face the Olgrym. He raised Knightswrath and saluted the Olgish chieftain, who had outdistanced the rest. To his surprise, the chieftain slowed, hefted his mace, and returned the salute with grave dignity. Then he broke into a wild sprint, his great strides devouring the distance between them.

Rowen held Knightswrath over his head, gripping it with both hands: a position the Shao called *hoso no-kami*. He took a deep breath. Then he gave in to Knightswrath's searing heat and the buzzing in his mind. The sword hilt grew hotter still. Rowen screamed.

All his senses blurred into one then vanished in a sea of violet fire.

CHAPTER TWENTY-FOUR

CHOICES

J ALIST WATCHED THE PROCESSION WITH a forced smile, applauding as
a fresh host of Dhargothi footmen marched through the streets of Hesod.
Ghastly banners rippled in the wind. Behind the footmen came a host of
war elephants, loud and armored, each one saddled with a howdah crowded
with archers.

"Let's get out of here," Igrid hissed through clenched teeth.

"Don't talk," Jalist answered in a low voice. "You're supposed to be a slave,
remember?" He eyed the crowds and noticed another off-duty soldier watching
them. He looked to be eyeing only Igrid because of her new, immodest attire,
but just to be certain, Jalist turned and scowled at her. He tugged the rope he
was holding, the other end of which was fixed to the iron collar around Igrid's
throat.

Igrid gave him a murderous look. "Do that again, and I'll kill you."

"Not unless you want to get *all* of us killed," Vardan hissed. He stood on
one side of her, Braggo on the other. Braggo ran a lock of her red hair between
his fingers, pretending to study it.

Igrid blinked. With obvious effort, she looked down and trembled.

Jalist wondered if the trembling was part of the act or really due to the fact
that she was standing in the city square, practically naked, in the middle of
winter, surrounded by some of the worst men alive. He felt a rush of sympathy
for her, but he forced himself to turn his attention back to the procession. "I'm
sorry, girl," he growled over his shoulder. "I know it's awful, but this is the
Bloody Prince marching into the city. They'll know something's wrong if we're
not here. Just keep your head down and endure a little longer."

"Good advice for all of us," Vardan muttered.

"No Jolym," Braggo noted a moment later. "Are they all out looking for the Isle Knight?"

"I hope the bastards rust," Vardan said, a bit too loudly for Jalist's liking.

Jalist silenced the men with a look then studied the crowds again. Some were off-duty soldiers, but most were common citizens of Hesod who had so far survived their captors. All tried to appear jovial as the armies of the Bloody Prince entered their city, though Jalist could see the loathing in their eyes. The Bloody Prince himself, cruel and handsome astride his bloodmare, had already entered at the head of his host, but Jalist suspected it would take hours for the rest of the army to enter Hesod—and the people of Hesod would have to witness all of it.

Most of the onlookers were old. Jalist guessed that all the young men had already been killed or enslaved. He preferred not to think about what had happened to the women. *Not a single Iron Sister in sight...*

Jalist had heard tales of the famed, uniquely all-female army all his life, but since the city's fall, the Dhargots appeared to have erased all trace of it. All the banners were gone. Nearly all the Iron Sisters' temples had been destroyed, their barracks converted into lodgings for Dhargots. The occupiers had left the Iron Sisters' statues standing, but only after hewing off each statue's face and painting vulgar messages across its bare breasts. Not a single Hesodi carried a weapon. Those who didn't wear slave collars still bowed at the sight of every Dhargot who crossed their path. Those who were struck or abused had learned to endure it without protest.

Though such sights made Jalist's blood boil, he dared do nothing to help these people. He wanted to be gone from Hesod, but blizzards had kept them there long enough to hear rumors. "The Dhargots think Locke is heading this way," he'd explained to the others. "That means Silwren's with him. Either they'll catch him... and we can free him... or else Silwren will torch a couple hundred of these bastards, and we can follow the trail left by their ashes."

But after days of the same routine, he wondered how long he could keep his sanity in such a place. He'd expected things to be awful in the city, given the Dhargots' infamous cruelty toward conquered peoples—women in particular—but conditions in Hesod were worse. He could only imagine how difficult it was for Igrid, perhaps the only Iron Sister who had escaped.

"Just breathe and endure," he muttered, white-knuckling his long axe, unsure whether he was speaking to his comrades or to himself.

Ahead of them, the procession continued. Behind the war elephants came another mass of Dhargots on horseback, followed by a thick, wrecked crowd of captives taken from other cities. All women and children—most dressed in rags, some naked—were being driven along by Dhargothi footmen with whips and spears, forced to walk through the snow, as well as the mess left behind by the elephants and horses. All who fell were beaten. Dhargots laughed.

"Gods," Braggo muttered. The man of the Red Watch had his sword half drawn.

"Relax, lad," Jalist warned in a heated whisper. "You look too much like a man with a conscience. Examine Igrid's hair some more. Vardan, shove him, like you don't want him touching your prize."

His comrades played along with the dishonorable charade—even Igrid, who managed to look frightened instead of murderously angry. Jalist forced himself to watch the slaves being driven into the city, pretending to view them like a man inspecting horses for sale. Though most of the Dhargots' captives were Human, he saw a handful of Sylvs as well as a few who seemed to have some Olgish blood.

He shifted his attention from the captives to the Dhargots around them. He counted rows of horses and squads of footmen. Trying to estimate how many Prince Karhaati had brought with him, he quickly lost count. At one point, he thought the procession had ended, only to see that the lull had been caused by a gap in the host. More cavalry entered the city, followed by more footmen and elephants, along with yet another mass of captives. Every once in a while, a squad of Dhargots blew trumpets while another beat out a savage rhythm on drums that Jalist suspected had been made of enemies' skin.

Jalist switched his long axe from one hand to the other. *Sweet Zet, did they send all of Dhargoth down here?* He thought of Rowen Locke's reckless hope of driving back the Dhargots by forming some kind of alliance between the Sylvs and the Isle Knights. Even if both nations had not been ravaged, Jalist doubted their combined force might have been enough to stop the Dhargots' advance.

Jalist considered the rumors about a burning sword that the Dhargots were supposed to claim in the name of their new Dragonkin master. Supposedly, the Isle Knight who wielded that sword had incinerated a good portion of the Shel'ai and Olgrym laying siege to the Wytchforest. Jalist didn't know whether those stories were true or if the destruction they described had been wrought by Silwren instead of Knightswrath. But he imagined those same fires burning away the wretched host before him. The thought made him smile.

The procession continued on and on, until the setting sun bloodied streets and rooftops. Finally, the people were allowed to return to their homes. Most of the soldiers either made their way for the crowded barracks or the taverns, but Jalist and his comrades headed for a small, ruined temple not far from the city gates. Their first night in Hesod, they'd made the mistake of staying at an inn. There, a high-ranking Dhargothi officer had seen Igrid and ordered the others to relinquish her into his care. They'd been forced to do so, intending to rescue her later. But by the time they forced their way into the officer's room, Igrid had already killed him.

They'd lowered the officer's body out the window and stripped off his armor so that he appeared to be just a common citizen killed for sport and thrown into the sewers. Luckily, no soldiers had been suspicious enough to question them, though ever since then, they'd taken care to avoid the inns.

Instead, they sought shelter in a tiny temple devoted to Armahg, where all trace of the goddess had been destroyed. There had been other refugees there at first, mostly children, but they had scattered when Jalist, Vardan, and Braggo walked in wearing Dhargothi armor, Igrid in tow. Jalist had been tempted to call them back, promising them safety, then he reminded himself that the fewer people who knew who they really were, the better. But Igrid had pointed out that at least a few of those children had probably died as a result of Jalist claiming their hiding place.

Jalist remembered this as they entered the temple again. Though it looked empty, Vardan and Braggo searched anyway, swords drawn, picking their way through the shadows and debris. Certain they were alone, they nodded. Jalist leaned his long axe against a defiled fountain so that he could help Igrid remove her collar, but she'd already pulled out the pin that kept the halves together. She cast the thing to the floor with a loud, iron clatter.

"Be quiet, damn you," Jalist muttered. He retrieved the collar, wrapped the rope around it, and set it aside. Then he took off his cloak and handed it to her. Igrid snatched it from him. Shivering, she wrapped it over her torn, inadequate clothing. Meanwhile, Braggo worked on starting a fire.

"I can't do that again," Igrid muttered.

Jalist hesitated. "You may have to."

Igrid looked at him. Despite her grimace, her eyes shone. "I'm telling you, I can't. I won't. The next time you have to leave, I'll hide here."

"And if the soldiers find you, you'll wish you were dead."

"Leave my sword. I can defend myself."

"Against one man, sure. Maybe even against two or three. But not a whole damn army. And that's what you'd be facing, once they found out there was a pretty woman running around loose with a sword in her hands."

Jalist glanced at Vardan and Braggo. Both men fussed with the fire, pretending not to hear. Jalist sighed. He squeezed Igrid's shoulder. To his surprise, she did not pull away. "I'm sorry," he whispered.

Igrid stood stone still, then she bent over the ruined fountain and retrieved the pair of shortswords she'd hidden under a pile of debris. She hugged them close to her. When she spoke again, her voice sounded steady. "Either we get some news on Locke in a day or two, or we move on. Staying here will only get us killed."

"Two days," Jalist said. "I promise."

Braggo stood up from the fire and approached. "I'm going out, Captain," he said in a low voice.

Jalist gave him a skeptical look.

"We need news," Braggo said. "You stay here with Igrid."

"Take Vardan with you," Jalist advised.

Braggo smiled. "Begging your pardon, Captain, but Vardan will stay and keep an eye on you."

Vardan looked up from the fire and offered a terse nod of agreement.

Despite his foul mood, Jalist laughed. "Still think we're going to try and get away?"

Braggo loosened his longsword, checked the pair of daggers on his belt, and accepted the small, round shield that Vardan offered him.

"Remember what you look like. When you're not in a tavern, keep to the open streets," Jalist reminded him. "These Hesodi might look broken, but I'm sure there are plenty who'd love to backstab a lone Dhargot walking through an alley."

Braggo nodded. "I'll try the taverns close to the old Iron Sisters' barracks this time." He glanced at Igrid.

"Don't bother," Jalist said. "They'll just be fights and chaos tonight. Head for the taverns by the new prince's palace. That's where the officers will be. If anyone has news, it'll be them."

Vardan added, "And if anybody who outranks you asks what you're doing by yourself, remember that parchment in your pocket."

Braggo checked to make sure he still had the letter Jalist had forged from General Brahasti, ordering Braggo to Hesod on secret business. As far as Jalist had gleaned, Brahasti was somewhere up north. Still, he doubted that any Dhargot would risk incurring the infamous general's wrath by interfering with his orders. Jalist had even remembered Brahasti's signature from when they served together in the Throng.

Certain he had the letter, Braggo slipped out of the temple. Jalist glanced out the windows and saw snow falling. "Hope we don't have another damn blizzard." He considered heading for the nearby stables to check on the horses, though he doubted they would come to harm, given that the stables' proprietor seemed afraid of Jalist and his friends. So far, the fact that Jalist was a Dwarr had not roused much suspicion, though they'd seen far fewer sellswords in the Dhargots' service than they'd expected.

Jalist was strangely relieved by that. Having been a sellsword for a good portion of his life, he'd met plenty with questionable consciences. Some were downright reprehensible. But given how especially cruel the Dhargots had been lately, he was hard pressed to recall many sellswords who would happily participate in such conquests. In addition to making him feel a little better about his profession, he was glad that he'd encountered no familiar faces in Hesod, as he had no desire to answer questions.

He wondered what had become of all the mercenaries who had enlisted in the Throng. Some had been his friends. All had scattered after the Throng was disbanded outside Lyos. He guessed that those who'd survived had returned to the Free Cities or their other towns on the Simurgh Plains with hopes for a life of peace, only to face fresh hardship when the Dhargots began their rampage.

What a world the gods have given us. We hardly survive one threat, and they give us another.

He glanced up at Igrid. She'd shrugged off Jalist's cloak and girded her shortswords over her tattered clothing. She stood by the fire, warming her hands. Vardan was trying not to ogle her as he sat on the opposite side of the fire, absentmindedly sharpening his longsword. Jalist snickered. Though Igrid appeared lost in thought, he wondered if she knew full well that Vardan had his eyes on her.

Sooner or later, when his guard's down, she'll knock him senseless and make a run for it. Maybe tonight, before Braggo gets back. Can't say I blame her.

Jalist still wanted to find Rowen, and for the moment, sticking to Vardan and Braggo's mission to help him find Silwren seemed as good a way to accomplish that as any. But as dangerous as it was for him and the men of the Red Watch to be in Hesod, it was worse for Igrid. Whatever the Lyosi king had offered her, it wasn't worth the risk.

The Dwarr joined her by the fire. He licked his thumb and tested the edge on his long axe.

Igrid gave him a sidelong glance. "Are you about to try and chop my head off?"

"Not if I can help it."

"How very kind of you, Captain Hewn."

Jalist smirked. "Didn't know you knew my surname."

"I have ears and a good memory." She rubbed her hands, then flexed her fingers, cracking them. "Twenty-five thousand."

"What?"

"That's how many men the Bloody Prince marched into the city, give or take. I saw your lips moving during the procession. You were trying to count them, weren't you?"

"I was, but I gave up when my brain started to hurt."

Igrid glanced at Vardan. She readjusted one of her shortswords then her clothing. "Not sure how many are out looking for Locke or guarding the supply lines, though from what we've heard, I'd guess another five or six thousand. Plus all the Jolym."

"Sounds about right." Jalist glanced at Vardan, too. The soldier had turned away, probably so Igrid's revealing attire wouldn't distract him from keeping watch. Unfortunately, that meant he'd turned his back on her. Igrid picked up a rock. Jalist seized her wrist and shook his head. Igrid frowned, tried unsuccessfully to pull away, then dropped the rock.

"I'll tell Locke when we find him." Jalist spoke louder than necessary to muffle the sound of the rock hitting the ground. "If he ever manages to put an army together, that might be useful."

"If he's even still alive, you mean."

"He is."

"Is that a premonition or a frantic wish?"

Jalist laid down his long axe and rummaged through his pack for a loaf of hard bread. He offered it to Igrid.

She shook her head. "Even if Locke put an army together, what makes you think he'd be any good leading it? He's no general."

"And I'm no captain." Jalist nodded toward the gaping hole where the temple's gates had been. "Might want to hide those swords."

Igrid turned, following his gesture, toward a little girl peeking into the temple. The child ducked out of sight when Igrid turned, then she looked again a moment later. Jalist clicked his tongue, drawing Vardan's attention.

Igrid said, "Leave her alone."

"So she can tell all the other orphans that we're here and one of them can tell the Dhargots in exchange for not getting their hands chopped off?" Jalist nodded to Vardan, who stood and started toward the temple entrance.

Igrid drew her shortswords. "I said, leave her alone."

Vardan paused and frowned at her. "The captain's right. I'm not going to hurt her, but—"

Igrid flipped one of her shortswords, caught it by the blade, and threw it. Jalist shouted a warning, but it was too late. Before Vardan could duck, the pommel of Igrid's shortsword struck him in the nose. The soldier cursed and stumbled, waving his drawn longsword in front of him.

Igrid plucked the bread from Jalist's hand. Before he could stop her, she leapt over the fire, danced around Vardan's blade, and swung her other shortsword. The flat of her blade caught Vardan at the back of his knees, sweeping his legs out from under him. Vardan dropped his longsword, and Igrid kicked it away.

Jalist ran to separate them, but Igrid was already heading for the temple entrance, shouting for the little girl to wait. To Jalist's surprise, the little girl obeyed. She stopped in the temple entrance, staring at Igrid with wide eyes. One small hand held a ragdoll while her other hand petted the place where the doll's head had been.

Jalist helped Vardan back onto his feet. The man, muttering a vile string of curses, retrieved his longsword and started toward Igrid, blood streaming from his nose. Jalist restrained him.

At the entrance to the temple, Igrid sheathed her shortsword and dropped to one knee. She called to the little girl again. The little girl's lips moved, though Jalist could not hear her. Igrid offered her the bread. The little girl approached cautiously and took it. She backed up a little but did not run. The two spoke a moment longer, then the girl turned and ran away.

Vardan started to follow, but Jalist stopped him again. "Unless you're going to kill the poor child, the damage is done." Jalist scowled at Igrid, who rejoined them. "You realize letting her go was just as stupid as what you did to Vardan, right?"

Igrid stooped, retrieved her other shortsword, and sheathed it. She looked at the ground. Finally, she said, "The little girl said the orphans are hiding in the sewers. There are clerics with them. She asked if I was an Iron Sister."

Jalist grimaced. "Tell me you didn't tell the truth for once."

"She says there are still Iron Sisters here."

Vardan stopped cursing. Even Jalist was speechless.

"She says they're being kept prisoner beneath the palace," Igrid continued. "Hundreds of them."

Jalist found his voice. "Lies. She wanted the bread, so she told you what you wanted to hear."

"I don't think so." Igrid's voice trembled. "She says it's a secret. That bastard, Ziraari, was supposed to have them all killed, but he kept some alive for sport. One of his men took charge of them after he died. This new prince must have them now."

Vardan wiped his bleeding nose on his sleeve. "How would she know that?"

"The sewers run under the palace. She said she's heard them screaming."

"You're talking about a palace full of Dhargots," Jalist countered. "That could be *anyone* screaming. Just because you want to—"

Igrid returned to the ruined fountain, rummaged through the debris, and retrieved her original clothes and armor. Without hesitation or modesty, she cast off the tattered clothing of a slave and started dressing herself. Vardan blushed at her nudity, but Jalist cursed and grabbed her arm.

"Enough! Even if she's right, there's not a damn thing the three of us—"

Igrid twisted free and gave Jalist a shove. "Touch me again, and you'll lose that hand." She pulled on a tight undertunic and trousers then started strapping on her armor. Despite the difficulty of working the buckles by herself, her hands blurred.

Jalist said, "Even if those women are here... and gods know I'm sorry if they are... I can't do anything about this. I have to find Locke. I can't risk my neck on this."

"Then don't." Igrid finished with her vambraces then strapped tassets to her thighs and greaves to her ankles, over her boots. Lastly, she tugged her brigandine over her head. She picked up her helmet with its noseguard, stared at it a moment, then changed her mind and dropped it back into the fountain.

"You can keep the Queshi bow," she said to Jalist. "Won't be much use where I'm going."

Jalist gritted his teeth. "Dammit, woman, think for a second! Stay with us. Once we find Locke and Silwren—"

"And how many of my sisters will be left by then?"

"As many as will be left after you get yourself killed. Have you forgotten that you're in a city full of Dhargots? The moment you walk out of here dressed like that, half the city will know about it."

Igrid paused. Then she threw Jalist's cloak over her shoulders and fixed the clasp at her throat. "Better?"

Despite himself, Jalist almost smiled.

"Listen to him, woman," Vardan grumbled. "I don't care if you fight like Zet himself. You'll never make it into the palace."

"I'm not going into the palace. I'm going under it." Igrid gathered her long red hair, started to tie it behind her head, then stopped. She drew a knife, tugged her braid over her shoulder, and sawed it off. She glanced at the hair, slightly surprised, as though she had not realized what she was doing, then she shrugged and let it fall. Pulling up the hood of her cloak to cover the rest, she took a step.

Jalist blocked her path. "All this based on the word of one hungry child you don't even know? Listen, before we left Lyos, you told me you wanted to be rich by the time this war was over. See this through, and you will be. But not if you do this."

Igrid was quiet for a time. Then she turned to Vardan, eyeing the drawn longsword in his hand. "I'm doing this, Lyosi. If you want to fight over it, step forward. I'm ready to die if you are." She rested both hands on her sword hilts.

Vardan frowned at her. He glanced at Jalist then back at Igrid. His frown became a smile. He sheathed his longsword. "Luck, Iron Sister. Gods know you'll need it." He plucked a knife from his boot and passed it to her, hilt first. Igrid accepted it with a terse nod and slid it into her belt. Then she turned back to Jalist.

"Tell Locke..." Biting her lip, she trailed off.

"Listen," Jalist tried one last time. "Just wait a moment, damn you. I'm telling you I need your help. Locke needs your help. If you'll just—"

A shrill horn blast echoed through the winter air. Unlike the trumpet blasts that had accompanied Prince Karhaati's procession, the blast sounded far away, well beyond the city walls. A second blast accompanied the first, then another, then another.

"That's a Dhargot horn," Jalist realized. "Someone's calling for help."

"There's no army around to threaten them," Igrid said.

Jalist caught her meaning. He looked at Vardan. "Find Braggo. Bring him back here."

Vardan leapt into motion, sprinting toward the temple entrance.

Jalist tried to summon the right words to convince Igrid to stay. She faced him, resolute, smiling faintly. Finally, Jalist sighed. He stepped forward and embraced her. Igrid tensed then hugged him back.

"Go help him," Igrid said as they parted. "And... tell him I'm sorry."

Jalist hesitated, then reached into the fountain and snatched up Igrid's bow, along with a quiver of arrows. He gave her one final look then hefted his long axe and strode out of the temple without looking back.

CHAPTER TWENTY-FIVE

IN THE SEWERS,
IN THE DARK

J ALIST RAN TO THE STABLES, where a squad of Dhargots was already saddling their horses, speculating in fearful whispers what they would find beyond the walls, but Jalist was faster. He pressed all the coins he had left into a stableboy's hands, ordering him to saddle Vardan's horse while he saddled his own, then Braggo's. He considered waiting then changed his mind. He told the stableboy to wait with the other horses then mounted his own. The Dhargots were still fussing with their saddles and trying to strap armor to their horses when Jalist rode out.

He'd hoped to be the first one out through the gates, but his stomach sank when he saw a second squad of Dhargothi spearmen already marching ahead of him in tight formation. A young officer led them on horseback. He spotted Jalist and shouted, probably demanding to know what Jalist was doing on his own, but Jalist spurred his horse and drove on ahead of him.

Beyond the city walls, the snows deepened despite a rough trail leading away from the gates. Jalist shivered, cursing Igrid for taking his cloak—even though it might very well save her life. He tried to urge his horse into a gallop, but the beast labored to carry him. Jalist glanced over his shoulder, glad that he'd at least outdistanced the Dhargothi footmen. He made it down one hill, then his horse became mired in the snows at the base of another. He dismounted and pulled his horse through the drifts, up the next hill one laborious step at a time. Shouts and screams drove him on. Then, sweating and exhausted, he paused at the top of the hill and looked westward.

At the base of yet another hill in the distance, a squad of Dhargothi cavalry was doing its best to outrun a rampaging band of Olgrym. Most were driving their horses as fast as they could through the snow, but some had either been thrown off their horses or been forced to stop and fight. Another Dhargot rode ahead of the rest, frantically blowing his horn and looking behind him at every step.

The charging mass of Olgrym howled, shaking Jalist down to his bones. He thought back to the Olgish charge he'd witnessed at Que'ahl, when one Olg after another had doused itself in pitch, lit its own body on fire, then hurled itself at the Sylvan fort. Jalist shuddered. He considered running. Then he saw a bright glint in the distance, accompanied by a wild slash of azure.

"Gods…"

He stared a moment, torn with indecision, then spurred his horse down the hill. He fumbled with his bow, trying to fit an arrow to the string. He'd just done so when the land in front of him blossomed into a scalding wash of violet fire.

Igrid considered trying to make her way through the city by sticking to shadows and alleys and entering the sewers closer to the palace, but she quickly changed her mind. Thanks to the arrival of the Bloody Prince's army, the streets roiled with armed men. Some rushed toward the western gates to see what was happening, but most still prowled the streets of Hesod, looking for trouble. Some of the Dhargots fought each other, but most simply tormented the Hesodi.

Igrid saw laughing Dhargots pelting a street vendor with melons from his cart. They didn't even seem to notice that the old man had stopped moving. A block later, she passed an old woman being stripped naked and hung from a defaced statue of the Iron Sisters. Igrid's face burned. She gripped the hilts of her swords but forced herself to lower her head and keep moving.

Shortly after, she saw a young woman—probably one of the last young women left in the city—being dragged into an alley by two Dhargots. Igrid started to pass them then changed her mind. She followed them into the alley, quietly drawing her shortswords. The first sliced through a Dhargot's neck. The second caught the other man in the throat as he turned, wide eyed.

Igrid freed her blades, turned, and saw a third Dhargot watching her from the street. She cursed. She made ready to throw her blade, but the Dhargot ran, shouting. She grabbed the young woman's arm and pulled her to her feet. The young woman's expression was dull and hopeless. She was not even crying. Igrid wondered how many times this had already happened. She shook her.

"I need to get into the sewers. The closest way. Show me."

The young woman blinked. She looked at Igrid then at the slain Dhargots, as though seeing them for the first time. She nodded. She led Igrid down the alley, up a deserted street, then down a second alley. Igrid heard shouting and the sound of boots stomping the flagstones behind her. She told the woman to hurry.

As they emerged from the second alley, they nearly collided with an elderly couple fleeing a single drunken Dhargot waving a drawn sword with one hand and a bottle with the other. Igrid sidestepped the couple, sank to one knee, and cut one of the Dhargot's legs out from under him. The couple kept running, but the young woman waited. The Dhargot howled. Igrid hoped their pursuers might stop long enough to help him.

The young woman led her down yet another alley then pointed at a cistern. She blinked at Igrid then ran. Igrid glanced over one shoulder. Either she'd lost her pursuers, or they'd chosen an easier target. After sheathing one of her blades, she used the other to pry up the cistern's heavy cover. An indescribable stench rolled out. She nearly dropped the lid but forced herself to look down. Wet, rough-hewn steps descended into darkness. Pinching her nose, Igrid lowered herself into the darkness, stopping halfway to drag the heavy lid over the hole.

Igrid closed her eyes, squelching her rising sense of panic. She took a moment to gather her senses, noting the cold water soaking into her boots. She took several shallow breaths through her mouth. Then, when she could manage it, she forced herself to breathe in through her nose. Somehow, she did not retch. She forced herself to take several more breaths until she reasoned she was as used to it as she was likely to become. Then she moved sideways until the ground sloped slightly upward, out of the water and filth. She found a wall and followed it.

The sounds of murder and chaos from the streets above barely reached her. For a time, she heard nothing but the trickling of water and the dreadful skittering of rat claws. Then she heard footsteps running through the water. Igrid hurried toward the sound, gripping her sword in the dark. Then she slipped. She managed to keep her face from falling into the foul water, but the stench filled her nostrils, striking her as though for the first time. Worse, she lost her sword.

She groped for it in the foul water, cursing, but it was gone. Finally, drawing her second shortsword, she started forward again. She headed in the direction of the footsteps. She heard them again. Fearful whispers accompanied the footsteps.

"Don't run," Igrid spoke into the darkness. "I won't hurt you. I'm an Iron Sister. My name's Igrid."

No one answered. She wondered if the children were holding their breath. *Smart,* she thought. She called out again. This time, the children ran. Igrid followed. A slant of light through a grate in the ceiling revealed two little boys and a girl, all dressed in rags, holding hands as they ran.

Igrid let them get well ahead of her. Sheathing her sword, she followed cautiously, careful not to slip. She passed beneath another grate. Waning sunlight from the city above revealed a badly decomposing corpse lying facedown in the muck. Igrid edged around it and kept going.

Ahead of her, the sewers branched off in two directions. Igrid figured the left tunnel was more likely to lead toward the palace, but she heard whispers coming from the right. She chose the right. Another grate illuminated what looked like a dead dog crawling with rats. Igrid drew her sword and hacked at one that came too close. She pressed herself against the cold wall and edged around the rest.

The sewers branched off again, though garbage almost completely blocked the left tunnel. Picking her way around a broken cart and a pile of what looked like broken furniture, she headed down the left tunnel. She heard voices. Ahead, the tunnel widened. Torchlight shone off wet stone. Igrid sheathed her sword and held up her hands. She approached slowly.

Three clerics, all old men, appeared before her. The filth caked to their robes made it impossible to tell which deity they served, but all held weapons. One also held a torch. A second torch blazed in a bracket on the wall. Beyond them, a throng of dirty children huddled behind two priestesses—one young, one old—in equally filthy robes. Like the men, both were armed.

"I'm not a Dhargot." Igrid lowered her hood. "I'm an Iron Sister. My name—"

"We heard you earlier," one of the old men said. "There aren't any more Iron Sisters."

"That's not what I hear."

The old men exchanged looks. The young woman stepped forward. "There aren't any more running free, he means."

Igrid gave them a crooked smile in the torchlight. "I'm hoping to change that."

"Then you're an army short," another of the old men said. He stepped ahead of the others. "Are you the one who gave Thessa the apple?"

"Bread," Igrid corrected. "Easy, priest. I'm no spy."

"Who knows what the Dhargots would do?" the old woman objected. "Protect the children. Kill her to be safe."

The children watched with wide, dark eyes. Igrid noted that many of them had armed themselves with rocks or shards of pottery. A moment later, she spotted the little girl she'd met earlier, though the child looked decidedly less friendly now. Igrid faced the old priest she took to be the leader. "Do I look like I'm in league with the Dhargots? I already killed two of the bastards getting down here—" She stopped herself, realizing her mistake, but it was too late.

"She'll bring trouble down on us," one of the priests said. He brandished a rusty cleaver. "Armahg will forgive us." He started forward.

Igrid grabbed his wrist and twisted, stopping short of breaking his wrist.

The priest screamed. The cleaver fell into the water and disappeared. Igrid released the priest and stepped back. She held up her hands again.

"The only ones I plan to bring trouble on are the Dhargots. Now, point me toward the palace." She withdrew a pouch of coins and tossed it to the leader.

The leader caught the pouch, but instead of opening it, he narrowed his eyes, scrutinizing Igrid. "If you're an Iron Sister, you should already know your way around the city."

"The barracks and the taverns, I know. Not the sewers."

"I don't recognize you."

"I don't recognize you, either. What of it?"

"Clerics bear witness when each new Iron Sister receives her steel."

"They're *supposed* to, but most don't bother. Besides, do you remember every single woman who knelt before Queen Sharra and said her vows?"

The leader hesitated. Finally, he sighed. He lowered a rusty shortsword and pointed. "Down there. Middle tunnel, then left, then right. Up the stairs. There's a grate, but it's chained shut."

"I'll pick the lock." Igrid repeated the directions in her mind so that she wouldn't forget them. "And the Iron Sisters?"

"In a dungeon under the palace, we think," the young priestess said. "After the grate, keep right. You'll find a locked door then a stairwell. Dungeon's at the top—"

"You'll hear it long before you find it," the leader interrupted.

Igrid caught his meaning. "Thank you. While I'm gone, I suggest you find a different place to hide these children. Better yet, get them out on the plains and head south, toward Atheion. I'll buy you some time." She started past them.

The leader touched her arm. "This won't make any difference, child. Even if you free them, arm them, and make it out of the palace, there are too many Dhargots. You won't make it out of the city."

"But we might make it to the Bloody Prince's bedroom. That counts for something." Igrid tapped her sword hilt.

"If you free the Iron Sisters, bring them back down into the sewers," the young priestess said. "You can get them out of the city that way." Some of the other clerics scowled at her, but she ignored them. "They'll follow you, but some of you might get away."

Igrid thought of Rowen and Silwren. If they could meet her on the surface, Silwren might drive back the Dhargots long enough for the Sisters to get away. She cursed herself for parting ways with Jalist so quickly. Even if the Dwarr told Locke what she was doing, and even if Locke decided to try and help her, they would have no idea where she might emerge.

Once we're outside the city, the Dhargots can ride us down like grass. Atheion's too far away. She tapped her sword hilt again. *At least if we get to Karhaati, we can do some good before we die.*

She considered the matter then made up her mind. She thanked the clerics again and winked at Thessa. The girl stepped forward.

"You cut your hair." She sounded disappointed.

"Easier to hide," Igrid said, then strode off toward what she was sure would be her death.

When Jalist regained his senses, he found himself lying in the snow, staring up at a twilit sky. He took a breath. His chest hurt, but he managed to sit up. Turning, he spotted his horse in the distance, milling with other riderless horses. He turned his head the other direction and saw charred corpses in the distance. A slash of azure caught his eye. Then he heard trumpets. This time, they sounded from behind him, back in the city.

Jalist forced himself to move. He crawled to his long axe then used it like a crutch to push himself back onto his feet. His ankle hurt, but he did not think it was broken. He spotted the Queshi bow in the snow where he'd been lying a moment before. In breaking his fall, the bow had snapped in half. He turned back toward the glimpse of azure and stumbled toward it.

He found Rowen Locke lying on his back, arms splayed, pale and wide eyed. Charred, unrecognizable corpses surrounded him. Fire had scorched Rowen's kingsteel armor and burnt away most of his azure tunic. The expression on his face made Jalist's skin crawl. Jalist thought he must be dead, too, but then the Isle Knight blinked. He stared up at the sky then at Jalist, uncomprehending.

Jalist grinned. But before he could speak, a sound drew his attention back toward Hesod. He looked up to see two Dhargots riding toward him. More followed on foot. Then a curious thing happened. One of the Dhargothi horsemen twisted in the saddle, raised a crossbow, and fired wildly at the footmen. The second horsemen spotted Jalist and waved, shouting.

Jalist laughed. Then he gave Rowen a gentle kick. "Get up, you fool. We'll swap mad stories later." He turned toward his horse and whistled. The beast, still fearful, hesitated then sauntered over. Jalist caught the reins. "Get up!" he shouted when he saw that Rowen had not moved. Slowly, the Knight sat up. A curved sword lay beside him, half buried in the snow. Rowen stared at it, then seized it.

By the time Vardan and Braggo joined them, Rowen had managed to rise to his knees. Jalist dropped his long axe and used both hands to haul Rowen onto his feet. Braggo dismounted and helped Jalist lift Rowen onto Jalist's horse. Rowen slumped forward, shaking, hugging his sword against his chest.

Vardan frowned, struggling to reload his crossbow. "Where's the wytch?"

"Not here." Jalist turned, debating which riderless horse he might catch first.

Braggo cursed and pointed.

The Dhargothi footmen had closed ranks and were marching steadily toward them, shields locked. Jalist guessed that Vardan had already killed their leader, hoping to slow them down, but a second force of Dhargots—all on horseback—had just crested the hill. Braggo held out his hand, offering to pull Jalist onto his own horse.

Jalist shook his head. "You won't get away with me weighing you down."

"And you won't get away on foot."

Jalist turned to Rowen. The Knight looked dazed and fearful. Jalist thought of the purple flames and glanced down at the charred remains of the Olgrym. "Just get Locke out of here. He's the one that matters."

"Like hell. We came for the wytch." Vardan lifted his crossbow, aimed, and fired. He started reloading immediately, without waiting to see if he'd struck his target.

Jalist glanced at Rowen's sword. "I think she's gone."

Braggo said, "But we saw wytchfire—"

"That was Locke. Don't ask me to explain. Just get him out of here." Jalist stooped, wincing from the pain in his ankle, and retrieved his long axe. "I'll hold them back as long as I can."

Braggo and Vardan exchanged looks. Vardan turned back to the Dhargots, lifted his crossbow, and fired. Braggo said, "They'll just ride around you." He dismounted, threw Jalist his reins, and ran toward the nearest riderless horse.

Jalist swore at him then pulled himself up into the saddle. He faced Vardan. "We'll split up. You and Braggo—"

"Too late. They're too close." Vardan fired again then dropped his crossbow. He drew his longsword. "Get going, Captain. We'll take care of this."

Before Jalist could answer, Vardan spurred his horse toward the Dhargots, shouting at the top of his lungs. Braggo flew past a moment later on a new horse. He drew his sword, turned in the saddle, and saluted Jalist. Then he added his wild shout to Vardan's. Both men of the Red Watch drove through the snow, steel glinting, straight for the advancing mass of Dhargots.

Jalist stared, watching the first furious clash of steel, then shook himself out of his stupor. Catching the reins to Rowen's horse, he tugged it around. He slapped the horse's flanks with the flat of his axe. The horse leapt into motion. Jalist followed, wind raking his damp eyes.

CHAPTER TWENTY-SIX

THE BLOODY PRINCE AND THE IRON SISTER

K ARHAATI WISHED HE WERE BACK in Cassica. That city had been wretched, too, but its people had already been broken once before when the Throng attacked and the Nightmare tore down their walls. That made them more malleable. In Hesod, Karhaati could practically smell rebellion. Normally, he would have relished the challenge of breaking these people, but he had already tasted plenty of that at Cassica and Quorim. He wanted spoils of another kind.

The Bloody Prince refilled his cup. Before drinking, he stopped to appreciate the cup's raised carvings of bare-breasted women swinging swords at dragons. Despite his foul mood, he laughed. He drank then lowered the cup and glanced at the maps and quartermaster reports scattered across his desk.

"What's so damn important about one Knight?"

He glared at the circle on the map that signified Hesod. There was no one around worth fighting. The Dragonkin had enlisted Karhaati's Lochurite berserkers, whom he was glad to be rid of, but had insisted that his Jolym needed no additional help in conquering Atheion. Karhaati's mission was simply to waste time and energy sending his legions to catch a single man.

Karhaati shook his head at the absurdity and shoved the maps aside. Weren't there plenty of Isle Knights left on the Lotus Isles, all ripe for killing? The Dragonkin had said something about a dangerous magic sword, but it all sounded like childish fairytales. Karhaati had other, more pressing matters: the continued defiance of his brother, Saanji, and his Earless; planning invasions of Lyos and Ivairia; and of course, the eventual necessity of killing his father and assuming rule over the Dhargothi Empire.

But as proud as he was, Karhaati was not about to defy his new ally. Not yet, anyway.

He shuddered, remembering how effortlessly the Dragonkin's Jolym had torn Karhaati's cavalry to shreds, sparing him alone. Karhaati's horse had been cut out from under him, his sword shattered. The Jolym quietly encircled him, their blades and armor splattered with blood, their backs unfazed by the arrows raining down on them from Cassica's battlements. Then Chorlga appeared, standing over him, grinning like a wolf that had just eaten its fill. Karhaati thought he was about to die, but instead, Chorlga had offered him an alliance.

He killed three hundred of my best riders and shamed me in front of my own host... all just to prove a point.

The disgrace in front of his men irked him the most, especially given all he had done recently to cull disobedience and cowardice from the ranks, but he could do little in reprisal. According to the stories, even Dragonkin were not immortal, but assassination was a tricky prospect. Chorlga was surrounded at all times by Jolym. Even had they been absent, Shel'ai could read minds and cast unnatural fire from their bare hands. Surely, that went double for Dragonkin. Karhaati had taken care to avoid any thoughts of violence toward Chorlga until the Dragonkin announced that he was going to Atheion, leaving the Isle Knight's capture in Karhaati's hands.

Karhaati considered the Isle Knight's sword. Whatever it was, Chorlga seemed afraid of it. That meant Karhaati might benefit from defying the Dragonkin's orders and forming an alliance with the Isle Knight instead. Word had it that the Dragonkin's Jolym had already destroyed most of the Lotus Isles and crippled the Knighthood. The Isle Knight might jump at the chance for a strong ally like Karhaati.

But what could the Knight offer me?

Karhaati did not understand the magic of the Knight's sword, nor did he care to. If the Knight wanted to live, he would have to do more. He would have to eliminate the Dragonkin... and fast, before Karhaati's men began to worship Chorlga. Once Chorlga was gone, killing a lone, trusting Isle Knight would be a simple matter.

"Foolish thoughts," he muttered. Until he had the Knight in chains, this reflection was pointless. He was better off focusing on sending more agents to Brahasti's compound so that the brilliant but disobedient general could either be dragged back into Karhaati's service or made to wish he had. But even that prospect seemed tedious.

There are always the Iron Sisters...

Karhaati's pulse quickened. He had not seen them yet, but several of Ziraari's generals had told him Ziraari's plan: to keep the Iron Sisters for his own amusement until the proper time, then send them to Karhaati as a gift. Only when Karhaati opened the slave wagons, he would find that the Iron Sisters had been armed. Even if they didn't kill him, so many of his men being killed by women would be a disgrace even more damning than what Chorlga had done to him.

But Ziraari was dead. The Iron Sisters were Karhaati's. He thought about sending the women back to his father. After all, Ziraari's plan had been a good one. But that could wait. He thought of all those strong, supple women chained in the dark. Rising from his chair, he drank his wine slowly, savoring it, running his thumb over the carved surface of the cup. Then he set the cup down, loosened his belt, and decided it was time to pay the Iron Sisters a visit.

Igrid wondered if her luck had finally changed for the better. She'd ascended without incident from the sewers into the Hesodi palace, followed the clerics' directions to the dungeons, and found two Dhargots asleep at their post. Torches burned low in brackets fixed to the wall next to them. They sat at a table just outside the cells, near a narrow stairwell that presumably led higher into the palace. Igrid crept out, stood in front of the guards, then peered around the corner. Another Dhargot stood with his back turned. He stood just outside a cell filled with women, sword drawn, whispering vulgar things through the iron bars. The women ignored him.

Igrid returned her attention to the first two guards. She eased her shortsword from its scabbard, drawing it between her fingers to muffle the scrape of steel on leather. Then she drew the dagger that Vardan had given her. She took a deep breath to calm her nerves. Then she leaned forward and stabbed both sleeping men in their throats.

They jerked awake, wide eyed, blood bubbling from their lips. One of the men stood, reached futilely for Igrid, and crashed to the floor. Igrid had already yanked her blades free. She turned. The third guard stepped around the corner. Though he still had his sword drawn, he frowned, as though he only meant to chide his comrades for making too much noise.

Igrid leapt forward, biting back the urge to fuel her limbs with a feverish battle cry. Her shortsword swung high, arcing for the Dhargot's face. He saw it coming and raised his own sword to block. But Igrid's sword pulled up short, just before their blades would have met in a loud clang. She kicked the Dhargot's knee. That stunned him long enough for her to bob, weave, and bury Vardan's dagger in his right eye.

Releasing the dagger, she pressed her hand over the Dhargot's mouth to muffle his death cries. He dropped his sword. She cursed as it clattered off the stone. She dragged him away from the doorway and dumped his corpse behind the table with the others. Snatching up the Dhargot's fallen blade, she braced herself, a sword in each hand. She heard drunken laughter and whimpering in the distance, but no running footsteps.

Satisfied, she searched the three men's corpses. She found daggers, a crude wooden carving of the Dragongod, and a pouch of coins, but no keys. She cursed again. Making sure the corpses were out of sight behind the table, she leaned against the wall, crouched low, and looked around the corner.

Before her lay a great, dim chamber lined on one side with iron cells. The stench of filth and misery, almost as bad as the odor in the sewers, filled her nostrils. All the cells roiled with strong-limbed women—some nude, others dressed in rags. At least one lay on the ground, wrapped in bloody gauze, unmoving.

A few women looked at her. Igrid pressed one blade to her lips, like a finger, calling for silence. The women nodded. With seasoned quickness, they turned away from her, sitting down or staring at the wall. Still, Igrid heard some of them whispering and knew it was only a matter of time before the guards sensed something was amiss.

Igrid ducked out of sight and listened again, just in case a Dhargot had spotted her. She took another deep breath. Then she leaned out a second time, taking stock of the situation. Her stomach lurched.

Opposite the overcrowded cells lay disorderly rows of animal cages, obviously dragged down there after the cells had been filled. Each cage contained one or two women. Some knelt, as though in meditation. Others wept and rocked themselves. Dhargots paced the rows, some with sticks or drawn swords, which they used to poke at the cages. But most of the Dhargots seemed to have tired of the sport and had gathered at the far end of the chamber. They filled three long tables, drinking and gambling, while others slept on adjacent straw pallets.

Igrid counted, cursed, then turned back to the cells. She grimaced at the cells' iron locks. While the cages looked to be of Dhargothi make, with doors secured only by small crude locks that could easily be broken off, the cells were another matter. They were Hesodi design, with heavy, complex locks that would have made a thief's heart sink. At best, she would only be able to pick one before she was spotted.

But one might be all I need.

Igrid went back to the slain Dhargots and took off one of their cloaks. She replaced her robe with the Dhargot's then picked up a helmet and slipped it on. It reeked of sweat. She hoped the dead man wouldn't give her lice. Sheathing her own sword, she slid a Dhargot's blade into her empty scabbard, armed herself with as many daggers as she could fit into her belt, and went to work.

She forced herself to walk boldly into the room. She stopped before the closest cell. Keeping her back to the guards on the other end of the chamber, she drew her thinnest knife and inserted the tip into the lock. Women pressed toward her. Some whispered questions. A tall, dark-skinned woman pushed in front of the others, hissing for them to be quiet. They fell back. The dark-skinned woman gripped the cell bars. A faint smile touched her lips.

"Igrid."

Igrid blinked. "Ailynn?" Igrid hardly recognized her former captain. Ailynn's hair hung in a long dark braid against her breasts. Her dark Soroccan body bristled with scars, some of them recent, including one that stretched from her bottom lip to her chin, interrupting her smile. Igrid blushed. "I thought…"

"I died with Queen Sharra?" Ailynn shook her head. "Some killed themselves to avoid capture. Others kept fighting. I chose the latter." She glanced over Igrid's shoulder. "Stop gawking and work that damn knife! They haven't seen you yet, but they will."

Igrid returned her attention to the lock, gently wiggling the tip of her dagger, trying to feel the mechanism through the blade. A moment later, she cursed. "I can't…" She glanced to the side and saw the occupants of the other cells watching, too.

"Breathe, child," Ailynn told her. "I know where you came from. You're better at this than I am."

Igrid met Ailynn's gaze, nodded, and returned her attention to the lock. A man shouted in the distance. The shout was followed by laughter. The Dhargots were calling out to her, thinking she was one of their comrades opening the cell for a bit of fun. Some teased while others reminded her not to open the cell without help.

Igrid felt a lump in her throat. She was running out of time. Her hands were sweating, making it harder to hold the dagger. The Dhargots called to her from across the chamber again. The teasing turned to angry shouts when she did not answer. She heard men pushing back their chairs and rising to their feet.

Then the lock clicked open.

Instead of opening the door, Igrid reached through the bars and gave Ailynn her dagger. "I'll slow them down. Get to work on the next cell." Ailynn plucked two more daggers from Igrid's belt, passed them to the women beside her, and nodded.

Igrid stepped back. The cell door opened. Women rushed out. The Dhargots shouted in rage and surprise then drew their swords. Igrid glanced at the doorway. She realized there was still time. She'd given the Iron Sisters a fighting chance. If she wanted, she could run back down to the sewers. She could save herself.

Igrid stared at the Dhargots scurrying up from the tables, arming themselves. To her surprise, she laughed. Then she tossed away the helmet. Despite the lump in her throat, she flashed the men a crooked smile.

"Well, I don't have all night. Come and die, you bastards."

Karhaati was only halfway down the stairs when he heard the clash of steel. At one, he turned sideways on the stairwell and drew his longsword. He considered calling for his bodyguards, whom he'd left at the top of the stairs, then decided against it. He heard the battle cry of a lone woman, punctuated by men's grunts, then a man's sharp cry of pain.

One of the Iron Sisters had gotten hold of a blade.

Karhaati leaned against the wall of the stairwell, listening. He imagined the look on the face of whatever careless guard must have been raping an Iron Sister when she plucked a dagger from his belt and slashed his throat. He imagined her rolling his body off hers, her face washed in his blood. He visualized her rising off the stone floor, naked, drawing the dead man's sword off his corpse—maybe screaming in defiance before she threw herself at the next target, as wild as an animal.

Karhaati smiled. He heard another man scream. Other men cursed, followed by what sounded like a table being overturned. The cries of women joined in—probably fellow Iron Sisters, shouting encouragement from their cells, unaware of the punishment awaiting them.

Steel clashed again, echoing up the stairwell. Karhaati's bodyguards had started down on their own, but he stopped them with a gesture. He was in no danger, and there were more than enough guards down there to handle one escaped woman with a sword. Closing his eyes, he leaned against the wall and listened. The woman's wild, sweet battle cry reached his ears. A moment later, he heard her gasp. He imagined her hurt, blood running down one arm as she fought to stay alive. He thought about loosening his belt in response to his growing feelings of lust, but a new sound interrupted the chaos: an iron gate swinging open.

More women cried out from the dungeon, offering battle cries of their own. Karhaati opened his eyes. He straightened. His smile became a scowl. Glancing back at his bodyguards, he snapped his fingers. He waited a moment for them to catch up then started down the stairs.

The woman tried in vain to lift her cheek off the cold stone floor. Somehow, she'd fallen in a pool of water, though she could not remember how. The water smelled like old coins. It reminded her of how her hands had smelled after she spent all day begging for coins outside a temple in the slums of the Dark Quarter.

My name was Ilreeth then... or was it Anza? She blinked. *Why do I have so many names?*

She tried to make her eyes focus, but all she saw was a wild blur of color swirling in front of her—some red, mostly gray. She blinked again. Slowly, a woman's face took shape, pressed against stone, staring back at her. The woman's eyes were brown. Half her face was red. She did not blink.

Is that my face? She felt a surge of panic. She tried once more to lift her head. A sharp pain made her wince. When the pain passed, she tried again. This time, beyond the dead woman lying next to her, she saw new shapes in the distance—more men, fighting. She saw more women, too. Women with swords. She blinked.

Igrid. My name is Igrid.

She fumbled for her sword and finally found it on the floor next to her. Blood covered half its surface. The sight of the blood reminded her of the wetness on her face. Pressing one hand to the gash in her forehead, Igrid snatched up her sword and tried to rise. A dying man collapsed in front of her, almost hitting her. His brown, pleading eyes found hers. Igrid recoiled. She pushed herself onto her feet, reeled, and almost fell. Someone grabbed her arm.

"You're still alive," Ailynn shouted, "but you won't stay that way if you don't start making that sword dance." She pushed Igrid aside and stabbed a Dhargot in the face.

Igrid nodded dumbly. Her whole body hurt. Glancing down at her tattered, bloody armor, she wondered how many times she'd already been cut. She decided it didn't matter. Turning, she spotted a Dhargot in swordlock with another Iron Sister. The Iron Sister lost her balance and fell to one knee.

Igrid stepped forward, stabbed the man in the back, and wrenched the sword from his grasp as he fell. She turned. She barely crossed both swords in time to stop an incoming axe. Sparks showered her. The shock of the blow shook her arms. The Dhargot howled, his face so close that she felt his spit as he screamed obscenities at her.

Igrid wanted to twist sideways and break free, but her legs did not seem to work. Her arms trembled. The Dhargot started to force her down. Then his eyes widened. The Iron Sister she had just saved withdrew her blade, nodded to her, then turned to find another opponent.

Igrid followed suit. She backstabbed another Dhargot then held a second in swordlock long enough for another Iron Sister to do the same. But then that woman fell, and Igrid was backpedaling, trying to fend off three Dhargots at once.

Ailynn saved her again. The Captain of the Iron Sisters stepped smoothly into the Dhargots' path. Like Igrid, she held a sword in each hand. Two more women followed her. One fell, but the rest of the Dhargots retreated.

"Formation!" Ailynn screamed.

As Igrid paused to catch her breath, other Iron Sisters rushed to join them. All had armed themselves, but a glance at the floor showed that many had already fallen. Meanwhile, the remaining Dhargots had pulled into a tight formation of their own and were retreating toward the far wall. As they passed cages still containing captive Iron Sisters, they thrust their swords between the bars.

Igrid bristled. They'd managed to open all the cells and hack open some of the cages, but a third of their sisters had not yet been freed. The Dhargots set about slaughtering these as quickly as possible. Igrid turned to Ailynn. She expected the captain to order a charge so that they could try to save as many of their sisters as possible.

Ailynn's eyes found hers. Ailynn shook her head. "Hold formation," she said in a low, steady voice. She handed one of her swords to a woman who was unarmed, then stooped to pick up a shield. She slid the straps over one bloody arm. Then, otherwise nude, she took up position in front of the others.

Some of the other Iron Sisters stooped to grab helmets. A few pulled cloaks or leather jerkins off the dead. But most of the Iron Sisters still had little or nothing by way of clothing, let alone armor. Igrid tried to ignore the plight of her caged sisters and count the remaining Dhargots.

"We outnumber them," she called out. "Let's finish off these bastards and go find the Bloody Prince!"

A few women cheered, but Ailynn scowled. "I said, hold your ground." She edged closer to Igrid. "How far to the sewers?"

"Right around the corner," Igrid said, "but we can't leave the rest of our sisters in cages!"

"The Dhargots have armor. We don't. They'll have reinforcements here any second. We go now, or we *all* die."

Igrid turned to the Iron Sisters being stabbed through the bars of their cages. Some shouted defiant curses at the Dhargots. A few wept. Others died quietly. None called out for help.

Igrid felt tears running from her eyes, mingling with the blood on her face. She considered charging the Dhargots anyway, in defiance of Ailynn's orders. Then she heard a scream of warning from behind her. She turned in time to see a squad of Dhargots barreling into the dungeon. Unlike the others, they wore extravagant armor draped in silk.

"Those aren't regular guards," Ailynn muttered. She shouted new orders, telling the women to pull back into a tight rectangular formation and prepare to repel attacks from two sides. Meanwhile, more confident, the Dhargothi prison guards charged again. The woman to Igrid's right went down, then a spear caught the woman behind her. The Dhargots came at them from two sides, driving them back inch by bloody inch toward their cells.

Igrid glanced at the door, now separated from them by twenty armed men, with more probably on the way. She shouted at Ailynn, "Either we break out now, or we die!"

Ailynn bashed her shield into a Dhargot's face, cleaved the top of his skull, and nodded. Moments later, the captain led half the Iron Sisters in a reckless charge toward the door. The Dhargots beat them back. Then Igrid spotted a single Dhargot in their midst, bigger than the rest. A bloodstained longsword sang in his grasp, faster than she would have thought possible. Unlike the other Dhargots, he wore an open silk tunic. And he laughed.

Igrid tried to tell Ailynn who she thought that was, but Ailynn did not seem to hear her over the din of battle. The Dhargots answered Ailynn's charge with twin charges of their own. The Iron Sisters threw them back, at great cost. Ailynn attempted yet another reckless charge at Karhaati's force. Karhaati answered by placing himself at the thick of the fighting. He drove forward, cutting down one Iron Sister after another.

Then he met Ailynn in a furious flash of steel—Ailynn shouting, Karhaati laughing. Igrid struggled to help, fighting desperately to stay at the side of her former captain. But then the prison guards charged with renewed fury, as though anxious to impress their prince. Igrid lost sight of Ailynn. The Iron Sisters' lines buckled. The prison guards drove a wedge between them.

But Igrid saw at once that the prison guards had overextended their lines. They could be flanked now. Better yet, a few Iron Sisters might even slip back and free more women from the few cages left untouched. Igrid pointed with one sword. She shouted fresh orders. To her relief, a few of the Iron Sisters obeyed.

Then, shouting Ailynn's name, Igrid led her own charge against the prison guards. Iron Sisters, savage and quick, fought on either side of her. While the Dhargots fighting Ailynn's force held their ground, the ones fighting Igrid's force withered. Then Karhaati's force fell back, too, retreating out the door.

The Iron Sisters followed, aided by more of their fellows. Igrid could not see Ailynn and Karhaati, but she imagined their fight must have spilled into the hallway beyond the dungeons. She followed, stepping over dead men and women, their bodies splashed with torchlight. Then she spotted Ailynn. The Soroccan woman lay unmoving on the floor, her eyes wide. Something had happened to her hair.

Igrid lifted her head. Karhaati stood on the stairwell, his tunic open, blood splashed across his face and chest. Dhargots formed a protective circle around him. Some shouted up the stairs for reinforcements, especially archers. Karhaati's eyes met Igrid's. The Bloody Prince grinned. He lifted something to his face. Igrid saw that it was a long, dark braid. Karhaati sniffed it. Then he draped it around his neck like a necklace.

Igrid screamed with rage. She started forward then stopped herself.

More Iron Sisters spilled out into the hallway. More Dhargots appeared in front of her, massing on the stairs. Karhaati started casually up the stairs, his bloody sword resting against his shoulder. Dhargots closed around him. Igrid took a deep breath and let it go. She glanced over her shoulder toward the other stairwell that led down into the sewers.

"Retreat," she said finally.

CHAPTER TWENTY-SEVEN

HANDS OF FIRE

A BROAD, FROZEN SEA LAY BEFORE him, stretching on as far as he could discern. A faint dusting of snow covered the ice. He shivered. His breath fogged the air. Sundown spilled through the clouds, splashing across the ice. It was utterly silent.

Rowen frowned. He was on the Wintersea. But that did not seem possible.

He looked down at his clothes. He wore a tattered leather jerkin, trousers, gloves, and boots. The gloves were too small, the boots too big. His only other item of clothing, a mouse-brown cloak, had been patched and sewn in a dozen places.

"I should be wearing armor."

He parted his cloak to reveal an Ivairian-style shortsword.

"Knightswrath. What happened to Knightswrath?"

He looked around, searching the ice at his feet. He looked behind him. For some reason, he'd expected to see mountains and green fields in the distance. Instead, he saw more ice. He considered heading south then changed his mind and went north.

He walked for what felt like hours. Strangely, the sun did not seem to move. Finally, he stopped. Something lay before him, frozen deep inside the ice. It was so big that he marveled that he had not noticed it sooner. He thought at first that it was just a trick, a web of water that had not quite solidified.

Then he realized that it was a dragon. Multicolored and six winged, it lay just beneath the ice. Its legs—huge, powerful legs ending in claws the length of his arm. He knew he should have been afraid, but he wasn't. He started forward, following the outline of the dragon's body. He stopped again when he saw its head. Its long neck, bent at an impossible angle, held its face frozen against the ice. One huge, dark eye met his. Though Rowen sensed that the beast was dead, eons dead, the dark eye seemed brimmed with sadness.

The eye blinked.

Rowen jumped. He reached for his sword, but it was gone. Stepping away from the dragon, he looked behind him, thinking he'd dropped his sword. But it was gone. When he turned around again, the dragon had disappeared, too. He stood for a moment, wondering if what he'd just seen was just a dream.

"Or maybe I'm going mad."

He started forward again. The sun still had not sunk any farther in the sky, though purple clouds drifted across it. An animal howled—not the shrill, mournful howl of a wolf, but the deeper, dreadful rumble of a greatwolf. Rowen shuddered. He was being hunted. He turned in a circle, searching for threats, but saw nothing.

Finally, he started north again. He walked and walked. Then he saw a cloaked man walking toward him. The man kept his hood drawn, his hands folded neatly in his dark, priestly cloak. An impossibly long shadow stretched behind the man. His ink-black cloak spread across the ice like a stain.

Rowen stopped. He knew that he'd been seen. Something told him to run. He searched the area around him for a weapon, but all he saw was snow and ice. He knew how to fight with his hands and feet—he'd done so many times before. Still, he trembled.

"*Singchai ushó fey.*" Those words were somehow important. They were supposed to give him comfort, but he could not remember what they meant. He wanted to hide, but there was nowhere to go. Gritting his teeth, he forced himself to take one step forward then another and another.

When just a few feet separated Rowen from the cloaked figure, the dark priest stopped. He stared at Rowen. Though splashes of red sunlight still shown against the ice, no light penetrated the priest's hood. Rowen heard him breathe, low and ominous, like the bellows of a furnace.

Then the breathing stopped. The dark priest removed bone-pale hands from his sleeves and lowered his hood. Rowen faced angular features, a thin jawline, and tapered ears. The man was either bald or had shaved his head. Rowen could not tell how old he was. The man must have been a Sylv or a Shel'ai, but his eyes were wholly black. Then he blinked, and his eyes turned purple. Finally, the dark priest smiled. Despite his coldly handsome face, his teeth were dark and rotten. "Do you know who I am?"

Rowen wanted to shake his head. Instead, he nodded.

"That's good. It's not every day that you're approached by a god." He took a step closer. "You should not have sent those messages. It was not your place to speak of me before I chose to reveal myself."

Rowen's knees buckled. He couldn't tell whether it was the product of his own fear or if the dark priest was doing something to him, but suddenly, he wanted to fall to his knees. He wanted to grovel. He wanted to worship the dark, terrible man, whom he had never before seen but recognized.

"I won't ask you to talk," the dark priest said. "Just listen." He made a sweeping gesture then folded his pale hands back into his cloak. "This world is mine. I took it from Nekiel. I took it from Nâya and Fâyu Jinn. I took it from the gods. And if I cannot have it, I will burn it to cinders before I let it fall to your kind."

Rowen's legs shook, worse than before. The dark priest's voice echoed through him like the beating of a war drum. He wanted to shut his eyes and plug his ears, but he could not move his arms.

"This is the world of your mind, your dreams. I cannot lie to you here. So instead, I will tell you the truth." He drifted closer to Rowen, though he did not seem to move, as though the earth itself had recoiled to let him advance. He seized Rowen's face, burning him. Rowen could not break free. He opened his mouth but could not scream, either.

Chorlga said, "Nekiel left me here for a purpose. He told me to dismantle the Dragonward from the inside. So I learned how. For eleven centuries, I've drunk freely from Namundvar's Well. I've made myself stronger than Nekiel ever was."

He let go, shoving Rowen backward.

"The Shel'ai went mad from a single sip. I've drunk oceans. So this is my vow to you, Human: surrender Knightswrath, or I will tear down the Dragonward. I will let Nekiel and his kind back into Ruun. I will cloak every kingdom on this continent in a night so dark, it will never know dawn."

Behind Chorlga, his shadow grew. Wings blossomed from its sides, spreading across the ice. The sun plummeted from the sky like a burning stone. Chorlga laughed. Rowen fell into darkness.

Shade stood on a snowy hill and watched the last of his people file out of the tiny fortress of Coldhaven. Winter winds clawed at his cloak and raked his skin. He winced, though not from the cold. Once again, they were abandoning their home. Coldhaven had never been much—just a wretched little collection of huts enclosed in a low wall of ice and stones, tucked between hills on the

Wintersea. Fadarah had not even intended it to be permanent. But some of the children had lived there for most of their lives. Now, they were experiencing for the first time a pain that Shade and the others knew all too well: the bitter sting of being driven from home.

They had abandoned countless temporary sanctuaries from Stillhammer to Ivairia, fleeing armies and mobs, burying their dead along the way. But this was different. This would be the last time.

Shade clenched his fists. Thin, angry tendrils of wytchfire steamed between his fingers. How many times had they said that before, vowing that this would be their final retreat? But they had no choice. They had already stayed in Coldhaven too long. Even if Chorlga did not already know about Coldhaven, it was only a matter of time before trappers or fishermen discovered it. Word would reach the nearest kingdoms. Some king or superstitious, influential cleric would blame the Shel'ai for the next plague to infect his lands and send more swords than their wytchfire could repel.

El'rash'lin is right. We've lost the war. Our only chance is to leave Ruun entirely.

But that would not be easy. Most of their strongest and bravest had already died. All that remained were ten children, some barely old enough to walk, and half as many old men and women. There had been no sign of the Shel'ai that Shade had left behind in Ziraari's camp. Either they had been killed, or they had chosen to strike out on their own.

Of course, we have the Sylvs.

Shade almost laughed at the thought. The Sylvan women they'd rescued from Brahasti's compound had reluctantly decided to accompany them, knowing that the fact that they were all pregnant with Shel'ai babies meant they'd never be welcomed back into Sylvos anyway. They walked beside Shel'ai in the column, shaking in their cloaks, for they had no magic to immunize them against the cold. El'rash'lin and Zeia grimly led the procession.

The two had hardly left each other's sides since their flight from Brahasti's compound. Often, they spoke in low whispers. In the evenings, while the others slept, El'rash'lin helped Zeia practice her magic. Despite her ghastly injuries, she suffered in silence, following El'rash'lin like a dutiful student—a student with no hands.

Shade marveled at the cruelty and injustice of it all. Not only had El'rash'lin refused to use his Dragonkin magic to restore what Brahasti's men had so painfully taken from her; somehow, Zeia seemed to have completely accepted his decision and abided by it without reproach. Shade's attempts to mock El'rash'lin had been met with silence. Indeed, Zeia had hardly spoken with Shade at all. At Coldhaven, she'd preferred to spend her solitary hours in meditation, the scarred, puckered stumps of her wrists resting pitifully on her lap.

And now, she was leaving.

El'rash'lin and Shade would conduct the Shel'ai and the Sylvan refugees across the frozen Wintersea, toward Sorocco. Zeia would head south on her own. She would find Rowen Locke and offer him her services and her protection.

Shade's bitter laugh dissipated in the cold wind. What use would Zeia be? A lone Shel'ai could do little against a Dragonkin like Chorlga, but without her hands, Zeia could do even less. She probably would not even make it off the Wintersea alive. But Shade had given up trying to talk her out of it. He'd tried for hours at Coldhaven, and she'd ignored him, continuing her meditation with just the faintest smirk.

"If she wants to die, I won't stop her." Shade started down the hill toward the ragged procession.

El'rash'lin and Zeia had drawn to one side, urging the column to continue on. Both faced Shade. El'rash'lin leaned on a staff. Zeia wore a sword, despite having no hands with which to wield it. Shade approached them slowly, shaking his head at the absurdity of it all. He decided to try one last time to talk some sense into them.

"Listen, it will take us days to reach the coast. We'll have to pass right through Ivairia. Even if the Ivairian king doesn't kill us, even if we find Soroccan merchants along the coast, we'll still have to buy or steal a ship."

El'rash'lin offered him a twisted smile. "I know a certain Soroccan who might help us."

Shade blinked, realizing to whom El'rash'lin was referring. He turned to Zeia. "Don't go. If you want to die, die with us, not alone in the wilderness."

Zeia and El'rash'lin exchanged knowing looks. El'rash'lin told her, "It's time." Facing Shade, he said, "Let us show you what Zeia has been practicing."

Zeia stepped away from El'rash'lin. Slowly, she raised her arms. Her sleeves fell back, revealing the stumps of her wrists. Shade winced at the sight of them. Zeia closed her eyes.

Shade frowned. "What—"

Wytchfire unfurled from Zeia's wrist-stumps.

Shade's eyes widened. Before he could speak, the wytchfire underwent a stunning transformation. The flames took on a new shape—the shape of fingers. Zeia opened her eyes. She smiled at the look on Shade's face. Slowly, she lowered her arms and held them out. She waved her new hands in front of Shade, flexing her fingers of fire. El'rash'lin stepped forward. Smiling at Shade, he offered Zeia his staff.

Zeia took it.

The staff smoldered a little where her fingers of fire wrapped around the wood, but it did not burst into flames. Zeia held the staff a moment then turned it slowly, passing it from one burning hand to the other. Her brow knit with concentration. Beads of sweat formed on her forehead. She turned the staff between her magical hands, faster and faster. Then she stopped, bowed, and returned it to El'rash'lin.

Zeia faced Shade again. The hands of fire disappeared. Her sleeves slid back down, concealing the puckered stumps of her wrists. She said, "You were saying?"

Shade stared, speechless.

El'rash'lin touched Zeia's shoulder. "Goodbye, my child. Remember your lessons. Remember what you are. We will not meet again in this world."

Zeia embraced him. When they parted, she bowed again. Then, without saying a word, she brushed past Shade and started south, alone, across the stark whiteness of the frozen sea.

Igrid ordered the Iron Sisters to scatter as soon as they descended into the sewers. Their feet splashed through the filth, the sound echoing off the walls. Rats scurried to keep ahead of them.

Originally, Igrid had intended to lead all the Iron Sisters up into the city and fight their way toward the gates or follow the sewers all the way out to the wilderness, but the Dhargots had followed them. She thought of how many more were quartered in the city above. If the Iron Sisters stayed together, they would only be easier to track.

"Make your own way," she told them. She knew that some would choose to stay in the city and try to sow insurrection. Others would take their chances in the wilderness. All would probably be dead within a few days.

But at least they'll die with swords in their hands.

Igrid longed to return to the palace, find Prince Karhaati, and avenge Ailynn's death. But the splash of Dhargothi boots and the glare of torches filled the sewers. So she ran.

She did not see the clerics. She hoped they'd had the sense to get the orphans out of the sewers and hide them somewhere else, though she had no idea where that would be. She realized that the only relatively safe place for them had been the sewers, and she'd spoiled that.

"No choice," she muttered. She hoped that was true. Crouching low, she ran headlong through the putrid darkness. Karhaati had sent crossbowmen down into the sewers. Steel-tipped bolts rebounded off the damp stone walls. Occasionally, Igrid heard screams and the clatter of steel.

She started up a stairwell. A few Iron Sisters followed her. Pressing her shoulder against the cistern lid, she shoved it out of the way and clambered up onto the street. It was night. They found themselves next to a tavern.

Igrid recognized the tavern where she and Jalist had stayed their first night in Hesod. It was the last place they should be. On both sides of the street, the windows of inns blazed with light. Dhargots milled nearby. Spotting the Iron Sisters, they drew swords. A few shouted.

The Iron Sisters stood shoulder to shoulder, defiant.

"Scatter," Igrid told them. She turned and ran. The clash of steel told her that not everyone had listened. Igrid sprinted down an alley, stopped just in time to avoid being seen by a passing squad of soldiers, then ducked out and ran in the opposite direction.

A few Hesodi milled in the streets or stood in the doorways of their houses. Most looked away. An old man threw her his cloak, then shut his door. Igrid grabbed the cloak, pulled the hood over her face, and kept running. Her body ached, and she remembered that she'd been wounded in the dungeon, though she'd not had time to examine her injury.

At the end of the next street, despite her hood, she was spotted. A squad of Dhargots gave chase on horseback. Igrid weaved down one street and up another, then she sprinted through an alley. She emerged, thinking she'd lost the horsemen, and was promptly spotted by a different squad of footmen.

Alarm bells rang throughout the city, and steel clashed in the distance. Igrid howled, hacking so furiously at the Dhargothi footmen that they fell back. She feigned another charge then broke and ran again. She discarded her cloak in an alley. Her lungs burned. She needed to find a place to hide soon, before she collapsed from exhaustion.

Rounding a corner, she encountered a dozen Iron Sisters battling twice as many Dhargots. Igrid stabbed one Dhargot in the back of the neck, cut another at the knee, and snatched up a cloak from the corpse of a third. A crossbow bolt whizzed past her ear. Igrid snatched up a fallen spear and drove it into a Dhargot's belly just as he turned to face her.

Letting go of the spear, Igrid donned the Dhargothi cloak and raced down another alley. Footsteps followed her. She glanced over her shoulder but saw, instead of Dhargots, two Iron Sisters. Both had dressed themselves in dead men's cloaks and helmets, though one of the women winced with pain and pressed one hand to her stomach. A crossbow bolt extended between her fingers. The other was helping her along.

Igrid could tell at a glance that they weren't going to make it. The prudent move would be to leave them behind. She took a step away from them, stopped herself, then caught the wounded woman's other arm.

"I don't recognize you. What are your names?"

Before the women could answer, a giant Dhargot in ornate armor emerged at the far end of the alley. Igrid could tell at once that he was an officer and an expert swordsman. Unfooled by their disguises, he blocked their path. He smirked, seemingly unperturbed by the thought of facing three opponents at once.

Igrid glanced over her shoulder. Four Dhargots blocked the other end of the alley. They approached slowly, knowing they had the Iron Sisters trapped. Igrid let go of the wounded woman. "See what you can do about those four," she told the two women, then turned to meet the officer.

The Dhargot swung too fast for her to counter. He bashed one of her greaves, gouged her tassets, and cut a fresh tear in her brigandine. But then he got careless. He lunged for Igrid's midriff, pulled back too slowly after Igrid parried, and lost an ear. Blood ran down his neck, but he hardly seemed to notice.

Igrid blinked back pain and exhaustion and threw herself at him. She feigned a stab at his face then changed direction and drove the tip of her sword into his scale armor. She could not pierce it, but the blow drove him backward. She followed, swinging hard. Their swords met. The Dhargot held her in swordlock then advanced with lightning speed. He grabbed her sword wrist.

Igrid kicked him in the groin. He winced but did not let go. She kicked him again, and he answered by kicking her knee. Then he spat in her face and shoved her against the wall. He swung. Igrid ducked. Sparks rained down on her. She dropped to the ground, rolled, and drove her sword into the Dhargot's foot.

He howled. His blade cut her leg before she could roll away. Dizzy, she reached for one of her daggers, but they were all gone. She'd left her sword in the Dhargot officer's foot. He wrenched it free and cast it over his shoulder. Then he started toward her, favoring one leg.

Igrid thought back to Rowen Locke's battle against a Dhargot named Jaanti. The latter had obviously been the superior swordsman, toying with him, but Locke had won anyway. This Dhargot had been toying with her, too, but that was over. He hissed curses through bad teeth and swung.

Igrid raised her forearms. She caught his blade on her vambraces, winced when she felt bones break, and threw herself forward. Her thumbs found the Dhargot's eyes. She dug in and pressed hard. The Dhargot howled again. He dropped his sword and lurched backward, grabbing her wrists. He lost his footing and fell onto his back. Igrid fell on top of him, still driving her thumbs into his skull.

When she was sure he was dead, she rolled off and tried to grab his sword. But her hands shook, her forearms drooped, and the sword fell out of her grasp. Igrid looked up.

Both Iron Sisters lay dead. Three Dhargots advanced on her. Igrid backed up. Before she could run, four more Dhargots fanned out across the other end of the alley. They locked shields, barring her escape. Igrid watched them advance.

I can't let them take me alive...

She spotted a long, curved knife in the dead officer's belt. She stooped and drew it, wincing when pain burned through her hands. The Dhargots stopped and braced themselves, thinking she meant to attack. Igrid looked up. The star-wash of Armahg's Eye lay almost directly above her. She blinked at it. Fresh tears made the stars blur.

"Well, Locke, so much for your daring, timely rescue." Igrid took a deep breath, held it, and raised the knife to her throat.

CHAPTER TWENTY-EIGHT

THE LOW FIRE

KARHAATI STOOD ON A TERRACE outside his new palace, grimacing as he listened to the chaos that had overtaken his city. Night had fallen, and snowflakes blew in the air, but the streets of Hesod still roiled with activity. Iron Sisters had poured out of the sewers like rats, killing every Dhargot they could. Though vastly outnumbered, they'd succeeded in catching many of his men off guard.

Worse, many citizens of Hesod had sheltered them. Some had even joined in what they perceived as a massive revolt against their Dhargothi oppressors. They had been beaten, of course, but the fighting was far from over. Iron Sisters remained. Now, hunting them down involved a slow, methodical process of sending armed men door to door to search every house and interrogate its occupants.

Meanwhile, at least a hundred armed women had escaped onto the Simurgh Plains. Many were still half naked, meaning they would freeze to death long before they found shelter, but Karhaati had still been obligated to send men after them.

And then, of course, there was the Isle Knight. By some stroke of bad luck, his appearance outside the city had almost perfectly coincided with the Iron Sisters' jailbreak, sowing further fear and chaos among the ranks. Thanks to his burning sword—which Karhaati cursed himself for underestimating—the Knight had escaped. He had also terrified many of the men and given others the impression that Karhaati was weak and incompetent.

In the hours since those events, Karhaati had already survived two assassination attempts by ambitious Dhargots who wanted to replace him, including one of his own bodyguards. Karhaati had killed both men himself and had their corpses hung from the palace parapets. In the morning, he would have to choose a hundred men, somehow blame all that had happened on them, and have them impaled in front of the city.

But that would not solve his problems entirely. Thousands of men were combing the Simurgh Plains, hunting for the Isle Knight and the escaped Iron Sisters. That left fewer men to keep order in the city itself... and fewer men to protect him, should the Dragonkin learn of his failure and seek reprisal.

"Which he will," Karhaati grumbled. He raised his goblet and took a small sip. He knew better than to get drunk on a night when so many wanted him dead, no matter how much he wanted to. He'd donned his armor and slipped on the heavy, ghastly necklace of dried ears to remind everyone who they were dealing with. But that had done nothing to dissuade his would-be assassins, and it would make even less difference if Chorlga came after him.

How can this be happening?

He shook his head at the injustice of it all. He'd conquered most of the Free Cities, absorbed the bulk of Ziraari's army, and rid himself of countless adversaries. He'd been chosen as the right hand of the most dangerous man on the continent. And yet, he stood poised to die in disgrace.

He'd heard that in instances of great failure, Isle Knights often took their own lives as a form of self-inflicted punishment designed to restore one's family honor. The Way of Ears preached something similar. Karhaati knew the tradition well, having seen it performed countless times over the years by generals who had displeased him, and wanted to avoid the greater shame and pain of impalement.

Unless he wanted all of Dhargoth to curse his name then act as though he had never existed, the course was clear. Karhaati knew he must gather his army at dawn, kneel naked before them, and cut off his own ears. Then he would drink poison—the ultimate disgrace for a warrior—and suffer the final indignity of having his body fed to the dogs. But that, at least, would keep him from being forgotten.

Karhaati shuddered. He did not want to die yet—unless it was in glorious battle, facing a worthy foe. He lowered his hand to his sword belt and touched the long, dark braid he'd cut from the head of the last Iron Sister he'd killed. He almost regretted doing it. She had been spectacular, easily the best fighter he'd ever faced. Yet she had been a woman!

Karhaati thought of the red-haired Iron Sister who had started it all. Hearing her fight had stirred his blood, as had the fierce look in her eyes when she finally stood before him. Karhaati wished he could have fought her, too. He would have liked to capture her. Instead of violating her, he would have kept her alive and well fed so that he could test his mettle against her whenever he wished.

Too bad she was probably dead by now.

Besides, sparing her might only get him into more trouble. His father had taught him that women were of little value. The Way of Ears prescribed the harshest punishments for women who took up arms against a man. Karhaati dared not defy such traditions, as Saanji and his followers did.

The thought of his youngest and last surviving brother made the bile rise in his throat. Karhaati spat over the terrace, resolving to think of him no more. He thought of the Iron Sisters again. He'd been given the bedchambers of Queen Sharra herself, though he'd found them surprisingly sparse and utilitarian. The presence of all her armor and weapons hanging on the walls served only to remind him that she, too, had escaped justice by killing herself.

Karhaati started to take another sip of wine then cursed and threw the goblet over the terrace. He felt almost as weak and ineffectual as Queen Sharra's husband must have been. That had to change. Glancing out at the city, he listened to the distant chaos and made up his mind. He strode from the terrace, summoned his remaining bodyguards, and went to take personal command of the hunt.

Jalist sat before a low fire smoldering at the mouth of a cave. The fire, though warm enough to blunt the winter chill, could not drive it off completely. He still shivered. But they dared build it no higher with a thousand Dhargots out searching for them. Jalist had argued that if they were going to die anyway, they might as well die warm, but Rowen had refused.

Jalist looked across the fire at his friend.

Rowen sat, faintly rocking himself, sweating despite the cold. His eyes were glazed. He still hugged Knightswrath against his chest as though it were a child, though the drawn kingsteel gleamed almost cruelly in the firelight. Rowen had woken earlier, screaming, but would not speak of his nightmare. He would say nothing about whatever had happened to him outside the walls.

That damn sword's doing something terrible to him...

Jalist touched the shaft of his long axe. Rowen had changed so much since the last time he'd seen him. He looked pale, older, and half mad. Surely, Knightswrath was to blame. Though Rowen had not spoken of it, Jalist had deduced that Silwren must have finally made her choice. She'd given her life to revive the sword's full power.

Rowen was a good and brave man, but he simply hadn't been born to wield magic—let alone magic of such tremendous power. Jalist shook his head, jabbing the fire with his long axe. And to make matters worse, they were going back to Hesod.

"Igrid's probably already dead, you know."

Rowen looked up. He blinked as though he'd forgotten Jalist was even there. "Maybe. But if not, we have to help her."

"Helping her will get you killed."

A wolf howled in the distance.

Jalist picked up his axe, looked around, then rested the axe on his lap. "Might get *me* killed, too."

"You aren't even supposed to be here," Rowen said, smiling faintly.

Jalist tugged at his cloak when a fresh gust of wind chilled him to the bone. "Didn't have anywhere nicer to be."

"Do you think Leander survived?"

Jalist winced. He had not spoken to Rowen about what he'd seen at Stillhammer. He had not even supposed that Rowen knew about the Jolym, though the sympathy in his eyes indicated that he did. Jalist shrugged. "If he did, he took the survivors to Quesh."

"Makes sense. They might be safe there."

Jalist grunted and stabbed at the dying campfire. "These days, I don't think anybody's safe anywhere. But take a Queshi with a bow and a bloodmare and a Dwarr with armor and an axe, pair them up, and you've got a border guard even the Jolym might not want to mess with."

"Maybe." Rowen sheathed Knightswrath. The life returned to his eyes. "Well, my friend, Quesh is south. I'm going north. So I guess this is goodbye."

Jalist scowled. "Are you as brain-rattled as a dragon cultist, or have you just not noticed yet that whenever I leave your side, bad things happen?"

Rowen smiled faintly. "Maybe both. Maybe neither. I'm not so good with questions anymore."

"I'll bear that in mind." Jalist cleared his throat. "When I was in Hesod, I heard a rumor about Isle Knights in Atheion. I'm guessing they're the ones hunting for you."

Rowen nodded slowly. "I know. But Igrid comes first."

"*If* Igrid's still alive, she's either leading the Iron Sisters across the plains, or she's locked up in some Hesodi dungeon. If the former, we'll run into her eventually. If the latter, the first thing we've got to do is get into the city without being seen."

Rowen did not answer.

Jalist said, "We can steal uniforms and helmets, but the Dhargots know what you look like. So unless you can't live without that rat's nest you call hair, I'll sharpen up my razor and make you bald. You'll have to leave that shiny armor behind, too. I'm sure you're partial to it, but there's no choice. I'd say leave the sword, too, but we might need it."

From far away, a wolf howled again.

"Another option is to see if we can find a company of sellswords and join up," Jalist continued. He heard himself talking quickly but did not know why. "The Dhargots are always hiring, especially now. We can join a company that's going to Hesod, lay low, and find out what we can. Or we could disguise ourselves as clerics. Might take some time, but—"

"You're talking nonsense."

"All right, then how about this? We ride east like our asses are on fire. We get back to Lyos, thrash any Jolym that are clawing at the gates, then cash in your favor with King Typherius. Maybe we enlist some Knights, too. We come back here with an army and slap the Bloody Prince until he bleeds out his ears. You and Igrid can rule the city as king and queen. I'll be the court jester and entertain your children by juggling axes. If that's not good enough, I'll set the axes on fire."

Jalist realized he was on his feet, though he did not remember standing up.

"Well, Locke, which will it be… or would you like to suggest a brilliant plan of your own?"

Rowen stared at him a moment, then looked back into the fire. "I tried commanding men once. I didn't do a very good job."

"Me, neither." Jalist sat back down. Neither spoke for a time, then Jalist said, "I'm not leaving."

"Yes, you are."

Jalist's dark eyes narrowed. "Don't use your ominous voice with me, Locke. Your brother did it better than you do. And truth be told, he wasn't worth a damn at anything besides making men think he was mighty." Jalist wondered why he'd mentioned Kayden, knowing how the mention of Rowen's brother would affect him.

But Rowen did not flinch. "I'm not threatening you, my friend. I'm *asking* you to go. I'm asking because you're right. This will get me killed. I know that. No sense in you dying, too. Go find this lover of yours. Kill each other's enemies, bake bread, do whatever the hell you want. Just keep each other warm."

Jalist felt his eyes sting. He said nothing.

"Chorlga spoke to me in my dream," Rowen continued. His voice lowered, as though he were afraid to continue. "He told me to surrender. He told me to give him Knightswrath or he'd tear down the Dragonward and let all the Dragonkin back into Ruun. And I think he meant it. He frightened me... but not just because of how powerful he is. Because he's desperate."

The fire had burned low. Shadows covered half Rowen's face. "I see now that I was wrong. We all were. I can't beat Chorlga. Even if by some miracle, I kill him, I'll just end up getting the rest of us killed in the process."

Jalist found his voice. "So your solution is to die?"

Rowen shook his head. "I don't have a solution. But I'm not dumb enough to think that Chorlga will leave us alone if I give him Jinn's sword. So I'm forgetting about the war. I'm just going to help everyone I can for as long as I can." He paused. "I'd help you find Leander, but I know you'll do fine on your own. Better than I would."

"Better than you will," Jalist corrected. He looked away.

"Better than I will," Rowen repeated. Slowly, he rose to his feet. His kingsteel armor looked dented and blackened, nothing like it had when he left Lyos. His brilliant blue tabard hung in tatters. The sigil of a balancing crane was unrecognizable. Rowen stepped around the dying fire, stumbling slightly.

Jalist rose, too.

Rowen squeezed his shoulder. "Thank you, my friend."

Jalist swallowed a lump in his throat. "The king sent me to bring you back," he protested weakly. "They need you in Lyos. My men died to keep you alive..."

"What were their names?"

Jalist pulled away, wiping his eyes and cursing the smoke from the campfire. "Vardan and Braggo. But there's plenty more like them in Lyos."

"Plenty in Hesod, too, probably."

"Sure, but those aren't *your* people."

"Not sure the Lyosi are my people, either. Or maybe they all are. Maybe that's what El'rash'lin meant." He shrugged. "Goodbye, my friend. If things make more sense in the next life, we'll puzzle it out then."

Rowen turned and walked away. Jalist sat back down. He stared into the embers, listened to Rowen ready one of the horses, and resolved not to turn around. But he did anyway, just in time to see a slash of azure vanishing into the winter darkness.

CHAPTER TWENTY-NINE

BREAKING THE SIEGE

B Y THE TIME DAWN CRESTED the battlements of Atheion, Aeko
Shingawa had already been pacing for hours, dressed in full armor,
a sheathed adamune resting on her hip. Her dark braid was coiled
beneath her helmet. Unlike the Isle Knights who wore strange or frightening
facemasks, she'd chosen a helmet that left her face exposed. Men said her
scowl was her sharpest weapon. But even her infamous scowl had limits, and
Aeko realized that as she spent the morning inspecting Atheion's troops.

The Noshan king had declared that until the siege was lifted, one third of
his army must stand ready at any given time. While most of Atheion consisted
of gigantic skiffs that floated on the sapphire surface of the sea called Armahg's
Tears, there was still a squat wall of sandstone forming a half circle along the
shoreline. The bulk of the city's defenders stood watch there. Others lined the
skiffs in case the enemy attempted to circumvent the wall and take them by
sea.

Most of the Noshans wore brigandines, but a few wore chainmail or
half-plate armor. All wore tabards emblazoned with Atheion's crest: a white
sailboat between mountains. Some carried longswords, but most preferred
spears, bows, and shortswords. Most had never been in battle. And all of them
looked half asleep.

Aeko stopped to shake a few of them awake. Some jumped at the sight
of her, blushing as they muttered apologies and fumbled to their feet. Others
blinked, frowned, and went back to sleep. Those Aeko kicked again, intoning
the appropriate threats of what would happen if they fell asleep on duty. She
doubted many believed her, though.

Other Isle Knights had been stationed along the wall. All stood at
attention, bowing as she passed, some rolling their eyes over the poor conduct

of the Noshan troops. But Aeko saw weariness in the eyes of the Knights, too. She could hardly blame them. Sieges were tedious things: days, even weeks of boredom, punctuated by brief, frantic moments of combat.

But there had been no such moments for nearly a month.

The Jolym had simply fanned out to form a steel perimeter on the shore, just out of bow range. At first, there had been only twenty, but more arrived every day. By the end of a week, four hundred stood along the shore.

Almost immediately, Atheion had braced for trouble. While some Noshans had greeted the Isle Knights as heroes, grateful that they'd shown up in time to protect the city against the Jolym, King Hidas in particular had not been happy to see the Isle Knights. Apparently, though, Crovis Ammerhel had addressed the city's fathers with a silver tongue, eventually winning over so many clerics that they, in turn, pressured the king into welcoming the Knights.

Meanwhile, the portions of the city that existed on the mainland—homes, shops, and a graceful row of white windmills—had been abandoned. King Hidas had mobilized all his troops, drafted two thousand additional men and boys, and armed them all with bows and spears. At Crovis's insistence, the king gave them strict orders to attack each Jol's eyes once the fighting started.

Since then, the Jolym had simply stood motionless, staring at the city. Snow piled around them. Some showed signs of rust. Men speculated that the Jolym had died somehow. A few had even suggested that they were nothing but empty suits of armor placed there as part of a cruel trick by the Isle Knights.

Before anyone could stop him, an eager Noshan officer had gone out with a dozen men to inspect the Jolym. As soon as they got close, the Jolym came to life and cut the Noshans to pieces. Aghast, the Noshans braced themselves, thinking the attack was finally about to begin. But the Jolym had simply returned to being statues.

Gradually, the Noshans fell back into complacency.

They even discovered that if they sailed to a different patch of shore, they could go to and from the mainland without the Jolym seeming to notice, let alone respond. Atheion's vibrant sea trade had resumed, albeit slowly. Ships still sailed to and fro, navigating a wide, calm river called Zet's Blood that joined Armahg's Tears to the islands and ocean beyond.

Traders brought strange stories of mass slaughter in Stillhammer and fires burning throughout the Lotus Isles, but the Noshans scarcely believed them. After all, the Jolym had done so little. And if they ever did actually attack, the Isle Knights would protect them.

"Fools..." Aeko glanced over the battlements, glowering at the steely figures beyond. She doubted that Jolym felt cold, though she desperately hoped they were at least half as miserable as she was.

She considered Crovis's suggestion that they ride out in force, bolstered by the Noshan army, and finish the Jolym once and for all. *A lot of good that did Bokuden...*

Aeko winced, chiding herself for thinking so glibly about the death of her friend and mentor. She reminded herself that Bokuden had not been undone because of a flaw in his strategy. Word had reached them from a handful of survivors: Saikaido had been attacked by the Nightmare, in league with Chorlga. Neither had been seen since, but the Jolym had continued to ravage the islands of the Shao, driving the Isle Knights from one temple-fortress after another.

Now, Crovis insisted that they attack the Jolym—not just to avenge the thousands of Knights who had been slain on the Lotus Isles but to clear a path for them to ride back and retake their homeland. Other Knights had proposed that they leave the Jolym besieging Atheion to King Hidas and simply sail back to the Lotus Isles on Zet's Blood. Winters in Nosh could be long and harsh. Zet's Blood was still passable, but in a week or two, their route to the ocean would be hopelessly blocked by ice.

All my Knights want to go back to the Isles. And here I am, forcing them to stay and fight to defend a home that isn't even their own.

Aeko sighed, glancing over the parapets at the distant Jolym. Then she heard someone approach and turned to see Captain Reygo ascending the steps. The Noshan's face was taut with cold. She guessed he'd run all the way from King Hidas's palace, crossing one bridge after another until he'd moved from the heart of Atheion to the shoreline. His eyes were dark with irritation.

"Lady Shingawa, the king sends his response to your plan." Reygo waited for Aeko to nod. "With respect, he says no."

Aeko nodded again, unsurprised. A few days ago, she'd proposed a daring strategy to the king, who had sworn to give her idea due consideration. But as soon as she'd seen the captain approaching her, she'd known the king's answer would be no.

"But, Captain, I was correct in assuming that the skiffs can be unmoored and sailed down Zet's Blood like boats, correct?"

Reygo's face flushed. "Yes, m'lady. But as the king pointed out last week, the skiffs are joined by bridges and walkways, some of them centuries old. Relocating the entire city of Atheion to the Lotus Isles would mean destroying them. The clerics would object. So would the people." He paused. "And so would I."

Aeko withdrew a scrap of parchment from her belt. She handed it to the captain. "I trust you've seen this?"

Reygo gave it a cursory glance and nodded. "My king showed that to me days ago." He handed it back.

Aeko glanced down at the message that had been sent from the Wytchforest. The raven carrying it had been shot down by Noshan hunters before the strange message could be delivered, but the nervous hunters had found the message and carried it to Atheion themselves. "These Jolym are the product of a Dragonkin… one who has been sowing destruction across the entire continent, careful not to reveal himself. He's cunning. He is not to be taken lightly, nor are his servants."

"I take my enemies seriously," the captain said pointedly, "but you're asking us to uproot our city, effectively end our entire way of life, over a scrap of Sylvan paper and a few hundred armored curiosities who are too afraid to do anything but stand there." He started to walk away.

Aeko grabbed his arm. She pointed at the Jolym. "When the ice is thick enough, those bastards will be able to walk right up to the palace and put your king to the sword. I wonder if you'll be glad you kept your precious bridges then."

The Noshan captain shook his head. "No disrespect, Lady Shingawa, but I have two thousand trained swords under my command. I can draft another five thousand, if necessary. And we have your Knights. That's more than adequate to beat five hundred dull-witted demons in rusting armor."

Aeko's eyes narrowed. "Do you have a great deal of experience fighting armored demons, Captain?"

"No," Reygo confessed, "but I've spent most of my life fighting berserkers. You ever see a Lochurite, Lady Shingawa? I imagine they're a lot like these Jolym. They're so drugged, they don't feel pain. They'll literally come at you until you cut off their heads or chop the legs out from under 'em."

Aeko remembered hearing that the fey, tribal folk had a long tradition of sending not just men, but women and children into battle. She studied the captain's stern expression, wondering how many of the latter he had faced. "Lochurites might be mad, but they're still flesh and blood. Jolym aren't."

"Whatever you say, Isle Knight. I have to get back to my duties."

"You're the Captain of the Guard. Your city is under siege. What duties do you possibly have that don't involve you standing beside us on this wall?"

Reygo smirked. "Atheion is a trade city. And there's the Scrollhouse. You might not believe this, but my job involves more than whoring and bar fights." He saluted. "If something changes, let me know. If the Jolym attack, one of my men will come get me." He turned and left.

A few Isle Knights who had been eavesdropping shook their heads in displeasure, though the Noshans standing next to them snickered. A few Noshans uncorked wineskins. Others nibbled on breads and sweet rolls brought to them by pretty, well-dressed women carrying baskets.

Disgusted, Aeko ignored the rumbling in her stomach and turned back to the battlements. She faced the stark white plains that spread beyond the Jolym beneath a crisp, pale sky. Minutes turned to hours. Anger became boredom. Aeko blinked and pinched her wrist with gauntleted fingers, trying to stay awake.

Matua did not know whether to feel honored or insulted.

The aging cleric had always wanted to see the inside of Atheion's Scrollhouse, a repository of knowledge and literature that predated the Shattering War. He had even become a cleric of Armahg in order to fulfill that dream, since they were tasked with maintaining and safeguarding the famous structure. But upon arriving in Atheion, he'd promptly realized that one could not simply wander into the Scrollhouse and read to his heart's content. Even the king could not enter unannounced.

But the discovery of a theft had necessitated some changes. Outraged, the high priests had declared that every last scroll, book, antique, artifact, and scrap of parchment be cataloged so that they could ascertain the extent of the theft. That meant countless hours of labor. So low-ranking priests like Matua had been drafted to comb through the aisles of the Scrollhouse and see it done—under guard, of course.

Thus, Matua had finally been allowed to enter the Scrollhouse. The novelty had quickly worn off when he realized the tedium and frustration of his assignment. Instead of being allowed to actually sit down and read the books and scrolls, reveling in their ancient knowledge and wit, he simply had to note their titles, offer a line or two of description, assign them a number that denoted their location within the Scrollhouse, then move on.

By the end of his first day in the Scrollhouse, Matua knew that dragons had once lived in the ocean as well as on land, that Ruun was only one of five continents located throughout the world, and that the key ingredient in kingsteel came from a mountain of fire that had fallen from the sky and landed on the Lotus Isles eons ago. One legend said that it had been cast down by Armahg as a test, for whichever realm possessed kingsteel was destined either to protect the helpless or to become itself a nation of bloodthirsty conquerors.

He'd learned of herbs that could increase or decrease the likelihood of pregnancy, including some that raised the odds of a Shel'ai being born to a Sylvan mother. He'd read that Dwarrish darksoil, which could grow food without need of sunlight, was made from the ground-up bones of dragons. And perhaps most fascinating of all, he'd learned that their sun was but one sun in a vast armada of stars called a galaxy and that Armahg's Eye was not actually the looming eye of a goddess but another such galaxy moving slowly toward them across a great, immeasurable void.

But every scrap of knowledge brought with it the frustration of having to return the book or scroll to its shelf before he could immerse himself fully, prodded on by guards who would not allow a cleric to spend more than a couple minutes with a given piece. By the end of the first day, practically weeping with frustration, Matua had very nearly refused to keep working. But every scrap of knowledge gained was still more than his head had held before, so he kept coming back, savoring what he could.

Besides, the work kept his mind off the siege. Matua had seen the Jolym standing beyond the walls, and he'd heard tales of what they could do. He'd been glad for any distraction from them. But then he'd stumbled upon an ancient book with pages that seemed both like and unlike paper. The book, written in his native language, Queshi, detailed the creation of the Jolym, describing how each Jol required not only a tremendous outpouring of Dragonkin magic but a significant sacrifice on the part of the maker. The Dragonkin had to carve off a little piece of his own soul, which would grow in the darkness of the Jol's armor like an unholy flower.

After a year, the Jol would have a rudimentary consciousness. It would function like the perfect slave, loyal and tireless, vulnerable only if an injury to its eyes freed its vaporous fragment of self. Thereafter, Matua could not help but ponder a frightful idea: if a single Dragonkin had fashioned all the Jolym laying siege to the city and all the ones rumored to have decimated Stillhammer and the Lotus Isles, how much of his own soul had the Dragonkin sacrificed? How much was left?

He was still in the Scrollhouse, contemplating this, when Captain Reygo arrived.

Matua tensed at the sight of him. After Rowen Locke and Silwren had fled Atheion, just as the visage of a ghostly dragon appeared over the city, the captain had seized Matua and interrogated him. Matua's wrist and jaw still ached, reminding him of the captain's less-than-friendly manner of asking questions.

Matua hoped the captain had only come to check on the clerics' progress, a daily formality required by the king to show his respect for the high priests, but the captain spotted Matua and walked straight at him. Matua smiled, suppressing a groan. "Good morning, Captain. The cataloguing continues. So far, we've uncovered no other missing—"

"If I wanted a report, I'd ask one of the high priests," the captain snapped. "The king wants me to inspect the chamber where the theft took place."

Matua blinked at the captain's tone, which was even harsher than usual. "That chamber has already been inspected, Captain."

"But not by me. They may have left clues. The king would like to know for sure that it was an Isle Knight who committed the theft, since we just so happen to have a couple hundred of them camped out in our city."

He's lying. Matua forced himself to keep smiling. "As you wish, Captain. I'm sure the Scrollhouse guards can show you—"

Captain Reygo stepped a bit too close, glaring down at him. "*You* show me."

Matua glanced over the captain's shoulder, looking to the Scrollhouse guards for help. Two looked away. One shrugged. Other clerics who were close enough to hear what was happening looked away, too. Matua sighed. He realized that he should have expected this.

"Right this way," he told the captain. "The Scrollhouse has lower levels built right into the skiff. Technically, we'll be going underwater—"

"I know my own city better than you, I think."

Matua nodded. "Forgive me. I just wanted to warn you that it can feel a bit strange. Watch your step. These stairs can be treacherous."

The captain chuckled coldly. As Matua led the captain through the Scrollhouse—away from witnesses, down one set of stairs after another—he saw the captain's shadow moving on the wall beside his own as though trying to devour it.

Aeko's eyes widened. "Sir Wei, your spyglass, please."

The young Isle Knight standing next to her obeyed.

Aeko looked then cursed. "Sir Wei, find Sir Crovis. He's probably drilling near the palace. Tell him I need him here right away." She paused. "Tell him the Lochurites are coming."

Sir Wei blinked with surprise, glanced over the walls at a distant shape on the horizon, then hurried off. Aeko looked through the spyglass again then turned to the closest Noshans. At the mention of the Lochurites, all had reached for weapons. Aeko spotted a sergeant and gestured for him to join her. She offered him the spyglass and pointed. The sergeant cursed, too.

"They don't look drugged yet," Aeko said. She listened, trying to tune out the bustle of trade and morning activity. She winced when she heard a far-off chorus of barbaric wails. *But they sound like it.*

Soon, others heard it, too. Hammers froze mid-swing. Dockworkers set down their crates and wiped their brows, turning westward. Men and women called for quiet. An ominous hush fell over the shoreline, punctuated only by the creaking of skiffs and sails. When the Lochurites' wailing knifed the air, distant but unmistakable, Noshans paled. Women screamed, grabbed their children, and ran. Men clutched their weapons. A few abandoned their posts, already shaking with terror.

Aeko ignored the chaos. "How many do you see?"

The Noshan sergeant paled. "Thousands…"

Aeko snatched the spyglass back from him. "Three thousand," she estimated. "Go find Captain Reygo. And send someone to warn the king."

The sergeant left at a sprint. He looked decidedly grateful for a chance to leave the wall. Aeko handed the spyglass to one of her own officers then loosened her adamune. "Bring everyone in, then close and seal the gates. If you're standing on the wall and you have hands, pick up a bow."

The Isle Knights reacted at once. Some went to man the handful of ballistas and catapults lining the walls, since Aeko had already deduced that they could use them with better effectiveness than the Noshans who maintained them. The Knights' eyes glinted not with fear but with measured eagerness.

Meanwhile, the Noshans reacted with far less calm. A few readied bows and crossbows, while others reached for spears, but a great many shied away from the battlements. More fled their posts. Aeko ordered them to stand their ground. Her fellow Isle Knights did likewise, but it made no difference.

Aeko reminded herself that as crazed and bloodthirsty as the Lochurites were, they'd always avoided Atheion, preferring to attack the smaller settlements throughout Nosh. The Noshans in Atheion were not accustomed to combat. They needed one of their own to give them courage.

"I need the king or Captain Reygo standing next to me. Or both," Aeko shouted. "And someone find out what's keeping Crovis."

No sooner had she said this than she spotted the Knight of the Lotus riding gallantly across the bridges of Atheion, toward the wall. Sunlight glinted off his kingsteel armor. More Isle Knights streamed after him. The retreating Noshans slowed at his approach. Some stood to one side, bowing. Others fell in behind him. Some of Aeko's Knights even began chanting Crovis's name.

Crovis pretended not to notice, though his ghost of a smirk said otherwise. He dismounted, handed the reins of his horse to one of his supporters, and hurried up the steps to Aeko's side. One of Aeko's supporters offered him a spyglass. Crovis produced his own. When he saw the Lochurites, he clicked his tongue. "Perhaps they only want to scratch their names into the Jolym's backsides."

A few Knights, and even a few Noshans, smiled at his joke.

Aeko said, "These could be the reinforcements the Jolym were waiting for."

"A few thousand half-naked savages with bronze weapons? Gods, I hope so." Crovis tucked away his spyglass and drew his adamune. "Stand your ground, men!" he shouted to Knights and Noshans alike. "The tongues of women and minstrels have no time for cowards."

More men laughed. Aeko looked around. While women could become Isle Knights, it was still a rarity. Of the two hundred Isle Knights there, she was one of only three women. She saw them in the distance, their faces covered by kingsteel facemasks. She wondered if they had bristled at Crovis's remark, the way she had.

A Noshan soldier ran up to her, nearly out of breath. He reported that he'd been sent by the sergeant, who had gone looking for Captain Reygo at the Scrollhouse. When Aeko asked about the king, the soldier shrugged. Aeko pointed. "Get to the palace. Tell the king I want him here now." The soldier started to go, but Aeko grabbed his arm. "I said I want the king. Not one of his stewards, not his cook, not his gods-damned fortune teller. The king. Understood?"

The Noshan nodded. Aeko let him go.

Crovis chuckled. "I'm guessing that's rather less friendly than what Hidas is used to."

Aeko glanced at the advancing tide of Jolym and Lochurites. "So is this."

As soon as they reached the deepest, darkest chamber in the Scrollhouse, Matua moved over to a thick stone table and set down the lantern he'd brought to light their way. The Queshi priest sighed.

Captain Reygo set down a lantern of his own, glanced at Matua, and tightened his gloves. "Lots of people dying these days," the captain said in a low voice. "Dhargots and Lochurites tearing up these lands, thanks to the Shel'ai. And what do *you* do? You let a Shel'ai into this city!"

Reygo took a step forward.

Matua took a step back, holding up his open hands. "You've already questioned me on this. The high priests did, too. They said I wasn't involved in what happened."

"You're friends with Knights and wytches," Reygo scoffed. "The king may be a fool, but I'm not. The Isle Knights are here to take us over. They think they can frighten us into paying them taxes, like they did with Lyos. But Atheion is stronger. We don't bow to Knights who sit in temples and try to look holy while they're counting their riches. We bow to nobody but our own king."

Matua said, "Unless you've failed to notice the copper color of my skin, let me remind you that I'm not a Noshan. I'm not a Shao, either. And I'm certainly not a wytch."

But the captain did not appear to be listening. "I lost good men in front of the gates. Those metal bastards cut them to pieces. I think the Knights had something to do with it. And I bet I'm not the only one who thinks that." He drew his sword.

Matua frowned. "Are you really going to kill me over this?"

"Kill an unarmed cleric of Armahg? No, Priest, that's not the kind of man I am." The captain cast his sword away. "But I *am* going to break your arm."

Matua did not answer. Instead, he held out his left arm.

Reygo blinked in surprise then laughed. He reached out and grabbed Matua's wrist. Matua kicked the captain in the groin. Twisting free, the cleric sidestepped, grabbed the captain's head with both hands, and bore him to the ground. Before the startled captain could catch himself, Matua drove his elbow into his nose—once, twice, three times. Then he stepped back.

Reygo cursed, tried to stand, and fell back down. Cursing again, he managed to rise, though he doubled over, clutching one injured region in each hand.

"That's what happens when you interrogate someone outside of your office," Matua said evenly. "What can I say, Captain? I've been a Queshi a lot longer than I've been a cleric. We know a little about fighting."

Reygo spat back an unintelligible answer then scooped up his sword. Matua reached for a lantern, prepared to throw it. But the captain sheathed his sword. He turned to go then froze.

"What in the hells..."

Matua followed his gaze to a man in a tattered cloak who sat near the wall beside the door, rocking himself. Neither had noticed him when they came in. Though the man wore a hood, Matua could tell right away that he was no priest. His clothes were so torn and bloody that Matua thought he must have been a beggar who had been savaged in the streets, though it seemed impossible that such a beggar could have gotten down there on his own.

"Who are you?" Reygo demanded.

The man rocked himself, his eyes trained on the floor. He did not answer. But the lantern-light splashed his shadow across the wall.

Matua gasped. "Reygo—"

But Reygo was already repeating his question. He kicked the beggar, who fell over but made no move to shield himself, as though he did not even realize he had been struck. Matua told the captain to stop. Instead, the captain grabbed the beggar's arm and tried to drag him to his feet.

The beggar's hood fell. The captain gasped and let go. The beggar fell and began rocking himself again. Lantern light shone off his long, tapered ears.

Reygo backed up and drew his sword. He looked at Matua. "A Shel'ai?"

Matua spoke despite the lump in his throat. "I don't think so."

The beggar looked up. Wide, violet eyes flashed with madness. "Please, get it out of me," he whispered. "Get it out... get it out... get it out..."

Reygo lifted his sword but drew back another step. "What is he talking about?"

"Stay back," Matua hissed. "Just stay away from him." He forced himself to meet the violet eyes. He held out his open hands. "We won't hurt you. My name's Matua. See these robes I'm wearing? I'm a servant of the gods. I can help you. Understand?"

The man stopped rocking himself. He cocked his head. On the wall behind him, a dragon of shadows unfurled its many wings. "Can you take it out of me?"

Matua glanced at Captain Reygo then back at the Nightmare. "Whatever it is, I'll help you. I promise. Only you have to trust me. Stay calm. Trust me to help you—"

Reygo howled and charged, swinging his sword with both hands.

The Nightmare looked up. Unfazed, he reached toward the captain. Violet flames leapt from his arm. The captain's battle cry became a strangled gasp of pain. He fell backward. His body struck the ground and burst into a pile of cinders.

Slowly, the Nightmare stood. He faced Matua, who stepped back. The priest said, "Wait, I know what you are. I know people who can help you. I know Silwren..."

"Silwren is dead. You lie." The Nightmare cocked his head again. "You cannot help me." Both hands came up. His eyes narrowed. "No one can help me." He turned, violet flames blossoming from his fingertips.

CHAPTER THIRTY

WINTER PRAYERS

ROWEN DISMOUNTED TO INSPECT THE bodies. They lay in a torn-up field of snow and mud: a score of men wearing black silk and scale armor, plus an equal number of women. Most of the women were naked, though a few wore rags, cloaks, or shields. Judging by the scene, the women had been surrounded, then a third of them were shot down with arrows before the melee began. The snow had frozen the dead so that blood coated everything like a fine layer of painted ice.

Rowen trembled as he examined each of the women. But Igrid was nowhere to be seen. He searched and searched but found no one left alive, although a trail indicated that at least ten Dhargots had survived the battle and marched back on foot toward the city. Rowen hesitated. Wolves paced the snowy plains in the distance, waiting for him to go. He did not want to leave the slain Iron Sisters to their hunger, but he dared not sacrifice the time it would take to bury them.

He whispered a prayer in Shao then mounted his horse and tried to drive the wolves away before turning back toward Hesod. He had not gone far when a squad of Dhargothi horsemen spotted him. But Rowen had already donned a slain Dhargot's armor and tunic in place of his own, which he'd packed away in his saddlebags. He'd also covered his red hair under a helmet, shaved off his red beard, and hidden Knightswrath. When the Dhargots converged on him, he pretended he'd simply gotten separated from his company and was on his way back to the city.

Rather than let him go, the Dhargothi sergeant leading the squad told him to join in the hunt. The men laughed, boasting that they'd tracked down and killed more escaped Iron Sisters than any other squad. A short while later, they spotted three figures in the distance—all long-haired, all on foot.

The Dhargothi sergeant ordered a charge. Six men lowered their spears and drove toward the women, shouting and jeering. Two more circled around quietly, readying crossbows. Rowen joined the latter. Hanging back, he readied a crossbow of his own and shot the first Dhargot out of the saddle. The second turned, fired too quickly, and missed. Rowen drove at him, threw his crossbow at the man's horse, then drew a Dhargothi shortsword and finished him.

He looked up. Though the other half dozen Dhargots had encircled the three Iron Sisters, they'd seen what he'd done. Two turned and charged him. Rowen threw his shortsword at one then drew Knightswrath to face the other. He was about to will its flames to life when he reminded himself that the Dhargots were also looking for him. If he could win without using Knightswrath's power, the Dhargots might just think he was another jealous, crazed soldier who wanted the women for himself.

If I don't get killed, that is.

The Dhargot thrust his spearhead at Rowen's face then pulled back when he missed—too slowly. Rowen managed to lop it off, but the Dhargot wheeled clear and rode away before Rowen could finish him. Meanwhile, the Iron Sisters had killed one of the other Dhargots, though it had cost them one of their own. The remaining three Dhargots glanced at the Iron Sisters, then at Rowen thundering down on them, and fled.

"I'm not a Dhargot," Rowen called out to the Iron Sisters, but they had already claimed horses from the battlefield and were riding away. Rowen shouted that he knew Igrid, but he doubted they heard him over a sudden gust of winter wind. Though the unmoving Iron Sister's brown hair told him that it could not be Igrid, he dismounted anyway to see if she was still alive. She was not. Rowen cursed, muttered another prayer, and mounted his horse again.

As he neared Hesod, he came upon yet another battlefield. He searched in vain for Igrid's body then found a slain Dhargothi captain. Remembering the Dhargots who had seen him and escaped, he traded his disguise for that of the captain and chose a new horse. He rode the rest of the way to Hesod, slowing when he approached the front gates. Being there, surrounded by enemies, when he'd been fleeing from that place only two days before, felt strange. But then he spotted all the corpses strung from the battlements, and his anxiety turned to rage.

At least fifty Iron Sisters had been hung from the walls of Hesod, all of them stripped naked, their bodies slashed and unrecognizable. Crows feasted on them. Rowen covered his mouth and forced himself to look. Then he spotted a woman with long red hair hanging amid the rest, twenty feet above him. He sat on his horse, staring, until another Dhargothi captain ordered him out of the way. Rowen moved clear, noting the man's necklace of dried ears as he rode past.

"The Bloody Prince…"

Rowen turned his horse to the south, white-knuckling the reins, intending to ride away. Then he gave Igrid's corpse another look. His vision blurred. He turned his horse back toward the gates and rode straight into the city of Hesod. "The Bloody Prince," he repeated in a low, lethal whisper, touching Knightswrath's cold hilt through his cloak.

Saanji paused to catch his breath then paid for it when Royce's sword bashed his right shoulder. Saanji turned to protect his shoulder, and Royce bashed his left arm, then his knee when Saanji tried to halt the blows by charging blindly. A fourth blow to the back of the knee dropped him to the ground. Saanji pushed himself up, furiously clawing at the fresh snow jammed in the visor of his helmet.

"You bastard."

Finally giving up on the visor, he fumbled with the strap beneath his chin, removed his helmet altogether, and threw it. But Arnil Royce was standing in a different place from where Saanji thought he was. His helmet sailed into a crowd, where a startled Lancer caught it then tossed it back to Royce. The Lancer captain jammed his kingsteel bastard sword into the snow, approached, and offered Saanji his hand. Blushing, Saanji took it. Royce helped him up then returned his helmet.

"You're getting better."

Royce's praise brought scattered laughter from the many Lancers, Earless, and common citizens of Cassica who had gathered around the practice yard to watch. Saanji blushed further. "If I hadn't been wearing armor, you would have killed me in five seconds."

"Three seconds longer than last week," Royce pointed out. He picked up Saanji's longsword, which Saanji did not even remember dropping, and passed it back hilt first. Saanji took the sword and pounded his own chest through his breastplate, afraid his heart was about to stop. He noted dismally that Royce was not even breathing hard.

"You're losing weight, too," Royce said.

Saanji rubbed one knee then the other. "Yeah, a daily regimen of porridge and grueling exercise will do that."

Royce removed his own helmet, tossed it to one of his squires, then retrieved his sword. He sheathed it. Glancing over his shoulder, he asked, "Up for a little mace practice?" On cue, another squire came forward, holding two heavy maces with heads of iron.

Saanji shook his head. "Not after last time."

Royce took both maces. "Actually, I thought you did quite well. This time, you'll do better." He threw one of the maces at Saanji's head. Saanji barely caught it in time. He opened his mouth to unleash a stream of vile curses, but Royce was already charging.

Royce swung at Saanji's breastplate. Saanji leapt back. Royce followed, swinging at his unprotected head. Stunned, Saanji managed to swing his own mace and knock Royce's aside, but then Royce stepped in, twisted, and drove an armored elbow toward Saanji's face. He stopped just before making contact.

"Move faster," Royce advised. His body reversed, slipping away from Saanji like an uncoiling whip.

Saanji forced himself into a fighting position. His arms strained to hold the heavy mace. He did not think he had any strength left to swing it. But then Royce charged, and Saanji swung. Royce's mace rang off Saanji's breastplate, then again off one of his pauldrons, but Saanji answered with a blow to Royce's backplate that almost drove the Lancer off his feet.

Royce spun away, smiling despite his wince. A few Earless cheered. Saanji stopped to bow—then dove sideways, wide eyed, when Royce came out of nowhere, swinging fast and hard. Saanji took blows to both shoulders and another to his chest before he summoned enough breath to shout, "I yield!"

Royce immediately ceased his attack, stepped back, and bowed. He was breathing more quickly. "Horseback next," he said.

"Like hell." Saanji tossed his mace down. He limped to the nearest stone bench and sat. One of Royce's squires offered him water while another helped him remove his armor. Royce joined him a moment later, already breathing normally again.

"I think, by spring, we'll have made a warrior out of you."

"I think, come spring, I'll have you killed in your sleep." Saanji examined the gigantic bruise already forming on his shoulder. "Gods, how did you get so fast?"

"Survive this war, and I'll tell you all about it."

Saanji switched from bemoaning his bruised shoulder to staring, speechless, at his equally bruised knee. Then he reminded himself that people were still watching. He forced himself to stand and laugh as though unhurt. "Is there anybody in Ruun who can beat you?"

"Anybody can be beaten." Royce set about removing his own armor, waving off his squires' assistance. "There's an Isle Knight named Crovis who's supposed to be as good as they come. And if the stories are true, your brother is Fohl's own executioner."

"I've never seen Karhaati lose," Saanji admitted. "Not even in practice. Then again, he picks his targets carefully."

"As do most men looking to craft legends around their own names." Royce unbuckled his sword and leaned it against his chair, still within easy reach. "Which reminds me… you need to stop referring to yourself as the Tomato Prince. And you shouldn't let your men call you that, either."

Saanji shrugged. "Some mean it kindly. Others don't. Either way, it's just a name. So long as they follow orders, they can name me after their mothers, for all I care."

Royce smiled in terse disapproval but let the matter drop.

Saanji examined the fresh callouses on his soft hands. "Anything more from the scouts?"

Royce shook his head. "Your brother's still massed at Hesod. Chorlga's Jolym are still besieging Atheion, with a token force at Cadavash, and another still razing the Lotus Isles. I think the Dragonkin will wait until spring for his next big attack."

"And where do you think that will be?"

"Could be anywhere. The Wytchforest, Quesh, Lyos… maybe everywhere."

"But not Ivairia?"

Royce's expression darkened. "My king thinks we're safe. But I say Chorlga will come after us sooner or later. Or Karhaati will. We might do better defending our keeps, fighting them from behind thick stone walls. Or we might suffer for giving him time to replenish his strength."

Saanji rubbed his shoulder. He knew a thing or two about the price one paid for failing to act. "So what next… a treaty with Lyos? An alliance with the Isles?"

Royce gave Saanji a critical look. Saanji had been pressing Royce for an answer to that question for days. So far, Royce had refused to commit himself to a single course of action. "It's too late to help the Isles and too soon to march to Lyos," Royce said finally. "I was thinking about Nosh."

Saanji's eyes widened. "If you'd said Hesod, I would have thought you were crazy. But marching to Atheion is even worse."

"That's where the Jolym are. Your brother is Chorlga's ally. If we lift the siege on Atheion, the Noshans will become *our* allies. Supposedly, there are Isle Knights at Atheion, too. If all of us join together, we can beat the Jolym. Then we'll be in a stronger position to deal with your brother."

"But you're forgetting about Chorlga. You know, that Dragonkin who's ten times as powerful as Fadarah ever was."

"I'm not forgetting him. But we'll need magic to fight Chorlga. He has to have enemies. If those enemies are anywhere, they're in the south."

"Or the north," Saanji countered.

Royce seemed to catch his meaning. "Maybe. But after what my king did to the Shel'ai years ago, I doubt they'll help us."

"Not your king," Saanji agreed, "but maybe you."

Royce smirked. "Do you really think we can trust Shel'ai?"

"No," Saanji admitted.

"Me, either."

"Then what do you have in mind?"

"I don't have *anything* in mind yet, besides a direction."

"South..." Saanji shook his head. "Why in the gods' names—" He froze mid-sentence. A Lancer was running toward him, his face flushed, one hand on his sword. Two Earless followed. The Lancer raced toward Arnil Royce, the renegade Dhargots toward Saanji.

Royce was already standing. "One at a time." He pointed at the Lancer. "Reginald, speak."

Reginald offered a quick salute. "Pardon the interruption, sir, but someone has just arrived at the gates. She's demanding to speak with you."

"An emissary?"

Saanji frowned, though not just because he couldn't remember either of the Dhargots' names. Lone emissaries were rare enough; lone *female* emissaries were rarer still. Saanji might have thought she was an Iron Sister if he hadn't already heard that they'd been wiped out. *Unless it's—*

"A Shel'ai," one of his Earless blurted out. "She surrendered to the gate guards. She's alone. She says she wants to talk to whoever's leading this army."

Royce and Saanji exchanged looks. "You're the prince," Royce said.

Saanji scoffed. "No, thanks. She's all yours."

Reginald looked from Saanji to Royce. He lowered his voice. "Shall I... have her killed, sir? We have archers on the battlements, and she's standing right out in the open."

277

"Shouldn't be too difficult," one of the Earless added. "The wytch doesn't even have hands!"

Saanji frowned. He wondered why someone would cut off a Shel'ai's hands, then he came up with a reason.

"Who is she?" Royce asked.

"She says her name is Zeia," Reginald answered. "She says a man named Rashlin sent her."

Saanji frowned. "El'rash'lin?"

The Lancer nodded.

Royce said, "You know the name?"

"Only that he's supposed to be dead. And that if he *isn't*, he's not someone you want to rile up."

Royce turned back to Reginald and the Earless. "Did she say anything else?"

The Earless shook their heads, but Reginald said, "One more thing... though it didn't make any sense. She said she's been sent to help an Isle Knight. I told her there aren't any here, but she said to tell you, anyway."

Saanji asked, "What Isle Knight?"

"She said his name is Locke. Something Locke. Rowen, I think."

Saanji whistled softly. "Now, that's a name we've heard before." He glanced at Royce.

Royce was quiet for a moment, then he started buckling on his kingsteel longsword. "All right, I'll see her. Show her in. And for the gods' sake, don't threaten her."

Jalist reined in his horse, scowling at the eastern horizon. He'd left the cave at dawn and pressed hard, intending to follow the Ash'bana Plains all the way south to Quesh, but a score of Dhargots on horseback had spotted him and driven him east. After losing the horsemen, he'd reluctantly chosen to head toward Quesh by way of the Noshan Valley. While in Hesod with the others, he'd heard stories of the Jolym besieging Atheion, so he resolved to give the City-on-the-Sea a wide berth. But the thick smoke darkening the eastern sky had piqued his curiosity. Then, cresting a hill, he reined in his horse, raised his spyglass, and beheld the devastation.

"Sweet gods..."

A cold, familiar dread filled his chest. He remembered standing outside the city of Quorim, seemingly a lifetime ago, back when he'd fought as a sellsword in the ranks of the Throng. He remembered watching El'rash'lin and the Nightmare fight in front of Lyos, too.

Common sense told him to point his horse south, ride until its heart gave out, then run until his own heart did the same. He even briefly considered riding north and warning Rowen. Instead, he rode east, readying his long axe and resting it in the crook of his arm.

Chorlga found the madman sitting cross-legged in the snow, half naked, shivering. He issued a quick mental command, ordering his Jolym to stay back, then sent his voice echoing through the minds of the dragon-worshippers, ordering them to do the same. He approached the Nightmare alone. He braced himself, ready to counter a sea of wytchfire if the madman attacked.

"You led me on quite a chase, Iventine. Tell me, why did you go to the library? Did you think you'd find a way to die there?" Chorlga scowled at the smoke still darkening the southern horizon. "Atheion was to be spared. Instead, you burned down a third of it... including half the Scrollhouse! A thousand lifetimes' worth of knowledge..."

The Nightmare looked up, his violet eyes wide as wounds. Chorlga realized that the madman did not even understand what Chorlga was saying. "Why am I alive? I died. I keep dying, but I don't stay dead. Why?"

Chorlga blinked. He'd told himself countless times that the Nightmare was nothing—a mere Shel'ai with amplified powers, an overgrown guard dog to be used as Chorlga saw fit. But the pleading desperation in the madman's voice gave him pause. "You are alive because I wish it. Remember that."

"I was"—the Nightmare flinched—"in the Light..."

"That was just a dream. You were here. You have always been here, serving me. You will continue to serve me until I release you. Do you understand?"

The Nightmare wrapped his arms around himself and started rocking. "Please... please—"

"Enough!" Chorlga lifted one hand to strike him, saw his own hand shaking, and tucked it into his sleeve. "You will obey me, Iventine. I am your master. I am your god. You will serve me a while longer... then I will let you go."

The Nightmare looked up. He stopped rocking himself.

"I will let you go," Chorlga repeated. "Do you understand? Simply do as you're told, and your end is near. I swear it on the Dragongod."

For a time, the Nightmare was silent. Then he whispered, "Who do I have to kill?"

Chorlga grabbed his arm and pulled him to his feet. "Whomever I tell you."

"Who did this to me?" the Nightmare asked.

"The world," Chorlga said. "The world did this to you." He hesitated then removed his own cloak and threw it over the Nightmare's shoulders. "They did the same thing to me. That's why we're going to burn the world."

He led the Nightmare back toward Cadavash. The Nightmare followed without objection. The Jolym fell in behind them, followed by throngs of dragon-worshippers, many of them chanting Chorlga's name.

Hráthbam Nassir Adjrâ-al-Habas stood at the prow of his fastest ship, watching it plow through the ice-blue waters of the straits his people referred to as the Cold Passage. Though Hráthbam had been raised in a family of merchants, they had always done the bulk of their business on the mainland, with the occasional run to the Lotus Isles or another of the islands on Ruun's eastern coast. Hráthbam was already farther north than he had ever gone but not even half as far as he would go before this was over.

He glanced back at his passengers. One hand rested uneasily on the hilt of his massive scimitar. He was glad that most of the passengers had confined themselves to the lower decks, though two in particular had inhabited the top deck almost since they came on board.

His crew—all strong, young Soroccans who had served his family for years—went about their duties in fearful, sometimes angry silence. Hráthbam could not blame them. He wanted nothing more than to be back home, arguing with his wives and children, and he was sure they felt the same about their own families. But he was grateful that so far, none of them had defied his orders.

He was even more grateful that none of them had raised a hand against his passengers. He liked his crew. He did not want to see them turned to ash.

The two male passengers—one young and coldly handsome, the other old with a ghastly, sore-covered face and twisted lips—had been arguing in heated whispers for hours. Finally, the younger man threw up his hands and walked away. He stood by the starboard railing of the ship and stared out at the ocean, his expression as hard as stone. The older man looked after him, shook his head, then approached Hráthbam.

The Soroccan merchant braced himself. Though he'd seen the old man's twisted face in his dreams and relived some of the old man's memories after they inadvertently entered his mind months ago, this was still the first time he'd actually seen El'rash'lin in person. El'rash'lin was kind, and the gods knew that Hráthbam owed the man a great debt. Still, his appearance made Hráthbam shudder despite his best efforts to appear calm.

El'rash'lin stood beside him, staring out at the calm, parting waters. "What is it your people say about patience and children?"

"Children were put here to drive their parents insane."

El'rash'lin's twisted lips formed a slight smile. "I was expecting something a bit more articulate."

Hráthbam glanced back at the Shel'ai who called himself Shade, though Hráthbam had heard El'rash'lin refer to him by another name he had not caught. "Is that one... your son?"

El'rash'lin shook his head. "Almost none of us have children. No time. Besides, it's hard to run for your life if you have a squalling infant in your arms."

Hráthbam thought of the Shel'ai children in the lower decks of his ship, some crying from seasickness. One had already thrown a tantrum that set the sails on fire, though El'rash'lin had managed to extinguish the flames and repair the damage in the blink of an eye. "So those children down below—"

"Were born to Sylvan parents," El'rash'lin said. "Born... then abandoned. Believe me, it could have been worse." After a moment, he added, "The odds are one in a thousand, they say... though it's a certainty if one or both parents are already Shel'ai."

Hráthbam remembered the pregnant Sylvan women who had accompanied the Shel'ai onto the ship. He considered asking what kind of children they were carrying then decided he would rather not know. "We should be there in three or four days," he said. "I'm not worried about storms, and we shouldn't have any problems with ice if we keep east of the Wintersea, but..."

"You're afraid of what we'll find to the north?"

Hráthbam shook his head. "Not afraid, just confused. I haven't been up there, but my people have. I've seen the maps, too. There's nothing but a few little islands and a mass of icebergs. No Dragonkin, no wall of fire. Are you sure you don't want to go south?"

El'rash'lin shook his head. "The Dragonward surrounds the entire continent, a ways out to sea. It doesn't matter where we go, though the people who want us dead are less likely to follow us into the cold."

Hráthbam hesitated. "Isn't that where the legends say the Dragonkin went?"

"Yes, but the world is shaped like an orange. If they went far enough north, they'd end up on the other side of the world and start south again."

"I know that," Hráthbam said. "That's not what I mean."

El'rash'lin smiled again. "I know what you meant."

A cold wind blew over them. Hráthbam tugged at his cloak, marveling that El'rash'lin did not shiver. "If you're just looking for a place to run, I can suggest a few that are a lot warmer. You won't even have food in the north, unless you want to live off fish and snow foxes."

"Not especially. That's why your cargo hold contains twelve cases of Dwarrish darksoil. I know, because I teleported them there." El'rash'lin added, "They'll only need ten. Keep the other two as payment for your troubles."

Hráthbam touched the bulging coin purse hanging from his belt. "Gods, I don't need any more payment! You brought me back from the dead. I owe you."

"Then give it to your wives by way of apology."

It took a moment for Hráthbam to realize that El'rash'lin was joking. "They'll appreciate that." They stood in silence for a moment, then the Soroccan said, "If there's a wall of wytchfire stretching up to the clouds, shouldn't we be able to see it by now?"

"It's not a wall of fire," El'rash'lin said. "The legends call it that because it sounds more impressive. Really, it's invisible. Your kind can pass through it without so much as a tingle. You'd never even know it's there. Same with Shel'ai."

Hráthbam frowned. He saw the old man shudder. "But *you* can feel it, can't you?"

El'rash'lin looked surprised. He nodded slowly. "I've been feeling it since we left Sorocco. Every hour, it gets stronger."

"What's it like?"

"An intense feeling of… dread. I couldn't feel it before, when I was just a Shel'ai. I'd grown up hearing stories about the Dragonward, same as everyone, but I wasn't even sure it was real. But now…" El'rash'lin shuddered again. "After we reach it, your job will be to help Kith'el… *Shade* and the others find an island. For now, any island will do. Do I have your word on this?"

Hráthbam nodded, puzzled. He remembered El'rash'lin saying that the Shel'ai would only need ten of the twelve casks of darksoil in his ship's cargo hold.

They...

"What... happens if a Dragonkin tries to pass through the barrier?"

El'rash'lin did not answer. Hráthbam was about to repeat his question when the old man asked, "What's the name of this ship?"

"*Winter's Prayer,*" Hráthbam answered. "My youngest named it. I wanted to call it *Dyoni's Bane,* but it was her birthday."

El'rash'lin smiled. "Good name." Then he gathered his cloak about his thin frame and walked away. Hráthbam watched him go. Another frigid gust blew off the waters, up over the ship's railing, making him shudder.

CHAPTER THIRTY-ONE

ASH AND RUINS

B Y THE TIME JALIST REACHED Armahg's Tears, the city of Atheion
had stopped burning, though smoke still hid the sun and choked the
afternoon sky. Remembering that the Dhargots and the Noshans
were very nearly enemies, he'd already stripped off his Dhargothi armor and
traded it for his own. He dismounted, long axe in hand. Only the blowing
wind and the distant creaking of skiffs greeted him. Still, he approached
slowly. The smell of smoke and charred flesh filled his nostrils. He winced. He
remembered that smell.

He slowed as he neared the sea. All along the shore, ash covered the snow
just beyond the shattered wall. Jalist saw heaps of charred bones amid the ash.
The bones were barely recognizable as Human, though he saw a few bronze
shortswords half buried in the snow.

"Lochurites?"

Standing before the shattered gates, he studied his immediate surroundings.
He remembered shops, taverns, homes, and windmills along the shore.

In their place lay ash and charred timbers, though Jalist had no way
of knowing whether they had been destroyed along with the gates and the
Lochurites or sometime earlier. He listened for survivors. He returned to his
horse and mounted the skittish animal, his long axe still in hand. He forced
himself forward, through the ruined gates.

He found only blocks of scorched stone. The wall bore great cracks,
and chunks of it had been blown apart along with the gates, but the bridge
remained intact. The stone archway led from the shore to the first of Atheion's
great skiffs, somehow intact despite the skiff's faint motion on the silent sea.
Jalist dismounted to search for signs of Atheion's defenders.

More charred skeletons lined the charred battlements. Some wore armor that had melted, cooled, and hardened again, so that the dead appeared to have been covered with steel blankets. Jalist could not tell at first who they were. Then he spotted a broken adamune on the ground. Half the sword's curved blade was gone, though what remained gleamed coldly in the snow. Jalist picked it up.

"Gods... I'm sorry, Locke." He started to toss the broken sword down then changed his mind and lowered it with slow reverence. He'd hardly finished doing so when he heard a sound. He turned, fumbling for his long axe, in time to see his horse galloping away from him.

Jalist cursed. He shouted at the animal, but it paid him no mind. He decided there was no point in chasing after it. If he was lucky, he would find another horse in Atheion. If not, he could stay, rest, and find fresh supplies before continuing south in the morning. He did not relish the thought of staying in Atheion, but at least he could get out of the cold for a while.

Another night spent in a gods-damned graveyard...

He tried not to think of all the corpses and wreckage he'd found in Stillhammer. In that case, the destruction had been wrought by Jolym, but Atheion was different. He recognized the signs of what had been done there, having seen them more times than he cared to remember.

Jalist started across the bridge, hoping the Nightmare was not still in the city. He also noted that it looked as though the destruction had started *within* the city then extended beyond the walls. He looked over the railing, down at the blue waters of Armahg's Tears. The surface gleamed with a thin sheen of ice. He wondered how long it would be before the sea was frozen solid.

Then he heard a sound.

Aeko Shingawa stood in the remains of the dead king's palace. A chill wind swept through the chamber, howling through cracks in the walls, but she kept her eyes fixed on the drawn adamune lying on the floor at the center of the chamber. *Her* adamune. Snow had fallen through great cracks in the ceiling, dusting the floor and dampening the blade.

Isle Knights stood all around her, as still as statues. She could hear their breathing and smell the blood and sweat on their armor.

Crovis Ammerhel continued his accusations: "Finally, with a heavy heart, I must accuse the Knight of the Lotus called Aeko Shingawa of extreme cowardice in the face of the enemy."

A murmur swept through the Knights. Some rumbled with anger, while

285

a great many more nodded in agreement. Crovis gave the Knights time to absorb his words. He paced around her sword, at the center of the gathering, never taking his eyes off Aeko. "Despite the courage she has demonstrated on countless past occasions... which are *not* in question... Aeko Shingawa's behavior since being promoted to the Order of the Lotus by our late Grand Marshal has been an unquestionable affront to the precepts of the Codex Viticus, as well as the philosophy of the Codex Lotius. She has not maintained the principles of our Order, either in spirit or in action. For that reason, I am left with the solemn and unfortunate duty of demanding justice from this assemblage."

Crovis Ammerhel faced Aeko with an almost believable look of reluctance, bowed to the assembled Knights, and stepped back. A few Knights applauded. Another Knight moved to the center of the chamber. Lanky and quick eyed, he wore his hair in a long dark braid. He held up his hands, calling for attention. When the Knights did not quiet down to let him speak, Crovis called for silence on the young Knight's behalf.

Aeko's heart sank. Her defense had not even spoken, and he'd already made a serious mistake. She sighed. She should have expected this. With Crovis acting as her accuser and the rest of the Knights as her judges, she'd had the option of defending herself or requesting another Knight to do it for her. Traditionally, the latter was preferable, since it gave the appearance that the accused had friends among the Knighthood.

But Aeko had few friends left. No Knight from the Orders of the Stag or the Lotus would speak for her. Finally, a Knight from the lowest of the three ranks—the Order of the Crane—had volunteered. His name was Sang Wei. Aeko knew nothing of his background except that he was poor and quiet. On the other hand, witnesses said he'd distinguished himself at the gates of Atheion, holding back the Lochurites almost single-handedly when the first blast from the Nightmare killed half of Aeko's company and left her unconscious.

Maybe he's braver with steel than with words. She'd met Knights like that before. She doubted such a man could help her now.

Sang Wei faced Crovis, then seemed to change his mind and fixed his gaze on Aeko. "Sir Ammerhel has leveled many grave accusations." His voice trembled. A few Isle Knights chuckled.

Sang Wei cleared his throat and continued. "She stands accused of incompetence in the manner in which she led the defenses of Atheion and in her failure to complete her original mission, which was locating Sir Rowen

Locke and bringing him back to the Isles for justice. She also stands accused of disloyalty for continuing to keep her Knights stationed at Atheion, even after she received word of the attacks on the Isles."

Aeko grimaced. Was her defense really going to articulately summarize Crovis's entire case? She considered shaking her head to warn him then decided to keep her expression immobile.

"Finally," Wei said, "Sir Ammerhel has accused her of cowardice." He stopped, turned, and faced Crovis. "Since no details were provided on this charge, I assume that Sir Crovis means cowardice in the face of the Jolym."

Crovis stepped forward and gave Sang Wei a toothy smile. "I do, sir. Had Lady Shingawa attacked the Jolym earlier, before the Lochurites arrived, they could have been defeated with ease. The Nightmare would not have sensed her weakness and taken that opportunity to strike… which resulted in the deaths of hundreds, including Atheion's beloved king." He bowed to Sang Wei. "My apologies for not being clearer."

Gods… Aeko clenched her fists, digging her nails into her palms. She began to wonder if Sang Wei was actually working on Crovis's behalf.

Sang Wei nodded slowly. "Perhaps Sir Crovis is unaware that before the Nightmare's appearance, Knight-Captain Shingawa was personally leading a force to meet the Jolym who were hacking through the gates."

"A charge that was unsuccessful," Crovis pointed out.

Wei smiled at Crovis. "Agreed. During the battle, Knight-Captain Shingawa demonstrated that she was unable to battle demons, barbarian berserkers, and rampaging Jolym after being knocked unconscious."

The young Knight's rebuttal brought scattered laughter, but Crovis scowled. "I remind the young Knight that many of our brothers were killed in the attack, along with countless Noshans. We have not yet even had time to commit their bodies to the Light. Such levity is uncalled for."

For a moment, Aeko thought that Sang Wei meant to point out that the reason they had not yet buried the slain Knights was that Crovis Ammerhel had requested this trial almost as soon as the Nightmare had vanished and the Jolym began their slow, mindless march north. But the young Knight blushed. "My apologies to this council. I meant no disrespect. I merely point out that honoring our fallen comrades has hardly been the priority of this company." He hesitated as though gathering his courage. "Even Sir Crovis has spent much of the last two days attending to other matters… meeting with the Noshan survivors, convincing them to sail what remains of their city to the Lotus Isles, I believe."

The Knights bristled, but Aeko fought to hide her smile. *Careful, young Knight.* Some of Atheion had survived, including a portion of the Scrollhouse that seemed immune to fire. Several thousand Noshans remained, including a good many soldiers. The skiffs themselves were a technological marvel. Most of the surviving Knights were probably thrilled that even in the face of defeat, Crovis Ammerhel had managed to gain additional wealth, strength, and territory for their struggling Order.

"I confess," Crovis said, "that *one* of my primary concerns has been for the living. Lady Shingawa's incompetence caused great harm to the Noshans. They've lost much of their famed city. They've lost more than half of their beloved Scrollhouse, their leaders, their friends, their families. As this council seeks justice for Lady Shingawa, I have sought justice for the Noshans."

Like hells, Aeko almost said.

Sang Wei nodded. "By Sir Crovis's own words, then, Aeko Shingawa also stands accused of crimes against the Noshans. I wonder, then, in keeping with the tenets of the Codex Viticus, why no Noshans are present in this chamber."

Another murmur swept through the crowd. Crovis spoke up quickly in his own defense. "The young Knight might not be aware of the fact that of the surviving Noshans, some are busy trying to salvage what remains of the Scrollhouse, while others work to unmoor the skiffs so that they might be sailed on Zet's Blood. Others tend to those portions of the river that have already frozen and will need to be cleared. Given these distractions, I do not think the Noshans are overly concerned with the internal application of Knightly justice."

Crovis's words earned many nods of agreement, but Sang Wei did not blink. "Do you acknowledge, sir, that no Noshans are present to either support or refute your version of events?"

Crovis offered Sang Wei a strained smile. "If it pleases you, I will withdraw all accusations and statements specifically tying Aeko Shingawa to the fate of the Noshans, so that we may complete these unfortunate proceedings. Is that acceptable?"

Sang Wei nodded. "It is, sir." He faced Aeko again. "Would you also agree, Sir Crovis, that your statements do *not* include an accusation that Knight-Captain Shingawa and the demon known as the Nightmare are in collusion?"

Crovis snapped, "I suggested no collusion. Lady Shingawa may be incompetent and a coward, but she is no traitor."

Sang Wei nodded again. "Not a traitor. Thank you, sir." He turned slowly, facing each of the remaining Knights in turn. "So in essence, Sir Crovis is angry because Knight-Captain Shingawa kept us in Atheion rather than racing back to the Lotus Isles to fight the Jolym."

He paused.

"Yet the Jolym were also besieging Atheion. In fact, it's entirely possible that the Jolym attacking Atheion had been diverted from the Lotus Isles, where they had previously been busy killing our people and burning our temples."

He paused again.

"It's quite possible, my brothers and sisters, that either by chance or through the will of the Light, those monsters that had previously ravaged the Lotus Isles found themselves facing *our* steel, and that by taking us back to the Lotus Isles, Knight-Captain Shingawa would actually have been allowing them to escape justice."

Aeko frowned. *What's he getting at?*

Crovis Ammerhel appeared equally confused. "The Jolym use no banners, no sigils. We have no way of knowing which ones attacked which kingdom, or when. We know only that the Jolym are the creatures of a Dragonkin, servants of Fohl, and an affront to the Light."

Sang Wei gestured to Crovis. "Our brother speaks the truth. The Jolym are an affront to the Light. Destroying them is a duty mandated by the laws and spirit of the Knighthood. In that spirit, I suggest that Knight-Captain Shingawa remained in Atheion to fulfill that directive."

The Knights murmured again.

Crovis flushed with rage. "Nonsense," he answered, shouting to be heard. "Lady Shingawa is a coward. If she wanted to battle the Jolym, she could have ridden out the gates a week ago. Instead, she hid behind the battlements. One wonders which side she's actually fighting on."

The murmurs from the Knights became shouts—some of agreement, others of outrage. Sang Wei waited until they fell silent before he answered.

"Sir Crovis," he began with sudden sternness, "do you wish to withdraw your previous statement and assert that Knight-Captain Shingawa *is* a traitor?"

Aeko smothered a grin.

Crovis blinked. "I spoke in anger." He bowed to Sang Wei then to Aeko. "I will assert once more that, *appearances to the contrary*, Lady Shingawa remains loyal to the Knighthood."

"So you do not question her loyalty," Wei said, "so much as her judgment in refusing to attack the Jolym more promptly?"

"More *decisively*," Crovis amended. "Incompetence and dishonor can sometimes manifest themselves as inaction, young sir. When such inaction gets Knights killed for no reason, I call it incompetence. I do not think I am alone in this."

Sang Wei answered before the rest of the Knights had time to voice their agreement. "So a competent, honorable commander is one who remains loyal to the Knighthood, does not retreat from the enemies of the Light, and does not get his—or *her*—Knights slain needlessly?"

When Crovis did not answer, Wei continued. "The Codex Lotius advises that we should *tend the blade but trust the scabbard*. In other words, a true Knight is one who values restraint over bravado. That statement is echoed in another passage from the Codex Lotius: *It is better to deliberate than to repent.*"

"One need not repent from courage," Crovis countered.

But Sang Wei continued as though no one had spoken. "Knight-Captain Shingawa showed restraint in facing a new, terrible adversary, about which very little is known. In so doing, she prevented Knights from dying rashly. She is, by Sir Crovis's own definition, a competent and honorable commander. Were it not for the appearance of the Nightmare, both the Jolym and the Lochurites might easily have been rebuffed from Atheion's walls."

"But the Nightmare *did* appear," Crovis insisted. He gestured to the cracks in the walls. "Or have you not seen the wreckage and smelled the bodies?"

Sang Wei faced Crovis. "By your own assertion, Knight-Captain Shingawa and the Nightmare are not allies. She had no way of knowing that the Nightmare would appear. You may find fault with her for not attacking sooner, but the Grand Marshal placed her in charge of this company. *Her*, not you."

Aeko heard a distinct change in the murmuring of the Knights around her. Her young defender was getting through to them.

But Crovis was not finished. He gave Sang Wei a withering look then slowly faced the rest of the Knights. "Brothers, the city of Atheion lies in ruins. More importantly, from what we've heard, much of our own beloved homeland lies in tatters. The temples where we prayed and trained for years have been destroyed. Ashes darken the Burnished Way. Both the Jolym and the magic-wielding demon called the Nightmare have escaped justice, as has the Dragonkin who supposedly leads them. The Codex Lotius calls for restraint and forgiveness, but I must confess, I find my heart filled with rage." He paused. "Not since the Shattering War has our beloved Knighthood faced threats like those that surround it now. Such times call for action. We need bold, honorable commanders." He pointed at Aeko. "We need better than this."

Sang Wei answered quickly. "What do you ask of this council, sir? Normally, the accuser voices their desired punishment along with their accusations, but you have not done so." Aeko sensed his hesitation. When the young Knight spoke again, his voice sounded lower. "Tell me, Sir Crovis, does your enraged heart require that a competent, reasonable Knight-Captain... one chosen by the Grand Marshal himself... be put to death?"

Crovis bristled. He touched the hilt of his own adamune, and Aeko wondered if he meant to challenge Sang Wei to a duel. Instead, he scowled at Wei then at Aeko. "I suggested no death sentence. I merely suggest that her rank of Knight-Captain *and* her induction into the Order of the Lotus be revoked until such time as she is able to demonstrate her worthiness of these honors."

Sang Wei said, "The Codex Viticus allows for a majority vote to suspend a Knight-Commander and replace him or her with another Knight of majority vote, but this does *not* apply to a Knight-Captain or higher. A Grand Marshal can revoke the rank of Stag or Crane, but the rank of Lotus can only be revoked by a majority vote in a body of at least five hundred Knights."

Aeko frowned. *How in Jinn's name does he know that?* The Codex Viticus was a frightfully ponderous tome. She had never heard a mere Knight of the Crane so familiar with its complex and tiresome edicts.

Crovis looked equally surprised but recovered quickly. "Our young friend demonstrates a refreshing respect for the law. Of course, he is correct. But I believe that in extreme cases, the Codex Viticus permits the temporary demotion of a Knight of the Lotus by order of a Sword Marshal."

Aeko swore inwardly.

Sang Wei frowned. "I see no Sword Marshal in this assemblage. In fact, I don't believe we've had a Sword Marshal for over a hundred years."

Crovis smiled faintly. "No, we haven't. But if I remember correctly, the Codex Viticus *also* allows a Knight of the Lotus to be promoted to Sword Marshal, in extreme circumstances like a time of war, by simple majority vote."

Aeko gave Crovis a cold smile. *Of course you remember correctly, and you damn well know it!*

Now it was Sang Wei's turn to look surprised. "That's correct, but—"

"Then I propose a more measured course of action," Crovis said. He paused, choosing his words carefully. "Lady Shingawa has refused to step down voluntarily. Sir Wei believes that she has acted appropriately, given the circumstances. Obviously, I disagree, but some of you may favor leniency. Some may even agree with Sir Wei. You are within your rights to do so."

He faced Sang Wei and gave him a gracious bow. "I do not wish to sow disunion in a time of war. So I suggest that if this assemblage will grant me the rank of Sword Marshal, I can then assume command of this company without dishonoring Lady Shingawa by stripping her of rank."

He added, "Naturally, as set forth by the Codex Viticus, such a field promotion is only temporary... unless ratified by the majority of all Knights on the Isles as soon as a proper vote can be called for. So, after the Jolym have been defeated, the Nightmare executed, and their foul master driven back across the Wintersea, I will surrender my fate into the hands of my honorable brothers and sisters in armor."

For a moment, no one spoke. Then, Crovis's supporters broke into wild applause. A few shouted their agreement. Some tried to argue but were shouted down. Sang Wei called for silence. No one listened. By the time Crovis Ammerhel was able to quiet the assembly, Aeko knew she'd lost.

She knew, too, why Crovis had not simply challenged her to a duel over some imagined slight. This way, he gained rank by appearing gracious, even merciful. Aeko eyed her sword, still resting on the palace floor.

I could challenge Crovis myself. But he'd win. Then Rowen Locke would have one less friend in the Knighthood... and right now, I'm not sure he has more than one.

Aeko resisted the impulse to stalk out of the room. One of Crovis's supporters, a gray-haired Knight of the Lotus named Wyn Kai, took over. He proposed granting Crovis the rank of Sword Marshal and called for a vote. The chamber resounded with shouts of approval. Wyn Kai smiled then called for voices of opposition. Though Aeko saw a few grimaces, no one bothered to speak. Sang Wei opened his mouth, but Aeko caught his eye and shook her head. She did not speak, either.

A heavy silence hung over the chamber for several oppressive seconds. Finally, Wyn Kai turned to face Crovis. "Sir Crovis Ammerhel, Knight-Captain in the Order of the Lotus and protector of the legacy of Fâyu Jinn, step forth."

Crovis did so, managing an expression of deep humility as he fell to one knee.

"It is the judgment of this special council that you be granted a field promotion to Sword Marshal, the permanence of which will be decided as soon as a proper vote can be organized on the Lotus Isles." He paused. "Do you accept this honor?"

Crovis had been looking at the floor. He looked up slowly. Tears glistened in his eyes. "I do." He drew his sword and gave it to Wyn Kai, who reversed it, passing it back to Crovis by the hilt.

"Then by the Light, we name you Crovis Ammerhel, Sword Marshal in the Order of the Lotus. Stand and be recognized."

Crovis sheathed his adamune and took his time rising. By the time he stood, thunderous applause surrounded him. Crovis bowed, turned, and bowed again. Then he picked up Aeko's adamune and slowly carried it back to her. His expression hardened. His eyes no longer appeared teary. "Knight-Captain Shingawa, I relieve you." He held out her sword, hilt first.

Aeko took it. "I stand relieved." She forced herself to bow then sheath her sword.

Crovis stepped back. Then he faced Sang Wei. "Sir Wei, in recognition of your honorable defense of Knight-Captain Shingawa… and contingent, of course, upon the agreement of those Knights here assembled… I hereby promote you to Knight of the Stag, with the corresponding rank of Knight-Lieutenant."

Sang Wei blinked.

After a moment's stunned silence, the chamber erupted into a second round of thunderous applause. Wyn Kai held up his hands, calling for silence. When he got it, he called for a second vote. This time, nearly every Knight in the chamber—including those who had sided with Aeko—voiced their agreement.

Clever bastard, Aeko thought, as she added her own.

Crovis faced Sang Wei again. "Sir Wei, do you accept this honor?"

Sang Wei looked to Aeko for help. Aeko nodded slightly. Turning back to Crovis, Sang Wei bowed. "I do, Knight-Marshal. Thank you." He started to kneel, but Crovis was already turning away. The Knights began to disperse.

Sang Wei edged closer. "Why did he do that?"

Aeko frowned. As the crowds shifted, for the first time, she noticed a short, muscular figure standing at the far end of the chamber. Her frown deepened. She approached the Dwarr, one hand on the hilt of her adamune. "You're Jalist Hewn."

The Dwarr looked surprised. "I am. Well met, Knight. I didn't think you'd remember."

"I make it a point of remembering the faces of turncoat sellswords."

Jalist smiled slightly. "Locke forgave me for that a long time ago. Besides, I'm the one who talked the Throng into revolting." He added, "You're welcome for that, by the way."

"So I've heard. Some tell it differently."

Jalist raised one eyebrow. "Like Crovis? I remember him, too, you know. He was just a Knight-Captain then, but I guess raiding the treasury of Lyos and pretending you single-handedly won a battle are enough to get you a promotion these days. And didn't I hear something about him plundering Phaegos because it didn't want to pay taxes?"

Aeko smothered a grin when the Dwarr's loud voice drew angry stares from nearby Knights. "I didn't know the Dwarr took such an active interest in the politics of the Free Cities."

"Didn't you hear? The king of Lyos made me his Captain of the Guard."

Aeko wondered if he was joking. "Then what are you doing here?"

"That's a long story." Jalist looked around. "To be honest, seeing this city from the outside, I didn't expect to find anybody alive in here. The whole front of the city's abandoned. Then I heard noise... men fussing with the skiffs, pulling up anchors that look like they haven't been raised in five hundred years. Saw the Scrollhouse, too. I've never seen so many crying clerics before."

Aeko glanced back at Crovis, who was busy being congratulated. "Why are you here? I thought you were with..." She trailed off, leaving Rowen's name unspoken. She did this even though she'd already lowered her voice so no one would hear, including Sang Wei, who stood a few steps behind her.

"I was. He's alive, if that's what you're wondering. He wanted to meet you here, but he's gone back to Hesod first."

Aeko momentarily thought the Dwarr was joking.

Jalist sneered. "I know. I told him the same thing. But there's someone there he cares about."

Aeko took Jalist's arm and pulled him away from the other Knights. "Silwren?"

Jalist shook his head. "The wytch is dead... though *how* she died might take some explaining, too, if you've got the time."

Aeko glanced back at Crovis again. A few Knights were watching her. Sooner or later, someone would realize who he was. "Get out of here," Aeko said. "Don't let any Knights see you. Meet me by what's left of the wall in half an hour. We'll talk then."

Jalist nodded.

Aeko watched him go then turned around.

Sang Wei frowned at her. "Wasn't that—"

"Never mind," Aeko said. "I'd like to know how a peasant-Knight knows so much about the Codex Viticus."

Sang Wei blushed. "My great-great-grandfather was a Knight of the Lotus. But he was stripped of rank after... an incident. After that, my family made a point of learning the law."

Aeko frowned. "I hadn't heard that."

"No one has. We were lucky. All the records from that time were lost in the Spring Fires. Better if I just pretended I was the first Wei to earn my adamune." He hesitated. "I'd appreciate it if you'd keep that to yourself, Knight-Captain."

"Gladly, Knight-Lieutenant." Aeko glanced past him. "I wonder if Sir Crovis has even stopped to realize something peculiar about our enemies." She paused. "The Nightmare and the Jolym both serve the Dragonkin. They're on the same side, along with the Lochurites. Yet when the Nightmare appeared, it lashed out blindly, burned up half the Lochurites and killed some of the Jolym... if *kill* is the right word."

"Do you think our enemies are fighting each other?"

"Maybe the Nightmare just can't be controlled. I recall hearing that Fadarah and the sorcerers had plenty of trouble with that." She added, "Strange that the Jolym take their dead with them."

Sang Wei snickered. "Do you think they bury them?"

"Maybe they just don't want us to be reminded that they're mortal." She sighed. "Speaking of the dead, we need to form a detachment and gather our own. But first, let's go congratulate our new leader before the words rot in my stomach."

Chorlga stared into the unresponsive darkness of Namundvar's Well. Finally, he spat in it. Then he straightened and closed his eyes. At his command, the sights experienced by all of his Jolym, all over the continent, poured into his mind in a dizzying fury. He reeled then sifted through it all with practiced determination.

First, he saw through the eyes of the Jolym massed around Cadavash, amid the cries and madness of the dragon-worshippers around them. Pushing these aside, he lingered on the token force he'd left on the Lotus Isles, still methodically hunting Knights in the shadows of their ruined temples.

Dismissing these, he moved on to the hundreds of Jolym scouring the rest of Ruun.

Through their eyes, he saw the endless snowy hills in which they walked, searching for Rowen Locke and, more importantly, for El'rash'lin. His Jolym had already probed the remains of Brahasti's compound then broadened their search from the Ash'bana Plains to the Wintersea. On the latter, they'd found what looked to be the remnants of a settlement. That must have been where all the Shel'ai had been hiding. El'rash'lin was probably with them. *But where are they now?*

Chorlga had sent some Jolym back into the ravaged kingdom of Stillhammer, others north toward Ivairia and Sorocco, and still more as far west as Syros. He checked on their progress. As he had anticipated, the Jolym stalked mercilessly through city streets, tore apart villages, and moved like battering rams through forests roiling with thieves, beggars, and wolves.

Through the eyes of his Jolym, Chorlga saw the screaming faces of people who ran, pleaded for mercy, or foolishly tried to fight. He paid them no mind. He was running out of places to search. He'd been reluctant to send his Jolym into Lyos, since the people there had demonstrated some ability to defend themselves. He saw little point in searching Quesh, Dhargoth, or what remained of the kingdom of Nosh, but that left only the Wytchforest. Given the Sylvs' history with Shel'ai, Chorlga doubted that El'rash'lin would have sought sanctuary there, but it was always a possibility.

Chorlga opened his eyes, staring down into the unyielding darkness of Namundvar's Well. "Why doesn't he just come out and fight?"

But Chorlga already knew the answer. The strain of being made a Dragonkin had followed El'rash'lin back from the dead. He was not much more stable than the Nightmare. If he pushed himself too far, trying to protect all the kingdoms of Ruun from the Jolym, he might lose himself completely. Chorlga might be able to control him. Then he would have not just one Nightmare at his disposal but two.

"But why isn't he guarding the Isle Knight, at least?" Chorlga shook his head. He'd expected to find them together. He'd thought El'rash'lin would stay with the Knight to help train him so that he might finally begin to control Knightswrath's power. But something told him that the Knight was still somewhere near Hesod—alone.

The Isle Knight did not greatly concern him, but El'rash'lin did. The old man was clever. Since he was not strong enough to destroy Chorlga, he might be searching for a way to eliminate his champion. Chorlga turned, scowling at the ragged madman rocking himself on the cold stone floor a short distance away. "Some champion…"

Chorlga considered the city of Atheion, the remnants of which were even now struggling through the icy waters of Zet's Blood, toward the open sea. The Nightmare's destruction of much of the Scrollhouse was a terrible blow— millennia of knowledge lost—but Chorlga had already spent countless hours poring over those ancient tomes. They said nothing of consequence.

Maybe El'rash'lin is only hiding, forcing me to spread my Jolym all over the continent to search for him. After all, he cannot leave. The Dragonward—

Chorlga froze. The power of the Dragonward, which increased in proportion to the being attempting to pass through it, would not permit El'rash'lin to leave Ruun. If he tried, it would kill him. Chorlga had not thought of it past that, but he did now.

He turned. His eyes narrowed on the rocking figure. The Nightmare began to whimper. "He's going to throw himself in," Chorlga said finally. "He thinks that will kill him for good… and you with him. And he may be right."

Chorlga's pulse quickened. Though the Dragonward surrounded all of Ruun, El'rash'lin would surely make for the closest part. Chorlga thought it over for a long time. Finally, he realized he had four choices.

He could reroute his Jolym back to the Wintersea, trusting that their sheer strength and numbers would be enough to "kill" El'rash'lin, causing him to reappear elsewhere on Ruun. At least that would give Chorlga time. But it would cost him many Jolym, and besides, he doubted they could intercept El'rash'lin in time.

He could go there himself, to the very edge of the fearsome Dragonward, but a teleportation spell would leave him weakened. Being near the Dragonward would slow his recovery, as well. El'rash'lin might actually be able to kill him then.

Chorlga considered his third option: sending the Nightmare. But he and El'rash'lin were almost evenly matched. If El'rash'lin had any additional Shel'ai helping him, he could prevail—or, without Chorlga there to keep the Nightmare in line, El'rash'lin might convince him to jump into the Dragonward himself!

That left only one option: Chorlga *and* the Nightmare would have to teleport to the Dragonward together. Chorlga could drain power off his servant, use him to absorb the brunt of El'rash'lin's attack, then finish him off himself. When El'rash'lin came back to life, he might even be mindless enough for Chorlga to control.

But all that will take time. I'll have to trust Ruun to the Dhargothi princeling.

The Nightmare whimpered again, interrupting his thoughts. Chorlga felt an unexpected stir of pity for the man, tinged with irritation. Then he realized there was a fifth option—riskier than the others but one that El'rash'lin could not possibly have anticipated. It would grant him such terrifying power, all the kingdoms would simply surrender to his will.

One I've considered before...

Chorlga made his decision. He turned and stroked the Nightmare's hair as though he were a cowering pet. "Have no fear, young one. You'll be dead soon."

CHAPTER THIRTY-TWO
SHORTSWORDS

KARHAATI LISTENED TO THE SWEET music of catapults. Not far from where he sat astride his bloodmare, surrounded by bodyguards, the catapults' great oak arms hurled wave after wave of rocks and fireballs at the gigantic temple. The marble walls had already been cracked, and the wooden roof had burned away. Still, he ordered his exhausted engineers to load and fire the siege weapons. He had half a mind to work them to death.

Of all the temples in Hesod, he had hoped to save this one, even going so far as to station guards outside to keep it from being looted and spoiled. An architectural marvel, as big as a palace and supposedly more than a thousand years old, it honored not just one but all the gods—including Zet and Fohl, whose statues had once adorned the others on the temple steps. Zet's winged statue stood thrice the height of a man, bigger than all the others, and armored. Fohl's had been much smaller, ominously cloaked, its back turned. All had been exquisitely carved by master stonemasons, right down to the slightest details: Zet's scales, the ripples in Fohl's cloak, and the taut skin of Tier'Gothma's milk-filled breasts. They were unlike anything Karhaati had seen in his own kingdom.

Nevertheless, at his command, his catapults destroyed them. He'd had no choice. By sealing themselves in the temple, the Iron Sisters had forced his hand. He had hoped that burning down the temple roof would smoke out the Iron Sisters, but even when smoke poured out the temple windows, they would not come out. He glanced around, appreciating how the remaining Hesodi citizens stood in the streets and gawked, aghast. Some looked as though they wanted to intervene. But given how poorly the last revolt had gone, Karhaati doubted they were foolish enough to try again.

He had always loved the sound of catapults. But they had been firing almost nonstop for two days, and still the temple stood. Cracked, blackened, and no longer recognizable as a place of worship, still it remained, as though taunting him. Even the poetic justice of attacking the temple with Hesodi catapults, appropriated when he took command of the city, could not stave off the discontent building within him. But he dared not suspend the attack after so clearly stating his intentions in front of the men.

Then he thought of his guest. He thought of her lying in his bed, drugged and asleep, naked except for the stained bandages wrapped around her ribs, thighs, shoulder, and of course, her throat. He thought of her red hair against the white silk of his pillow. His blood quickened. He imagined riding back to the palace like the conqueror he was and having his way with her. Then he shook his head.

No, not this one.

He turned to his newest bodyguard, a one-eyed sellsword who had just recently arrived in Hesod after abandoning Brahasti. Karhaati had been tempted to kill the man for that alone, but he appreciated the sellsword's gall. "You, go back and check on the woman. Make sure nobody's touched her. And don't *you* touch her, either, if you value your remaining eye."

The sellsword nodded gruffly. "Yes, Prince."

Karhaati decided to stay and oversee the temple siege a while longer, but now that he'd thought of her, he could not erase the woman from his mind. The men had given her to him as a gift, and he could scarcely fail to appreciate its value. She was perhaps the only bit of good fortune he'd had. For that reason, he'd left his most trusted men to see that she was not harmed or even touched by anyone, save his best physicians—all of whom had been told that their survival depended on keeping *her* alive.

Still, she had been sorely wounded. A soldier had managed to tackle her before she could open her own throat, but the knife had still cut deep. It was doubtful that she would survive, let alone recover enough for him to use her as an adequate test of his sword arm. But he prayed that she would. He had even sacrificed a bloodmare and three young slaves in the hopes that the gods would respond to his plea.

Perhaps one day, if she lives, she'll even give herself to me willingly. Women of action love men of the same, do they not?

He cursed himself, trying to shake off the thought. The woman was beautiful, sure, but he could always find another beautiful woman. It was her fierceness he valued most. He did not even want revenge on her for all the harm she'd caused. She was a true warrior—more of a warrior than any man he'd ever fought—and how could such a warrior do anything other than what she'd done?

Stones cracked against the temple walls. Smoke stung his eyes. Soldiers laughed while Hesodi looked on and wept. But Karhaati could think of nothing but the woman. He did not even know her name. He smiled, imagining what it might be.

Saanji was grateful that Arnil Royce had a new sparring companion, though he felt a pang of jealousy as he watched the Lancer dueling the wytch. Saanji had purchased the false affections of more prostitutes than he could recall, especially exotic women—dark-skinned Soroccans, olive-skinned Queshi, or any woman who showed signs of having Dwarrish blood in her ancestry—but Zeia had enchanted him right away. He'd been unable to wrest his eyes off her during council meetings, though she'd hardly said a word to him. In fact, he found it more than a little amusing that he would feel such attraction toward a woman with no hands.

Despite her lack of anything past the wrist, Zeia seemed to be fairing quite well against Royce. Hands of violet fire blossomed from her sleeves, each one somehow gripping the hilt of a shortsword. The pommels smoked. Flames spread from her "hands" down the blades, engulfing them, causing the air around them to shimmer.

Though it was a stunning sight, Royce appeared to have gotten used to it. He circled Zeia with increasing speed, his kingsteel bastard sword flashing in the afternoon light. Then he charged. Steel rang. Sparks rained down onto the snowy ground. Royce's sword blurred one direction, then another. Zeia backpedaled, both swords in motion, but Royce was faster. His sword tapped Zeia's greaves, then her spaulders. Zeia cursed.

He's not going easy on her, Saanji realized.

Despite her frustration, Zeia seemed glad for the practice. Sweat glistened on her forehead. The ghost of a smirk played on her lips whenever Royce was forced to retreat from her burning shortswords. Though she looked uncomfortable in armor and still refused to wear a helmet, she had already adapted faster than Saanji had. And despite probably spending most of her life relying on wytchfire, with no need to develop melee skills, she'd learned quickly.

Faster than me, Saanji thought ruefully. *Then again, she's learning from the best.* He grimaced. *Then again, so was I.*

Zeia's daily sparring with Royce had drawn a great deal of attention, too. Lancers and Earless crowded the practice yards, as did the people of Cassica. Though the city's populace had initially greeted Zeia with hostility, that had changed after Saanji suggested she use her magic to heal some of Cassica's wounded. Karhaati had left plenty in his wake, and the Bloody Prince had killed nearly all the clerics who might have otherwise treated them.

Zeia had refused at first, but after Royce voiced his support of Saanji's plan, she consented. For days, she'd helped any Human willing to share her company, somehow able to dispense healing energies through her hands of fire. Zeia's face had remained stern, her demeanor far from cordial, but she'd successfully healed young and old alike, saving scores of Cassicans from infected wounds. That, plus her unique appearance, had made her a curiosity throughout the city. Everyone came to see the stoic Shel'ai who could summon working hands of wytchfire to replace the ones that had been cut from her body.

Saanji thought of the stories he'd heard coming from Lyos about an incredibly powerful sorceress named Silwren who had healed their wounded despite earlier encounters with Lyosi mobs bent on killing her. Supposedly, the Lyosi thought of Silwren as a hero now. Saanji would not have thought it possible, especially after the destruction of Fadarah's infamous Throng, but he foresaw a day when Zeia might be equally beloved in Cassica.

Well, maybe not by everyone. He noted a group of scowling Cassicans in the distance, giving Zeia murderous looks. All had knives in their belts. Saanji gestured to get the attention of one of his officers then nodded toward the group. His officer got the message. He gathered a squad of Earless and stood at the perimeter of the practice yard, watching the group carefully in case they tried to cause trouble.

Saanji turned back to watch Royce and Zeia. Royce had knocked one of the shortswords out of Zeia's hands and was steadily driving her backward. Zeia's expression looked even more taut than usual. Then Saanji saw something curious: her left hand, which no longer held a sword, flickered and disappeared, then reformed. Moments later, Zeia's right hand vanished. Her shortsword landed in the snow.

Meanwhile, Royce's kingsteel bastard sword was already angling for Zeia's throat, which was suddenly defenseless. Saanji opened his mouth to scream a warning, but Royce already saw the danger. With a grunt, the First Lancer wrenched the sword higher, changing the angle. Zeia managed to duck. The blade sailed just over her head. The swing threw Royce off balance.

Zeia shouldered into him, tripped him, and knocked the Lancer onto the snow. Her flaming hands reappeared. She gestured, and an invisible force plucked the kingsteel sword out of Royce's hand, floating it into her own. The Shel'ai smirked. "Fine blade." She stepped back, flipped the sword high in the air, caught it by the blade—which steamed in her grasp—and returned it to Royce, hilt first. Royce took the sword and rose to his feet without comment. Onlookers exchanged glances, unsure whether to applaud.

Saanji went from breathing a sigh of relief when Royce didn't accidentally behead their newest ally to chuckling softly. "Well, that's *one* way to win." He approached, laughing more loudly than he needed to, hoping to dispel tension. A few onlookers joined in.

Royce gave Zeia a terse smile. "I could have killed you."

"But you didn't." Zeia's hands disappeared, the violet flames seeming to retreat back up her sleeves like bullwhips uncurling in reverse. "If you like, we can call it a draw."

Royce blinked. "No need. Well fought, m'lady." He bowed. Zeia returned the gesture. Royce looked from her to Saanji. "Now, if you'll forgive me, I should check on the preparations."

That defeat stung his pride—or was it his sense of honor, given how she'd won? Saanji wondered if he should try to soften the mood with another joke, but Zeia spoke first.

"How much longer will your men need to prepare?"

Royce was already turning away, but he glanced back to answer. "Not long. The horses and supplies are ready. It's just a logistical matter at this point." He indicated Saanji with a nod. "We've decided that the prince's men—"

"Earless," Saanji corrected. "Don't worry, we've adopted the insult, made it our own." He glanced at Zeia, hoping to see her smile. She did not.

Royce continued. "We've decided that the Earless will be integrated with my Lancers, so the men can get used to each other before the siege. It takes time to choose commanders and assign them into squads, but it's almost done."

Zeia used her wrist-stump to wipe the sweat from her brow. "The sooner we can march, the better."

"Or worse," Saanji muttered. He stooped to gather a handful of snow. "I don't relish the thought of marching an army through this stuff. I relish the idea of sleeping on it even less."

Zeia looked about to offer a biting reply, but Royce said, "Relieving the Noshans will be difficult. None of our men are used to fighting Jolym. But a winter siege of Hesod will be even harder."

"Neither can he helped," Zeia snapped. "El'rash'lin says that Rowen was bound for the Free Cities. The closest are Hesod and Atheion, both of which are under siege. Wherever he is, he will need our help."

"So will the cities," Saanji muttered. He wondered if Zeia cared about that. He reminded himself that less than a year ago, she'd been fighting beside Fadarah *against* the Free Cities. *Why is she so bent on helping Rowen Locke now?* Her answer made Saanji wonder if she'd read his mind—a thought that frightened him.

"I swore to El'rash'lin that I'd help the Isle Knight defeat Chorlga. That means defeating your brother and his army, too." She gave Saanji a cold look. "I did not expect any of this to be easy. If you did, perhaps we were hasty in forming this alliance."

Before either man could answer, she walked away.

Saanji whistled. "Ice and fire, that one."

Royce said, "Good thing our men are calling all this the New Alliance."

"Why's that?"

"New things have an excuse when they go badly." Royce stooped to retrieve Zeia's shortswords. Both had blackened from her touch, though not as much as the first time they sparred. "Do you think her hands disappearing was a trick? Or had she just got too weak to keep up the spell?"

Saanji had not thought of that. He glanced after Zeia, who had left the practice yard for her private quarters. Reluctant bodyguards—two Lancers and two Earless—fell in behind her. Saanji turned toward the group of Cassicans he'd noticed earlier. They were gone. "I don't know. Doesn't seem like she likes appearing vulnerable. Makes sense why."

Royce nodded. "Holding objects is one thing. Throwing them is another. She won't be much use to us if she can't throw wytchfire."

Saanji scratched his growing goatee. "I don't know. A crazed woman with hands made out of fire, swinging a sword? That would scare the piss out of me!"

"But will it scare the piss out of your brother?"

"No," Saanji admitted after a moment. "He'll probably think she's beautiful." *Like I do.*

"And the Jolym?"

"I don't think *anything* frightens them. So we'll just have to fill their eye sockets full of arrows and hope that does the trick."

"And hope Chorlga isn't with them," Royce added.

"Well, we could always stay here."

Royce frowned. "I'm not losing my nerve, Dhargot. The Shel'ai is right.

If Knightswrath really is that powerful, we need to find Rowen Locke and make him our ally before your brother kills him and Chorlga takes the sword. Besides, the gods know we'll need *his* help against Chorlga and the Nightmare."

Saanji nodded. "I know. I wasn't questioning your guts, just our collective sanity."

Royce scoffed. "Ah. Well, that's another matter. Look on the bright side, though. All the scouts say the Jolym appear to have gotten tired of killing everywhere else. Looks like they're all massing in the south."

"Perfect. Maybe they'll all form one big, unkillable army that can tear us to pieces."

"At least they'll sing songs about us." Royce clapped his shoulder. "We march for Nosh at first light. I need you sober for that."

"I'll do my best."

Saanji waited until Royce left, Lancers falling in behind him, then turned and headed for the nearest tavern. Glancing at the direction Zeia had taken, he had half a mind to invite her to join him, but he did not have the nerve to ask.

As he walked, he considered Royce's question about Karhaati. He imagined how his brother would react to the sight of Zeia. Like so many Dhargots, his brother worshipped power. Zeia would impress him, surely, but his would be the kind of admiration that hinged on servitude and conquest. Since Zeia was not powerful enough that Karhaati would be forced to serve her, the only remaining option would be to honor her power by killing her.

Gods, how did we both come from the same womb?

The thought made him wince. For all he knew, they had not. Men who adhered strictly to the Way of Ears placed almost no value on women. Saanji did not even know his mother's name; he had no memories of being held or suckled by any woman save his frightened wet nurses. He wondered who his mother might have been—a slave with the misfortune of being born beautiful, a captive from a conquered people, or perhaps even some unwanted daughter of royal blood? He touched the opal ring on his finger. The thought of Maryssa made tears well up in his eyes. He blinked them back, glad his bodyguards could not see.

Turning the corner, he spotted his favorite tavern in the distance. Cassicans, mostly children and the elderly, milled in the streets, moving between shops and temples. They spotted him and drew aside. A few nodded. Saanji made a point of nodding back. Though he'd earned a reputation for kindness during the city's occupation, Saanji had not forgotten that he was still a Dhargot.

Some of his Earless had already been attacked by Cassicans who saw no distinction between them and the other Dhargots. For that reason, Saanji had ordered that no Earless travel through the city alone. If possible, he preferred that they travel in the company of Lancers.

But Lancers made poor drinking companions, and despite his promise to Arnil Royce, Saanji intended to get good and drunk. After all, it would be a cold, grueling march through ice and snow to reach Nosh, and there was a very good chance that his own shallow grave was all that awaited him there. Better he approach that fate with a sore belly and a headache caused by hláshba.

Saanji smiled, remembering the tavern's unexpected stock of that powerful Soroccan liquor, which even the most committed drunks tended to avoid. He'd already spent more coins and hours in that tavern than he could recall. He felt honor-bound to pay one last visit. Besides, the tavern's owner was an old man who'd had his tongue cut out by Dhargots, but he still seemed friendly enough toward Saanji. The old man played a strange stringed instrument in a way that would have made the gods weep, and Saanji wanted to hear him play again before one or both of them died. He was still contemplating this, playing a favorite melody in his head, when the attack began.

His only warning was the wide eyes of an old woman who happened to be looking in his direction, but it was enough to send his hand for the hilt of his shortsword. He drew it and turned. One of his bodyguards had already fallen toward the street, a spear in his back. The others howled in warning and drew steel, backpedaling to form a circle around Saanji.

"Gods-damned Dhargots!" someone yelled.

All around them, Cassicans screamed. Doors slammed. The attackers— the men he'd seen earlier—charged out of an alley. Two more had spears. The rest had crossbows. Saanji wondered where they'd gotten them. He held up his empty hand. Despite the sudden lump in his throat, he found his voice.

"Wait, listen, we're not like the others. I'm not my brother. You don't have to—"

One of the men interrupted with a crazed, unintelligible shout. Then the men with crossbows lifted them, taking aim. One of the Earless shoved Saanji backward. His heel caught on something, and he fell. More screams swirled around him. He heard the clatter of steel and saw a shower of sparks.

He looked around for his sword. He spotted its brass hilt glinting in the distance—too far to reach. He crawled toward it but had gotten only halfway when a man with a spear blocked his path.

"For my wife," the man grunted. He thrust the head of his spear at Saanji's face. Saanji watched it coming closer and closer, knew he was about to die, then remembered he could still move. He rolled to one side. A stab of pain—cold, then hot—told him he hadn't gotten away clean. Nevertheless, he rose to his feet then surprised himself by charging his attacker.

He surprised his attacker, too. The man tried to turn his spear in time to impale Saanji through the stomach, but he was too slow. Saanji caught the spear, wrapped one arm around it, and pinned it to his side. They struggled, so close that Saanji could smell hláshba on his opponent's breath. He noted the man's bloodshot eyes. Saanji tried to wrest the spear away from his attacker, realized he wasn't strong enough, and kicked blindly.

His attacker grunted. Saanji kicked again. The man's grip loosened. Saanji kicked him a third time then tore the spear free. Rather than waste time trying to bring the point to bear, he drove the shaft into his attacker's nose. The man cursed and fell backward. Saanji hesitated, then aimed his spear and thrust downward.

He looked up as he dragged the blade free. In the distance, three of his Earless lay on the street, all bloody. One moved weakly, clutching his stomach, his eyes glazed. The other Earless had formed a line and charged, one despite the crossbow bolt in his shoulder. They'd already cut down three attackers, including the ringleader. The remaining four backpedaled, blindly waving spears or daggers in place of crossbows.

Then Saanji saw a second knot of men, dressed in rags and armed with daggers and cudgels, racing up from the other end of the street. For a moment, he thought they were coming to help. His heart soared. Then one of them pointed right at him and spat on the street.

"Watch your backs," Saanji called to his men. They glanced over their shoulders. One of them cursed. Another tried to haul the wounded man onto his feet, but his glazed eyes widened with pain, and he screamed until his comrade laid him back down again.

Saanji watched, trying to remember the men's names. Shame filled him when he could not. Then the sound of approaching footsteps reminded him of the danger. He turned to face the second knot of men. He counted.

"Seven on one side, four on the other," he called to his men. "Can't hold them here. Fall back."

"Where?" one of his men grunted, looking around. The tavern was too far. All the nearby houses had closed and barred their doors. Most had closed their shutters, too. Then Saanji spotted an open window.

He pointed with his sword. "There. If you want to live, run like your asses are on fire." He ran. His men followed. The second group of attackers angled their charge, trying to block Saanji's path.

We're not all going to make it...

"Climb through the window," Saanji shouted. He turned, intending to charge the men, but one of his Earless—he could not tell who—shoved him back toward the window.

"Get to safety, my prince. We'll hold them off."

Saanji glanced at the charging men. His courage faltered. He nodded dumbly and ran the rest of the way to the window. He clambered through. The house stank of sweat and filth. He saw no furniture or source of light. The house's owner, an old man with one arm in a sling, cowered in the corner.

Saanji spotted the door, unlatched it, and threw it open. Waning daylight made him wince. "Inside," he called to his men.

No one answered, though he doubted anyone could hear him over the din of fighting. Then someone screamed in pain. Saanji hoped it was one of their attackers, though the glare of the setting sun blinded him. He stood in the doorway, shaking, then stepped back out into the street.

"Enough," he shouted toward the blur of noise and fighting men. "Leave my men alone. We've done nothing to you. We aren't like the others. Don't you understand?"

A cudgel sailed through the air, emerging from the setting sun as though born of it. A man held the cudgel. Saanji took a step backward—too slowly. The cudgel met his shoulder. Bones cracked and shifted. Saanji withered. Then he realized he was still holding his sword in his broken arm. He switched his sword to his good hand and lifted it, but the cudgel knocked it out of his grasp.

Someone shouted, "Do it, Lem. Do it fast!"

Saanji looked up. "Lem, is it?"

Lem blinked. He'd raised his cudgel but paused when Saanji spoke his name. Saanji took advantage of the opportunity by driving his foot into Lem's groin. Lem staggered backward, cursing. Saanji tried to push himself up. But another man kicked his legs out from under him. Saanji saw a rust-covered cleaver arcing toward his face. Then a sword blurred downward, knocking it aside. A second sword followed the first, cutting the cleaver out of the attacker's hand. Violet fire blurred past him.

Zeia finished off the man with the cleaver then turned to face the man with the cudgel. She was not alone. Four figures surged out of the shadows behind her. Two wore the dark scale armor of Dhargots, while the other two wore plate armor that gleamed in the setting sun.

Saanji let himself sag against the wall of the house and sink onto the street. Lancers and Earless streamed past him. The cries of battle became screams for mercy. A moment later, Royce knelt before him, grim faced. Blood splattered his armor and ran slowly down his kingsteel bastard sword. He spoke Saanji's name.

Saanji nodded. "I'm still alive."

"I can see that." Royce wiped his sword clean on his sleeve then sheathed it. "Can you stand? We have to get you inside."

"Why? Isn't the battle over?"

"Not quite." Royce grabbed his good arm and gently helped him up. "They weren't just after you. This is citywide. A hundred rebels, at least."

Saanji shook his head. "Zeia… but Zeia healed them…"

"Maybe that's why it's only a hundred and not five thousand." Royce snapped his fingers, and two Lancers came to his assistance. "Get the prince back to the barracks. Keep him safe. Give him hláshba for the pain and bandage his ear."

My… ear?

Saanji remembered the spear thrust earlier in the battle. With his good, left hand, he touched his right ear. The pain made him wince. He looked at his fingers and saw blood. He laughed.

"Earless…"

The Lancers helped him along. Saanji went with them then stopped, twisting back so abruptly that his shoulder shifted and the pain made him scream. "Royce," he muttered when he could, "my men… my bodyguards… are any alive?" When no one answered, he added, "Find out their names…"

He took a step and lost his balance. The Lancers tried to catch him, forced to grab his right arm. Broken bones shifted. Saanji whimpered, then his world went dark.

CHAPTER THIRTY-THREE
THE MUSTERING

AEKO STOOD ON THE SHORES of Armahg's Tears and watched as the last of Atheion sailed out of sight, fading into a horizon dominated by high, snowy mountains. Though the houses and temples that rode on some of the skiffs had been reduced to charred ruins, the skiffs themselves were intact. They looked more like ships now, powered by weeping Noshan oarsmen. At the heart of the seafaring caravan floated what remained of the Scrollhouse, beneath an azure banner.

Aeko took a deep breath. Despite the cold, the smell of smoke and charred flesh filled her nostrils. They had finally finished burying the dead—not just their own but the Noshans and the Lochurites as well—but the smell remained. Aeko wondered if that smell would cling to the armor and tabards of Crovis's followers, all the way back to the Lotus Isles, as she was sure it would cling to hers. She wondered, too, if anyone would stop congratulating Crovis long enough to notice.

She doubted it. Thanks to Crovis, what remained of Atheion's treasure and people were about to become part of the Isles. "The Noshans think Crovis is giving them protection," she muttered.

"In a way, he is," Sang Wei answered from her right. "I heard there are still a couple tribes of Lochurites out there. If they come back, with Atheion like it is—"

"People who give up their freedom to men like Crovis never get it back. Ask the people of Lyos."

"I will the next time I'm there," Sang Wei answered. "I'll be able to ask them, because *you* kept them safe."

Aeko blinked. "I wasn't aware the Codex Lotius showed the bright side of conquest."

"It doesn't, not really. But the Codex Viticus does." Sang Wei cleared his throat. "But I don't think that matters now."

"No," Aeko agreed. She turned in the saddle to study what remained of her company: twenty-three sour-faced Knights. All that she could convince to stay behind and continue the search for Rowen Locke rather than follow Crovis Ammerhel back to the Isles. By the looks on her Knights' faces, none were especially confident in the wisdom of their decision.

Aeko turned to study the newly promoted Knight of the Stag beside her. Sang Wei looked only a little more certain than the others. She'd even thought for a moment that he meant to remain at Crovis's side and sail with the remains of Atheion on Zet's Blood, out to sea. The young Knight seemed to grasp what he was risking by staying behind.

Although Crovis had granted all of them permission to continue their search for Rowen Locke, the coldness in his eyes had made his intentions clear: once he got back to the Isles and assumed command of the remaining Knights there, he would drive out any remaining Jolym and install himself as Grand Marshal. But Aeko doubted he would stop there. The Knights would demand justice. Crovis would have to take his army onto the mainland in the guise of marching against Chorlga.

But he'll stop at Lyos first. He'll sack one Free City after another to finance his campaign... and he'll do it all in the name of honor.

"And no one will say a word against him."

Sang Wei looked at her. "Knight-Captain?"

"Nothing," Aeko said. She turned to look at the stern-faced Dwarr seated on horseback to her left. At her suggestion, Jalist had kept out of sight until Crovis was gone. "Sure you don't want to accompany us to Hesod? Should be great fun."

"Oh, I doubt that very much, unless you manage to find an army between here and there." Jalist tugged at the strap of his long axe. "Listen, I'll ride with you until we reach the western mountains, but that's as far as I can go. I told Locke I was going south."

Aeko nodded. "And as I recall, you promised King Typherius that you'd go back to Lyos."

Jalist scowled. "Your point?"

Aeko drummed her fingers on the hilt of her adamune. Finally, she said, "Oaths are made of air."

Jalist's dark eyes narrowed. "Strange thing for an Isle Knight to say."

"I'm talking about oaths, not honor."

"I thought Isle Knights saw those as basically the same thing."

Aeko glanced at Sang Wei, who looked even more uncomfortable than before. She chided herself for having spoken so openly. "Never mind. We should go."

She started to turn her horse about, but Jalist said, "What do you think you're going to do when you get to Hesod? Start a siege? The Bloody Prince has an army the gods would envy. Don't you know he'll tear you to pieces in five seconds?"

"This isn't my first campaign, Dwarr. I'm not foolish enough to think I can take Hesod with twenty-four swords. I'm just here to help Locke. If he made it out of the city with his friend, they'll need help getting east in one piece."

"Suppose he and Igrid didn't make it out. Suppose Locke got captured. What then?"

Aeko smirked. "Then we'll rescue him."

Jalist's eyes narrowed again. "Forgive me, but I don't think sneaking into a city is your style, Knight-Captain."

"My Knighthood doesn't depend on my armor. This may surprise you, Dwarr, but I'm capable of fighting without it."

"I don't doubt that. But to get into Hesod, are you capable of posing as some heartless sellsword or a well-raped woman in chains? Are you capable of slitting sleeping men's throats or stabbing them in the back?"

Aeko turned to Sang Wei. "Ride ahead of the column. I'm trusting you and your spyglass to alert us of any Dhargots or Lochurites between here and Hesod. We can't flee in this snow, so if they see us before we see them, we'll have to fight, no matter the odds. Understood?"

Sang Wei paled but nodded. "You can trust me, Knight-Captain."

I hope so. "I know," Aeko said.

Sang Wei turned his horse and rode ahead of the others. With a final glance at the disappearing azure banners flying over Atheion, Aeko rode down to join her Knights. At her approach, they stiffened in their saddles. In their stern expressions, Aeko saw loyalty tinged with doubt. She could hardly blame them.

"We are lost in a land of enemies," she began. "Our brother, Sir Locke, is somewhere to the north, fighting alone. By now, all of you have heard about the sword he carries... where it came from, how he came to possess it. Some of you may believe that the Light is at work here. Others may not."

Her Knights stirred uncomfortably. Since leaving the Lotus Isles, there had been almost no mention of Knightswrath from either Crovis or Aeko.

While the former did not want to fuel faith and interest in a potential rival, Aeko had not wanted to risk her Knights' loyalty by expressing belief in what many might regard as a superstition. She regretted that now.

"We have already buried many of our brothers and sisters in the cold ground... and before this is finished, it could be that there will be no one left to bury *us*." Aeko paused. She saw her Knights' discomfort grow. "I have no words to warm away the chill you're feeling. But like you, I have memorized the words of the Codex Lotius... some of which Sir Wei repeated at my defense."

A few Knights smiled.

"I do not pretend to know the will of the Light, the gods, or the shade of Fâyu Jinn. But let those words be the fire that warms your sword arm," Aeko continued. "We will meet our enemies. We will find Sir Locke, and we will defend him with our hearts' blood. I swear this oath on the graves of our comrades, on the ashes of my failures, and on the steel I still have strength to swing." As she finished, her voice echoed in the morning air just as the snow began to fall.

For a few anxious seconds, no one spoke. Then her Knights cheered.

Aeko led them north, after Sang Wei. Jalist rode beside her. "I thought you didn't put much stock in oaths," he said in a low voice.

Aeko pretended not to hear him.

Rowen Locke had been prowling the streets of Hesod for days. He'd entered the city with every intention of marching straight to the palace, summoning Knightswrath's full power, and avenging Igrid by killing the Bloody Prince— even if it cost him his life. But he'd put that aside when he heard about some two hundred Iron Sisters trapped in the temple. He decided to save them in Igrid's honor.

He'd been tempted to use Knightswrath's power to free them by carving and burning an escape route clean through the Dhargothi lines and perhaps even the walls of Hesod, but unleashing that much uncontrollable power was just as likely to kill the Iron Sisters as it was to destroy their enemies. So he'd rented a room at a nearby inn, hid his kingsteel armor under a loose floorboard, and gone out to assess the situation at the besieged temple.

He saw at once that the situation was hopeless. The Iron Sisters were trapped on all sides. At least a thousand Dhargots crowded the streets, huddled behind mantelets and overturned carts. Between storms of arrows unleashed into the temple, they hurled vile insults. Meanwhile, the Bloody

Prince's catapults fired day and night, as though their only purpose were to reduce the great temple to rubble, one stone at a time—and they were well on their way.

The temple walls bore cracks wide enough for a man to march through. Once in a while, an Iron Sister would appear and fire an arrow through the cracks, then disappear before scores of Dhargothi archers could return fire. The Iron Sisters were obviously outnumbered and all but beaten, and the Bloody Prince was just toying with them. Sooner or later, he would either flood the breached temple with warriors or have his catapults hurl enough smoke inside that the Iron Sisters would either suffocate or be forced to surrender.

Rowen thought of Igrid. *They won't surrender. They'll die in battle if they can, but if it comes to it, they'll cut their own throats before they let the Dhargots take them alive again.*

He touched Knightswrath's hilt through his cloak, readjusting the latter to make sure the telltale weapon was thoroughly hidden. He wondered again if he could sow some kind of rebellion within the city. He'd considered trying to fight his way to the dungeons in case any Iron Sisters had been caught and returned to their cells. But two nights earlier, he'd met a Dhargothi jailor at one of the taverns, caught the man in an alley afterward, and determined after harsh questioning that the dungeons of Hesod were empty.

After disposing of the jailor's body, along with the body of another Dhargot who'd caught him dropping the corpse of the first into the sewers, he'd begun looking elsewhere for potential allies. The Bloody Prince had arrived in Hesod with plenty of slaves, mostly captives taken from Cassica and other cities. Rowen heard that some of them had risen up to support the Iron Sisters, to no avail. Rowen even considered freeing slaves by killing their masters, one at a time, then trying to convince the slaves to join him in saving the Iron Sisters trapped in the temple, but he quickly dismissed the idea as even more ludicrous than his determination to save the Iron Sisters in the first place.

As for the people of the city, it seemed that all the Hesodi with a will to fight had either been culled long ago or had died fighting beside the Iron Sisters when Igrid managed to spring them from the dungeons. Despite the grim sight of the besieged temple before him, the thought of Igrid's accomplishment made him smile. It seemed almost impossible that she, alone, could have freed the Iron Sisters from imprisonment, but he'd heard the story in the streets. Besides, he could imagine no other scenario that could have thrown Hesod into such a commotion. Yet she had died, and the Iron Sisters' freedom had been short lived.

Gods, Igrid, why didn't you wait for me?

He wondered what he would have done had Igrid waited. Would he have helped her rescue the Iron Sisters or refused, saying that his first priority was aiding one of the other Free Cities, taking Knightswrath back to the Isles, or confronting Chorlga? He blushed, afraid he knew the answer.

But I'm here now. If I can just get those women out of the temple...

He shook his head. He could neither distract so many Dhargots, let alone defeat them, nor use the sewers to slip into the temple—if such a route existed, the Iron Sisters surely would have used it before. In fact, Rowen had already been in the sewers, and though he guessed that one of the tunnels did indeed run beneath the temple, no grate or cistern led upward. After searching and searching, he'd found nothing but a ceiling of solid rock.

Unless...

He touched Knightswrath's hilt through his cloak again. A slow smile formed on his lips. He watched the siege a moment longer, said a quick prayer in Shao for the women trapped inside and an additional prayer that no more would die before he could get to them, and returned to the inn. He would have to wait until nightfall.

Saanji opened his eyes, blinked, then cursed. "Why in Zet's name is the ground moving?"

Arnil Royce's face appeared over him. The First Lancer wore clean, gilded armor. He smiled thinly. "Because you're in a wagon."

Saanji managed to sit up, pushing back a bearskin blanket to look for bandaged wounds. Though he was in his underclothes, he appeared uninjured. He tested his right arm. His shoulder ached, stinging so much when he moved it that tears welled in his eyes, but he kept moving it, and the muscles loosened. The pain subsided. Then he remembered his other injury. He lifted his hand and felt nothing but a nub where his right ear had been.

"Blame Zeia," Royce said. "Or thank her, if you prefer. She healed your shoulder, but she said she couldn't do anything about the ear besides dull the pain."

Saanji blinked and looked around. He was surrounded by mounted Dhargots—his Earless. They beamed at the sight of him. Saanji made what he hoped was an unflappable expression and nodded at them. A few saluted. Others cheered. Saanji turned to Royce, who was still riding alongside the wagon.

"Where are we?"

"Riding south. Or have you forgotten how to tell direction?" Royce gestured to the slow-setting sun to his right.

"I mean, why am I in a damn wagon?"

"Because it's rather difficult for an unconscious man in his underclothes to ride a horse."

Saanji bit back a curse. "I mean, why am I not resting in a temple or a tavern, being nursed by some pretty cleric with a healthy bosom?"

Though Royce continued smiling, a glint of dark seriousness shown in his eyes. "The Cassicans wanted us gone... enough of them, anyway. We lost a handful of men, but thanks to Zeia, we didn't have many wounded. Those who couldn't travel I sent north under guard. Don't worry. Your wounded Earless will be safe. Everyone else is with us."

He made a sweeping gesture all around them. "We started out a few hours ago. I wanted to be well underway before the gods decide to throw a blizzard at us. Zeia said you were well enough to be moved. So we moved you."

Saanji checked his hand—his opal ring was still there. His shortsword lay beside him, clean and sheathed. He spotted his armor lying at the far end of the wagon as well. "How many did we lose?"

Royce's smile thinned even further. "Fifteen Earless, nineteen Lancers. You lost that officer of yours from the practice yards, too. He followed some of the Cassicans who were about to attack Zeia and forced them to start their rebellion a little early. It could have been worse."

"Much worse without Zeia, I'm guessing." Saanji spotted her in the distance. She wore armor over a plain fighting robe with long sleeves. She glanced his way and nodded, her face as expressionless as stone. Saanji nodded back, blushing. He tugged up the bearskin blanket to cover his soft, pale body, suddenly self-conscious. He noted that Zeia appeared to be guiding her horse with her heels. The reins had been looped around her saddlehorn. He was surprised that she had not summoned her hands of fire to hold them, then he reminded himself that such things drained her strength.

Royce said, "Things would have been much worse without you, too. The rebels wanted to assassinate the two of us, plus Zeia, before the rest of the attack began. Your Earless threw them off balance. And you held them in the street long enough for me to get some Lancers together." Royce paused. "I'm told you did a bit of fighting yourself."

Saanji snorted. "Just a few lucky swings. I'm only here because my men kept me alive." *Some of them died doing it, and I never even bothered to learn their names.* He squinted, studying the long line of armored men stretching on behind his uncovered wagon. "How are our numbers?"

"Better than you'd think. Some desertions, but two hundred Cassicans volunteered to come with us. They want revenge on your brother, I think."

"Don't we all?" Saanji turned the opal ring on his finger. "By the way, is there a reason you didn't put me in a covered wagon? I don't relish the thought of getting dressed while half the army gawks at my backside."

"It's your fault for waking too early. Do you want me to surround the tent with shield-bearers? Or maybe I could find an elephant somewhere."

Saanji glowered at him, wrapping the bearskin blanket around himself like a cloak as he sat on the edge of the wagon and pulled on his boots. The horses and footmen had worn a path through the snow, but the ground was still bumpy. His stomach twisted. "Royce, unless you think it will raise my men's morale to see their commander retching over the side of a wagon, you best get me some food and wine."

"I can manage one of those when we stop—which may be soon. I'm told that a few miles south, the snow gets too deep for wagons. We might have to send them back to the city."

"And what do we do for food?"

"Each man can carry his own provisions."

Dry rations and water, you mean, Saanji thought darkly. "Too bad my brother kept all the elephants." Saanji pulled on his britches, strapped on his greaves, then feigned immodesty and dropped the bearskin blanket to don his tunic. He fumbled with his cuirass, a leather vest covered in scales of blackened steel, unaccustomed to donning his armor without help. He girded his sword last. Turning, he saw that Royce had ridden on ahead to speak with a squad of scouts, who were just returning from the south.

"I'll walk," Saanji told the wagon's drivers. They stopped the wagon. But before he could climb down, one of his Earless brought a saddled horse alongside the wagon and offered him the reins. Saanji considered leaping gallantly from the wagon onto his horse, then realized he would almost certainly fall flat on his face. He climbed down from the wagon, waving off assistance, then mounted his horse. His stomach rumbled again.

Concealing it with a grin, he waved again to his men, provoking scattered cheers, then rode ahead to join Zeia. "That's the second time you saved my life."

Zeia's white pupils became daggers of ice. "When was the first?"

"Two nights ago, in my dreams. I was being chased by an Olg. Big one, big as a house. A chieftain, I think. But you handled him without much trouble."

Zeia did not laugh—or respond. But hands of flame unfurled from her sleeves, causing the fabric to smolder as she grabbed the reins. She stared straight ahead. Saanji rode beside her, trying to think of something else to say. Finally, he gave up and rode on ahead so that he could pretend to consult with his officers.

CHAPTER THIRTY-FOUR

STONE AND FIRE

ROWEN FINISHED DONNING HIS KINGSTEEL cuirass, then he paused and looked at his other pieces of armor. He absentmindedly touched his face, where he'd just finished shaving off the stubble of a red beard. He'd trimmed his unruly red locks as short as he could, cutting them himself with a knife, and he was counting on his helmet to cover the rest. He intended to conceal his cuirass beneath an oversized tunic emblazoned with the impaled dragon of Dhargoth, but his gauntlets, greaves, tassets, spaulders, and vambraces were another matter. The best he could do was wear a large cloak to cover himself, but if a night breeze caught his cloak or a single flicker from a torch or lantern betrayed the telltale shine of kingsteel, he was finished.

He might pretend to have bought or plundered a single piece, but even if they didn't recognize him as the Isle Knight they were looking for, his armor would draw too much attention. Besides, concealing Knightswrath would be difficult. He planned to turn his belt so that the long-handled sword would be hidden by his cloak, but even that was risky.

I'll have to leave the rest of my armor here. Same goes for my tabard. He inspected the torn silk garment, rubbing its azure fabric between his fingers. How many times had that tabard been torn since he donned it less than a year ago? He examined the white sigil on his tabard, trying to make out the shape of a balancing crane through all the tears, bloodstains, and burn marks. He smiled thinly. *I never was much of a Knight. Maybe it's fitting I leave it here.*

He placed the rest of his armor back in the hole, followed by his tunic, then replaced the loose floorboard. He doubted anyone would find it after he left, but just to be safe, he moved the creaking boards and straw that passed for a bed so that they covered the floorboard. Then, with a heavy sigh, he finished getting ready, extinguished the lantern that provided the room's only illumination, and left.

He emerged from the tavern into a city street already filled with drunken soldiers. He forced himself to smile, pretending to enjoy the spectacle. Since the Hesodi who still enjoyed some measure of freedom knew well enough to stay indoors, the Dhargots mostly fought each other, engaging in drunken brawls until an officer interrupted them. But some had slaves of their own, whom they dragged behind them like leashed dogs. One man had a young girl with him—little more than a child in rags, her face dirty, her eyes dark and expressionless.

The Dhargot caught Rowen's eye. "Twenty iron crowns for an hour." He winked.

Rowen tensed. He touched his dagger and remember that in the Dark Quarter, the punishment for men who abused children was a blade between the ribs. He looked around. *Too many eyes.* "No, thanks." He started to walk away.

The Dhargot grabbed his arm. "Fifteen," he said. "Or twenty, and she's yours to keep. I caught her last week, crawling around the sewers. Hardly touched her myself. If you don't want her for your bed, she'd still make a good house slave."

"I'm a sellsword. Do I look like I have a house?" Rowen forced himself to smile despite his revulsion.

"Then sell her to someone else." The Dhargot scratched at stitches in his cheek, which had begun to scab over. "I'm through feeding her, dragging her around. I just want to sit by a fire and drink."

Rowen eyed the man's sewn cheek. Something told him the little girl had done that. *Don't look at her eyes,* Rowen thought. But before he could help it, he felt his gaze drawn to her dark one. She looked back.

"Twelve," Rowen said. "Twelve, and she's mine."

The Dhargot grimaced. "Twelve? By the Dead God, I could drag her over to the slave pens and get thirteen! I was giving you a deal because of the dragon on your chest. If you're not interested, I'll find someone who is." He started to walk away, tugging the rope that joined his wrist to the girl's throat.

Rowen grabbed the man's cloak and jerked him to a stop. The man whirled, reaching for his sword. Rowen held up his hands. "Fourteen. That's all I've got. Profit is profit. Do you want it or not?"

The Dhargot made a show of scratching his stitches in deliberation. He looked the little girl up and down. "Fine," he said finally.

Rowen finished counting coins out of his pouch, careful to conceal how many remained. Though he'd taken twice as much as the Dhargot requested off those he'd killed earlier, he knew that if he let on how much he really had, he would get nothing but a knife in the back. Feigning last-minute reluctance, he gave the Dhargot the coins. The Dhargot handed him the rope then grinned.

"Good luck with this one. Don't let her near a blade." The Dhargot pointed at his stitches, laughed, and backed away. He kept one hand on his sword in case Rowen objected. But Rowen only stood there, holding the rope. He waited until the other Dhargots milling in the street lost interest in him, then he started toward the alley, gently tugging the girl after him.

"Don't run," he whispered. "I'm not going to hurt you. I'm not a Dhargot. My name is Rowen. I'm an Isle Knight. Do you know what that is?"

The little girl looked at the ground.

"I can't set you free, so I'll have to take you with me, into the sewers. Don't make a sound." He considered cutting her free, then decided against it. He led her toward the nearest cistern, looked to make sure they had not been followed, then pried up the lid.

"Not the sewers," the girl said, her voice barely a whisper.

Rowen hesitated. He wondered if she was afraid of the dark or if the reek bothered her. Then he remembered what her captor had said. "The Dhargots won't get you. I promise." Rowen descended into the sewers, leading the girl.

Having been down there once before, Rowen knew the way, but he cursed when he realized he hadn't thought to bring a torch or lantern. An occasional flicker of torchlight shone through the grates as men passed by on the surface, though it was not enough to see by. The stars and moon were no help at this distance, either.

"What's your name?" Rowen whispered.

The little girl grabbed his arm, digging her nails into his flesh, but she said nothing.

"I already told you mine. It's Rowen. I'm from Lyos. Do you know where that is?" As he spoke, Rowen tugged her as gently as he could toward the wall of the sewer, out of the reeking water. He started forward in the darkness.

He kept whispering, hoping less to earn the girl's trust—which he figured must be impossible, after all she'd gone through—than to keep her distracted enough that she would not scream and draw attention. They'd just edged around the flickering torchlight of a Dhargot who was pissing down a grate when the little girl stopped.

"I know her," she whispered.

Rowen kept one eye on the grate, fearing the Dhargot had heard her. But the soldier finished his business and walked away. Rowen pulled the little girl away from the grate, just in case. "What?"

"The woman you're talking about. I know her."

Rowen had been talking so idly that for a moment, he didn't realize what she meant.

"Red hair. She has red hair, like you."

Rowen let go of the rope. He turned to face the little girl in the dark. She had not run. "What's your name?" he asked again.

"Thessa," she answered.

"Pretty name," Rowen answered. "Hold still. Let's get that rope off you." He drew his dagger. Reaching out in the dark, he found the rope hanging from her neck and cut it with a single, swift stroke. "Listen, Thessa, I'll keep you as safe as I can, but you have to stay quiet and stay close. We're going up to the big temple where the Iron Sisters are. We're going to free them. We're going to help them get down into the sewers, then we're all going to escape from the city. Understand?"

Rowen hoped she would not ask what he intended to do once they were out of Hesod, since he'd not yet figured that out himself. Instead, Thessa said, "The sewers don't join up with that temple." She grabbed his arm again.

"I know. But they will soon." Rowen touched her hand, loosening her fingers when her nails began to dig into his arm again.

They crept on through the sewers. The darkness deepened. No more grates appeared above them. Rowen listened carefully, wondering if they would run into Dhargothi soldiers who had been sent down to inspect the sewers, but all he heard was Thessa's frightened breathing and the slow drip of water.

We're close now.

He reached up and touched the low, cold stone ceiling. While the walls of the sewer had been reinforced with bricks, the ceiling was just thick, unshaped rock. "Thessa, I have to do something now. I'm going to make a fire. Don't be afraid."

"Are we under the temple now?"

"Yes," Rowen said. *I hope so.*

"Is Igrid in there?"

Rowen thought of the red-haired woman whose corpse he'd seen. "Maybe," he lied. "Now remember what I said. Stay quiet. Don't be afraid."

Thessa did not answer, but Rowen imagined her nodding. He took a deep breath to steady himself and gently removed her hand from his arm. He stepped away from her. Then he drew Knightswrath and willed it to life.

Violet flames ignited all along the curved kingsteel, bright but silent. Thessa gasped. He glanced at her, half afraid she would run, unsure what he would do if she did. But Thessa stayed, staring at the flaming sword with wide eyes.

"Stay back," Rowen warned. The dragonbone hilt grew hotter and hotter in his grasp. His pulse quickened. He felt his blood turning to fire. His vision blurred. He blinked, staring at the ceiling. He felt as though he were looking through it, all the way up to the stars. He blinked again.

Knightswrath's hilt grew hotter still, searing him. Part of him wanted to drop it, but he felt a stronger desire to give in completely, as he had when facing Fadarah in the Wytchforest. He nearly did, then he jerked back from the feeling. *Silwren, help me…*

He gritted his teeth and thrust Knightswrath upward. With a great, steely ring, the flaming blade sank into the stone. He pushed hard, expecting to meet more resistance, then stopped when he was hilt deep, the crosspiece flush against the rocky ceiling. Violet flames bled from the ceiling, flowing down his arms and covering his face. The flames clawed at him. Rowen bore it as long as he could then screamed.

He partially withdrew Knightswrath from the rock, braced himself, and swung, as though he were slashing an enemy standing just before him. A ringing sound echoed through the sewers again, even louder than the first time. Dust and pebbles peppered Rowen's face, but he did not stop. Withdrawing Knightswrath completely, he sidestepped and made a second incision in the rocky ceiling then a third.

By now, he saw nothing but purple fire.

He shouted for Thessa to stay back again, though his own voice suddenly sounded foreign. Blindly, he slashed the rocky ceiling twice more, then stopped. A deep, ominous rumbling overpowered the searing glare of his wytchfire. The world went dark. Icy water closed all around him as though he'd fallen through a crack in the Wintersea. A terrible reek filled his nostrils: the decay of all those he'd failed.

No, I'm still in Hesod. I'm still alive, he told himself, but he could not remember falling.

He tried to rise, realized that both his hands were empty, and groped in the reeking darkness for Knightswrath. He could not find it. Panic over losing the sword eclipsed his fear of drowning. He reached all around him, groping and clawing at the void.

Silwren, where are you?

Then, all at once, the icy, reeking water receded. In its place came the sound of steel scraping against leather, the angry and fearful shouts of women. Thessa's voice rose over the din. The child spoke his name then Igrid's. A woman answered, but Rowen could not make out the words. Then rough hands seized him. He was being dragged through the darkness.

"No. Silwren..."

He resisted a moment then gave in.

Karhaati was inspecting the swordswoman's wounds when he received the news. He frowned, thinking at first that one of his men had spread some sort of lie, intending to make him look foolish. He considered cutting the messenger's throat, then noted the genuine fear in the man's eyes. "What happened?"

"General Umaari had command," the messenger said. "He noticed that the Iron Sisters hadn't fired any arrows since sundown. He sent runners to inspect the breach, and... the Iron Sisters were gone. The temple is empty!"

The red-haired Iron Sister remained sufficiently drugged and asleep, but Karhaati took care as he peeled the linen off her abdomen and examined the stitches, as though the pain might wake her. In places, her flesh looked yellow or blue-black. In others, faintly green. Dull, red streaks led away from the wound.

Karhaati grimaced. "Did you not clean these with boiled wine?"

His chief surgeon nodded fearfully. "Yes, Sire, and a poultice of frogleaf and blue clover. As you can see, her throat and shoulder are healing well, and the cut to her third rib is almost gone. But the metal that cut there was dirty. It may even have been poisoned at one time or another with felberries. It's in the hands of the gods now."

"Wrong. It's in *your* hands. And your hands are exactly what you will lose if this woman dies, followed promptly by your tongue, your feet, and your cock." Karhaati glanced at the messenger. "How did they get out?"

The messenger glanced at Karhaati's fearful surgeon then back at the Bloody Prince. "The general found a hole in the temple that leads down into the sewers. They must have tunneled out, sire."

Karhaati turned his attention to the stitches in the Iron Sister's throat.

True to his surgeon's word, her other wounds appeared to be healing quite well. The sight of her pale throat drew his eyes to her full lips. Karhaati's blood quickened. "Umaari said the ground was too thick for that. Solid rock. He said they'd need a month to tunnel out."

The messenger shrugged helplessly. "The general has already sent men to block off all exits from the sewers. If they try to emerge elsewhere in the city—"

"They won't. The sewers empty into a crag a quarter mile beyond the city walls. Send a thousand men there to wait. In the meantime, I want another thousand down in the sewers, searching every inch."

"Sire, the general has already seen to that. The entire army has been mobilized. All slaves have been locked in their pens. All townspeople are under house arrest as well."

Karhaati turned his attention to the line of stitches in the Iron Sister's chest, just beneath her right breast. He drew back the sheet to look. His blood quickened further at the sight of her bare bosom, but he resisted the urge to touch her, remembering his vow. "The townspeople may have helped them escape. Have Umaari pick out one hundred at random and impale them at first light."

The Bloody Prince glanced up. His newest bodyguard stood in the corner. For the first time, he realized that the one-eyed sellsword was openly gawking at the Iron Sister's naked body. Karhaati covered her.

"Get going," he told the messenger. Turning to his chief surgeon, he said, "And you… if there are any clerics of Tier'Gothma left alive, I suggest you find out if they know something about infected wounds that you do not."

His chief surgeon bowed and followed the messenger out the door. Karhaati faced his one-eyed sellsword again. "Don't look at her," he warned.

The sellsword blinked with his good eye then bowed. "Of course, Prince."

Karhaati poured himself a glass of wine then glanced back at the woman lying in his bed. "Wait until Umaari is done impaling the townspeople, then take him outside the city and do the same to him." He took a sip of wine. "He'll offer to cut off his own ears instead. Let him, then impale him anyway."

The sellsword smiled slightly. "Whatever you say." He tapped the pommel of his shortsword. "Sure you don't want me to stay close, though?"

"No need. The Iron Sisters can't reach me here." He touched the dark braid still hanging from his belt. He wished he had not ordered the stairwell from the basement into the sewers blocked off. He would have preferred to die in battle against crazed women with swords than be stabbed in the back by his own men. *And that's exactly what will happen now that the Iron Sisters have escaped.*

He had won countless victories for his men, but no self-respecting Dhargot could follow him for long after this. Even if the soon-to-be-executed General Umaari took full responsibility for the Iron Sisters' escape in the hopes of gaining favor with the gods before his death, it would make little difference. In a week, perhaps two, Karhaati would be slain. Then only Saanji would remain.

The Bloody Prince sneered at the thought. He considered asking Chorlga for help. The Dragonkin still had legions of Jolym at Cadavash, plus a growing army of dragon-worshipping fanatics. But Karhaati sensed that, like a Dhargot, Chorlga had no use for weak allies. Besides, Karhaati had no desire to shame himself just so he could remain in this world a little longer.

He glanced once again at his one-eyed bodyguard. Though he'd known this sellsword just a short while, he already trusted him more than anyone else in his army. A Dhargot fought for his own glory and to honor the Way of Ears. But this man fought for pay, and nobody could pay more than Karhaati.

He scrutinized the unconscious woman again, thinking he might very well die long before she was well enough to fight him. *Might as well enjoy her now.* But the thought repulsed him even more than it excited him. This nameless Iron Sister had outfought some of his best men. She was a warrior, through and through. It was not her fault that she'd been born a woman.

"Sellsword, I want you to promise me something." Karhaati plucked one of the jeweled rings off his finger and tossed it to the bodyguard. "I'm buying your vow in advance, with the gods as my witness." He knelt beside his bed and touched her red hair, which looked as though it had been hastily cut short with a knife. Then, almost as an afterthought, he withdrew a second jeweled ring and tossed that to the sellsword, as well.

The sellsword was busy admiring the first ring, but his good eye widened even more when he caught the second. "For these, I'd kill my own mother."

"How shameful, that you know who she is." Karhaati stroked the Iron Sister's hair one more time then rose to his feet. "If I die, you are to cut this woman's throat. Cut deep. I want no one to despoil her... not even you. Is that understood?"

The sellsword looked down at the woman and back at the jeweled rings gleaming on his right hand, then shrugged. "A rich man can always find or buy a pretty woman. Consider this one dead already. I swear it on the gods: I won't touch her with anything but my knife."

"Good. Break that vow, and I'll make you wail in the next world."

Another messenger entered Karhaati's bedchamber so abruptly that the sellsword drew his sword and nearly cut him in half before the man could fall on one knee. "Sire," he gasped, "an army marches toward us!"

Karhaati frowned. "I've left no army standing but my own."

"It's your brother, Sire," the messenger said. "Thousands of Earless, riding alongside Ivairians with lances! They've marched from Cassica. They're coming here!"

Karhaati stared a moment. Then he laughed. "How far are they?"

"Two days, Sire. They've made camp north and west of Armahg's Tears. Word just reached us."

Karhaati thought it over then laughed again. "Assemble my captains." When the messenger left, Karhaati sat down in the chair beside his bed and began donning his armor. Though his brother was still two days away, it never hurt to look imposing when bracing for a siege. Besides, Karhaati preferred to meet any potential assassins while armored.

"Who the hell marches to war in winter?" the sellsword asked.

"Only the desperate and the foolish. I must confess, I had not thought my fat little brother was either. And to form an alliance with the Ivairians..." He snickered. "I shall enjoy killing him."

The sellsword cleared his throat. "Do you... still want me to kill general what's-his-name?"

"Umaari." Karhaati thought it over. "Yes," he said finally. "Only do it yourself. Now. And make it quick. If there's a siege coming, I don't want the men disheartened by his wailing. Afterward, cut his ears off and hang him from the wall."

The sellsword nodded. "Count on it." He hurried out, drawn sword still in hand.

Looks like an Ivairian blade, Karhaati thought. *I wonder where he got that.*

Dismissing the question, he turned back to the sleeping Iron Sister. He stroked her red curls one more time then made sure she was covered before he slipped out of the room and quietly closed the door behind him.

CHAPTER THIRTY-FIVE
ALLIES

Jalist stiffened and swore.

After a sleepless night camping in tents pitched in the snow, they'd broken camp and set out at first light. But they'd hardly begun their journey north, toward Hesod, when Sang Wei came galloping back to the column. The young Knight of the Stag held his spyglass in one hand, the reins in the other. Aeko Shingawa signaled a halt and rode ahead to meet him. Jalist followed.

Aeko asked, "Dhargots?"

Sang Wei shook his head. "Berserkers, I think. And they're not coming from the north or the west this time." He pointed south. "I just happened to turn around and saw them."

Jalist frowned, turning in the saddle. For the first time, he saw a faint glint of steel in the distance. He reached for his own spyglass. "Not berserkers. They're riding horses. Must be Dhargots that circled around. Could be they mean to trap us between themselves and another force."

Aeko took Sang Wei's spyglass. She moved it slowly, checking to the west, north, and east. After a moment, she shook her head. She looked south. "How many do you count?"

Jalist felt a lump in his throat. "Hundreds, I think. They're riding in columns to hide their numbers."

Sang Wei said, "I wonder if they've spotted us yet."

A distant trumpet reached their ears. Jalist snickered. "There's your answer, young Knight."

Aeko swore. She rode back to the column, Jalist and Sang Wei right behind her. The other Knights had followed their gestures and spotted the approaching force. A few of them looked through spyglasses of their own. "Ride west, for the mountains. Don't stop. We might cross paths with berserkers along the way. Keep your steel ready."

She raised her hand, about to signal them to move out.

Jalist grabbed her arm. "Wait…" He raised the spyglass again.

"Seconds count," Aeko said with a scowl. "What is it?"

Jalist lowered the spyglass and handed it to Aeko, since she'd already returned Sang Wei's. Tears glistened in Jalist's eyes, drying quickly in the winter air. "Just look."

Aeko looked again. "Gods… those look like—"

"Bloodmares," Jalist said. "Hundreds of them. And the red horse banner of the Queshi."

Sang Wei's jaw dropped. Other Knights turned, wide eyed, to look again. Aeko frowned, still looking through the spyglass. "I see the Queshi banner, all right, but there's something else…"

"White banner with a black dragon," Jalist said. His voice choked. He wiped his eyes.

Aeko lowered the spyglass. "Jinn's name…"

Sang Wei looked confused. "Apparently, I don't know my heraldry as well as I should. Isn't that the Dhargots' standard?"

"Not on a white field, son… and not without a spear sticking through it." Jalist threw back his cloak and tugged up his sleeve. He showed the Knight of the Stag the same symbol tattooed to his right bicep: a black wingless dragon.

Aeko turned to her standard bearer, telling the Knight to raise their colors. Then she turned her horse south instead of west. A faint smile tugged at her lips as she glanced back at Jalist. "Care to handle the introductions, Master Dwarr?"

"Who in the gods' names starts a campaign in winter?" Saanji tugged at his cloak. He caught a few snowflakes on his gauntleted palm, which glistened in the rising sun, and watched them melt.

"Your brother started it," Royce answered, riding beside him in the column. "Perhaps that's something you could discuss with him."

Saanji touched the opal ring, which now hung from a chain around his neck, beneath his cuirass. "Oh, I'm sure we'll exchange words. Perhaps even insults."

"For my own part, I had something more dramatic in mind."

Saanji frowned. Before he could ask what Royce meant, Zeia said, "Killing the Bloody Prince is no more our priority than taunting him. I'm here to help the Isle Knight... and in so doing, help the Shel'ai."

Royce turned to look at her. "Begging your pardon, m'lady, but I doubt one in ten men in this army gives a burning damn what happens to the Shel'ai. We Lancers are here because the Bloody Prince attacked Ivairia. I'll let our friend, Saanji, speak for himself."

Saanji blushed. He happened to be riding between the two and suddenly felt caught in a place where he most definitely did not want to be. "Call it sibling rivalry, if you like." To Zeia, he said, "My brother is Chorlga's ally. He also happens to be in command of what is currently the largest army on the continent. And he's a sadistic bastard, besides. Killing him is about the closest thing to justice that Ruun can muster."

"And Chorlga commands a host of Jolym, the Nightmare, and his own powers, besides. What will we do if he attacks one flank while the Bloody Prince attacks the other?"

Saanji raised one eyebrow. Part of him wished that Zeia had voiced the sentiment earlier.

Royce said, "If we lift the siege at Atheion, we'll have the Isle Knights and the Noshans with us... plus, if we're lucky, that one particular Isle Knight you're so keen on finding. With our combined strength, we'll be able to fight anyone—including Chorlga and his demon."

Saanji noticed that Royce was speaking louder than he needed to. He glanced around at the Ivairian and Earless officers riding within earshot. He smothered a grin, bit back his cynical retort, and nodded. "Oh, of that, I have no doubt."

Despite Saanji's best efforts to sound sincere, Royce flashed Saanji a withering look.

"We need to form a better strategy for fighting the Jolym," Zeia said. Holding her reins with hands of fire, she nodded toward Royce's vanguard, which consisted of a hundred armored men with heavy lances. "Spears and swords won't be any help against them."

Royce said, "We have a thousand Earless archers. If needs be, we can arm more men with crossbows. They take little skill to use, and if you fire enough of them at a target, some are bound to strike home."

"We're only talking about a few hundred Jolym," Saanji reminded her.

Zeia's violet eyes narrowed dangerously. "Just one Jol nearly killed Shade and myself... two of the most powerful Shel'ai on the continent."

Saanji shuddered, though he was not sure whether Zeia's tone or her statement frightened him.

"When we reach Atheion," Royce said, "we'll have the Jolym trapped between us and the city's defenders. We have horses. The Jolym are on foot. Have no fear, m'lady. We'll mow them down with ease."

Saanji studied Royce's expression. *He doesn't really believe that,* he decided. "So what do we do after Atheion? Do you think we should give my brother the chance to surrender?"

"Actually, I was thinking I'd cut him down in front of all his men, then string him up by his feet and let his bloody corpse drain in front of the city like a butchered pig." Royce smirked at Saanji. "I hope that won't cast a pall over our friendship."

"You... mean to challenge him?"

Royce nodded slowly. One hand rested on his kingsteel bastard sword. "Do you think he'll accept?"

Saanji thought it over. "Yes," he said finally, "but why risk it?"

"It's a worthy risk. If I kill the Bloody Prince, his men may lose heart. The slaves and captives in Hesod might revolt. We could save thousands of lives— which we'll need if we're fighting Chorlga after this." His eyes narrowed. "Or do you think your brother is better?"

Saanji thought back to the practice yard and of how fast Royce moved, his steel blurring in the winter light. He shook his head. "I'm not questioning your sword arm, my friend."

"Perhaps you were hoping to make amends with your brother before he goes to the gods?"

Though Saanji guessed that Royce was joking, he touched the opal ring through his cuirass again. "No," he answered in a low voice. Tears stung his eyes. He cursed himself and blinked quickly, willing them back.

Rowen opened his eyes. Daylight made him wince. Then he shivered. He realized he was lying in a fissure of rocks and snow. He sat up. Thessa was kneeling in the snow next to him. She said something he did not hear. He clawed at the snow, looking for Knightswrath. Then he remembered it was lost. He closed his eyes, biting back a stream of curses and tears.

Silwren... I'm sorry.

When he opened his eyes, he found himself staring up a drawn length of steel.

"Who are you?" a woman's voice demanded.

Rowen faced the speaker: a tanned, dark-haired woman in mismatched armor, holding a well-notched longsword. Before he could answer, Thessa spoke for him.

"I *told* you his name. He's not a Dhargot. He knows Igrid. He's one of the Knights from the east. Can't you see the armor he's wearing?"

Rowen glanced down. Someone had removed his tunic. His kingsteel cuirass gleamed in the winter light.

"Names mean nothing, child. And armor can be stolen by any fool who chances upon a corpse." The dark-haired swordswoman prodded Rowen's cuirass with the tip of her sword. The blade sparked. "You're too pale to be an Isleman. I'd say you're from the Free Cities, probably a sellsword. So let's have the truth."

Rowen looked around. Dozens of Iron Sisters, all armed, surrounded him. A few scowled in his direction, but most faced north, toward a gaping hole in the rock spewing a partially frozen stream of filth.

"I'd tell you my name, but you already said names mean nothing. Judging by the reek, that's the opening to the sewers. We're outside the city. You haven't killed me yet. You haven't thanked me, either. Feel free to skip both, and I'll be on my way."

He started to rise.

The dark-haired swordswoman stabbed his cuirass, knocking him back down. "I'm not in the habit of thanking demons. I *might* be in the habit of killing them, given the chance... or letting them go if they answer my questions."

"Where are the Dhargots?" Rowen asked. "They should have swarmed over us by now."

"They started to, then pulled back. There's another army close. I think they're afraid of a siege. But there's still plenty of those bastards prowling around the sewers."

In the sewers...

Rowen shook his head, trying to focus on more immediate concerns. He could not imagine who would be poised to lay siege to Hesod. The Sylvan army was in tatters and occupied with the Olgrym. From what El'rash'lin had told him, the Isle Knights and the Dwarrs had their own problems, and he doubted Lyos would send the Red Watch this far in the middle of winter to help a foreign city. He could not imagine the Noshans doing it, either.

The swordswoman jabbed his cuirass again. "Speak, or I'll stick this sword where you don't have any armor."

Rowen bit back an angry retort. "The girl speaks the truth. My name is Rowen Locke. Igrid was my friend. I came to help her. But I saw her... hanging from the walls." He glanced at Thessa then back at the dark-haired swordswoman. "So I helped you instead. Don't make me regret it."

The Iron Sister frowned. "You don't have purple eyes or pointed ears. You're not a Shel'ai. So tell me how you carved through rock so thick, it was going to take us another two weeks to tunnel our way out."

Rowen pictured Knightswrath lying in filthy water, lost in the darkness of the city sewers. Surely, by now, the Dhargots had entered the temple and found the hole he'd carved. How long would it be before they found the sword, too?

He felt a surge of hope when he remembered how merely picking up the sword had left Briel's hand blistered. But how long would that keep the sword safe? How long before the Dhargots wrapped it in a cloak or found some other way to carry their great prize back to their prince?

How long before it finds its way to Chorlga?

Rowen started to rise to his feet again. This time, when the Iron Sister tried to knock him back down, he kicked her legs out from under her. Iron Sisters swarmed around him, leveling swords. But none looked willing to get too close.

The dark-haired swordswoman stood, unperturbed, dusting the snow off her mismatched armor. Rowen noted with grudging admiration that she had kept hold of her longsword in the fall. "My name is Haesha," she said. "I like people to know my name, just in case I have to kill them later."

Rowen felt a chill run down his spine, remembering a time when a sellsword named Dagath had told him almost exactly the same thing. "Haesha... Igrid went by that name for a while."

"She was your friend?"

Rowen blushed. "Close enough."

Haesha smiled thinly. "Maybe you really did know her, then. I saw her a week ago, fought beside her for a while. I thought she'd lead us after Ailynn fell. She ran instead."

"Igrid was no coward."

"I didn't say she was. Sometimes, it's smarter to run. Igrid was smart more than once." Haesha sheathed her sword. Taking that as a signal, the other Iron Sisters drew back a step. "You should know, she's not dead. At least, not as far as I know."

"I told you, I saw her—"

"Did you see her face?"

Rowen glanced at Thessa again, then back at Haesha. He recalled the Iron Sisters hung naked from the walls, their bodies covered in hungry crows. "There... wasn't much left of her."

Haesha caught his meaning. "Might have been her. Maybe not. Between us, I hope it was. Last we heard, the Bloody Prince had her trussed to his own bed like some kind of trophy."

Rowen's throat felt dry. "When was that?"

"Four days ago, at least. We caught a Dhargot who tried to trade some news for his life. You can imagine how we responded."

"Give me a sword." Rowen held out his hand.

Haesha blinked then laughed. "You forgot to say *please*."

Rowen glanced past her at the dark mouth of the sewer entrance. "Take care of the girl. I'm going back in there to get Igrid... and something I left in the sewers. I'll need a sword. You can either give me one, or I can pry yours out of your broken hand once you're done threatening me with it. I'll give you to the count of five to decide."

Haesha raised one eyebrow. The other Iron Sisters bristled, advancing on him, but she waved them back. "Did you not hear the part where I said the sewers are full of Dhargots? They've blocked off that way into the city in case we tried to get back in. You'll die before you get out of earshot."

"I have two reasons that are well worth the risk." Rowen paused. "I'm at three right now. What's it going to be?"

Haesha smirked. "You have spirit. No wonder Igrid liked you." She snapped her fingers and held out her hand. An Iron Sister armed with two maces reluctantly handed one to Haesha, who in turn presented it to Rowen. "This will have to do."

Rowen gave the weapon a practice swing. Maces were better suited to Jalist, but the weapon felt sturdy. He nodded. Turning to Thessa, he said, "See? Told you I'd get you out."

"*We* got *you* out," Thessa said. "You cut the ceiling open then yelled and went to sleep. We had to carry you." She came forward and grabbed his arm. "I'll go with you."

"No, you won't." Rowen gently pried her fingers free. "Stay with Haesha and the others. I'm going to get Igrid."

Haesha took Thessa's hand. "We'll keep her safe. Good luck, Knight. Die well."

Before Rowen could answer, a distant trumpet split the winter air. Another followed, then another. Haesha said, "Those aren't Dhargothi trumpets. Might be friends... or at least enemies of our enemies. Sure you don't want to wait?"

"Can't. If I had time to explain, you'd understand." Rowen switched the mace to his left hand, mussed Thessa's hair, and started back toward the sewers. He considered his chances of accomplishing even one of his goals, let alone both. But what choice did he have? He couldn't abandon Knightswrath.

And I can't leave Igrid, he admitted to himself. He stepped over a ribbon of frozen filth then paused to study the ground before him. He would have to climb a little to reach the opening to the sewer, and he did not relish the idea of slipping and falling. He chose his path and took a step.

Something crunched in the snow behind him. Thessa screamed a warning. Rowen turned, already swinging, but a sword blocked his mace. A second sword forced it down. A third Iron Sister swung her spear like a quarterstaff, knocking his legs out from under him. Two more stepped on his arm and wrenched the mace from his grasp.

He started to rise anyway. Haesha's boot pressed him back down. She sighed. "Sorry, Knight. Consider this your thanks."

"Wait, you don't understand," Rowen started to plead, a moment before the pommel of a sword drove him back into darkness.

Hráthbam stood on the deck of the *Winter Prayer* and watched as the two thin, cloaked figures climbed out of the little boat that had carried them to shore. As they started out across a seemingly endless field of ice, their dark cloaks shown against the stark, glaring white. Neither man looked back.

Hráthbam shook his head. Though El'rash'lin had refused to confirm his suspicion, Hráthbam knew the old man was going off to die. What puzzled him was why El'rash'lin had suddenly seemed to change his mind about the manner in which he met his end, choosing to walk into the Dragonward rather than remain on board the *Winter Prayer* and simply sail into it. The Soroccan merchant also did not understand why the sorcerer called Shade had decided to go with him. Still, there was something cold about Shade, and Hráthbam was glad to be rid of him—if only for a little while.

He replayed El'rash'lin's final instructions in his mind. While Hráthbam carried the other Shel'ai and Sylvs north, following the coast of the frozen sea, El'rash'lin and Shade would make their way north on foot. Eventually, Shade would meet them at the northernmost edge of a tiny peninsula that, according to Hráthbam's maps, overlooked an even smaller nearby island.

The thought of his remaining passengers living out the rest of their lives on that frozen, nameless island, with nothing but their wits and a few casks of darksoil, seemed nearly as absurd as El'rash'lin so calmly walking off to his own death. Hráthbam considered what he'd managed to piece together of El'rash'lin's story: the Shel'ai-turned-Dragonkin had been brought back to life, along with the Nightmare, and now both were immortal. But El'rash'lin hoped that throwing himself into the Dragonward would permanently end not only his own life but the Nightmare's.

"Set sail, lads," he called to his crew. "The sooner we finish, the sooner we can lose our wits to enough hláshba to leave the gods stinking drunk."

As his crew set to work, Hráthbam cast a final glance at the figures disappearing across the ice. He shook his head again. Not for the first time, he thought of his former bodyguard, a red-haired sellsword named Rowen Locke. He prayed that wherever he was, hopefully still in possession of the rusty adamune that Hráthbam had given him, his life made more sense than Hráthbam's.

CHAPTER THIRTY-SIX

WINGS OF BONE,
EYES OF FIRE

S HADE CAUGHT EL'RASH'LIN AS HE stumbled. The stark pallor of El'rash'lin's face unnerved him. "Your color has changed, old man. Is that fear or the Dragonward?"

El'rash'lin's twisted lips formed a brief smile. "Apologies... if my appearance... troubles you. You could have stayed... on the ship."

Shade shook his head. "I'll see this to the end. Besides, *you* could have stayed on the ship, too. Or did you just prefer to die on the ice?"

"Chorlga should have tried to stop us. He hasn't. I wanted to be away from the others in case—" El'rash'lin choked, doubled over, and choked again. As Shade pulled him back up, he saw a bright splatter of blood on the ice.

El'rash'lin wiped his mouth, though a smear of blood remained. His smile was gone. He took several deep, wheezing breaths. "I thought... it would weaken me, getting close to the Dragonward, but not like this. Something's wrong."

"*Countless* things are wrong," Shade said, though El'rash'lin's worry filled him with panic. "How far are we from the Dragonward?"

"Not far. We'll reach it... by nightfall. But something—" El'rash'lin choked again. His violet eyes watered. "Gods... I feel myself dying, Kith'el. That shouldn't be happening. Not yet."

"Is it the Nightmare?"

El'rash'lin blinked. He started to answer then choked again. He answered in mindspeak. *"It must be. I think Iventine is dying... really dying!"*

Shade frowned despite his surge of hope. The sooner the Nightmare left the world, the better. "You said Chorlga wouldn't absorb him, that he was afraid it would drive him mad—"

"Iventine is being drained, but not like how the Dragonkin used to drain dragons. This is different somehow—" El'rash'lin winced, then his eyes widened. He sank onto the ice, suddenly too heavy for Shade to hold him up. Tendrils of wytchfire flashed randomly off his body. Shade considered backing away then knelt beside him.

More wytchfire appeared. Shade turned away as raw heat rolled over him. He clenched his eyes shut and tried to escape, but El'rash'lin grabbed him and pulled him closer.

"Godsbane..." El'rash'lin let go.

Shade fell onto the ice. He stared, speechless. Great wings of ash spread beneath El'rash'lin's body, forming out of thin air. Terrified, Shade crawled backward. El'rash'lin's gaze—wide and unblinking—followed him. Wytchfire flared from his hands, his feet, then his eyes.

Then the wytchfire dimmed and vanished. The ash wings blew away. Shade rose slowly to his feet. He approached slowly. "Old man..."

El'rash'lin did not move despite the tears glistening in his eyes. But his face began to change. The twisted lips straightened. The sores shrank then disappeared altogether. He appeared as he had looked years ago—just a white-haired Shel'ai with tapered ears and sad violet eyes.

"Old man," Shade called again. His heart leapt into his throat.

El'rash'lin's violet eyes turned dark. The white pupils became as black as oil. Shade knew he should close those eyes, gather up the body of his one-time friend, and find a patch of ground that was not frozen in which to bury him.

Instead, Shade retreated. He thought of El'rash'lin's final word. "Godsbane," he said to himself. For a moment, he faced south. Then he turned northeast, toward the peninsula where he was supposed to meet the *Winter Prayer* in two days.

He stood on the ice, alone, unsure what to do.

Chorlga stood with his back to the great, yawning chasm that was the dragon graveyard and watched his army assemble. Hundreds of Jolym massed before him, arrayed in neat, steely rows. He'd recalled all those from the Lotus Isles, from Stillhammer, and from both the Simurgh and the Ash'bana Plains.

He studied them, appreciating his creations. He'd not seen them together since before they'd launched their first attack on the Dwarrish kingdom. He thought of the countless hours he'd toiled, how each one represented an entire year's labor. He thought of all he'd endured—gathering the metal, shaping it in secret, stealing into Cadavash to draw power from Namundvar's Well when necessary. Slowly, century after century, he'd crafted a nearly unkillable army with which he would build an empire. Each Jol contained a scrap of his own soul, a wisp of his own private allotment of Light.

My creations, my immortal champions, my children.... In a moment, all of them would be dead.

He studied his dragon-worshippers next. Hundreds strong, they knelt in the snow amid the Jolym. Men, women, children, some of them were draped in extravagant robes, but most wore rags. All trembled. He sensed that some knew what was about to happen, while others could only guess. But none attempted to flee.

Some had already been in Cadavash, worshipping the bones and legacy of dragons, when he'd appeared. Others had flocked to him in the days and weeks since, lured by stories of his power or merely running from the cruelty and turmoil of the world beyond. Chorlga reminded himself that in a way, their deaths would be a kindness. Especially for those who had spent their lives madly worshipping the bones of dragons, their hearts' deepest wish was about to be granted.

Chorlga issued a mental command to his Jolym. The great, steely host shifted. Each Jol seized the closest dragon-worshipper by the arms and held them immobile. A few scrabbled to freedom, but most were caught in the blink of an eye. Some wept or pleaded. Others protested that there was no need for force, reminding Chorlga that their loyalty to him was absolute, but it made no difference. Chorlga needed them restrained because he knew that once he began, instinct would take over. Some might still try to run, and he would need all that he could get.

He glanced at the Nightmare. The young man sat in the snow, half naked, his knees pressed against his chest. He was rocking himself, as always, seemingly oblivious to what was happening all around him. Chorlga braced himself then probed the Nightmare's mind for any indication that the madman would attempt to fight or flee. He found none. He withdrew his mind at once, fearful that the Nightmare's madness might contaminate him—then felt silly for doing so, given what he was about to attempt.

He closed his eyes and took a deep breath, wondering as he had before resurrecting the Nightmare if the breath would be his last. He had already accomplished a feat that no other Dragonkin had ever managed. Now he would attempt another, still-greater feat. And he would have to do so without the aid of Namundvar's Well, using nothing but his own body as a conduit.

He had not bothered to calculate the odds, knowing that his chance of success was abysmal. More than likely, he would burn himself to ashes from the inside out. *But if I succeed...*

Chorlga opened his eyes and glanced at the kneeling Nightmare. "It's time, my friend... time to make the world burn."

He moved to the first dragon-worshipper: a middle-aged man who had lost his nose and several fingers to frostbite. The man wept. Snot froze to his face. He struggled feebly in the grasp of a hulking Jol who stood behind him, but he said nothing. That particular Jol wore a brass, laughing facemask.

"You were born a man," Chorlga said to the dragon-worshipper. "Tonight, you will become a dragon." He pressed his fingers to the noseless man's face. The man jerked. Wytchfire flared from Chorlga's fingers, flowing into the man's eye sockets. It flowed back out a moment later—brighter, hotter—and was absorbed back into Chorlga's body.

Chorlga stepped back. A faint rush of exhilaration made him smile. He signaled, and the Jol released the noseless man, letting his corpse fall onto the snow. Blackened eye sockets stared upward. Chorlga met their dark gaze.

"Thank you," he said, and moved on to the next.

The process took hours. Slowly, Chorlga moved up and down the line, edging around the growing heap of corpses, pressing his hands to the face of each dragon-worshipper in turn. He drained them one after another, without pause, adding each Human's tiny scrap of power to his own. Some screamed—most in panic, but some in rabid exaltation. Gradually, though, the screams died down. Most simply whimpered. Others threatened, attempted to bargain with him, or pleaded for the lives of their loved ones.

One old woman with drowning eyes shook her head piteously. "They told me you were a god..."

"I am," Chorlga said and demonstrated his power.

When the last dragon-worshipper slumped dead onto the snow, her eye sockets black and blistered, Chorlga took a moment to steady himself. He had to move quickly. As intoxicating as this newly gained power was, he could not contain it for long. So he resumed the process.

This time, though, he drained the Jolym. Each one knelt at his approach. They made no sound and offered no protest. To his own surprise, Chorlga wept at the unmaking of his greatest creations.

Through the holes in each Jol's bright facemask, he withdrew the scrap of his soul that he'd given to create it, drawing its power back into himself. Much was lost in the transfer, though far less than if he'd simply reabsorbed their power without touching them—as he had to heal the injuries he'd sustained at Saikaido Temple.

Chorlga felt his own power building and building, past anything he'd felt before. The Jolym remained kneeling after their deaths, now absolutely hollow, as though some madman had simply dragged hundreds of suits of armor out into the snow and posed them. Only the scorch marks on their elaborate facemasks told a different tale.

By the time he stepped away from the last Jol in his column, the sun had sunk beyond the snowy hills, withdrawing its bloody tendrils of light. No sound reached his ears save the winter wind blowing through the abandoned temples. Chorlga turned slowly, surrounded by lifelessness. He shivered.

Then, with renewed determination, he made his way to the Nightmare.

The world seemed to shimmer around him. Unbidden, wytchfire streamed from his fingertips and ran like tears from his eyes. Draining the Jolym and dragon-priests had more than doubled his power. It roiled like madness through his veins. But even that was not enough. He would need far more if we wanted to accomplish the impossible.

The Nightmare looked up. Their eyes met. The Nightmare said, "Stop."

Chorlga paused. "You sound remarkably lucid for a madman."

"Stop," the Nightmare said again. He did not sound afraid. He remained where he was, seated in the snow. He no longer trembled.

Chorlga felt his heart jostle and wondered for a moment if he had absorbed more power than his body could sustain. He fought back a surge of pain. The world blurred, but he blinked until it came back into focus. "It's too late, Brother. I cannot stop."

He pressed his hands to the Nightmare's face. The latter made no move to defend himself. Purple flames burrowed into the Nightmare's eyes. Chorlga felt the man shudder, though he did not scream.

Then the wytchfire flowed back out.

Chorlga jerked, nearly losing his grip. It felt as though his blood had turned to ice, freezing in place. His vision darkened. Suddenly, he was drowning beneath the ice, lost in the darkness of a bottomless frozen sea.

No, he thought. *I will not fail. Not here. Not now.*

He struggled back to the surface. His hands found the ice. Wytchfire flared, blinding him. Frantic, furious, he melted the ice and clawed his way out.

And then, he was on the plains again, standing outside Cadavash. He stood alone. The Nightmare lay facedown on the snow, unmoving. Wings of ash had formed beneath his body; Chorlga barely had time to register the curious sight before the wind blew them away. A stabbing pain in his chest drew him back to his senses.

Not much time...

He would have to finish the task on his own. Though he had spared one single Jol—his oldest and strongest—he had already sent him away, lest Chorlga be tempted to command the Jol to carry him to his destination. With the addition of the Nightmare, Chorlga's powers had become too volatile. Touching the Jol would either release that power too early or melt it completely.

"I have commanded armies, slain kings, defied gods. I can walk a hundred feet on my own."

Still, he stooped to retrieve the staff he'd placed there earlier, suspecting he would need it. He took a deep breath and started out. Step by agonizing step, he hobbled away from the dead dragon-worshippers and the rows of silent, kneeling Jolym. Rather than return to Cadavash, he made his way south across the snowy plains.

Slowly, the darkness began to tighten around him. He felt as though the world itself were squeezing him inside some great, invisible fist. Though he did not have far to go, what might have taken him just a few moments in the past now took ages. His senses betrayed him. His vision blurred. Normally all but immune to the cold, he felt it piercing him on all sides, like arrows made of ice that pierced him bone deep. Sometimes, though, the cold vanished, and in its place, he felt searing, maddening heat. The vise-like pressure of the air around him intensified.

Worst of all, though, were the screams.

He mistook them for the wind at first, until they grew louder, and he realized with frightful clarity that they emanated from within. Chorlga shook his head, trying to block them out. He had anticipated this, having experienced some of these symptoms when he drained power from Namundvar's Well, but the internal cacophony was worse.

He spun. His staff shuddered as though it supported far more than just his weight. Then it snapped. Chorlga could not catch himself. He pitched forward into the snow, which struck his face with the hardness of stone. A new kind of pain spread in waves throughout his entire body. He closed his eyes and screamed, adding his voice to the grisly chorus in his head.

I can't do this. I'm going to fail. I'm going to die.

Fresh panic filled him. In his quest for power and vengeance, he'd defied both the gods and the Light and broken laws even the cruelest Dragonkin had never dared to test. What torments would they inflict upon his soul if he perished now?

Chorlga opened his eyes. He began to crawl through the snow, inch by inch. The earth raked him, tearing through his clothes, shredding his flesh as though freshly fallen snow had somehow been transformed into a field of broken glass. But still he crawled.

Finally, when he feared he could go no farther, he saw it: a nub of white bone lying in the snow, swirled faintly with crimson. His heart leapt. That bone joined another, then another. He lifted his head. Countless bones spread out before him, each one meticulously joined to the next with collars and chains wrought of kingsteel.

Somehow, Chorlga found the strength to kneel. The countless voices in his mind stopped screaming. The terrible cold melted away, replaced by a giddy warmth. Slowly, he lifted his gaze from the enormous skeleton of Godsbane to the darkened heavens. He gave Armahg's Eye a wolfish grin. "You have failed."

He waited for the heavens to answer. He half expected the gods, or the shades of El'rash'lin, Silwren, and perhaps even Fadarah and the Nightmare, to appear before him, blazing in the darkness, begging him not to proceed. But all he heard was a distant, mournful wind blowing across the empty plains.

Chorlga closed his eyes. He extended one hand and touched the very tip of one wing bone. An icy jolt raced up his arm, but Chorlga answered with wytchfire. Purple flames raced down his arm, pulsing from his fingertips. The dragonbone soaked up the flames like parched earth welcoming the rain.

Chorlga unleashed more. All that he had absorbed, he funneled slowly, carefully, through his fingertips. Wytchfire filled the first bone then overflowed to the next. Inch by inch, purple flames spread throughout each of the countless bones that formed the dragon's six great wings. Then they spread to its serpentine tail, its four limbs, and its cavernous ribcage.

Finally, they crawled up a long neck to its gargantuan skull, which rested on its side in the snow. Wytchfire filled the skull, pouring into it like water siphoned back into a bottomless well. Chorlga wondered if it would be enough. Then, finally, purple flames overflowed the eye sockets, flickering toward the heavens in bright, unforgiving tongues.

But Chorlga was not finished yet.

The creation of a single Jol had taken a full year—the scrap of himself needed that long to blossom into a crude form of consciousness. For a dragon, that would take longer—perhaps an entire century. But Chorlga could not afford to wait. So he gave more of himself than he ever had. Into Godsbane's bones, he poured not just the power he'd absorbed from his dragon-worshippers and all he'd taken back from his Jolym but as much of himself as he could give without dying.

A second, wild surge of panic filled him. What good would it do to establish a new empire on Ruun if he lost all that he was in the process and became a thing no more mindful than one of his Jolym? What revenge on the gods and all these paltry races could he savor if he sacrificed all ability to feel?

That will not happen. My fury is as deep as the water beneath the frozen crust of the Wintersea. I will endure.

He renewed the process, pouring out still more wytchfire. The flames darkened, reminding him of the telltale, darker blood that leaked from a mortal wound. But he did not stop. He forced himself to continue despite his blurred vision, the ache in his chest, a deep feeling of deflating organs, and bones gone brittle.

Finally, he withdrew his hand. Wytchfire continued to course through the bones, darkening them from stark white to ash gray. Wytchfire pooled in the eye sockets, continuing to blaze there though it dimmed everywhere else.

Chorlga struggled to stay on his feet. Indescribable weariness flooded him. But he forced his eyes to stay open. He felt a new presence beginning to awaken. It felt simultaneously ancient and new. Raw anger roiled in the air, tangible as his own fogging breath. For a moment, he feared that too much of Godsbane's own wrathful consciousness had been recalled from the Light and that he would not be able to control his own creation.

Then the wrath dimmed, and the wytchfire blazing in the dragon's eye sockets brightened. Tendrils of wytchfire flickered between the bones. The now-blackened kingsteel chains that joined the bones creaked but held. The wings stirred.

A fresh surge of exhilaration made Chorlga forget his exhaustion. "Godsbane," he whispered, "whom do you serve?"

Slowly, the Dragonjol lifted its head. Enormous pools of wytchfire regarded Chorlga. Its jaw opened. The Dragonkin trembled. Instead of speaking or exhaling fire, the Dragonjol bowed its massive head. Horns twice the length of lances dipped toward the ground. Its voice rang through Chorlga's mind like a thousand trumpets.

"I serve the Emperor of Dragons. His enemies are my own. Let all who would defy him tremble."

344

"Let us put that to the test." Into the Dragonjol's mind, Chorlga projected an image of his first target. The Dragonjol responded at once by lifting itself off the snow. Its tail snapped back and forth. Its massive wings spread, flexed, and began to move. Though no membranes of flesh joined the wing bones, the Dragonjol rose.

Chorlga watched, speechless.

The six wings beat in perfect synchronicity. Somehow, though, the Dragonjol made no sound save the rattling of the kingsteel chains that joined its bones. The ghastly, flaming apparition hovered then rose higher. Chorlga watched until it vanished from sight, winging westward. The rising sun glinted off the collared bones of its long, whipping tail.

Chorlga's strength failed. He pitched face first into the snow. For the first time, he realized that where Godsbane had lain, the snow had been transformed to ash. The smell of charred flesh filled his nostrils.

He imagined what was to come. A pang of guilt rose up within him, but he squelched it away. With the last of his fading strength, he summoned his only remaining Jol to carry him into Cadavash, where he could rest. Then, confident that he was safe, he surrendered his own senses and assumed those of the Dragonjol. He felt as though his own body were drifting at fantastic speed through the clouds, filling lungs the size of a house with crisp morning air. *His* eyes seemed to stare down at the lands of Ruun, now awash with red-gold sunrise.

Chorlga's eyes filled with tears.

CHAPTER THIRTY-SEVEN

CROSSROADS

R OWEN WOKE ON A STRAW bed in a gigantic tent, facing a massive fire. Smoke from the fire escaped through a hole in the ceiling. A cauldron of sweet-smelling stew bubbled over the fire, which was so hot that sweat beaded on his forehead, even as his stomach growled. Rowen looked under a thick blanket and saw that he was in his underclothes. He turned left and saw his kingsteel cuirass resting on a table, cleaned and polished, along with the rest of his possessions.

He turned right and saw Jalist Hewn.

The Dwarr smiled from his chair. "Locke, my friend, you've got either the greatest or the worst damn luck in the whole world." He stood. In place of his former attire, he wore a ringmail vest of leather and steel. His bare, powerful arms reached for the long axe leaning against his chair. The long axe was bright, newly forged metal, with a long shaft of wood wrapped in dark leather and banded in silver. Jalist moved it aside, leaned forward, and squeezed Rowen's shoulder.

"I know. You didn't get Igrid out. The Iron Sisters told me. By the way, the one named Haesha says she's sorry for cracking your skull. She did it to save your life, but it turns out she struck a bit too hard. Good thing we had a Shel'ai handy to heal you."

Rowen resisted the impulse to curse at the mention of the Iron Sister who had thwarted his attempt to reenter the sewers of Hesod and find Knightswrath. "What Shel'ai?"

"One we haven't met before. If we had, we'd remember." He shook his head before Rowen could ask his next question. "Don't worry about her. You'll meet her soon enough. Now, about Igrid…"

Rowen sat up, winced through his headache, and got out of bed. Despite his dizziness, he started to get dressed. "I'm glad you're alive, my friend, but Igrid is the least of my worries."

"Could have fooled me."

"What happened to the girl?"

"You mean the child you rescued? She's safe. She's with some clerics. She tried to see you a couple times. And she's not the only one. You've been asleep for two days."

Rowen froze. "Two days?"

Though they were alone, Jalist lowered his voice. "Listen, Locke, it wasn't just the lump on the skull that Haesha gave you. I don't know what happened to you in Hesod, but you went mad as a dragonpriest for a while. They had to tie you down to the bed. You were raving like some beggar who's smoked too much *fran-té*."

Rowen's hands shook. "Two days…" He thought of Knightswrath, lying in the city sewers all that time. Surely, the Bloody Prince had it by now. "I've got to get back into the city."

"Igrid can wait. Trust me."

"This isn't about Igrid." Rowen started for the tent flap. Jalist grabbed his arm. With astonishing strength, he pushed Rowen backward.

"Hold still and calm down, Locke. Whatever you plan on doing, it can wait until you get your armor on and a little sense back in that porridge you call brains." He handed Rowen a sweetbitter leaf. "Chew that first. Your breath smells like you've been eating raw urusk for the past month. Might want to remedy that before you meet royalty."

Rowen forgot about Knightswrath for a moment. He chewed the leaf until its sweet taste turned bitter, then he spat it out. He gratefully accepted the cup of cold water that Jalist handed him and drank half of it in one gulp. "Are you secretly a king or something?"

"Thank the gods, no. I don't think my heart could handle any more surprises."

"I hope mine can." Rowen winced as the headache returned.

Jalist plucked the cup of water from Rowen's hand, poured it out, and filled it with wine. Rowen drank deeply then went back to donning his armor. Jalist helped him.

"I'm surprised you aren't ordering me to rest," Rowen said, "especially if I was as crazy as you said." He wondered if Jalist had exaggerated. Rowen remembered having no nightmares related to Knightswrath, Chorlga, or Silwren, as he had before. Chorlga had not attempted to speak to him through dreams. But the comparison to those who smoked too much *fran-té* alarmed him. He'd seen slum dwellers in the Dark Quarter who became so addicted to the intoxicating, hallucinatory substance that not having it for even a short period of time drove them raving mad.

"My friend, after all I've seen the past few days, something tells me the best thing I can do is just help you get this armor on." Jalist went to a different table across the tent and came back with two Ivairian blades: a bastard sword and a shortsword, both waisted, with brass crossguards and wire-wrapped handles. He gave them to Rowen.

"Where did you get these?"

"Royce left them for you."

"And who in Fohl's hells is Royce?"

As though in response, the tent flap opened. Two figures walked in. A slender, balding man of medium build wore full armor. His cuirass bore the gilded engraving of a crowned horse. Beside him walked a pudgy man in dark scale armor. At the sight of the latter, Rowen started to draw one of his swords. Jalist stopped him.

"This is Prince Saanji of Dhargoth."

"So?"

Prince Saanji smiled faintly. "Despite how that sounds, I'm a friend. Glad to see you aren't howling like a rabid animal anymore." Before Rowen could answer, he said, "I won't stay. I just wanted to meet the famous Isle Knight who's been the source of so many implausible barroom tales."

Saanji glanced at his Ivairian counterpart. "If you want to chat with the newest recruit in our army of madmen, I'll just go meet with Haesha and the Iron Sisters, maybe see what we can do about getting them outfitted with some armor and decent weapons."

The Lancer nodded, and the Dhargothi prince left. When the Dhargot was gone, the Lancer faced Rowen. He gave Rowen a suspicious look then bowed. "My name is Arnil Royce. I met Igrid on the road, north of the Red Steppes. I'm sorry to hear that you couldn't get her out of Hesod." He paused. "And given what I've been hearing lately about Chorlga, the Nightmare, and all those gods-damned Jolym, I'm even sorrier to see that you no longer have a certain sword of fire hanging at your side."

Rowen looked from the Lancer to Jalist, then back to the Lancer. "I feel like I just walked into a tavern, but the bard was already halfway through his song."

Royce smirked. "I don't doubt it. Your friend can answer most of your questions, I'm sure. In the meantime, I have some of my own, and a few thousand men whose lives depend on what you have to say."

Rowen recovered from his surprise enough to gird the two swords Jalist had given him. "Point me toward Hesod, because that's where I'm going. If you want to talk, we can talk along the way." He started toward the tent flap.

Royce moved to block him. "Apologies, Knight, but Jinn's sword will have to wait. I'm sure Zeia will be here to talk to you about that in a moment, anyway. In the meantime, I've already spoken with the Iron Sisters, but they've spent most of the past few months in a dungeon. So I need to know what *you* know about the strength of the Bloody Prince's forces, if he has any Jolym in the city, and how likely it is that the slaves might rise up and fight with us."

Rowen considered trying to force Arnil Royce out of the way. Though not an Isle Knight, and a bit smaller, the man had the look of a seasoned warrior. Rowen knew a little about the fearsome reputation of the Lancers who served the king of Ivairia, where his parents had lived long ago.

Royce seemed to sense Rowen's thoughts because one hand moved toward the brass, anthropomorphic hilt of his bastard sword. The Lancer raised one eyebrow. Rowen touched one of his own swords, but Jalist intervened.

"Well, Locke, you heard him. Did anybody discuss troop strength and the morale of their slaves while you were hiding in a tavern or sulking around in the sewers? No?" The Dwarr faced the Lancer. "I've been in the city, too, you know. I already told you, Karhaati has more men than you and the renegade prince combined, plus elephants and siege engines besides."

Royce turned from Rowen to Jalist. "That's why I need to know if I can count on a few thousand slaves rising up against their masters. If not, this will be one of the least successful sieges in the history of Ruun."

A voice said, "Well, at least you don't have to worry about Atheion." A newcomer entered the tent and smiled. "Hello, Squire. I'll have you know, you gave us a less-than-merry chase."

Rowen's eyes widened. He sidestepped away from the others then bowed deeply before the armored woman. "Commander—"

"Captain, actually, for what it's worth."

Rowen straightened. In place of a golden-horned stag, his former teacher wore a tabard emblazoned with a white, nine-pointed flower. "And a Knight of the Lotus, besides!"

Aeko's smile vanished. She glanced past Rowen. "Sir Royce, if you're done questioning my former squire before he's had time to dress, let alone heal, I'd like to wring his neck for a while."

Royce cleared his throat as though he meant to object, then left the tent without another word.

"That one seems less than happy," Jalist muttered.

Aeko said, "Could be the fact that he's outnumbered, with an even stronger army at his back, led by a Dragonkin. Or maybe he just thought that by the time he reached Hesod, he'd be sharing camp with a few thousand Isle Knights."

Rowen asked, "How many are with you?"

"Twenty-four."

Rowen's expression soured. "I was hoping for twenty-four thousand."

"Sorry to disappoint you. On the bright side, thanks to you, Royce has about a hundred Iron Sisters, plus more coming in from the wild every day. And that's not all." She nodded toward Jalist.

To Rowen's surprise, Jalist blushed. "I found Leander," he said simply. "He has five hundred Housecarls with him, plus another five hundred Queshi who got tired of all this trouble on their borders and came to see what's the matter. Step out of this tent and turn east if you want to see what a whole damn corral full of bloodmares looks like."

"You found him…" Rowen grinned. He squeezed Jalist's shoulder. "I'm surprised you're wasting time with me, then."

Jalist cleared his throat. "Yeah, well, it seems my people haven't changed their minds on men bedding down with men just because they had their kingdom torn in half." He turned to Aeko. "Tell him the rest."

Aeko hesitated. Then she said, "The Jolym invaded the Isles. So did the Nightmare, though I don't pretend to understand how. Saikaido Temple is—"

"I know," Rowen interrupted. "El'rash'lin told me."

Aeko raised one eyebrow. Though tears had welled in her eyes at the mention of her old home, she blinked them away. "Then it seems you have some interesting stories to tell as well. But I'll finish mine first. The Jolym spent a few weeks tearing up the countryside then massed at Cadavash. The Nightmare hasn't been seen since the Lotus Isles, but if it's still alive, it's probably there, too. Chorlga has been entirely too quiet. But… someone's come to help us. Help *you*, I should say. El'rash'lin sent her."

Rowen thought of Silwren. For one wild moment, he wondered if El'rash'lin had somehow brought her back to life, as Chorlga had done for the Nightmare. Heartache filled him. He nearly wept at the thought of seeing Silwren again. Then a cold breeze touched his face.

He turned to see a woman entering the tent. He saw at once that she was a Shel'ai, though in place of a bone-white cloak embroidered with crimson greatwolves, she wore armor and a pair of Ivairian shortswords. Her dark hair—unusual for her kind—had been cut short. Though Rowen had never seen her himself, he recognized her face from El'rash'lin's memories. "Zeia?"

The Shel'ai's violet eyes widened in momentary surprise. "My master said you might know me."

"Just a few glimpses from his mind. He and Silwren saved you, when you were little." Rowen forced himself to bow, though he kept one hand on the hilt of a sword. "El'rash'lin thought of you as... one of Fadarah's closest allies."

Zeia's eyes sparked with anger. "That was a long time ago, Isle Knight. Fadarah is dead. Shade killed him, to punish him for what he planned with Brahasti." She added, "Though I think Fadarah would surely have died from the blow *you* struck, if it bolsters your pride to think so."

Rowen stiffened at the mention of Shade, but Zeia turned to Aeko. "I must speak with him alone. Wait outside."

Aeko touched the hilt of her adamune. "I'm afraid I don't take orders from Shel'ai."

"And I don't waste time discussing courtly politics and troop strength when the world is set to burn." Zeia faced Jalist. "You wait outside, too, Dwarr. My words are for the Knight of the Crane alone."

"These people are my friends," Rowen interrupted. "You are not. Speak or don't. I don't have time for this, either."

Zeia looked surprised, then nodded. "So be it. El'rash'lin sent me to help you. By helping you, I help all Shel'ai left in Ruun, and perhaps all those yet to be born."

"And how, exactly, do you plan on helping me?"

"By retrieving what you so carelessly left behind. I pulled the image from your mind while you slept. You lost Knightswrath in Hesod. But the Bloody Prince does not have it. Not yet. The sword is alive now. For whatever reason, it's chosen *you* to be its champion. No one without strong magic dare touch it."

Jalist answered first. "So it's been lying in a river of muck and shit for days... a bright, priceless adamune with a dragonbone hilt long as my forearm... and no Dhargot thought to wrap it in a cloak and pluck it out?"

"Fel-Nâya's ancient powers have been revived. Silwren saw to that. The sword protects itself. I doubt the Dhargots could see it even if they looked right at it. But Chorlga could... and will, which is why we need to move quickly." She faced Rowen, her expression cold. "Without the sword, you are just a man. The Dhargots would kill you in an instant. So I will go into the city by myself and retrieve the sword. Meanwhile, you must prepare yourself to use it."

Rowen shook his head. "Knightswrath isn't my only reason for going back into the city."

Zeia nodded. "I saw the comely, red-haired swordswoman in your dreams, too. While I'm thrilled that you've found love, Human, I'm not about to risk all the lives throughout all the kingdoms on Ruun just to retrieve your favorite bedmate."

Rowen blushed, half from embarrassment, half from anger. "At the risk of offending you, Sorceress, I'm afraid you're not turning out to be my favorite ally."

"Nor should I be. You've killed many of my friends. I suspect I've killed some of yours. I don't imagine we'll be sharing wine in this lifetime. But I'll see this war through to its end. You must do likewise. All that matters is slaying Chorlga. To do that, we'll need magic far stronger than mine. We'll need Knightswrath."

"You talk like a fairytale," Jalist grumbled. "Chorlga is a man, not a god. Are you telling me that since the gods threw Zet down out of the sky, nobody's ever killed a Dragonkin just by sticking a knife in his back or hitting him with a poisoned arrow?"

Zeia gave Jalist a stern look. "I remember you, Dwarr. You were at Cassica and Lyos. Have you already forgotten about the Nightmare? Chorlga is stronger still. He's drunk so deeply from the Light that he's barely even a Dragonkin anymore. He survived the purge after the Shattering War, when Jinn's armies scoured the entire continent for any Dragonkin who escaped justice. He's kept himself hidden for centuries, growing stronger. Now he can instantly heal any wound that isn't severe enough to kill him in the blink of an eye. If he wishes, he can see, hear, and sense every living thing surrounding him for miles. And he has an entire army of Jolym around him. If you think your axe can kill such a thing, by all means, ride to Cadavash and try."

Jalist glared at her but said nothing.

"You told me to prepare," Rowen said. "How am I supposed to do that? If you want me to kill Chorlga, just take me to him. I don't need to pray or meditate. Just get me Knightswrath, and the Dragonkin dies."

Zeia faced him with open derision. "You don't even remember, do you?" She shook her head. "How many times have you really unleashed the sword's power?"

Rowen did not answer.

She answered for him. "Once, against Fadarah. Once, against Doomsayer. And once, in the sewers of Hesod. Each time nearly killed you. Instead of becoming stronger, you've gotten weaker. Already, being without the sword nearly drives you mad, doesn't it? If you were pushed just a little, you could be as drunk off power as Chorlga, as mad as Iventine, as blind as Fadarah." She paused. "Well, Knight? Tell me I'm wrong."

Rowen saw his friends bristle out of the corner of his eye. His face flushed—first with anger, then with shame. "I can't," he said finally. "So what should I do while you're gone... pray to the Light for help? Practice my sha'tala? Maybe learn to forget my own name?"

"I'm not the champion, Human. You are." Zeia took a step backward. "I go to get the sword. Remember what I said. Prepare yourself while I am gone."

Rowen shook his head. "This is madness. Maybe you can get into the city without being seen, but you won't be able to touch the sword. When I was in Shaffrilon, a Sylv tried to touch it, and it nearly burned his hands off."

Zeia smirked. She lifted her arms. Her sleeves fell, revealing puckered scars. "Then it's a good thing I no longer have hands."

She turned and hurried out of the tent.

Jalist whistled softly. "Strange friends you're making these days, Locke. Which reminds me... Leander said they ran into a Sylv who claimed she knew you. A rather surly woman, covered in scars."

"Kilisti," Rowen said. "What happened to her?"

"They didn't kill her, if that's what you're asking. He thinks she rode back for the Wytchforest. Oh, and the Queshi got that grim little message you sent about Chorlga. So did the Lancers, the Noshans, and the king of Lyos... which probably makes you the only person without royal blood who's known to damn near every kingdom on the continent!"

Rowen wondered how many of his warnings had not reached their destinations and how many lives had been lost because of it. "What has Chorlga been doing?" he asked wearily.

"We don't know," Aeko answered. "Royce says he's been sending scouts toward Cadavash for days. None have returned."

"He must have Jolym hidden on the way to ambush them," Jalist mused.

"Or else Chorlga is killing the scouts himself," Rowen said. "Otherwise, one or two would make it back."

Jalist shrugged. "Either way, there must be something happening there that he doesn't want us to see."

Rowen rubbed his eyes as his headache blurred his vision. "That would explain why he hasn't moved against us."

"Oh, he's moved against us," Aeko corrected. "Stillhammer and the Lotus Isles are in ruins. Meanwhile, his Jolym have thrashed half the countryside."

And I've done nothing... "But we're still here. He could wipe out this whole army himself, if he wanted to."

"Maybe he doesn't know we're here yet," Jalist offered.

"Gods help us if he finds out." Rowen remembered Chorlga's offer: if Rowen surrendered Knightswrath, Chorlga would stop the killing. Perhaps he'd been holding back in order to give Rowen time to decide. But Knightswrath was gone. Until Zeia retrieved it, Rowen couldn't surrender even if he wanted to.

Rowen finished his wine then smelled the stew again. His stomach rumbled, but the thought of eating made him queasy.

Jalist said, "We should attack the Bloody Prince now. If we can take the city, we can at least hide behind thick walls and a few thousand archers. Might not be much, I know, but it beats fighting Jolym and a Dragonkin while we're also fighting off frostbite."

Rowen wiped sweat from his brow. Just then, frostbite did not sound altogether unappealing. Despite the roaring fire, neither Jalist nor Aeko appeared overheated. He rubbed his eyes again as his headache throbbed.

Jalist said, "You look pale as bone, Locke. Lie down. You're safe here."

Safe? Rowen shook his head, partly in refusal and partly in sheer disbelief that such a thing as safety could exist. "Too much to do..."

"Not for you," Aeko said. She squeezed his arm. "Rest, Squire. But keep your armor on." She looked down at his new weapons. "I'm sorry I don't have another adamune for you. Or more armor. I might be able to find a tashi—"

"These suit me fine." Rowen unbuckled his swords, even though he'd just girded them. Their weight alarmed him. Had he just gotten used to kingsteel? He thought of the few pieces of armor he'd left back in Hesod. Then he froze. "The scroll..." He faced Jalist. "The scroll Silwren gave me! I left it in my saddlebags. I gave my horse to Kilisti so she could get away."

Jalist and Aeko exchanged looks. "Just a scroll," Jalist said. "If you like, we'll go back to the Wytchforest and get it once all this is over. Might even steal a few of those glowing stones while we're at it. I bet we could sell them for a fortune."

Just a scroll...

"Luminstones," Rowen muttered. He realized that Jalist and Aeko were guiding him back toward the bed. "Had one of those in my saddlebag, too." He felt his pocket. "Wait. No. I have one here. This was Kilisti's." He drew out the small, seemingly nondescript stone and cupped it in his hands. A blue glow formed, spilling between his fingers. He gave it to Jalist. "For your prince."

He managed to smile then lay down on the bed, closed his eyes, and collapsed into nightmares.

Saanji found Zeia in her tent.

The Shel'ai had conjured her hands of fire and was using them to gird a shortsword about her waist. The leather smoked where she touched it. The brass buckle had already blackened. She looked up and scowled. "Entering my tent unannounced is a good way to get yourself killed, Human."

Though it was still midday, Zeia's tent was dark. Only her flaming hands held back the shadows. The wytchfire shone off her face, matching her violet eyes. For a moment, Saanji could only stare.

Zeia scowled again. "Well?"

Saanji shook himself out of his stupor. "Royce seems to think you're going into the city—"

"I am." Zeia finished with her shortsword then picked up a dark cloak. She threw it over her shoulders. The seams smoldered.

"Is that… wise?"

"Necessary," Zeia corrected. "That foolish Knight lost Fel-Nâya in the sewers. It's probably still there. I have to go and get it."

Saanji nodded. "The Iron Sisters say there's an opening to the sewers just outside the city, but it's probably heavily guarded. Wait a moment, and I'll pick out my best men—"

"I'm going alone."

Saanji chewed the inside of his lip. "At the risk of repeating myself—"

"I'd rather this not turn into a bloodbath, Prince. I can slip in unseen. Your men can't."

"I don't know much about magic—"

"Good. I appreciate your honesty. Now, avoid looking foolish and keep your thoughts on magic to yourself."

Saanji blushed. "I was just going to say—"

"That I can't possibly get past scores of armed men without being seen, and what will I do if I'm spotted," Zeia finished.

"Oh, I *know* what you'll do if you're spotted. That's the problem." Saanji blushed further. "You've gotten to be pretty good with a sword. And honestly, just the sight of your hands might scare half the Dhargots out of their wits. But from what I've seen, you can't throw wytchfire anymore. All you'll have to defend yourself with is that sword. And that's not enough."

Zeia answered with a derisive smirk. "If that were really all I had, you'd be right. But it isn't."

"Fine," Saanji conceded, "you can read minds, maybe make one or two guards think they hear—" He broke off, interrupted by the distinct feeling that someone was stirring a razor-sharp knife through his brain. He tried to scream, but no sound came out. He sank to his knees, shaking uncontrollably.

Zeia's smirk disappeared. She rushed forward. "Are you... I didn't think—"

"What did you just do?" Saanji tried to say, but the words came out jumbled.

"El'rash'lin taught me. It's called a mind-stab. It's something all Shel'ai can do, with some training, but most don't even know it. He says we've forgotten most of our old skills—"

Saanji did not hear the rest. He lurched forward and retched. Tears of pain and humiliation streamed from his eyes. A searing sensation lingered within his mind, sending random, white-hot jolts through all of his senses. Then, all at once, the searing ceased.

"Keep your eyes shut," Zeia said. Tingling warmth emanated from her flaming hands as she held them to his temples, as though her touch were composed not of flesh but of countless small, hot needles.

Saanji nodded dumbly. He did not even remember closing his eyes in the first place. With the searing pain now absent, he felt a dizzying vertigo. Then that, too, subsided. The tingling withdrew. He felt Zeia wipe his mouth with a piece of cloth.

"I shouldn't have done that. I only wanted to demonstrate. I thought that at its lowest strength, it wouldn't... I'm sorry."

Saanji tried to answer, but the words he formed in his mind stayed there as though frozen. He felt Zeia's tingling caress on his forehead. Eyes closed, mute, he savored it.

CHAPTER THIRTY-EIGHT
THE BELLY OF THE RAT

Z EIA MADE HER WAY OUT of the camp. Arnil Royce had assigned
a contingent of bodyguards to stay with her even after they left
Cassica, and these armored men followed quietly a few yards behind
her. Meanwhile, Lancers and Earless hurried to get out of her way. None of
the sentries challenged her. Finally, at the edge of the camp, she dismissed her
bodyguards. They looked only too happy to be relieved of duty. Alone, Zeia
moved stealthily through the darkness.

She did not bother visiting the gorge, even though that was the most
direct route back to Knightswrath. Even Humans were not foolish enough to
leave so obvious an entrance into their city unprotected on the eve of a siege.
She suspected that by now, a pile of rubble blocked off the old entrance into
the sewers, and scores of Dhargots with crossbows had been given the sorry
duty of patrolling the sewers.

She thought back to how she, Royce, and Saanji had ridden ahead with
the vanguard and discovered a small host of Iron Sisters massed outside the
city. Zeia had recognized the Isle Knight in their midst before any of them—
though the absence of an adamune with a telltale hilt of dragonbone had filled
her with dread. Almost immediately, she'd pressed one flaming hand to the
Isle Knight's forehead, sending her thoughts into his. She'd ascertained where
the sword was, and she might have rushed straight into the sewers right then
and there to retrieve it, but a company of Dhargots happened by.

Only a hundred strong, they posed no real threat, and they ran as soon as
they spotted Royce's banners and the flashing armor of his men. But Saanji,
fool that he was, had ignored Royce's advice and given chase. She suspected
that the foolish Human was trying to impress her. And even more foolishly,

she'd delayed her entrance into the sewers to see that the Earless prince—who now truly only had one ear—made it back in one piece.

By then, it was too late. Dhargots had massed along the city walls, and catapults added their fury to an endless arc of arrows, driving them back. Now her only chance to retrieve the sword of Fâyu Jinn lay in entering Hesod the same way that a host of Shel'ai and Unseen assassins had once entered Lyos: through its wells. Zeia winced at the thought of how much what she was about to do would hurt.

She trudged through the snow, alone in the no-man's-land between the encampment and the city. The walls of Hesod loomed above her. In places, ice glazed the stone. Dhargots massed around the battlements. A few shouted insults and fired arrows at her, but she was too distant for the latter to reach her and unperturbed by the former.

Zeia searched north of the city until she found what she was looking for. Just ahead, illuminated by moonlight, the snowy fields gave way to a frozen ribbon of water. Fishing huts lined the icy lake, along with a line of modest watchtowers, but all looked to have been abandoned. Nevertheless, Zeia approached them cautiously.

While Lyos drew its water from an aqueduct that ran all the way to the coast and fed a massive manmade reservoir within Pallantine Hill, Hesod's water came from wells fed by a river that ran near the city. In winter, ice formed over that river. Even if one broke through the ice, swimming the river all the way to the wells would have been impossible, as no one could hold their breath for that long.

Not without magic.

Zeia hesitated. Fadarah had never attacked Hesod; thus, the Shel'ai had not performed any reconnaissance there. For all Zeia knew, the watery tendrils that ran underground and fed Hesod's wells were far too narrow for a person to swim, anyway. She could lose her way. She might even become trapped, held in the darkness until her magic ran out, followed promptly by her air.

Besides those risks, and despite her earlier boasts to Saanji, she had never been among the strongest of Fadarah's Shel'ai. The spell she was about to attempt had always been too difficult for her in the past.

But I have to try. I have no choice.

She thought of the Isle Knight—what a disappointment he'd turned out to be thus far. Instead of rallying nations and inspiring armies, as Fâyu Jinn had done, he'd floundered in the wild, alternately drawn to and fearful of the incredible magic at his disposal. Silwren had sacrificed herself for nothing. The

Human stood no chance against Chorlga. Better that they'd all just forgotten about Fel-Nâya completely and explored some other means of slaying the Dragonkin. But it was too late for that.

Zeia reached the frozen waters, took a deep breath, and let it go. Looking down, she thought she saw fish passing by, a dark blur far beneath the ice. She knelt in the snow. Summoning her flaming hands, she pressed her palms to the ice. She shivered even as she urged heat to flow through her ghostly touch. Slowly, the ice began to melt.

She withdrew her hands long before the ice had completely gone, knowing she had to conserve her strength. Dismissing one flaming hand but retaining the other, she drew her sword. She fumbled as she gripped it, still not quite accustomed to the strangeness of holding something with a wispy hand formed entirely of magic—a hand she did not feel so much as sense. Gathering her strength, she drove the blade downward. The ice cracked.

Zeia withdrew her blade. Rather than stab with it, she swung and swung, as though she held an axe. Sweat formed on her brow, but she went on chopping until chunks of ice fell away, revealing the pale-blue water beneath. Then she sheathed her sword, dismissed her flaming hand, and sat to catch her breath.

She stared at the ugly, puckered scars capping her wrists. A wave of resentment filled her. El'rash'lin wielded the powers of a Dragonkin. He could have restored her hands and made her whole, but he had refused. At the time, she'd agreed with his decision. But perhaps she had been hasty.

No, El'rash'lin was right. He was right about everything, from the beginning. If Fadarah… if all of us… had just listened to him, none of this would have happened.

She lowered her arms, letting her sleeves slide down and conceal her scars. She rose to her feet. For a long time, she stared at the pale, cold waters. To her surprise, she thought of Saanji and felt another pang of guilt over the pain she'd caused him during her demonstration of the mind-stab technique.

Pushing the prince from her mind, she summoned her flaming hands once more, ungirded her sword, and let it fall. Then she took another deep breath, stepped off the bank, and let the icy water close over her head.

Igrid woke to find a sweaty, rat-faced man with yellow teeth leaning over her. She feared for one wild moment that she had died and Fohl, the Undergod, had come to torment her by endlessly hauling out her insides. Then she recognized the robes of a healer. His nimble fingers fussed with her bandages, though his eyes and chilling smirk betrayed his greater interest in her breasts, which were as bare as the rest of her.

Then the healer noticed that her eyes were open. He leapt back. Igrid reached for his throat, but something stopped her short. She realized she'd been tied down. She turned her head, looking left then right. She was lying on a bed. The room smelled of wine and putrid incense. Lanterns blazed on tables all around her.

Gods, where am I?

She struggled, but the bonds tied to her wrists had been wrapped underneath the bed. Identical ones held her ankles and thighs. She studied the healer then looked past him and saw still more figures in dark robes lurking by the lanterns. Panic surged within her, but she forced herself to smirk.

She tried to threaten the men by telling them how pretty their ears would look on her necklace, inviting them to come closer so she could bite them off, but she found that she could not speak. For a moment, she thought it was just the consequence of her dry, parched throat. Then she remembered the alley—and the knife.

Gods, I tried to cut my own throat...

She gnashed her teeth and hissed.

The lead healer paled. He held up his hands. "Don't move, child. We're just changing your dressings. The good news is that your bones have almost healed. But lie still, or your wounds will reopen."

The note of pleading in his voice puzzled her. The men weren't city clerics. They looked like Dhargots. But Dhargothi healers were known for observing the same stern philosophy as the warriors: only the strong deserved attention. The weak were better left to perish. Why would they care if she lived or died?

Igrid looked down at her body. Bandages wrapped half her torso, but where the healer had not yet finished, tight stitches were wreathed in purple skin. A thin trickle of blood ran from one of them. Igrid winced as a wave of nausea swept over her.

"Don't retch," the healer warned. "If we have to keep stitching up your guts, you'll have more holes than flesh."

One of the other healers laughed and said something crude. Igrid gritted her teeth and stubbornly willed herself not to vomit. Slowly, the nausea subsided, relaxed by numbing pain. Despite her best efforts, her eyes watered.

"I'll give you wine for the pain, but you have to promise to lie still."

Igrid nodded weakly.

One of the other healers handed the leader a goblet. A third, younger healer came forward and helped lift Igrid's head. He held it while the leader brought the goblet to her lips. Igrid drank. The wine was strong but bitter, obviously mixed with herbs to dull her pain. The leader lowered the goblet so that she could swallow.

The other healer made another crude comment. Igrid shifted her eyes, batted her lashes, and smiled at him. The next time they offered her the goblet, she filled her mouth, waited until they lowered the goblet, and spat at him.

The healer let go of her head, which fell back down on the pillow, sending waves of pain radiating out from her throat. The younger healer cursed, wiped his face, and lifted his other hand to strike her. The leader stopped him with a sharp command. He spoke a name, and the younger healer paled and backed away.

Karhaati. He said Karhaati's name…

A chill raced through her body. Had the Bloody Prince himself ordered that she be saved? If so, what sick torments would a man like that have in mind for her once she'd healed? She considered forcing her wounds to reopen so that she could die then and there.

The lead healer looked down at her again. After ogling her, he looked into her eyes when he spoke. "Please don't struggle. I promise, child, we're trying to help you."

Igrid forced herself to nod. If she meant to reopen her own wounds and bleed out, she would have to wait until the healers left, anyway. With supreme effort, she managed to lie still as the lead healer finished bandaging her while two more healers assisted him. Igrid noted that although they freely leered at her naked body, which made her skin crawl, none touched her beyond what was called for.

When they were finished, the lead healer sent the others away. Igrid accepted another drink of wine then endured the humiliation of the rat-faced old man spoon-feeding her a bowl of vile-tasting broth. By then, she felt tired. She wondered if the wine had also been drugged.

"That's enough," a voice said.

The old man turned and bowed. "Of course, my prince." He flashed Igrid a look—was it pity or pleading?—and hurried to go. A big man in red robes stepped into the lantern light. He grabbed the old man's arm, turned him back around, and pointed at Igrid.

"Why is she uncovered?"

The old man paled. "Prince, as you commanded, we were changing her dressings, checking stitches—"

"Are you *still* changing her dressings and checking her stitches?"

The old man hesitated. "No, my prince. Forgive me—"

"You're finished, yet you left her there, naked. Did I not tell you that she was to be treated with dignity?"

"We *have* treated her well," the healer insisted. "I swear on the Dead God, no man has touched her except to—"

The big man punched the healer in the stomach, held his fist there as the healer jerked, then pulled back. Igrid saw a wide, bloody knife in the big man's hands. He knelt, wiped the blade on the dying healer's robes, then straightened. He snapped his fingers. A big man with a patch over one eye stepped out of the shadows. He gave Igrid a leering glance then grabbed the old man's arms and dragged him out of the room. His whimpering confirmed that he was still alive. A moment later, Igrid heard a wet, rasping choke from the hallway.

The Bloody Prince closed the door, flipped the knife, and sheathed it. "I'm running out of healers, Iron Sister. Strange that even bruised and stitched, you manage to be beautiful."

Igrid forced herself to meet his gaze. Though her heart pounded painfully in her throat, she refused to look away. After a moment, the Bloody Prince nodded in what looked like grudging approval, stepped forward, and grabbed a blanket off the floor. He covered her.

"Believe it or not, as much as the thought pleases me, I have no intention of raping you. Nor will any other man so long as I'm alive. I have other plans for you. That's why I put you in my own bed, so that I could be close enough to protect you."

Queen Sharra's bed, Igrid realized.

"Do you have any idea how strange it is that you're still alive? Fever, infection, the depth of your wounds, one of which was actually poisoned... yet here you are." He sat down at the edge of the bed.

Igrid went rigid.

"Clearly, the Dead God wishes it so, as do I." The Bloody Prince withdrew something from his belt and dangled it in front of her.

When Igrid realized what it was, she tried to claw Karhaati's eyes out despite her bonds. He smirked. He dangled the dark lock of Ailynn's hair over Igrid's face a moment longer, then sniffed it, grinned, and tucked it back into his belt. He stood. "Do I have you nice and rankled, Iron Sister? That's good. You see, I mean for you to regain your strength, all of it, before I kill you. I want you at your very best, understood? Either you give me a good death, or I give you yours. That's what warriors like us deserve."

He moved slowly around the room, extinguishing one lantern after another. Igrid panicked again as darkness began to swallow the room. He gave her a chilling look, his face half lit by firelight. Then he extinguished the last lantern. Igrid braced herself, prepared to fight as hard as she could, if only to open her wounds and speed up her death.

For a long time, nothing happened. She could hear the Bloody Prince standing near her bed, breathing heavily in the dark. Then he opened the door, left the room, and closed the door behind him. A moment later, she heard the door lock.

CHAPTER THIRTY-NINE

THE CHALLENGE

"**T**HIS IS MAD. YOU KNOW that, right?"

Royce blinked at Saanji's accusation then smiled faintly across the council table. "I thought we'd already settled this. We can't wait for the Dragonkin to bring up his army and attack us from the rear. Either we withdraw and brace for a siege ourselves… which we might have to do later, anyway… or I kill the Bloody Prince right now, in front of his city, and remove one enemy from the game board."

"This isn't a game," said the female Isle Knight seated to his left.

Saanji nodded, pointing at her. "Gods-damned right, it isn't!" Realizing he was standing up, he sat back down. He picked up his goblet and took a long drink. "You're good, Royce. I've seen you dance circles around men in the practice yard, and the gods know how much trouble you made for my brother. But this is a needless risk. Spring will be here in fewer weeks than I have fingers. Just wait. My brother's own men will kill him soon enough."

But Royce was already shaking his head. "And what if they don't? Or better yet, what if they do? We'll just be replacing one enemy with another. Better the Bloody Prince dies in humiliation while the Dhargots are already vulnerable."

Someone said, "Loyalties aside, perhaps our one-eared friend just doesn't feel like watching his kin die. He can hardly be blamed for that." The speaker was the young, bronze-skinned prince of the Queshi, who also happened to be the tallest man Saanji had ever seen. While the others had arrived at the council wearing armor, the Queshi wore only plain riding clothes and a dagger. His sand-colored hair had been pulled back in a tight braid. Nothing about him betrayed his rank besides the fierce-eyed bodyguards standing with crossed arms behind him.

Saanji lifted his cup. "Do not be concerned, Prince Kentua. I promise you, I'll gladly kiss the hands of any man who guts that bastard."

"The goddesses know he's in dire need of gutting," Haesha added, lifting a goblet of her own.

The Dwarrish prince, Leander, spoke next. Despite his muscular frame and dented armor, and in spite of all the horrors Saanji guessed the young man must have witnessed, his eyes remained shy and downcast. "My men and I didn't come here to fight Dhargots. We didn't come here to save the Hesodi, either... as much as we sympathize with their plight." He nodded toward Haesha, who answered with a stony scowl. "I'm sure Kentua can say the same. We came here for Chorlga."

Kentua nodded. "Chorlga and his metal devils didn't just do harm to our Dwarrish neighbors. We Queshi once had a city of trade near the southern border of Stillhammer, at the base of the mountains. It's gone now. Women, children... all happened as you would imagine. Chorlga must answer for that. And by my arrows, he will."

"But the Bloody Prince is the Dragonkin's strongest ally," Royce countered. "Chorlga might be powerful, and his Jolym might be gifted killers, but he cannot hope to rule all of Ruun without help. He'll use the Dhargots to enforce his will throughout every kingdom, including yours." He nodded to the two princes, who sat beside each other.

"Agreed. Better we break the bastard now." Haesha rose unsteadily to her feet, one hand on her sword. "And I should be the one to do it, not you. No disrespect, Lancer, but I'm the closest thing to a captain that the Iron Sisters have left. I speak for them. Better I honor our slain by slicing the Bloody Prince throat to cock and feeding him to the crows."

Maybe if you hadn't already drunk more wine than I have, Saanji thought, listening to the faint slur in her voice.

Royce gave the Iron Sister a respectful nod. "I admire your passion. If I fall... which I don't expect I will... then you are free to issue any challenge you like. But I've brought thousands of men from Ivairia, and if I might speak bluntly, more than a few of them are anxious to go back. Our own king has ordered it. My men need to be reminded why they're here in the first place. As much as the Bloody Prince has to die, I have to be the one to kill him."

Saanji glanced at the only two people at the table who had not yet spoken. Seated at the far end, Rowen Locke looked as pale as the snow still piled outside Royce's tent. Sweat glazed his forehead. The sight reminded Saanji of how he himself felt when he ran out of wine.

It's that sword. Having it, then not having it, has done something to him.

Seated beside Rowen was Jalist Hewn. The Dwarr had so far divided his attention between concern for Rowen and furtive glances toward Prince Leander. Saanji had already guessed that the two must have been lovers at one time, though the Dwarrish prince seemed to be making a point of pretending otherwise.

Deciding that he would receive no help from either, Saanji changed tactics. "At the very least, we should wait for Zeia."

Rowen glanced up sharply at the mention of Zeia, but Royce said, "Why?"

The question caught Saanji off guard, but he formed an answer quickly. "Because she's a Shel'ai, because she's fey as a greatwolf, and because she'll be coming back with a magic sword that, if what I've heard is true, can slice through city walls like a hot knife through butter. How are those for reasons?"

The members of the council all turned to Rowen for confirmation. The Knight of the Crane said nothing.

After a tense pause, Aeko Shingawa said, "It makes sense to face an enemy when you're at your strongest."

Haesha shook her head. "The wytch might be back within the hour, or a few days from now, or maybe never. We can't wait."

"Nor should we," Royce added. "If Zeia's task is as important as she claimed, the more we distract the Dhargots, the better. Short of launching a full attack on the city, I know of no better distraction than summoning all of them to the walls to watch me cut their beloved prince to shreds."

Saanji frowned. He settled back in his chair, studying his friend. "Why do I get the impression that you've already made up your mind?"

Royce smiled. "Because I have."

Prince Leander cleared his throat. "No offense, Lancer, but you don't command this host."

Haesha laughed. "Well, he certainly commands the biggest share of it."

"I don't presume to speak for the Dwarrs," Royce added quickly. "This is my fight, my risk."

"But this alliance belongs to all of us," Aeko countered.

"Says the woman in command of just twenty-odd Knights," Haesha snorted.

Aeko faced the Iron Sister, unperturbed. "Says a Knight of the Lotus with years of battle experience and as much desire to watch our enemies burn as you have."

Haesha looked prepared to argue, but Kentua stood up, his tall frame nearly brushing the top of the tent. "This bickering will count for nothing if the Jolym attack us from behind. If the Lancer wants to issue his challenge, so be it. I'll leave this siege to the rest of you. My riders have no interest in Hesod, anyway. Our skills can be put to greater use if we ride east to protect the rear."

Leander nodded. "My Housecarls will go with you." He turned back to Royce. "I assume the Cassicans you command will want to stay with you, since it's the Dhargots they want revenge on, but if you have any archers, you should send them with us. They'll be put to best use fighting Jolym."

Aeko rose to her feet as well. She held up her hands. "I suggest we not disband our alliance before it's even one week old."

The Army of Three Princes, Saanji thought. *Only a week ago, they were calling it the New Alliance. Probably doesn't bode well that we can't settle on a name.*

Kentua said, "We're not disbanding, Knight. We're facing two great armies, one at Hesod, the other at Cadavash. It makes sense that we divide our forces. Besides, my horse-archers wouldn't be much use in a siege, anyway. We're better suited to putting arrows through the eyes of Jolym while our strong Dwarrish friends hold them down." Smiling, he clapped Leander on the shoulder.

Saanji turned to Rowen, who was seated across from him at the far end of the table. "Gods, say something," he muttered, too quietly for anyone to hear. He could feel it all unraveling. Who better to unify them than the man chosen to wield the sword of Fâyu Jinn? But Rowen continued to sit, pale and silent, arms crossed as though barely holding himself together.

"Our Queshi friend speaks the truth," Royce said finally. "If the Queshi and the Dwarrs agree to guard our eastern flank from Chorlga and his Jolym, we'll contend with the Dhargots. Once they're defeated, or at least once the Bloody Prince is dead and the city in chaos, we'll march east to relieve you."

Leander stood and nodded. "If such aid proves necessary, it will be most welcome."

Everyone else still seated rose from their seats, Rowen last of all.

Royce said, "Then it seems our council is concluded. I'll issue my challenge to the Bloody Prince within the hour. With luck, he'll answer at once, and I'll have him roiling in Fohl's hells by sundown."

Leander said, "The siege is your business, but we'll stay long enough to watch you kill him." He reached across the table and offered Royce his hand. Royce shook it.

Haesha said, not unkindly, "Just so you know, Lancer, I plan on spending the next hour praying that the goddesses let me take your place."

Saanji said, "And I'll be praying that that legendary sword arm of yours doesn't get overconfident. My brother is no bumbling squire, you know."

Royce tapped the hilt of his kingsteel sword. "I never said he was. Luckily, I'm not, either."

Sweet gods, I hope so! "Good," Saanji said. "Then dance circles around the bastard until he's pissing blood." He stepped forward and embraced his friend. Then, after casting a final disappointed glance at Rowen Locke, he went out to pace the camp and see if Zeia had returned.

Rowen rose last from the council table, stirring only when Aeko touched his shoulder and startled him out of an odd daydream. In the daydream, he kept shifting from burning alive to transforming into the very flames that burned him, then back again. He blinked at Aeko then looked around and saw that the others had already left. Two of Arnil Royce's squires were busy removing the cups and wine from the table. One gave them a sour glance, hinting that he wished them to leave so that they could finish tidying up.

"So much for the meeting."

"Yes," Jalist said, appearing at his other side. "I think everybody wanted to retire and consider your thoughtful words."

Aeko gave Jalist a dark look, but Rowen said, "What did you expect me to say? I'm no general." He looked down and flexed his fingers.

Aeko said, "You know more about magic than anyone here, including me."

Rowen shrugged. "Royce seems like a competent general."

"But he's used to fighting muscle and steel, not magic. I doubt, present company aside, if any of these commanders have ever even seen wytchfire before."

"Don't forget Zeia," Jalist muttered.

"Won't matter," Rowen said. "You heard them. They're only going after the Dhargots right now. Chorlga is *my* problem."

Jalist picked up his long axe, which he'd leaned against the council table, and rested it over his shoulder. "Wake up, Locke. Chorlga is *everybody's* damn problem."

"But mine more than yours." Rowen glanced down at the Ivairian bastard sword hanging where Knightswrath used to be. "Somehow…maybe when Zeia gets back with the sword, I can…"

Jalist grabbed his arm and shook him. "Gods, Locke! Did someone burn the brains out of your skull while I was asleep? What's wrong with you?"

Aeko moved to separate them. Rowen blinked as though he'd just been startled awake again. In a low voice, he said, "If so, kill him for me. I'm not sure I'm up to it."

Jalist's expression went from angry to worried. In a softer voice, he repeated, "What's wrong with you?"

"I should have gone with her," Rowen muttered.

"Who? Zeia?"

Rowen nodded. "Zeia. Igrid. Maybe Silwren. All of them. I should have gone with them."

Jalist and Aeko exchanged looks. Aeko said, "Speaking on behalf of every woman on Ruun, I release you from any foolish obligations you have in mind. Now go and get some sleep, Squire."

Rowen shook his head. "I should be there when the Lancer kills the Bloody Prince. Besides, I'm not sure sleep would help me."

"Fine," Jalist said. "We'll watch the Dhargot die, then while the rest of the city is tearing itself in two, you can sleep. I'll bring you sweet rolls and warm milk and tell you a gods-damned bedtime story, if you like."

Rowen half smiled. "You don't need to play nursemaid, my friend. Go be with your prince."

Jalist blushed. "I already told you—"

A trumpet peal ripped through the morning air. Jalist swore, but Aeko said, "That's Ivairian. Sounds like the Lancer doesn't like to waste time."

"Good," Jalist mumbled. He cast a sidelong glance at Rowen. All three exited the tent together. Though Rowen tried to walk ahead of his companions, both hurried so that they stayed on each side of him.

Karhaati stood on the battlements overlooking the little-used eastern gates and stared at the impossible. An army of Lancers and renegade Dhargots unfurled across the snowy plains, as he had already anticipated it would, but they were not alone. A seemingly endless line of lean, bronze-skinned archers on red horses followed them, accompanied by a tight knot of women in mismatched armor, plus an even stranger sight: at least two hundred stout, Dwarrish Housecarls in gleaming ringmail. And here and there rode Isle Knights in azure and kingsteel.

The Dhargots manning the battlements began to speak in fearful whispers and point, but Karhaati laughed. "It seems the whole continent has decided to show us what their blood looks like frozen in the ice. So be it."

He was about to issue commands to his archers when Dagath pointed. A single Lancer was moving ahead of the army, trudging on foot through the snow, toward the eastern gate. Though his full armor looked identical in design to the other Lancers', it had been gilded with golden scrollwork. The Lancer stood in the snow, staring up at the battlements, so still that Karhaati might have mistaken him for a Jol.

Karhaati's pulse quickened. *Does he mean to—*

"Want us to fill him with arrows?" Dagath asked. His voice rumbled with anger. The sellsword's good eye was bloodshot, as though he had not slept. Nevertheless, he plucked a crossbow from a Dhargot's hands, spanned it, and reached for a bolt.

"No," Karhaati said. "Don't spoil it. Something tells me this is going to be quite interesting."

For a long time, the Lancer stood, unmoving and defiant. Finally, he reached up, removed his helmet, and dropped it into the snow. In a deep, booming voice, he shouted up at the battlements. "I am Arnil Royce, First Lancer to the King of Ivairia. I have come to challenge Karhaati, also called the Bloody Prince, to come forth and answer for the crimes done against my people." He paused. "If he has the courage, let him arm himself and step out. Let him meet me, so that all may watch him die."

Heavy silence fell over the battlements. Karhaati felt the weight of thousands of eyes turning to look at him, awaiting his response. *Is this it... my good death?* He laughed again. Then he shrugged off his cloak. "So be it," he said again. He turned to Dagath. "Remember your vow, Sellsword. If I die, kill the red-haired woman. Make it quick."

Dagath's good eye narrowed. "I remember. But... begging your pardon, Prince, I've heard of this one. They say he's Fohl's own mistress with a blade. Maybe he's—"

Karhaati ignored the rest. He touched the dark braid tucked into his belt. Then he removed the braid, tucked it under the neck of his cuirass, and removed each of his swordbelts. He handed his matching shortswords to Dagath. He gave him his thick, heavy necklace of dried ears as well. As much as Karhaati enjoyed wearing it in battle, knowing the sight of it could intimidate his opponents, it could also be an encumbrance. Besides, something told him that *this* opponent would not be so easily intimidated.

"Bring me Widowswail," he said.

A slave stepped forward and offered him a plain, ancient-looking bastard sword wrapped in dark silk. He took it by its black pommel, admiring the black pearls inlaid in the crosspiece, and drew it. Ghastly scrollwork covered the blade, depicting graphic acts of murder and rapine.

"The Lancer is mine. Let no one interfere," he told his archers. Leaning over the battlements, he stretched out his arm. Slowly, he lowered Widowswail until its tip pointed at the Lancer. The Lancer stared back, unmoving.

"Be right down," Karhaati called. As he descended from the battlements and ordered his men to open the city gates, he realized that he might have said the same thing to Fohl, the Undergod, and the ghosts of all the men he'd killed, roiling somewhere in the dark earth.

Saanji tugged at his cuirass, certain that his armor had somehow shrunk and was attempting to suffocate him. "Gods, get this over with," he muttered. Though he stood at the head of the army, surrounded by Earless, he was torn between striding ahead to be closer to Arnil Royce and retreating back into the ranks so that his brother would not see him.

He'd already been relieved when the Dhargots had not tried to kill Royce with arrows the moment he stepped within range. Lancers on horseback, carrying massive tower-shields, had been ready to race in and protect him with their own lives. Now the First Lancer stood, stock still, waiting to see if the challenge would be answered.

Saanji wished Royce had decided to issue his challenge from horseback, lance in hand, though he understood that not everyone would have viewed that as honorable. The Ivairians were unquestionably better at fighting on horseback, so much so that Karhaati might have simply used Royce as target practice for his crossbowmen.

He thought of the suggestion that Haesha had offered in a conspiratorial whisper outside the tent: that the moment the Bloody Prince emerged from the protection of the city walls, they could erase him with a hail of arrows fired by the powerful composite bows of the Queshi. Saanji had refused. He knew enough about the Queshi to know that they would never agree to such a thing, either.

Besides, Royce would never forgive me for that. And I can't fight this war without him.

As the minutes passed without answer, Saanji wondered if his brother was still asleep or just busy tormenting some poor innocent subject elsewhere in the city. Then he spotted a single armored Dhargot gesture from the battlements. A moment later, the city gates rumbled open.

Saanji's stomach twisted. He fixed his gaze on Royce. "Finish it, my friend." As he stood at the head of a crowding host of onlookers, he began to pray, touching the little opal ring still hanging around his neck.

Rowen stood at the front of the host, next to Jalist and Aeko. As the duel began, the Lancers and the Earless cheered, thousands upon thousands adding their voices to a growing chorus in the chilly air. His throat tightened.

The Dhargot who emerged from the gates of Hesod towered over the Lancer. He swung his blade with the lazy contempt of a swordmaster. His size and derisive stride instantly reminded Rowen of Jaanti, the fearsome Dhargot he'd fought in a village outside Atheion. That Dhargot had almost killed him. Rowen's victory had been chance as much as anything. Jaanti had simply underestimated him and toyed with him for too long.

Rowen blinked away his weariness and glanced at Jalist. The Dwarr looked back, his dark eyes narrowing. Rowen wondered if they were thinking the same thing. But Rowen had glimpsed Royce's expression while the army was still massing just beyond bow-shot, before he strode ahead to issue his challenge. The First Lancer looked deadly serious. Surely, he knew what was at stake. He would not be foolish enough to toy with an opponent as dangerous as the Bloody Prince.

And Royce's men love him, Rowen thought, listening to the cheers. *What if Knightswrath had passed to him instead of me?* He shook off the thought and returned his attention to the battle.

A kingsteel bastard sword gleamed in Royce's hands. Somehow, despite the snow and the weight of his armor, the Lancer moved like a dancer. He dodged Karhaati's powerful swings with apparent ease and jabbed at the Bloody Prince's armor, leaving dents and bright scratches all over the darkened steel.

The Bloody Prince's frustration grew. He shouted curses and insults as he swung. Each time the Lancer retreated, the Bloody Prince chased after him, swinging wildly.

"He's got to get tired soon," Jalist said.

But the Bloody Prince seemed inexhaustible. He gouged a dent in Royce's breastplate that made thousands of onlookers gasp in unison, but Royce recovered in the blink of an eye and nearly cut off Karhaati's head before the Bloody Prince beat him back.

The two swordsmen paused a moment. Dhargots shouted encouragement and jeered at Royce from the walls, though the Lancer seemed oblivious to everything but his opponent. The Lancer stooped, his kingsteel sword held low, as though it were him and not the Bloody Prince who was beginning to tire. Then he leapt forward.

A blur of steel, faster than should have been possible, he danced around his startled opponent, moving first one way, then the other. His kingsteel sword rang off Karhaati's armor again and again. Sparks rained on the snowy earth. Blood followed. The Lancers' cheers became deafening. The Earless cheered, too. Rowen turned and saw Saanji cupping his hands around his mouth, his eyes wide.

Despite his distance, Rowen could see the Bloody Prince's eyes widen, too, though for obviously different reasons. Blood trickled from the gaps in Karhaati's armor. Again and again, he tried unsuccessfully to get away from the stinging blur that was Arnil Royce. Then he stumbled over something— Royce's helmet, left in the snow—and reeled backward.

Surely, he already knew that was there... "No," Rowen muttered, though no one heard him.

Rather than allow the Bloody Prince a chance to recover, Royce leapt forward. The tip of his kingsteel blade lunged for Karhaati's exposed face. Karhaati was looking down. But somehow, he knew exactly where Royce's sword was going to be. One gauntleted fist caught the blade and jerked it sideways. The Dhargot's sword blurred.

Royce crumpled. Blood streamed down his armor at the elbow. But he did not cry out. Instead, he lifted his arm to fend off Karhaati's next blow. Meanwhile, he tried to twist his own sword free. But Karhaati held on, even as blood streamed from his fist. Karhaati laughed. He swung again then again.

In the blink of an eye, onlookers on both sides went deathly quiet. The sound of ringing steel and Karhaati's laughing grunts echoed in the morning air. Jalist shouted, "Gods, let go of the sword!"

Royce finally surrendered his weapon. With a bestial growl that betrayed no sign of injury, he launched himself at his bigger opponent. The Lancer reached for the Bloody Prince's face. Momentarily holding both men's swords, Karhaati stumbled backward, stunned by the smaller man's ferocity. He let go of Royce's sword. As the kingsteel blade fell into the snow, the Bloody Prince used his free hand to shield his face from the gauntleted fingers clawing for his eyes. He brought the pommel of his sword crashing down.

Royce suffered the first two blows to the head without acknowledgment.

At the third, he stiffened. He stood at a half crouch in the snow, hands still raised, as though frozen. Karhaati took a step backward. He took a breath, gripped his own sword with both hands, and split open Royce's head.

Rowen felt the bottom drop out of his stomach.

For a moment, no one spoke. Then all along the battlements of Hesod, the Dhargots cheered. The Bloody Prince jerked, as though hearing them for the first time, then turned. He waved at them with his bloody sword. He turned back to his opponent. Reaching behind his back, he drew a knife. He knelt.

The Lancers' cries of despair became howls of rage. Dozens started forward, steel drawn, but it was too late. The Bloody Prince held up Royce's ears. He blinked, unafraid, at the charging host. All along the battlements, crossbows shuddered. Hundreds of bolts thudded into the snow, forming a line between the Bloody Prince and the vengeful Lancers.

Rowen heard Saanji's voice shouting over the din, ordering the men back. The renegade Dhargothi prince had his own sword drawn, his face deathly pale as he shouted commands. A moment later, the din quieted.

The Bloody Prince still hovered over Royce's body, though he'd sheathed his sword. Holding Royce's ears in one fist, he used his other hand to recover Royce's sword from the snow. For a long time, he appraised the sword, openly appreciating his new prize. Then he shouted Saanji's name.

Saanji stood ahead of his troops but turned sideways as though afraid to meet his brother's gaze. Rowen felt a hand on his arm and realized that without even knowing it, he'd drawn his own sword and started forward, only to have Aeko stop him.

The Bloody Prince stood over Royce's body, lazily swinging Royce's sword as though it were his own. He taunted his brother, challenging him. Saanji did not move. Finally, Karhaati turned and started slowly back toward the city gates. They rumbled open once more. The Bloody Prince was almost back inside when he stopped, turned, and threw Royce's sword, end over end.

It stuck in the snow and quivered just a few yards from Saanji. "Just in case you ever grow a spine, little brother," Karhaati called. The Bloody Prince disappeared back inside the city. The oak-and-iron gates rumbled shut behind him. And all along the battlements, the Dhargots cheered again.

CHAPTER FORTY

WITNESS

R OWEN STOOD WITH AEKO AT the edge of the camp. A heavy snow had begun to fall, but none of the men seemed to notice it. He shook his head and watched as the Army of Three Princes began disbanding. Prince Kentua left first. Rowen had seen it in the tall man's eyes when a stunned company of Lancers hurried to recover Royce's body and carry it back to his tent. The Queshi prince merely sighed and walked straight to his horse. The other Queshi followed. Rowen thought Saanji would try to stop them, but as turmoil swallowed the camp, the Earless prince was nowhere to be seen.

The Dwarrs left soon after. On foot, they marched after Prince Leander, who looked straight ahead and said nothing. *Where's Jalist?* Rowen looked around and spotted his friend in the distance, wet eyed, leaning on his long axe. Rowen started toward him, but Jalist turned and walked away.

"That leaves the Lancers, the Earless, and the Iron Sisters," Rowen muttered.

"And us," Aeko added.

"I'm amazed the Dhargots haven't just ridden out and attacked us already."

Aeko grimaced. "No need. The longer they wait, the smaller this army becomes."

Then a Knight of the Stag joined them. Rowen could not remember the man's name, although Aeko had introduced him earlier as her second-in-command. His expression said that he had bad news.

"Captain Shingawa, the Iron Sisters are leaving."

Aeko looked as though she were caught between swearing and laughing. "Where are they going?"

The Knight of the Stag glanced at Rowen then lowered his voice. "Back into the city, I think. They say they're going to fight their way back into the sewers—"

"And die there," Aeko interrupted. "Has Prince Saanji tried to talk them out of it yet?"

"I don't think so. I haven't seen him. But I spoke to the Iron Sisters' captain. She seemed... a little drunk. She kept talking about vengeance. She threatened to kill me unless I walked away."

Aeko rubbed her eyes. "I'll talk to her myself. In the meantime, gather the Knights. They'll need a speech after this."

The Knight of the Stag nodded and hurried off.

Rowen looked up at the sky. *Gods, Zeia, where are you?* "If this snow keeps up, it'll bury half the camp."

Aeko tapped the hilt of her adamune. "I have to go try and talk the Iron Sisters out of doing something stupid. Then I have to try and convince my handful of Knights to do something just as stupid and stay here. That leaves Saanji for you."

Rowen blinked. "What makes you think I want to talk to a Dhargot?"

"This one isn't like the rest. At least, he doesn't seem like it. Neither are the men who follow him."

"Good for them. But what do you want me to do?"

"Anything you can. Help him talk to the Lancers. Convince them to stay."

Rowen looked around at all the armed men milling about in the thickening snowfall, moving stoically between tents, pretending they didn't hear the Dhargots of the Bloody Prince jeering at them from the walls. "I don't think—"

"I don't give a damn what you think," Aeko snapped. "Either you're a Knight of the Crane, or you aren't. I haven't surrendered yet. If you haven't, either, put that wytch out of your mind and do something useful. That's an order."

Rowen wondered to which wytch she was referring—Zeia or Silwren. He muttered, "Yes, Knight-Captain." He started to bow, but Aeko was already walking away. Rowen stood for a moment, trying to understand how everything could have changed so quickly. Then he went to find Prince Saanji.

When he found the renegade Dhargot's tent empty, he approached the closest squad of Earless and asked where their prince had gone. No one knew. He stopped a Lancer next, but the man walked away without answering as though he had not heard Rowen's question. Rowen continued on and heard a commotion. Touching his sword hilt, he followed the sound and found an

Earless and a Lancer engaged in what appeared to be a heated argument over a horse. Men massed on either side, armed and scowling.

Rowen considered intervening, then decided that he'd better find Saanji as quickly as possible. As he continued searching the camp, he spotted a squad of spearmen in mismatched armor. The men stood in silence around a campfire, glumly sharing a wineskin. Thinking they must be part of the Cassican militia, he delayed long enough to ask what they meant to do. Their quick looks and vague responses gave him his answer.

Moments later, a squad of Lancers nearly trampled him as they rode away, armored and stoic. Rowen wondered if they were going on patrol or simply deserting. Then he passed an old cleric who wore the large-breasted sigil of Tier'Gothma. He thought of Thessa. Following the cleric, he found Thessa in a tent, helping the other clerics tend the wounded. She wore clean clothes, and her small face shone with kindness and urgency.

Rowen smiled. He started toward her then stopped. The last time he'd spoken with her, he'd promised to rescue Igrid. True, it was Haesha who had stopped him—admittedly, to save his life—but he had done nothing since to follow through on that promise. By now, Igrid might very well be dead.

Another promise I couldn't keep.

Rowen left the tent before Thessa had a chance to notice him. He finally spotted Saanji in the distance, amid a knot of anxious Earless officers. He started toward him. Then he stopped. His vision blurred, as though he were seeing the world through a haze of water.

He rubbed his eyes, thinking it was due to the snow. Instead of dissipating, the blurring intensified. A strange darkness nipped at the corners of his vision, accompanied by a growing feeling of vertigo. The sounds of the camp died away.

Magic, Rowen realized. Panic swelled within him. He reached instinctively for Knightswrath, only to touch the hilts of the ordinary swords at his belt. All sounds continued to fall away, save the sound of his own heartbeat, which grew louder and louder, like an approaching war drum.

Then, as though a sack had been thrown over his face, darkness flooded his sight. He felt in front of him but touched nothing. He screamed but could not hear his own voice. A moment later, the darkness vanished, and he was standing on the Wintersea again.

Sundown spilled across the ice. Though he could not see it, he smelled blood. Chorlga stepped from the sun's glare, wearing an extravagant robe of black and gold silk, plus a crown of burnt gold. Rowen felt his bowels tighten. He reached for his swords again, but they were gone.

Chorlga smiled, flashing his rotten teeth. "Hello, Isle Knight. My apologies if I startled you. I just thought we should talk."

Rowen pretended to look around so that he could avert his gaze. "Why did you bring me here?"

"I didn't. I am simply a spot of light in that muddy pigsty you call a mind." Chorlga stepped closer. He studied Rowen, looking concerned. "Pardon me for saying so, Sir Locke, but you look terrible. Did someone die? Are you dwelling on unpleasant memories?"

Rowen tried to clear his mind. *This isn't real...*

Chorlga grinned. "Or maybe you've lost something very dear to you." One hand came up and withdrew Knightswrath from the dark folds of his robe. An ornate sheath of black tooled leather covered the blade. The Dragonkin held the sword by the scabbard.

"Strange to see this again after so long. Incidentally, have you heard the legend that kingsteel was sent by the gods as a test? They wanted to see whether those who possessed it would become protectors or conquerors. Curious that even after all these centuries, your Order has elected to become neither."

Chorlga held out the sword as though offering it to him then withdrew it. "Do you like the scabbard? To let so venerated a blade go naked was unseemly. Besides, it's much easier to hold this way. Which reminds me"—Chorlga snapped his fingers—"I believe you two know each other."

Zeia appeared, kneeling on the ice. Her clothes were torn, her expression dazed. Her arms ended in bleeding stumps, as though her hands had only just been cut off. The blood formed endless pools at her side.

"Don't be rude," Chorlga told her. "Say hello, my mangled little pet."

Zeia looked up weakly. She blinked. Her eyes met Rowen's. She melted, dissolving into the ice without sound, becoming a puddle of ash and blood. Chorlga smiled down at the puddle. Then he lifted his head. His eyes widened as Rowen came at him.

Rowen clamped one hand around the Dragonkin's throat. He drove his fist into Chorlga's face over and over again. Chorlga shuddered. Rowen felt the man's bones breaking, sagging inward. He kept punching. He tried to wrest Knightswrath out of Chorlga's grasp, but the Dragonkin would not let go. So Rowen went on punching.

Then Rowen stood alone on the ice, both hands empty. His knuckles bled, dripping onto the ice with impossible slowness. Rowen looked around, but the

Dragonkin was simply gone. For a moment, he thought he'd done it. Then a massive, many-winged shadow stretched over his own.

Chorlga laughed. "How spirited of you, Sir Locke. Spirited, but pointless."

Rowen felt a fresh wash of fear. He forced himself to turn. Chorlga stood before him, unharmed, Knightswrath still in hand.

"Even though you could not see me, I was there when my little prince cut your mighty general's skull in half. I was close enough to breathe on your neck and stroke that pretty she-Knight's dark hair. I was *that* close, and you didn't even know it."

Chorlga held the dragonbone teasingly close to Rowen's hand before he pulled it away. "Now I have your burning sword and your new wytch. I have everything but you. I told you I would stop the killing if you surrendered. You did not surrender. So now, I will show you the true meaning of wrath."

Chorlga vanished. Then the sun vanished, too. Rowen stood in darkness once more, surrounded by nothing but the sound of his own heartbeat. Then Chorlga's voice rang out in his mind. *"El'rash'lin was a fool. He thought that by destroying himself, he could rid you of the Nightmare. But the Nightmare is gone now. So are the Jolym. In their place... I have this."*

The ice flared as though the water beneath had been transformed into fire. Then it shattered like glass. Something huge burst out, dark and flaming. Rowen heard only the rattling of the chains joining the dragon's bones.

Chorlga was behind him then, whispering into his ear. "I want you to know, Knight, that were it not for El'rash'lin, I might not have done this. Summoning her should have killed me. But he drove me to it. You all did."

The Dragonjol rose higher and higher, unfurling its skeletal wings. Rowen realized he was on his knees. He tried to rise or look away, but something held him immobile. He wept.

"Magnificent, isn't she?"

The Dragonjol's gigantic ribcage began to expand as though the fleshless creature were drawing a breath. Violet flames seared the night air, spurting along each bone end to end. The flames began to gather within the Dragonjol's ribcage, swirling in a harsh but utterly quiet maelstrom, burning brighter and brighter. The creature's maw opened.

Rowen choked, "No..."

Chorlga grasped Rowen by the shoulders. His fingernails dug in like claws. "Tell the fat prince to surrender to his brother. Tell all who value their lives to lay down their swords. Then come to Cadavash. Find me in the temple. Worship me, and all shall be forgiven."

Rowen wanted to say yes. He wanted to beg for forgiveness and promise to do whatever Chorlga asked. But before he could speak, the sea of violet flames gushed from the Dragonjol's mouth to coat the ice, the Wintersea, and the entire world.

For a moment, Jalist thought for certain that they would kill Rowen. Lancers and Earless had drawn their swords and formed a circle around Rowen the moment he started screaming. Their eyes widened. When Jalist followed the sound and saw his friend, he was concerned his friend had simply gone mad.

Rowen stood stone still, arms straight at his sides as though pinned there, screaming at the sky. His blank eyes stared. Jalist waved his hand in front of Rowen's face. Unblinking, he continued to scream as quickly as he could draw breath. When he stopped, his breath came in ragged gasps.

"What happened?" Jalist demanded.

Saanji shuddered, white-knuckling Royce's sword. "Gods know! He started toward me, like he wanted to talk, then… he just started screaming!"

"Don't touch him. He's bewytched," an Earless warned.

"Kill him before it spreads," a Lancer suggested. Others nodded.

Jalist unslung his long axe and gave it a warning swing. "Back off, lads. If anybody's going to split *this* one's skull, it's me."

Armed men exchanged glances. No one moved. Jalist turned to Saanji for help, but the Earless prince just stared.

Jalist looked around. Earless and Lancers spoke in fearful whispers. He imagined them gathering their courage, preparing to charge. He saw the little Hesodi girl Rowen had saved, clutching the hands of a cleric as she stood nearby, watching with wide eyes. Two Iron Sisters held spears as if they meant to throw them. Then he spotted Aeko Shingawa.

In full battle dress of azure and kingsteel, the Knight of the Lotus shoved her way through the crowd. Her Knights followed. Drawn adamunes glinted in the afternoon light, shining through the thickening haze of falling snow. The Isle Knights formed a protective ring around Rowen. "What's happening here?" Aeko demanded.

Saanji answered, his face ashen. "What's happening is that your magic-crazed hero-Knight just lost his damned mind!"

Aeko glanced at Rowen's expression then turned to Jalist. "What's wrong with him?"

"I don't know any more than you do, but if I had to guess, I'd say magic. And nothing kind, by the sound of it."

Aeko nodded. "We'll take care of him," she told Saanji. She raised her voice. "We'll see that he harms no one. Nor will anyone harm him."

For a long time, no one spoke or moved. Earless, Lancers, and a smattering of Iron Sisters milled around the protective circle of Isle Knights. Jalist could see that everyone's nerves had frayed near the breaking point, even as the snowfall thickened and the cold continued to grow, seeping in through their clothes.

"Leave them alone," Saanji ordered finally.

Gradually, the crowds dispersed. Saanji drew Aeko aside. The two spoke in heated whispers. Sang Wei helped Jalist take Rowen by the arm and half lead, half drag him back to his tent. A few Knights followed.

Sang Wei said, "I'll see to this, Dwarr. We'll keep him safe. Ride on, if you like."

Jalist caught his meaning. He glanced east, in the direction Prince Leander and the other Dwarrs had gone. He turned back to Rowen, whose eyes remained wide and unblinking. Jalist shuddered. "No," he said, "I'll stay."

By the time sundown washed the tents of the camp, Saanji's army had shrunk considerably. Even in the thickening snowfall, Lancers had continued to leave. Saanji spoke with officer after officer, pleading with them to stay. He offered them riches. He made threats. He spoke of Arnil Royce and the opportunity for revenge and tried to shame them into staying.

When none of that worked, he considered capturing and hanging a few Lancers for desertion. But he had hardly begun issuing orders when he discovered that no Lancer and almost none of his Earless were willing to obey.

As the day ended, he sat in his tent, shivering despite the half-empty bottle of hláshba he held in one wavering fist. Royce's sword rested naked across his knees. One of his own officers was going down the list of all the Ivairians who had either deserted or seemed likely to do so.

"Sir Altrick said he's leaving at first light. Sir Hector and Sir Bowen plan to go as soon as the snow stops… and I think they'll be taking most of the Cassican militia with them."

"What about Sir Bors?" Saanji slurred. "He wanted to storm the gates after Royce fell."

"Sir Bors left an hour ago. He said he meant to raise a bigger army and come back."

Saanji took a long drink of hláshba despite the roiling feeling in his otherwise-empty stomach. "I'm surprised none of them wanted to challenge my dear brother themselves."

"Begging your pardon, Prince, but I think it's a matter of Ivairian law. Challenges of revenge cannot be issued until a month has passed, so the previous victor has time to recover and prepare."

Why didn't I know that?

Saanji took another long drink. His eyes swam. "Enough for tonight. Whoever's still here in the morning, send them to me. I'll beg them more then."

The officer nodded then cleared his throat. "M'lord, shall I have the cook prepare dinner?"

Saanji shook his head. "Just go." The officer saluted. Saanji returned the gesture halfheartedly. The officer started to leave. "Wait," Saanji said. "Royce's body. A funeral... I just realized his men are leaving, and we haven't even buried him yet."

"I think that's their way, too, m'lord. The actual body doesn't matter much to them. They just bury it where it falls. A formal ceremony is held a month after the Lancer has fallen. The body itself isn't necessary."

Saanji thought of a very different funerary practice observed by some Dhargots: the body was burned, then if the dead person was an enemy, his ashes were painted on one's weapons; if he was a friend, his ashes were mixed with wine and drunk. Saanji imagined burning Royce's body and mixing a pinch of his remains in a cup of hláshba.

Saanji clutched his stomach, tried to hold it back, then threw up. He retched until his eyes watered. When he looked up, his officer was gone. He wondered how much the man had seen. He decided it did not matter anymore.

CHAPTER FORTY-ONE
SIR FEY

ROWEN WOKE IN DARKNESS. HE feared that he was still on the Wintersea. Then he found himself on a straw pallet. A low fire burned at the center of his tent, hissing when snowflakes fell through the hole and melted in the flames. He looked around and found himself alone.

He sat up, pushed aside his blanket, and looked for a weapon. He spotted his swords resting on a nearby table, exactly where he'd found them the first time. His new, mismatched armor lay next to it. He got up. The cold, damp ground pressed against his feet, making him shudder. He tugged on his boots.

Despite the fire, his breath fogged before him. He paused, watching it dissipate. "This is almost the end," he whispered to himself. He shuddered again. Then he got dressed. He had just girded his swords when he heard the tent flap rustle. He turned around, expecting to see Jalist or Aeko.

Instead, he saw Shade.

Rowen thought he must be dreaming. He blinked. When Shade did not disappear, Rowen drew both his swords and started forward. Shade held up his hand.

"Wait—"

Rowen threw his shortsword.

Shade made a sharp motion, and the shortsword froze midair. Another motion made it fall to the ground. But Rowen had already expected this. By then, he'd crossed the tent and was thrusting the tip of his bastard sword at Shade's throat.

Shade stepped backward. His hands rose, but no wytchfire appeared. Instead, the Shel'ai summoned a wall of force that knocked Rowen's lunge awry. Rowen recovered quickly. Twisting, he sent his sword sweeping back at Shade's throat in a blurring backhand. This time, Shade made no move to defend himself.

Rowen stopped short. He held the edge of his sword to Shade's throat. A thin line of blood appeared. He frowned. "You're letting me kill you."

"Isn't that what you want?"

Rowen shifted, turning so that he faced Shade fully, without removing his sword. "More than you could possibly know."

Shade nodded slowly. "For what I did to your brother."

"For what you did to a *lot* of men's brothers. And to Silwren."

Shade smiled thinly. "Before you declare yourself champion of all the honored dead, hear what I have to say." He paused. "El'rash'lin sent me."

"I don't care if the gods themselves sent you. Nothing you have to say could possibly interest me."

For a long time, Shade met Rowen's gaze, unblinking. Finally, he said, "Then why am I still alive?"

Rowen took Shade's sword. He noticed that while the Shel'ai still wore all black, his clothes no longer bore the emblem of a crimson greatwolf. "You've changed your colors."

"I'd like to think I've changed more than that. But we'll see." Shade paused again. "I killed Fadarah."

"Funny, I thought I did."

"He would have died from the wound you gave him. We couldn't prevent that. But I hastened his departure."

"Why?"

"The same reason you went looking for Brahasti. The Sylvan captives, the rapes. Even in war, there must be rules. Fadarah broke those rules."

Despite his anger, he managed two words: "The Unseen."

Shade flinched. "Those are old sins. Kill me for that later, if you must. But first, we need to talk."

Rowen hesitated then stepped back. He lowered his sword. "Speak."

"El'rash'lin is dead… but you already know that, I think." Shade wiped his neck, glanced down at the blood, then wiped his hand on his tunic.

"I suspected. He said he was going to throw himself into the Dragonward."

Shade nodded. "That was his intention. But that's not how he died."

Thoughts of the Dragonjol made Rowen white-knuckle is sword. "I think I know that, too."

Shade raised one eyebrow. "Then you've seen Godsbane?"

Rowen did not answer.

"You have no idea how far I've traveled, Human." Shade's eyes shone with unspeakable weariness. "What I saw in the north... Chorlga sent the Dragonjol to Ivairia. He did this for no reason beyond a desire to test his new creation. It turned a whole countryside to ash. The Lancers don't know it yet, but most of them no longer have a home to return to."

Something told Rowen that Shade had witnessed this with his own eyes. "So why are you here?"

"I searched the minds of some of the men when I slipped into the camp," Shade said instead. "Half this army is about to abandon whoever still leads it. The other half has even less faith in their leader than I have in you. But I promised El'rash'lin I'd help you if I could."

"There's nothing you can do." Rowen hesitated then decided it no longer mattered if Shade knew the truth. "Chorlga has Knightswrath. I lost it in Hesod. He took it before Zeia could get it back for me. He's waiting for me in Cadavash. He's probably already destroyed the army that was marching east to confront him."

Shade paled. "He has Knightswrath..."

"And Zeia, if she's still alive." Rowen sheathed his bastard sword. "He says that if I surrender, he'll show mercy."

Shade's eyes narrowed. "You don't actually believe that."

Rowen picked up his shortsword and sheathed that as well. "I don't pretend to understand even half of what's happened all around me, as far as magic goes. But something tells me that Chorlga's idea of mercy isn't something I'll enjoy."

Shade touched his throat again. "You're going to try and kill him without Knightswrath."

Rowen did not bother answering.

"When?"

"As fast as I can ride to Cadavash."

"With your army?"

Rowen shook his head. "Alone. Besides, this isn't my army. I'm not Fâyu Jinn. I never was." Rowen thought of Igrid. He realized that if he went to Cadavash, he would be abandoning her to her fate. But how could he rescue her alone?

Then again, what can I do against Chorlga?

"Can you get me into Cadavash without Chorlga knowing it?"

Shade shook his head. "I might be able to slip in by myself, but I can't do anything against the Dragonjol."

"Could you kill Chorlga if I distracted him?"

Shade answered more quickly this time. "As strong as he is now, I could only kill him if all his defenses were down—which they won't be. Only Knightswrath can do that. And you're the only one who can use the sword." The Shel'ai turned. For a long time, he seemed to study the dying fire at the center of Rowen's tent. "Is Zeia still alive?"

"I don't know. He showed her to me, showed her dying, but I think that was just to hurt me. I think… he believes she means as much to me as Silwren did." Rowen hesitated, remembering that long ago, Shade and Silwren had been lovers.

Shade stared into the fire again. "If Chorlga thinks that, then she might still be alive. If she is, we have a chance."

Rowen shook his head. "She looked hurt. He's probably just keeping her alive to taunt me. I don't think she'll be able to help us fight him. Besides, she has no hands."

Shade nodded. "That's why she might be able to help us." Slowly, he explained his plan.

Rowen listened, keeping one hand on his sword hilt. When Shade finished, Rowen nodded—his only answer.

Shade faced him for a moment, then nodded back. He seized the hood of his cloak and drew it up over his tapered ears. Then he turned and vanished into the night.

Saanji woke to one of his bodyguards shaking him. He cursed and fumbled for a weapon, asking if they were under attack. The servant said no. He asked next if Zeia had returned. When the servant answered no to that as well, Saanji rubbed his eyes, directed his gaze toward the tent flap, and saw darkness beyond. He realized he must have slept for only a few hours. A stabbing headache made him reach for the bottle of hláshba beside his bed. The servant repeated something about a visitor.

"Gods, who is it?"

"One of the Isle Knights, m'lord. He insists it's urgent. We tried to send him away, but he won't leave. When your guards tried to *make* him leave, he knocked one down and broke another man's nose. Do you want him killed?"

Saanji took a long drink, closed his eyes, and waited for his headache to slacken. "You said *he*. I take it it's not the woman?"

"No, m'lord. It's… the Knight who went fey earlier."

Saanji opened his eyes. "He's here?"

The servant nodded. "We've taken his weapons. If you like, we can bind his hands—"

"Just send him in." Saanji stood up, wrapped himself in his robe, and went to urinate in the privy. He kept his shortsword lying on his bed, within easy reach. The sight of it reminded him of Royce's sword. He wondered where he'd put it. He turned and spotted it lying on a table, glinting in the candlelight across his tent.

Then he realized he was still pissing, corrected his aim, and finished. By the time he turned, the Isle Knight was being escorted into his tent. Although he still wore a battered kingsteel cuirass, the rest of his armor was mismatched. Four Earless warriors stood around him, all scowling. One had a bloody nose. The Isle Knight's hands had been tied in front of him.

Saanji took another drink and picked up his sword. "So, Sir Fey, have you come to kill me?"

The red-haired Isle Knight shook his head. "No, m'lord, though what I have to say will probably sound no less sane than I sounded earlier."

Saanji sat down in an empty chair. "Then speak, Knight. I'm curious to see if there's anything left in this world that can surprise me."

The Isle Knight hesitated. "I just spoke with Shade."

Saanji blinked. "Congratulations." He lifted the bottle and took yet another long drink of hláshba. "Tell me, what did Fadarah's right hand say? Did he tell you why he calls himself a ghost? I've always wondered."

"He didn't, m'lord, but I'd be happy to tell you. Only I think we should discuss this in private."

Saanji chuckled. "You assault my guards then ask me to talk to you in private?"

"Your guards didn't want to let me see you."

"That's because I was busy having nightmares about my friend getting his skull split open." He rubbed his stomach and realized there was only one swallow of hláshba left in his bottle. He finished it then snapped his fingers and pointed to a bottle of wine on a far table. One of his bodyguards brought it, along with a cup. Saanji drank straight from the bottle. A moment later, content that he'd finally drowned his headache, he studied the Isle Knight's expression. For a madman's, his eyes looked exceptionally clear.

"Fine." Saanji waved his hand. "Leave me alone with the Knight. If I need you, I'll scream."

The bodyguards hesitated. One issued a threat that Saanji could not hear. Then they filed out, leaving the Isle Knight's hands tied.

"Talk fast," Saanji said, waving his wine bottle. "I don't intend to be lucid for much longer."

"You might want to alter that plan, m'lord. I need you clearheaded by morning."

Saanji laughed. "Did Royce's ghost put you up to this?" His smile vanished. "I shouldn't have said that." He looked up at the roof of his tent. "I'm sorry. I'm sorry." He poured a little wine on the ground then took another long drink.

"I'm going to kill Chorlga," the Isle Knight said.

"Good for you. I'll light candles and sacrifice something in your honor. Would you like a city named after you? If so, I'm afraid you'll have to remind me what your name is—"

The Isle Knight took a step forward, his expression severe. "I'm going to kill Chorlga, but I can only do that if you kill your brother. And it has to happen in three days."

Saanji blinked. "Now I *know* Royce put you up to this. He always believed in the impossible." Suddenly wanting to hold his dead friend's sword, Saanji stumbled across the tent and picked it up. As he turned, he lost his balance. Using the sword as a crutch, he caught himself then returned to his chair. He held up the sword, letting the light shine off its blade.

"Pretty, isn't it?" He laid the sword on the table then changed his mind and picked it back up. "Not sure what *you* saw earlier today, Sir Fey, but Arnil Royce couldn't beat my brother. And Royce was the best swordsman I've ever seen. What in the Dragongod am I supposed to do?"

Fearing he was about to retch, Saanji stood and began to pace. He held the bottle of wine in one hand, Royce's sword in the other. "I'm not saying I'm giving up. Royce was my friend, and my brother is a rotten bastard. Only I'm about to lose the Lancers, meaning I'll be laying siege to a city that's defended by an army bigger than mine. Oh, and it's a gods-damned blizzard outside!"

"It stopped snowing," the Isle Knight said.

"How lovely. Maybe if we start shoveling now, we can clear a path to the walls by morning. Some attack that'll be!" Saanji tired, forgot why he was pacing in the first place, and returned to his chair.

"I didn't say you have to take the city in three days. I said your brother has to die in three days."

"And why is that?"

"Because Chorlga will be watching."

Saanji shuddered. "There's a pleasant thought. Maybe if he sees me sending assassins, he'll get sufficiently rankled and send all his Jolym to wipe out my little army... and that's if my brother's men don't do it for him." Saanji finished the bottle of wine and looked around for another.

"I don't think his Jolym exist anymore."

Saanji frowned. "Are you joking?" When the Isle Knight did not answer, Saanji's frown deepened. "For a man sharing good news, you look more like a man who just caught his wife bedding an Olg."

"This isn't good news," the Isle Knight said. "If you kill your brother, what Chorlga will send after you in retribution will be far worse than either the Jolym or the Nightmare. But it's the only way we're going to win."

Saanji rubbed his eyes. "Maybe you should start this particular mad tale at the beginning. And do it fast, before the room turns so much that I get sick again."

The Isle Knight explained. Saanji listened. The tale sounded so absurd that Saanji made him repeat it. When the Knight was finished, Saanji frowned. "You're even more crazed than I thought."

"I swear, everything I've told you is the truth."

"Ah, yes. The favorite mantra of madmen."

"So it is." The Isle Knight smiled faintly. "You're going to have to trust me."

Saanji laughed. "Trust you? Knight, I don't even know you! The only knight I knew who was worth trusting just got his whole damn head split open."

"And on the third sunrise, you're going to avenge him."

Saanji glanced down at his opal ring. He suddenly felt more sober than he wanted to. "I have plenty of reason to kill my brother, Sir Fey. I just don't have the skill—or the guts, if you want to know the truth." He stood up and started pacing again. "If you want him dead so bad, why don't *you* kill him? I hear you're good with a blade. Or get that dark-haired she-Knight to do it."

"My business is with Chorlga. Yours is with the Bloody Prince. Besides, when Aeko finds out I'm gone, she'll come after me."

"So I take it you aren't going to tell her."

The Isle Knight shook his head. "Jalist and Aeko can't know. They've suffered enough for me."

"But apparently, I haven't." Saanji bowed, waving Royce's sword. "My apologies, Sir Fey! I can't imagine what was going through my mind." Saanji realized that his feet were cold. Saanji took his boots back to the chair, stuck Royce's sword in the ground, sat down, and started to tug his boots on. Midway through, he stopped. He stared at one of his boots, dangling halfway off his foot. A slow smile formed on his lips.

"Know what I think, Sir Fey? I think you're about to go get yourself killed. And I think I will, too. But at least we'll both find out if the gods are actually real." He kicked off his boot, hopped off his chair, and lurched toward the Isle Knight, sword in hand. He presented the sword. The Isle Knight backed up, stretched out his hands, and cut himself free.

Saanji grinned. Then he wiped the grin from his face, stepped back, and offered a grave salute with Royce's sword. "Die well, Sir Fey. You know, that's important to Dhargots—a good death. I never thought I'd get one. Did you?" Before the Isle Knight could answer, Saanji shouted for his bodyguards. They rushed back into the tent, swords drawn. They moved to seize the Isle Knight, but Saanji shook his head.

"Forget him. Just escort him to the eastern edge of the camp and put him on a horse. Don't ask questions." He looked past his bodyguards at the servant who had awakened him. "As for you, I have some things I'd like you to get."

Rowen shivered as he guided his borrowed horse away from the camp. As the light and heat from the sentries' fires faded behind him, a cold chill took their place. Though he'd dressed in three cloaks, the chill stole through his clothes and armor and wrapped itself tight around his bones. His horse neighed in protest despite the thick blanket stretched beneath the saddle.

The Ivairian palfrey whose name he did not know reminded him of Snowdark. He presumed that Kilisti had taken his piebald horse back to the Wytchforest. He hoped both were safe. He tugged at his cloaks and looked up at the dark sky. Armahg's Eye shown high above, beautiful but indifferent.

Nevertheless, Rowen said a prayer of thanks that neither Jalist nor Aeko had been in his tent when Shade had arrived. Though Aeko had left two Isle Knights standing watch outside Rowen's tent, Shade had rendered both of them unconscious. By the time they regained their senses or one of his friends came to check on him, Rowen would be long gone.

He knew they would follow him, though he dreaded what would happen when Jalist in particular encountered the grisly sight that Rowen suspected must be waiting farther to the east. *Unless it hasn't happened yet. Unless I still have time to warn them...*

He urged the horse to move faster through the thick snow. As he rode, he glanced around, scanning the shadows for a sign of Shade. He knew the Shel'ai was out there somewhere, probably nearby, perhaps just a little way ahead of him. The thought unsettled him, but he reminded himself that he was following Shade's plan. The Shel'ai had nothing to gain by killing him now.

Besides, if this works, I can always kill him once it's over.

Rowen lifted his gaze and saw a faint orange sheen on the eastern horizon. He might have mistaken it for the first hint of sunrise, but he checked the position of the sliver moon and saw that it was still several hours too early. He narrowed his eyes. For the first time, he saw a pale smear of violet beneath the orange glow, as though one had given birth to the other. He slowed his horse and closed his eyes. Forgetting the cold, he whispered another prayer. Then, remembering Shade, he opened his eyes and listened for the slightest sound as he continued riding.

CHAPTER FORTY-TWO
BURIED IN SNOW

ALL DAY, ROWEN RODE ALONE across the snowy expanse that was the Simurgh Plains. He stopped only when he had to, determined to end the trek as soon as possible. The cold was nearly unbearable. At sundown, he built a fire. He'd hoped to find a village with an inn, but all he'd passed was a burnt-out cottage hours earlier. As he sat by his low fire, trying desperately to warm himself, he heard the distant cry of wolves.

He wished he'd thought to bring a crossbow. He thought of the last time he'd fought a greatwolf and considered the possibility that he would die in the frozen wild, slain not by a Dragonkin or one of his great henchmen but by a simple ferocious beast with a hungry belly. For some reason, the thought made him smile. Nevertheless, he slept with both swords within easy reach.

He woke at dawn, shivering and hungry, and pressed on. He'd traveled less than an hour before he came upon the remains of three massive greatwolves lying together in a grisly heap, their maws wide, their bodies half buried in snow. All had been charred. None had been eaten. The tracks of lesser wolves led off in the distance, as though an entire pack of wolves had fled for their lives.

Rowen looked around, searching the wilderness for signs of a man in a dark cloak. "Don't expect me to thank you," he muttered into the cold air, and rode on.

Late in the afternoon, he came upon the remains of a burned village. Only a few scorched walls and charred wagons remained. Ashes blew amid the sound of burnt, creaking wood. The telltale smell of charred flesh reached his nostrils, reminding him of the funeral pyres that had blazed day and night after the Battle of Lyos. He whispered a prayer and rode on.

Near sunset, he came upon two thirds of the Army of Three Princes.

They filled a nameless, snowy valley. A few banners flew in the breeze. A handful of axes and blades still glinted in the snow alongside a few broken lances. Wind-blown pieces of singed fabric hinted that once, tents had filled the valley. Here and there, a forlorn red horse pawed at the snow, saddled but riderless.

Rowen stared. The smell of smoke and charred meat filled his nostrils, making his eyes water. Resisting the urge to ride on, he dismounted. He led his horse through the devastation, trudging through ankle-deep snow. Retrieving a blackened lance, he used it as a staff to help him along.

Near the center of the valley, a violet light caught his eyes. He traced it to a tangle of charred bodies half covered by soot—a luminstone.

Rowen started to reach for it then thought of Jalist. He wondered if it was kinder to pass on word of what he'd seen or let his friend see for himself. He told himself that he probably would not live to carry word back to Jalist anyway. Slowly, of its own accord, the luminstone dimmed. Rowen waited until it had gone utterly dark, then mounted his horse and resumed his slow eastern ride.

Dawn found Saanji standing in front of the high city walls, shivering in his armor. It was snowing again. Royce's kingsteel sword hung at his side. He stood alone, well ahead of what remained of his army. He waited. The sun rose behind him, faintly warming his neck. All along the battlements above, Dhargots went on jeering at him—as they had for the past half hour and the three days before. A few fired crossbow bolts into the snow a few yards away, but none dared fire directly at him. Saanji did his best not to flinch at the sounds. Then, all at once, the Dhargots fell silent.

A moment later, the gates of Hesod rumbled open. Karhaati finally emerged from the city just as the snow stopped falling. He moved slowly, his armor jingling with every step. His thick necklace of ears swayed as he moved. At least two of them looked fresh, still crusted with dried blood. Saanji felt a lump in his throat.

Karhaati approached with a yawn, a familiar sword glinting in the crook of his arm. When just a few yards separated them, Karhaati stopped. He looked around. "Seems you've lost your army, dear brother."

"Only some of it," Saanji managed.

"Looks like most of it. I wonder what the rest of these men will do once you're dead. Do you think they'll join me?"

"I doubt it."

Karhaati nodded. "I didn't think so. That's fine. I don't want them, anyway." He raised his voice, shouting to be heard by all. "But I'll cut their ears off myself. Then I'll impale each of these traitors, one at a time."

He made a sweeping gesture with Widowswail then returned it to the crook of his arm. He cocked his head, looked at Saanji, and smiled again. "I must say, Brother, I'm surprised. I thought you'd run or maybe send assassins. I even thought you might beg for my forgiveness after I killed your friend. But here you are. Father would be impressed."

Saanji swallowed hard. "Oh, I'm sure he would. Tell me, should we embrace before we kill each other?"

Karhaati smirked. "I don't think that'll be necessary." He glanced past Saanji again. "Tell me, is the Isle Knight with you?"

"Which one? There are so many running about these days, in their pretty armor and bright-blue tabards."

Karhaati's expression turned serious. "You know who I'm talking about." He stepped forward. "Emperor Chorlga spoke to me last night. I heard his voice in my head, as clearly as I hear yours."

"Chorlga is an emperor now? How exciting!"

"Guard your tongue. He might be listening. He is more than a Dragonkin, you know. He's practically a god now." Karhaati paused. "Shall I tell you what he said?"

"That depends. Was it poetic and frightening?"

Karhaati took yet another step forward. "He told me he's destroyed the rest of your army—everyone you sent east. They're all ashes now. And he told me... he *showed* me... how he did it." Karhaati shook his head. "That kind of power, it's too much for anyone."

Saanji thought of Rowen Locke. He forced a smile. "Probably. We'll see."

"One of us will, anyway." Karhaati gave Widowswail a wide, slow swing. "You know I can't forgive you, Brother. Not this time."

"I didn't come here to ask your forgiveness."

"That's good."

Saanji tapped his sword hilt. He swallowed hard. "Let's just get this over with."

"Why hurry?" Karhaati held out his arms, closed his eyes, and turned slowly in the crisp morning air, as though daring Saanji to charge while his back was turned. When he faced Saanji again, he opened his eyes and smiled.

"I wish I'd met Ziraari this way. I would have liked to kill him. He deserved that. But you will suffice."

Saanji took a deep breath, held it, and drew Royce's sword. "I'll do my best."

"We'll see. If you like, I'll let you keep your ears. Looks like you've already lost one, anyway." He took a few more steps then froze. His smirk vanished. He looked down and saw the tip of a caltrop poking through his boot. His weight had just born the barbed tip clear through the sole of his boot, then his entire foot. In addition to blood, the tip wore a telltale, burgundy smear.

Karhaati blanched.

Taking a few deep breaths, Saanji swallowed the lump in his throat. "I believe the Sylvs call that quickdeath. They use it to bring down Olgrym. At least, that's what *you* told me." He whirled Royce's sword in a deliberate circle, letting its kingsteel blade catch the sunlight. He waved it at the city walls, too, where Karhaati's men watched with uneasy puzzlement, unable to discern why the Bloody Prince had stopped moving.

Saanji said, "Take another step, if you like. I have five more caltrops hidden in the snow all around you. One should do the trick, though."

Flushed with rage, Karhaati hefted his sword and took a step forward, his expression so furious that Saanji shrank back. But then Karhaati paled again. He tripped and almost fell.

"Saanji…" The sword fell from Karhaati's hands. The Bloody Prince swooned. From the battlements of Hesod came a rumble of shock and disappointment. Behind Saanji, men cheered.

Saanji took a step forward, staring at his brother. Finally, he said, "For Maryssa," and lifted Royce's sword.

Karhaati's eyes widened. He tried to back up, stumbled, and fell. He looked up and winced as the sun shone in his eyes. Saanji followed, blocking the light.

"Not like this," Karhaati gasped. "Please, brother, my men are watching. Please—"

Saanji stared, unblinking. Then he stretched out his sword and cut off the Bloody Prince's necklace. Dried ears fell to the snow. Karhaati looked down at them then back up at Saanji. His expression hardened. "You have no honor."

"And no more siblings. Whatever shall I do?" Gripping Royce's sword with both hands, Saanji swung hard. Karhaati's head fell to the snow. The body followed.

Saanji turned his back on the stained snow and walked back toward his camp. His men cheered louder. Saanji lowered his face, clenched his eyes shut for a moment, then lifted his head. He forced a wild grin and waved his bloody sword over his head.

Dagath watched his second Dhargothi master fall. He leaned on the battlements, taking in the stunned silence all around him. Then, grunting, he headed for the stairs. He had no time to waste. With the Bloody Prince slain, the city would fall into upheaval. Dhargothi officers would start killing each other in their mad scramble for power. Sooner or later, a friend of the late General Umaari would take advantage of the chaos to stab Dagath in the back.

If Sneed were here, he'd know what to do. The thought of his half brother made him jerk. He'd been missing for many months—probably killed by the squire they'd captured on the road when the latter escaped. Dagath's eyes stung as though an arrow had pricked him through his armor. He shook off the feeling and hurried on toward the palace, thinking of the promise he'd made. Remembering how the red-haired woman had made his blood boil, he considered breaking his vow, then he glanced down at the jeweled rings on his fingers.

He'd already defied the gods enough for one lifetime. Better he get one last look at the woman before slitting her throat, fill his pockets with whatever he could take from the palace, and be on his way. And he knew just how he would get out.

After the Iron Sisters' initial escape from the dungeons beneath the palace, the Bloody Prince had ordered the entrance into the sewers be bricked off. But Dagath had issued different orders an hour later, telling the builders that the prince had simply changed his mind. The entrance into the sewers was blocked only by a heavy, locked trapdoor, to which Dagath had the key. Once in the sewers, he just had to find a tunnel that emptied outside the city—one that had not already been discovered and blocked off.

But what if there isn't one?

At least the streets were deserted. A few Hesodi, plus a handful of Dhargots with their slaves, milled about, but none challenged him. The people did not know yet that Karhaati had been slain. Though Dagath had been in Hesod just a short while, everyone knew that Dagath was the Prince's man. And he already had a reputation for enacting swift justice on anybody who failed to respect his station. Still, he felt relieved at the sight of the palace in the distance.

Evergreen trees and wells lined a long walkway. Dagath hurried along beneath the canopy of leaves. He paused beside one of the wells and glanced inside. He could not see to the bottom, but ice clung to the sides of the well. He had the odd thought that if the water were frozen, he might lower himself down into the well and simply walk on ice, out of the city.

He shook his head at the absurdity of the thought and hurried into the palace. He passed two guards and one of the Bloody Prince's few remaining healers. He ignored their questions and proceeded up the stairs to the second floor. He passed a heavily perfumed slave. The young man stood aside and bowed, but for no particular reason, Dagath knifed him, then headed up to the third level. Karhaati's room sat at the end of another long hallway. All the other rooms on the floor had been deserted. Two guards lay on the floor outside Karhaati's door, slain.

Dagath stepped to one side, in case someone was creeping up behind him, and drew his shortsword. He turned sideways. He listened carefully but heard no sound. All the doors were closed. He started forward. When he reached the guards, he noted that one had been stabbed in the back while his sword was still sheathed. The other had managed to draw his blade before someone slashed his throat so deeply that his head had nearly been cut clean off.

Dagath snickered. He wondered how the Iron Sister had gotten her hands on a blade, not to mention how she'd freed herself in the first place. Karhaati's bedroom had once belonged to the queen of the Iron Sisters. Perhaps she'd hidden a weapon in there somewhere. Dagath wondered if she'd also hidden gold and jewels, which the Bloody Prince and his men had failed to find.

Worry about that later. He pushed open the bedroom door with his foot, standing well back in case the Iron Sister pounced out of the shadows. The door creaked. Sunlight streaming in from the terrace filled the room. He entered, sword raised, but the big room had been emptied of most of its furniture, and a quick inspection told him that the Iron Sister was gone.

"Well, pretty one, you didn't go out the way I came, or else you would have been spotted. You must still be in the palace." He proceeded out to the terrace and looked down. Perhaps ten feet below and several feet to one side stood another, smaller terrace. Its stone railing glinted with frost. A spot of blood dotted the snow on the floor.

Dagath cursed. He did not have time to waste on a hunt, though he imagined it would be a short one. Jumping that far must have reopened all the Iron Sister's wounds.

A moment later, he heard shouts and a clash of steel. He wondered if the gods would consider him in fulfillment of his vow if someone else killed the Iron Sister. He decided not to risk it. He sheathed his sword, climbed onto the railing of the terrace, and jumped down.

He made his way back into the palace, cursing his sore knees, and spotted the Iron Sister at the far end of a corridor. She'd knotted a Dhargothi cloak around her breasts like a sarong. Blood splattered her bare arms, matching the color of her unkempt hair. A shortsword blurred in each hand.

"She's mine," Dagath shouted, but the guards ignored him. The Iron Sister had already killed one of them. Three more pressed in, eager for revenge. The Iron Sister backpedaled. One of the guards charged too quickly. The Iron Sister sidestepped and opened his forehead. But she winced. Dagath imagined her wounds leaking beneath her makeshift dress.

The other two Dhargots hesitated. They glanced at Dagath as he approached, then relaxed, sure he was coming to help them. Dagath waited until they'd turned back to the Iron Sister, then he stabbed one in the back. He beheaded the other before the man could turn.

Dagath grinned. "You're mine," he repeated to the woman.

He stepped over the corpse of the slave he'd killed earlier and headed toward the Iron Sister. But before they could meet, a chorus of angry shouts made him glance back over one shoulder. Three more Dhargots had arrived just in time to see what he'd done. Dagath cursed. As he turned to meet the Dhargots' charge, he saw the Iron Sister flash him a crooked smile, turn, and run.

She's heading for the dungeons, he thought. As he backpedaled, slashing to keep his opponents at bay, he wondered if the Iron Sister intended to flee the city via the same route he'd chosen. He thought of the key around his neck, hidden beneath his armor, then wondered if she could break the lock.

He managed to wound two of the men before one slashed his arm. Another grazed his leg, but the man overextended himself, and Dagath cut him down. He stood for a moment, regarding his final two opponents. All three men were bleeding. Shouts echoed from the streets beyond the palace.

"If I were you, I'd look to filling my pockets and getting out of here," Dagath advised. The men exchanged glances. They backed away. Dagath did likewise. When he was well away, he turned and limped after the Iron Sister. He started down toward the dungeons, but he made it only halfway before he froze.

More shouts reached his ears, accompanied by a woman's battle cry and a furious clash of steel. He thought it was just the Iron Sister fending off more guards, but then another woman's cry echoed up the stairs, followed by a third. Somehow, the Iron Sisters had overtaken the dungeon.

He drew back a step. He thought of the red-haired woman and scowled. He might still get to her, but there was no telling how many Iron Sisters were down there. Besides, she was obviously a skilled opponent. Even tired and bleeding, she would not go down easily. Fulfilling a vow made in the sight of the gods was one thing; dying in the attempt was something else.

"Another time," he muttered, and went to find a different way out of the city.

CHAPTER FORTY-THREE

THE QUEEN OF RATS

T HERE WAS NO SIGN OF the dragon. Rowen half expected it to
come crawling out of the fissure as soon as he drew close. Then he
remembered seeing the massive skeleton suspended on huge iron
chains in the depths of Cadavash and wondered if even the great fissure carved
into the landscape was big enough to conceal it. Step by step, he forced himself
closer.

Rowen thought of the last and only other time he'd been to Cadavash.
He'd been acting as a bodyguard for the Soroccan merchant Hráthbam Nassir
Adjrâ-al-Habas, who wanted to buy dragonbone from the mad people of
Cadavash and sell it elsewhere. But they'd arrived in the dragon graveyards
and been so overwhelmed by the horror of the place that they had stayed no
longer than necessary.

Rowen remembered throngs of worshippers stumbling about, mourning
dragons dead for millennia. Their lamentations—sometimes absurdly theatrical,
other times chillingly sincere—had been accompanied by widespread ritualistic
self-mutilation. Rowen had heard of such fey worshippers before, but he had
only ever seen a few here and there during his travels. Seeing them massed
at Cadavash, where such madness was not only tolerated but encouraged, had
given him as many nightmares as all the ghastly uses of magic he'd seen during
the past year.

Now, though, Cadavash stood silent.

The same massive, gray fissure loomed in the distance. Around it stood
a smattering of taverns, lean-tos, and shops, many of them frosted with
ice. Nothing moved. Above it all sat the temple: a gaudy, red-painted thing
supported by pillars and surrounded by statues of Zet. Great bronze doors led

into the temple. The doors stood open. Though it was morning, the interior was dark.

The sight of it amid all the silence sent a chill down his spine. Before he even realized it, he'd drawn his bastard sword. He moved forward slowly, trying to minimize the crunch of his boots in the snow. He was glad he'd relieved himself when he felt his body tighten from fear. Hunger gnawed at his stomach, too. The weariness pressing down on his eyelids reminded him how little he'd slept.

Gods, I'm in no shape for a fight, let alone the fight of my life.

He continued edging toward the temple, glancing about the shadows of the makeshift town for enemies. Then something caught his eye: a glint of steel on the plains to the east. Despite his hesitation to turn his back on the temple, he went to investigate. He did not have to go far before he found himself wishing he'd just kept walking toward the temple after all.

East of the temple and the fissure, half buried in snow from the most recent blizzard, lay the frozen bodies of countless dragon-worshippers. Most lay facedown, but those who didn't displayed the final emotion they'd felt in this life. They lay wide jawed, their eye sockets blackened by fire, blue fingers curled like frozen hooks. Men, women, and children, they lay in contorted heaps in the snow, forgotten, buried only by the falling snow.

And scattered in their midst, all facing away from him, kneeled hundreds of Jolym.

As he drew closer, he wondered how he had failed to notice the ghastly sight from half a mile away. He took a step back, about to turn toward the temple, but something compelled him to check the Jolym first.

He singled out the closest one and edged up to it as quietly as he could. He shuddered when he had to step over the wide eyes of a little boy, noting that his body looked undisturbed. So did the others. Even the wolves had stayed away.

Wolves have more sense than I do...

When Rowen was close enough, he jabbed the Jol in the back. The tip of his sword chipped away a chunk of ice, revealing glinting shoulder blades and muscles shaped into the steel. The Jol did not move. Rowen took a deep breath then moved to stand in front of it. Even with the Jol kneeling, its grinning brass facemask was nearly at eye level. Rowen stared into its dark eye sockets then backed away.

He looked down. At his feet lay the corpse of an old man, his hands still folded as though he'd died while either praying or pleading for his life.

Looking past the Jol, he narrowed his gaze on the temple. He forced himself to sheathe his sword. "All right, you purple-eyed bastard, I'm here." He stepped around the Jol and started toward the temple. "Care to show me what all these lives paid for?"

He braced himself, expecting to hear Chorlga's voice in his mind, provoking deep feelings of fear and violation akin to finding a thief in his home. But Chorlga did not answer.

Rowen wondered where Shade was, if the Shel'ai was watching. Then, remembering Shade's warning, Rowen took care to clear his mind. As he walked, he imagined building a wall around his thoughts, brick by brick. By the time he'd gone halfway toward the temple, he imagined Chorlga's frustration when he found Rowen's mind transformed from an open book to a sealed, indecipherable scroll.

Then he heard the rattling chains. He spun around but saw only his own footprints. He turned back to the temple, then the adjacent town. Nothing moved there, either. But the metallic rattling grew louder. Then he looked up.

Rowen fell to his knees, shielding his eyes as Godsbane passed over. The skeletal dragon flew so low that Rowen felt the searing heat wafting off its body. Its shadow blotted out the sun, spreading across the snow like a stain.

Rowen forced himself to stand then to look. The Dragonjol's skeletal wings flapped as it settled onto the ground next to the temple, dwarfing the structure. The ground shook. Tendrils of wytchfire sputtered and coursed along its bones. From time to time, the chains joining them creaked and grated from the effort.

Godsbane turned its head and looked at him.

Rowen looked away. He started to kneel again but stopped himself. *No,* he thought, then said it aloud. He thought he heard Chorlga's laugh, though he could have sworn the sound came from the Dragonjol's toothy maw. He stood there, shaking, until he found his voice.

"If you're going to kill me, get on with it."

Chorlga's voice echoed painfully in his mind, taut with mockery. *"I have no wish to kill you, young one. In fact, I wish to reward you. Pledge your loyalty to me, and I will make you my general... maybe even a king, in time, should you prove yourself."*

Rowen wanted to say yes. He sensed in his heart that this was the only way he could survive—and put a stop to Godsbane's rampage. But he remembered all the Dwarrs and Queshi lying blackened in the snow. He imagined Jalist finding Leander. He thought of Silwren. Though his voice trembled, Rowen said, "No more tests, Dragonkin. I've already proven myself. Prince Saanji is dead. Prince Karhaati is dead. Hesod is mine. But you may have it, for a price."

Chorlga was silent. Then he said, *"You're lying."*

Rowen forced himself to meet Godsbane's gaze. He flashed a derisive smirk. "Am I?" As he spoke, he imagined smashing down the mental barrier he'd just made. Then he thought of how he'd entered Saanji's tent and stabbed the sleeping drunkard. He imagined the blood spilling past the brass quillons of his sword to warm his hands, leaving a briny smell that persisted long after he'd washed them.

After that, he remembered sneaking back into the sewers of Hesod, surrounded by reek, slitting the throat of a guard with darkly painted eyes, the feel of the dried ears on the guard's necklace as they brushed against his hand—then climbing the steps to Karhaati's room. Once more, he saw the Bloody Prince's eyes go wide as he woke and fumbled for his sword, one moment before Rowen slashed his throat.

He imagined these things as he had been doing for days, over and over again—as though they had really happened.

Godsbane stirred. The massive skeletal body rose to stand on two legs. Six wings spread, shadowing all of Cadavash. The dark eye sockets flashed with purple fire.

"That's not what I told you to do."

Rowen swallowed a fresh surge of fear and smiled again. "I am not your pawn, Dragonkin. I kill who I want. If you want my loyalty, you best earn it." He paused. "The streets of Hesod run red with the blood of all those who opposed me. If you doubt me, see for yourself. I'll wait."

Godsbane cocked its head. Then its neck tensed like a Queshi bow. Wytchfire gathered at its sternum. Its mouth opened wide. But Rowen did not move or blink. Finally, the Dragonjol settled back onto the earth like a sleeping dog.

"That won't be necessary. I'll claw the truth from your mind and leave you drooling and as senseless as the Nightmare, unless you tell me the truth."

Rowen calmed himself before he called back toward the temple, "I grow weary of your threats, Dragonkin. While you hide in your temple, *my* followers are busy carving my likeness in Hesod. *My* likeness, not yours. They've already forgotten you. They wept when I left, and they shall weep again when I return."

"You will not return unless I wish it."

Godsbane jerked. The Dragonjol twisted its head back and forth as though screaming, though no sound resulted, save the rattling of the chains joining its bones. It stood on two legs again, crouched, then leapt into the air. Its wings blurred. The great beast rose into the sky.

"We shall see if you speak the truth. If you do, expect pain unlike anything you have ever experienced. If not"—Godsbane's eyes blazed with purple fire—*"expect worse."*

The Dragonjol twisted in midair and flew off to the west. Rowen watched until it disappeared from sight. He summoned all his willpower to keep from smiling. Then another metallic glint caught his eye. A huge armored figure stepped out of the darkness of the temple. He slowly, gracefully descended the temple steps and stared toward Rowen.

The glint of kingsteel was unmistakable. The Jol had been wrought entirely of it. The Jol was even larger than the kneeling ones, and instead of wrists that ended in weapons, it had real hands. As it drew closer, Rowen saw its facemask: an exaggerated expression of sorrow.

Rowen resisted the impulse to draw his swords. He waited until the Jol stopped right in front of him and held out one gigantic kingsteel hand. Rowen unbuckled both his swords and placed them in the Jol's hand. The Jol's coal-dark eyes regarded Rowen, then the Jol closed its hand, gripping both swords by their pommels. The Jol's other hand came up, gripping the scabbards. With frightful ease, the Jol snapped both swords in half. One hand kept hold of the sword hilts while the other released the blades, reached out with surprising speed, and seized Rowen by the cloak.

Chorlga's voice rang in Rowen's mind again: *"While we wait, Isle Knight, come inside. It's time we meet face to face."*

The kingsteel Jol turned, pushing Rowen ahead of him. Rowen felt the sun on the back of his neck a moment before the Jol fell in behind him. Its shadow swallowed his own.

Shade knelt in the remains of a dragon-worshipper's lean-to, eyes closed, building wall after wall in his mind. Sweat ran down his face. He'd arrived in Cadavash just behind Rowen. Though he'd been strengthening his mental defenses for days, he still feared that either Chorlga or Godsbane would sense him. So far, they had not. But Shade sensed the Dragonjol as it flew overhead.

He'd both seen and sensed Godsbane in the north, too, while passing through Ivairia, where he'd witnessed the Dragonjol effortlessly reducing an entire countryside to ash. Then, the Dragonjol had been miles away and distracted. Now, it seemed close enough to touch, and a feeling of dread, even worse than what he'd felt in the presence of the Nightmare, filled him. He nearly wept with relief when the Dragonjol flew on, taking with it its own primal essence of anger and deep, roiling sorrow.

But when it was gone, Shade sensed something else: its master.

He's too powerful, too mad. I can't do this. The Isle Knight is on his own…

"But what about Zeia?"

His own voice came out in a whisper, tired and raspy, as though it belonged to someone else. Slowly, Shade straightened. Zeia must be in the temple. He sensed her as a weak, ghostly flutter. Chorlga must have taken her as close to death as he could without actually killing her.

That means she won't be able to help us…

"But she has to," Shade muttered. He peered out of the lean-to, toward the temple, just in time to see a Jol leading the Isle Knight up the stairs and through the dark mouth of its doorway. He shuddered.

Silwren, if you can hear me… if you can forgive me… please, my love, I need your help!

Shade closed his eyes. Though even the slightest use of magic risked detection, he had no choice. Visualizing Zeia, he stretched out his mind and whispered just one word.

Zeia found herself alone in a temple, surrounded by soot-covered altars, winged statues, and empty wooden pews. She lay in torn, bloody clothes on a short, white staircase that led up to the temple's principle altar. Icy-white light spilled in through arrow-thin windows. She frowned. Then she remembered.

Using her forearms, she pushed herself up into a sitting position. She tried to block out her memories of the terrible, drowning swim into the city, her pitched battle against the Dhargots who spotted her, then her desperate flight into the sewers. She also tried to block out how she'd felt when she finally found Fel-Nâya lying naked in the dark, filthy water. That moment of elation had crumbled just as quickly as it had formed when Chorlga emerged from the shadows right in front of her.

With just a wave of his hand, the Dragonkin had dispelled her flaming hands, driven her to the ground, and filled her body with pain every bit as terrible as what she'd felt when the one-eyed sellsword had cut off her hands.

"And now, little one, here you are."

Zeia resisted the impulse to turn her head as Chorlga walked past her. She wondered where he had been hiding, if she'd just not seen him, or if he wanted the sport of watching her try to escape. She said nothing as the Dragonkin, extravagantly robed, knelt before her, grinning with his rotten teeth.

"How are you feeling, little pet?"

When Zeia did not answer, Chorlga grabbed one of her wrists and pressed one finger into her scarred, puckered stump. She clenched her teeth. A tendril of wytchfire bloomed from Chorlga's knuckle, danced down his finger, and burrowed like a burning insect into her wrist-stump. The searing jolt swept all the way up to her shoulder, followed by stabbing cold.

Zeia wept but did not scream.

Chorlga nodded slightly as though in approval. "You have spirit, little pet. I must say, in twelve centuries, I've never seen a Shel'ai do what you can do. As far as rats go, you are a queen. The Queen of Rats. Shall I make you a crown?" He released her wrist and stood up. "We shall have a visitor soon. Can you guess who it is?"

Zeia shuddered, remembering the Dragonjol—and the visions of all the death and destruction that the aberration had wrought, which Chorlga had taken great delight in forcing into her mind.

"Oh, no, not Godsbane," Chorlga said. "Care to guess again?"

Without waiting for a response, Chorlga gestured. Invisible hands picked Zeia up, spun her around, and carried her up the stairs. As she floated past the altar, she saw something she had not noticed before: a throne made out of dragonbones. She wondered if Chorlga had made the throne himself or if it had already been there when he'd arrived.

The invisible hands released her. She winced as she dropped face first onto the marble floor. All the breath left her lungs. She braced her elbows against the floor and tried unsuccessfully to push herself up. Footsteps rang off the stone behind her.

Chorlga grabbed her hair and jerked her head up. "Do you want to know why I hate your kind so much? Shall I tell you?"

Chorlga started to lift her then dropped her back onto the floor. He laughed then snapped his fingers. A new pair of hands—cold and metallic—seized her and dragged her up. Zeia blinked, momentarily finding herself face to face with an enormous Jol. Then the Jol spun her around, still holding her. Each of the Jol's hands easily encircled one of her arms.

"I asked you a question." Chorlga crossed his arms. Though he grinned, his eyes narrowed.

Still, Zeia said nothing.

Chorlga came one step closer. "Let's try a different question. Like, why have I done all this? Why did I go to such lengths to turn everyone else against the Shel'ai, to turn the Shel'ai against each other? Would you like to know?"

Zeia whispered quietly, so that he would not hear.

Grinning, Chorlga stepped closer. "Again, please, little pet. I couldn't—"

She spat in his face.

Chorlga's grin vanished. He wiped his face and stepped back. "You have some inkling of what I could do to you. Before I actually punish you, though, I'll let you think about that for a while. If you're lucky..." He frowned, then his grin returned. "Ah, our visitor has arrived!"

He snapped his fingers again, and the Jol dropped her to the floor, turned, and headed for the temple doors. Despite its metallic bulk, it moved with impossible quiet and grace. Chorlga knelt beside her again. He followed her gaze.

"Quite a creation, is he not? Nothing like Godsbane, of course, but still, he was my first one. I made him after the Dragonward went up, trapping me in this rat-infested sewer of a world."

Zeia glanced at her captor. For the first time, she noticed that the Dragonkin looked paler than he had when she'd last seen him. Faint tendrils of blood shone in his eyes. Even the color of his pupils had dulled from mist white to stone gray. For a moment, those eyes roiled with sadness and pain. She felt a stirring of pity.

"Where is the sword?" she asked.

Chorlga snickered. His eyes brightened. He stood and waved his hand. Fel-Nâya appeared out of thin air. Once again, the Dragonkin held it by the scabbard. Zeia had the sudden thought that if he were ever careless enough to hold it by the pommel, and if she were close enough, she could tear away the scabbard and leave him holding the naked sword. She wondered if that would kill him.

"No, it wouldn't," Chorlga said. Before Zeia could chide herself for not guarding her thoughts, the Dragonkin said, "Shall I demonstrate?" He continued holding the ancient adamune by the scabbard then, with just a moment's hesitation, used his other hand to seize the dragonbone pommel.

Chorlga winced. Smoke billowed between his fingers. Still, he drew the sword. Wytchfire flared along the length of the blade then clawed its way downward, past the oval crossguard. The purple flames swept up Chorlga's arms, bright and angry, toward his face. Chorlga gritted his rotten teeth but did not cry out. He let the flames swirl about his face then slammed the sword back into its scabbard. He let go of the pommel. The purple flames disappeared.

Chorlga faced her, grinning despite his smoking, blistered flesh. When next he spoke, his voice was a chilling whisper. "If you have any thoughts of harming me, Queen of Rats, surrender them now. I assure you, I have spent centuries enduring every torment imaginable."

Even as he spoke, his blistered flesh began to heal. By the time he'd settled the sheathed adamune in the crook of his arm and ascended the stairs, he was fully healed. Only the burnt-off arm of his robe suggested that anything had happened.

Chorlga sat on his throne of dragonbones and waited.

Moments later, Zeia felt the air go hot. A primal feeling of panic welled inside her. Godsbane had returned. She saw only the Dragonjol's shadow, which blocked out the light entering the windows of one whole side of the temple, but she could feel it right outside. Swallowing her fear, she studied Chorlga's expression. The Dragonkin looked distracted... and perhaps just a little afraid.

Zeia glanced toward the distant gates of the temple. She wondered how far she would make it if she ran. *Surely not far enough, especially with Godsbane right outside. Not yet,* she told herself.

Moments later, she felt Godsbane pulling away. She turned back to Chorlga. His expression looked terse but distracted. She guessed he must be in telepathic communication with the Isle Knight. *Who else could be coming here if not him?*

Zeia tensed, preparing to make a run for it. But something stopped her. Without knowing why, she let her shoulders sag. She drooped her head, as though she barely had the strength to keep her eyes open. A moment later, the opportunity was gone.

"Come closer, Queen of Rats." Chorlga snapped his fingers, and invisible hands of magic hauled her closer to his throne, forcing her to lie at his feet, facing the temple gates. He rested his feet on her side.

A moment later, the Isle Knight appeared in the doorway, the towering Jol a step behind. The Jol shoved the Isle Knight into the temple. He entered slowly, looking about, then fixed his gaze on Chorlga.

Zeia blushed. She wanted to speak telepathically to him, to apologize for her failure to retrieve Fel-Nâya, but she did not have the strength. *Besides,* she thought, *what would it have mattered? What could this weak Human possibly have done?*

The Jol guided the Isle Knight through the temple, past pews, altars, and leering statues, until he stood before Chorlga himself. The Isle Knight paled. The Jol continued to hold him with one hand. The other came up, clutching the hilts of two broken swords. The Jol showed them to Chorlga then tossed them onto the ground. They sparked as they struck the stone.

Chorlga sighed. "Well, Sir Locke, we meet at last. Strange. I expected more from you." His feet rose from Zeia's side. A moment later, an invisible hand brushed her aside. She turned in time to see Chorlga rise from his throne, Fel-Nâya still held in the crook of his arm. The Jol had forced the Isle Knight to his knees. Chorlga bent forward, his face hovering over the Isle Knight's.

"So, I believe you were saying something about Hesod, about defying my orders." Though the Dragonkin grinned, his eyes narrowed. Wytchfire flared from his hands, dancing around his wrists. The Isle Knight tried to meet Chorlga's gaze, managed to hold it for a few seconds, then looked away.

Zeia lowered her gaze to the floor. She eyed one of the broken swords. She wondered if she could summon enough magic to hurl it toward the Dragonkin's throat. She doubted she could do so fast enough to make contact, but it would at least permit her one final act of defiance. Chorlga might even kill her for it, acting on reflex, granting her the mercy of a quick death.

"El'rash'lin..."

Shade's voice was barely a whisper in her mind, as quiet as a breeze through the branches of a forest, then it vanished. She looked about. Chorlga continued to loom over the kneeling Isle Knight, gloating. He had not heard.

For a moment, Zeia thought she'd imagined it. Shade should have been hundreds of miles from here, well beyond the Dragonward, safeguarding their people. What was he doing here?

Still letting her head sag, just in case the Dragonkin remembered her and turned to look in her direction, Zeia sat up. She spotted a flicker of movement at the far end of the temple. A cloaked figure had just slipped in through the gates. Crouched low, he slowly made his way through the temple, moving from pew to pew. Then he straightened behind a statue and turned to face Zeia.

They held each other's gaze for just a moment, then Zeia looked away. No mindspeak was necessary. She nodded slightly. As Shade continued to creep through the temple, making his way closer and closer, Zeia took a series of deep, slow breaths. She would have only one chance—and it would probably kill her.

She thought of El'rash'lin and the others—even her enemies—along with all the Shel'ai children yet to be born. One chance would be enough. It had to be. She considered trying to speak a telepathic word into the Isle Knight's mind, then decided against it. With Chorlga's attention fixed solely on the Knight, the Dragonkin would surely sense that. She would have to trust the Isle Knight to do his part—and that El'rash'lin's faith in the man had not been misplaced.

Or his faith in me...

Zeia closed her eyes, breathing easily, gradually drawing together all the strength she had left. When she was ready, she opened her eyes, turned slightly, and saw that Shade was in position. The Shel'ai had crouched some twenty feet away, behind another statue, as close as he could get without being detected.

Zeia rose slowly, dragging her feet on the stone, letting Chorlga hear her. The Dragonkin had the Isle Knight's face in one hand, pinching his jaw with burning fingers. Surprisingly, the Isle Knight would not scream. But he slumped when Chorlga let him go.

Chorlga straightened and turned to face Zeia. "What are you doing, Queen of Rats?"

Zeia looked down. Chorlga followed her gaze to the hilt of one of the broken swords. He laughed. "Defiant to the last." He spread his arms. "Very well, Shel'ai. Do your worst."

Zeia snickered. "I will." Facing Chorlga, she unleashed the strongest mind-stab she could muster.

The Dragonkin's eyes widened. He jerked. Confronted by such an unexpected attack, he panicked. Rather than answer with a mental attack of his own or create a mental barrier, he hurled a storm of wytchfire at Zeia.

Zeia pitched herself sideways. Fire streamed past her, singeing her arm, burning her clothes. She landed on the marble floor but kept her eyes open. She saw Shade sprinting up the steps toward Chorlga. Wytchfire streamed from Shade's fingertips. Purple flames engulfed Chorlga's body. The Dragonkin stiffened then turned to meet the new attack.

Shade's wytchfire sputtered and died. Still, Shade charged. He passed the Jol and threw himself at Chorlga. His hands closed around Fel-Nâya's scabbard. He wrested the ancient adamune from Chorlga's grasp and turned. At the same time, Zeia stretched out with her mind, picked up the broken sword and threw it at the Jol's face.

She tried to drive the shard into one of the Jol's eyes. But she missed. The bit of broken blade sparked off the cheek of the Jol's facemask. But that was enough. The Jol turned to face her. When Zeia picked up the second hilt and sent it flying toward the Jol's face, it released the Isle Knight to bat it away.

In that instant, the Isle Knight leapt forward. One hand closed around the pommel of Fel-Nâya, just as Shade thrust it toward him. The Isle Knight turned. Even as the Jol reached for him, he hefted the sword.

The scabbard burned away.

Purple flames engulfed the blade, the hilt, then the arms of the man who held it. The Isle Knight howled. Fel-Nâya cut a blinding arc through the Jol's armored chest. Then it swept back up, severing an arm. The Isle Knight took one step forward. Instead of stabbing the Jol through one of its eyes, he cut off its head. Then he turned.

Zeia turned, too.

Chorlga pressed his hand to Shade's back. Wytchfire engulfed him. Shade screamed and fell. Chorlga stretched out his arm and sent a second searing sea of wytchfire at the Isle Knight.

The Isle Knight lifted Fel-Nâya and met the flames, unblinking. The sword drank in the fire. The Isle Knight took another step forward. Chorlga fell back, his eyes wide. Then he waved his hand and hauled Shade's burned body onto its feet. Using Shade as a shield, Chorlga unleashed a second torrent of wytchfire.

This time, it was too much.

Fel-Nâya drank in most of the flames, but some spilled over, scorching the Isle Knight's arms. He screamed and staggered. Then he took another step. Chorlga wrapped one arm around Shade's throat. Shade's eyelids fluttered weakly. Somehow, he was still alive.

"Stay back, Knight. Stay back, or I swear, your friend—"

The Isle Knight took one final step forward and thrust his burning blade clear through Shade's chest, into Chorlga's. The Dragonkin's eyes widened. Zeia thought she saw Shade snicker. The Isle Knight stood there a moment, stone faced, pushing the sword even deeper. Then, slowly, he dragged it out.

Chorlga and Shade stood together, smoldering. Then Shade fell to the floor. Chorlga teetered backward. Aiming blindly, he unleashed another blast of wytchfire. It sailed clear of the Isle Knight and struck a statue of Zet in the distance. The statue toppled and shattered. Chorlga clutched one hand to his chest. He tried to take a step and collapsed backward into his throne of dragonbones.

Rowen Locke followed.

Chorlga turned, his face blackened and crying. His eyes met Zeia's. She thought he actually meant to plead for help. But then the Dragonkin turned back to the Isle Knight. Blood bubbled between his lips. Nevertheless, he grinned.

"In my world, Knight, what is given can always be taken back."

The Isle Knight frowned.

Zeia pushed herself up. "Kill him!" she screamed.

Shaking himself free of his daze, the Isle Knight drew Fel-Nâya back, holding it with both hands. But before he could plunge it into Chorlga's heart, one whole wall of the temple evaporated in a radiant sea of fire.

CHAPTER FORTY-FOUR

WHAT WAS GIVEN

S AANJI SAT IN A CHAIR at the edge of the camp, a glass of strong wine in hand, and watched smoke rise over the battlements of Hesod. Bodyguards milled around him, many holding shields thick enough to ward off crossbow bolts, in case the city gates swung open and the Dhargots charged onto the field. But Saanji doubted that would happen.

Only a few hours had passed since he'd slain his brother, and already, he could hear the city devolving into chaos. He imagined his brother's officers fighting each other for dominance. Inevitably, the soldiers they commanded would be forced to choose sides. With luck, enough would die in the ensuing melee that the slaves and captives throughout Hesod would be emboldened to rise up and revolt again.

If the gods were truly kind for once, whichever general eventually assumed command might even be willing to surrender the city to Saanji, provided that he and the Earless let them slink back to Dhargoth unharmed. Saanji smiled at the thought. Then the smile vanished.

He remembered what Sir Fey—he could not remember the man's real name—had said about Chorlga's dragon. Saanji had woken the next day and, to his own surprise, still felt determined to follow through on his plan to confront Karhaati, but certain, at least, that *that* part of Sir Fey's tale had been ludicrous. There were no more dragons in Ruun, let alone dragons reanimated by the same magical processes—whatever those were—that had created the Jolym.

But word had reached him of some new devilry thrashing the lands to the north, scorching men by the hundreds. He almost pitied the Lancers who had deserted him, since they would only be returning to whatever smoldering ruins Chorlga's newest champion had left behind.

And if Sir Fey is right, that thing will be coming here!

Saanji doubted it, but he'd taken precautions just in case. Ballistae had been made ready to fire ropes and nets lashed to weights, in the hopes that they might tangle a dragon's wings and drag it down from the sky. In case the dragon operated anything like the other Jolym, Saanji had squadrons of spearmen ready to try to stab the thing through the eyes.

Though his Earless had initially mocked him for these preparations, the jeering had stopped once they started hearing reports of the dragon. Now, they praised him. Even the dark-haired she-Knight, Aeko Shingawa, appeared to approve of his plan—before she, her Isle Knights, and the Dwarrish sellsword had deserted him, too.

Saanji felt a rush of irritation, then he thought of where they were going and decided to drink in their honor. No matter how skilled they were, a handful of Isle Knights and one Dwarr could hardly have made so great a difference in the siege. Besides, he still had a few hundred Iron Sisters on his side.

"Where is Captain Haesha?" He looked around and saw only his own men. "I don't see any Iron Sisters. Why aren't they watching?"

One of his bodyguards cleared his throat. "Begging your pardon, Prince, but we already told you. They've gone to sneak back into the city. They've attacked the sewers where they're sealed off—"

Saanji frowned. "Lousy plan. My dear brother's army is still too strong. Why didn't I try to talk them out of it?"

"You did, m'lord. Captain Haesha wouldn't listen. She said there were captives and citizens who couldn't wait. You said if she opened up a path into the city, you'd send in a thousand men to assist her."

Saanji's frown deepened. "Gods, I need to stop making promises to beautiful women."

"She said she'd make you their Iron Prince if you helped her take the city," someone said.

Saanji decided to ignore the touch of mockery in the man's voice. He watched smoke rise over the city. Then he stood up, tottered, and caught his balance before one of his bodyguards had to assist him.

"If the gods want another bloodbath, they can make one up themselves. I say let's let our men grow fat, old, and shameful." He looked around for agreement. When no one spoke, he continued. "If the Iron Sisters actually do cut a way into the city, we'll mass at the palace and work our way out from there. In the meantime, write a message, tie it to an arrow, and fire it over the walls. Blunt the tip so it doesn't kill anybody. Hard to read an offer for truce if it's got blood on it."

He took a drink, turned, and saw one of his servants poised with a quill and parchment. He wondered why then remembered. "On the message, write—"

A warbling trumpet blast cut the winter air.

Saanji had been trying to memorize the meaning behind all the various pennants, gestures, and trumpet blasts employed by an army, but this one eluded him. He only knew that the blast had come from behind him, in his own camp. "What is that?"

"Attack from the rear," someone said.

Maybe the Jolym are still alive. Saanji dropped his wine and reached for Royce's sword. He wished he hadn't drunk so much. He wished, too, that he'd wiped his brother's blood off the blade.

Another, slightly different trumpet blast sounded. He turned to his bodyguards. They frowned. One said, "Doesn't make sense. The sentry must be a fool."

"Why?"

"He's warning of an attack from above, but we're too far from the city walls—" The bodyguard broke off, eyes widening. Men exchanged terrified looks.

Saanji turned to a table that had been placed beside his chair in the snow. His helmet rested on the table. Suddenly, though, it had become three helmets. He chose the one in the middle. As he slipped it on, he looked around. Everywhere, horses screamed, and men panicked.

Cursing, Saanji surprised himself by climbing onto his chair then stepping onto his table. He waved his arms to get men's attention, nearly falling off the table. "Well, lads, look on the bright side. You're about to see something nobody's seen in more centuries than Zet had inches on his cock. Think of how popular you'll be in taverns!"

A few men laughed.

"Stay calm. Remember the plan. Remember what I told you..." Saanji trailed off, wondering if he'd remembered to make sure his strategy had been fully discussed throughout the camp. He decided that if he hadn't, it was too late to worry about that.

"Right about now, my dear brother's soul is crisping in one of Fohl's hells. So are lots of men who wanted you dead. One day, maybe we'll see them again. If so, let's tell the bastards that before *we* died, we managed to bring a gods-damned dragon out of the sky!"

Men cheered. Saanji waved Royce's sword then leapt off the table. Somehow, he managed to land without falling. One of his bodyguards brought his new horse: a spirited bloodmare left for him as a present by the Queshi prince. The bloodmare's dark eyes regarded him suspiciously. It pawed the ground.

Sighing, Saanji took the reins. He tried to fit his foot into the stirrup. It took three tries, but then he pulled himself up into the saddle with hardly any help. Straightening, he looked up. At first, he saw nothing but clouds. Then he spotted the most fearful thing he'd ever seen winging in from the east.

He paled. He considered turning south and riding as fast as his bloodmare could carry him. Instead, he howled and rode east through the camp, waving his sword. As he did so, he wondered if his men found his appearance emboldening or if they merely thought he'd gone as mad as Sir Fey. He hoped it was the former.

As someone rolled the dead man off her and helped her up, Igrid wiped the blood from her eyes.

"Is that yours or a Dhargot's?"

Igrid glanced at the speaker, a familiar Iron Sister, and said, "Hard to say. Same color."

Haesha put Igrid's sword back in her hands then carefully peeled away the bloody cloak that Igrid had wrapped around her naked body. Haesha whistled. "I've seen raw meat bleed less than this. Lie down. We'll finish this. I'll leave a Sister to guard you."

"Like hells, you will. Just wrap me up tight and cover me in armor."

Haesha raised one eyebrow then gestured. Iron Sisters streamed past her, charging up the steps that led into the palace. Haesha took off her own tabard and put it on Igrid. Removing her own sword belt, she wrapped it around Igrid's waist and cinched it tight.

Igrid winced and looked down. Already, blood was soaking through the tabard. "I'll be fine," she said before Haesha could speak. "I'll be no safer here than I'll be in the city streets."

"Then go down through the sewers. You can make it out. It cost us, but we cleared a path."

"And I'm sure dragging my open wounds through sewer water will do wonders for my health." Igrid grasped the belt and cinched it even tighter. "Armor."

Haesha went to the nearest slain Dhargot and peeled off his cuirass. She helped Igrid don it. "If you want greaves and vambraces, fuss with those yourself. I have a city to take back."

Igrid nodded weakly. She was tempted to ask Haesha what was happening outside the city. From eavesdropping on the lecherous Dhargothi healers, she'd heard rumors that Arnil Royce was there, along with Rowen Locke. But Haesha was already bounding up the stairs after the other Iron Sisters.

Igrid took a moment to catch her breath, then stripped the Dhargot of his armor. She winced with every motion, feeling as though her insides were spilling out. She wondered if she should reconsider Haesha's advice and try to slip out of the city through the sewers. That had been her original plan before she'd chanced across a mass of Iron Sisters, just as they were trying to batter their way back into the dungeon.

She stopped and listened to the sounds of battle raging in the palace above her. From what the Iron Sisters had told her in the few moments they'd been together, Igrid knew that the Bloody Prince had been killed. His officers were fighting each other for supremacy, even as the city itself was under siege.

The Bloody Prince is dead...

The thought provoked a strange ambivalence within her. She had not forgotten what the despicable prince had done to Ailynn. She'd wanted to kill him herself and would have done so without hesitation. But he *had* saved her.

"Whatever he did, he did for his own reasons," she muttered. Finished donning her armor, she considered a helmet then decided against it. Better that she leave her hair uncovered. At the moment, the last thing she wanted was to be mistaken for a Dhargot. Leaning against the wall for support, she started up the stairs.

As she moved, she thought of the one-eyed sellsword. She'd seen him earlier. He'd either been killed by the other Iron Sisters or fled for his life. She hoped he was not still in the palace, hunting her. Another time, she might have welcomed the challenge of such an obviously skilled opponent, but right now, she was hardly at her best.

When she reached the top of the stairs, she realized that the sounds of battle were growing more and more distant. The Iron Sisters must have cleared the palace of enemies and moved out to the city beyond. She should be there, with them. She tried to hurry, but the pain made her stop again.

I'll be useless in a swordfight, she realized. She remembered hearing that this palace had once housed three armories. One was supposed to be on the same floor as Queen Sharra's bedroom, filled with her trophies of war. If she could make her way there and find a crossbow, she might still be of use.

Though she dreaded the thought of climbing so many stairs, Igrid decided she had no choice. She made her way cautiously through the palace, still leaning against the wall for support. She passed dead Dhargots and Iron Sisters alike, along with a handful of slaves who might very well have been killed by the Dhargots for sport or at the hands of Iron Sisters by mistake. She tried not to look at their faces. Near one end table, she spotted a pitcher of wine.

Muttering a prayer of thanks, she took a long drink, then she poured the rest of the pitcher's contents beneath her cuirass, hoping it might clean her wounds. She winced at the sting, then tossed aside the pitcher and kept going.

By the time she reached the topmost floor of the palace and located a crossbow, she hardly had enough strength left to move. Nevertheless, she used a winch to arm the crossbow and dragged it down to the hall, to Queen Sharra's bedchamber. With some hesitation, she reentered the room that had been her prison, edging around the guards she'd killed earlier. She dragged the crossbow out to the terrace. She looked out over the city.

Her eyes widened. She could see fighting in the streets. A few rooftops burned. Crowds rushed to and fro. She could not tell from this distance who was fighting, but the screams of the dying were unmistakable. Igrid wondered if she shouldn't try to find the strength to go out and fight after all. Then the screaming changed.

What had been shouts of battle just moments before, intermingled with cries of pain, became a collective cry of panic. The streets flooded with people all running in the same direction: back toward the palace. Igrid lifted her gaze.

"Sweet gods…"

She dropped the crossbow. It discharged. The bolt glanced off the stone terrace and clattered off in the corner, though Igrid hardly realized it. A great winged, burning thing swept across the sky. She shook her head, unwilling to believe her eyes. But then the dragon's bony maw opened, and great sheets of purple flame poured out, scouring one street after another.

Igrid wondered where the flames were coming from, since the dragon appeared to have neither scales nor flesh. Then she noticed something equally curious: whenever the dragon turned and banked back over the eastern wall, spears joined to ropes and nets flew into the air. Most fell short, but a few rattled between its bones. Soon, the dragon was tangled.

Its mouth opened as though to scream with rage, but no sound issued forth. Only then did Igrid realized that aside from the strange rattling of chains that hung from its bones, the dragon made no sound whatsoever. Yet its fleshless wings flexed, somehow beating against the air.

For a moment, it looked as though all the ropes and nets had finally tangled its wings too much to move. Then the thing flared with wytchfire that seared along all its bones, burning away the ropes and nets. The dragon rose higher. It belched a seemingly endless sea of purple flame over the eastern walls, then turned back on the city. It chose a new direction and started flying again—heading for the palace.

Igrid lifted her crossbow, remembering too late that it had already gone off. She cursed, fumbling with the winch. Her hands shook. By the time she'd nocked another bolt, the dragon was nearly upon her. Great, dark eyes with pupils of purple flame seemed to stare right at her. Igrid lifted her crossbow. Then she laughed at the absurdity of killing such a creature with such a weapon.

Still, she pulled the trigger. The crossbow shuddered. The bolt leapt forward into the winter air. It fell short. The dragon continued soaring toward her, filling up her vision. She wanted to run but could not tear her gaze away. She fell to her knees and waited for the end.

But the dragon stalled in midair. Purple flames blazed along its bones, brighter than ever. The dragon jerked, flapped its wings, and twisted its head from side to side as though screaming. The flames grew brighter still, until Igrid had to look away.

When she looked back, she saw the dragon plummeting out of the sky. Chains flailed and rattled. The bones separated, jumbled, and crashed onto the city streets. A blinding glare caught her eye. Igrid turned her head just in time to see an enormous ball of flame rising into the eastern sky, traveling faster than thought.

"What..."

Before she could complete the thought, Igrid felt a wave of numbness sweep throughout her entire body, emanating from her wounds. She winced. Then she fell against the railing as everything went dark.

Rowen felt a terrible heat sweep past him, different somehow from any other wytchfire he'd ever seen. The glare blinded him. He lost sight of Chorlga. Forced to shield his eyes, he fell back. The glare seared through his eyelids, scalding into his mind the impression of flames that poured endlessly like water into a dark, empty hole.

When all the flames had been swallowed, the glare vanished. He opened his eyes. Chorlga still sat on his throne of dragonbones. His robes smoldered, almost entirely burned away. Most of his flesh remained charred or crusted with dried blood, but he was still alive.

Rowen hefted Knightswrath and started toward him. The hilt felt red hot in his hands, but he could not let go. He could not stop until Chorlga was dead. Somehow, though, he seemed to be moving in slow motion. Before he had gone halfway, Chorlga stood. The Dragonkin's eyes dulled to the color of stone.

"So much lost. And still, here we are."

The ghost of a smile formed on Chorlga's lips. Then his body blurred, grayed, and disappeared altogether. Where he had been, the air shimmered then returned to normal. Knightswrath pulsed with scalding heat, then the flames vanished from its blade.

Rowen stood, breathing hard, staring at the empty throne. Wytchfire had scorched the bones. At the foot of the throne lay Shade, facedown. His clothes had been mostly burned away, leaving nothing but blackened flesh. Rowen figured he must be dead. He considered stabbing him to be sure but shook his head.

Gods, what did I do? He was my ally...

"And Kayden's tormentor," he muttered.

He turned to see Zeia stumbling toward him. No hands of fire capped her scarred wrists. Nevertheless, Rowen lifted Knightswrath and stepped into a guarded position.

Zeia smiled slightly. "It seems we still have a long way to go before we trust each other, Human." She lowered her gaze to Shade. Her expression softened. Slowly, she knelt and turned him over. Rowen winced when he saw the massive, scorched wound he'd made in Shade's chest. He knelt, placing Knightswrath on the floor to one side. Zeia held Shade's head with a scarred wrist, then ignited one flaming hand and closed his staring eyes. The hand flickered and disappeared. She continued to support his head with her wrist then lowered his head back to the floor.

"Chorlga isn't dead yet. We have to follow him. We have to finish it." Her voice sounded flat, exhausted.

Rowen glanced down at Knightswrath. No blood showed on the blade. Zeia's face reflected in the steel. For a moment, she looked like Silwren. Rowen picked up the sword, moved it to the crook of his arm, and offered Zeia his hand.

"I'll find him."

Zeia regarded him in silence then stretched out one arm. A hand of violet flame reappeared, fluttering weakly from her wrist. Rowen hesitated, then grasped it and hauled Zeia to her feet.

CHAPTER FORTY-FIVE

THE DRAGONWARD

ROWEN STARED OUT AT THE vast, icy expanse, red with sunset. Aside from dreams and visions, this was the first time he had ever actually been this far north. For a moment, he felt utterly alone—despite the great army massed behind him.

Someone touched his arm. He turned. Igrid appeared next to him. She wore the gleaming mail and tabard of an Iron Sister. Her red hair hung in short war-braids from the back of her helmet. It had been three months since he'd entered Hesod with the armies of Prince Saanji and found Igrid in the palace, near death. He'd used Knightswrath to save her, but she was still weak. He'd pleaded with her to stay behind—but she'd refused simply by flashing her crooked smile.

"It's almost over," Rowen whispered. "He's just ahead. I can feel him…"

Igrid started to embrace him then stopped. Her crooked smile looked forced. "Is one allowed to hug a Sword Marshal without permission?"

Rowen scoffed. The title, bestowed upon him only six days ago, seemed as ludicrous as the extravagant new armor he was wearing. In place of a crane balancing on one leg, the azure tabard hung over his cuirass showed a white, nine-petaled flower with a golden heart. But the armor never seemed to fit as well as what he'd had before.

Funny. I never thought that armor fit, either.

He squeezed Igrid's hand and turned north again. He wondered what the others saw. *Probably nothing*, he realized. To him, though, the Dragonward appeared as a broad, soaring wall of pale purple fire. The closer he drew to it, the more his senses tingled. He felt a dreadful heat welling up within Knightswrath, too, warming the entire sword as it hung at his side. He fought the impulse to draw it. He had not drawn the sword in weeks. Nor did he intend to now—not until he faced Chorlga.

Someone else stepped forward and joined them. "How do you know he won't teleport away?"

Rowen turned and regarded Jalist. The Dwarr wore the Lyos-red uniform of a Captain of the Guard, bestowed upon him when they'd passed through the city days ago. But Jalist looked no more comfortable in his new uniform than Rowen figured he looked in the armor of a Knight of the Lotus.

No, it's more than that, Rowen realized. Some of the mirth had gone out of Jalist's eyes. They looked dark now, even for a Dwarr's. Rowen glanced at the luminstone hanging around Jalist's neck, bound in a silver chain, and wondered again if leaving it on Leander's body had been the right thing to do.

"He won't," Rowen said. "He can't anymore. He used up all the power he'd taken from Godsbane just to heal himself. He used up most of his own since then, trying to get away."

Jalist grunted. "Well, he won't get away this time." He turned and looked behind them.

Rowen turned, too. He stared at the vast, rippling host of armored riders waiting behind him. Mostly Lancers and men from the Free Cities, the men had been with him almost since he'd left Hesod. But others were new.

Small forces of Dwarrs and Queshi had joined him a few weeks ago, as eager as anyone to avenge their slain princes and countrymen. After them came two hundred Sylvs, sent by Captain Briel himself. Kilisti led them, mounted on Snowdark—whom she announced she had no intention of relinquishing.

Others were noticeably absent. Prince Saanji had gone west with his Earless. His father, the Red Emperor, was still alive—and he still had ten thousand fanatical Dhargots in his service. Saanji's war had only just begun. Rowen intended to help, eventually. In the meantime, to everyone's surprise, Zeia had elected to go with Saanji. So had a contingent of Iron Sisters, led by Haesha.

Rowen was not entirely certain yet whether all the men who followed him were truly his allies. Days ago, as they marched along the coast near the Burnished Way, nearly a thousand Isle Knights had come to join them, accompanied by an equal number of squires and Noshan militia-men. Their leader, Wyn Kai, said they'd been sent by Crovis Ammerhel, the new Grand Marshal of the Lotus Isles. With a strained smile, Sir Kai had gone on to say that the new Grand Marshal had formally validated Aeko Shingawa's recent promotion of Rowen to Knight of the Lotus. Furthermore, Crovis had declared that he be made a Sword Marshal and invited back to the Isles to take command of Saikaido Temple.

"He's calling you back for a reason, Squire," Aeko had insisted. "Stay away. I'll go back and see what's happening on the Isles while you chase the Dragonkin."

So Aeko had gone, too. A week had passed, and there had been no word from her since.

Perhaps strangest of all his new would-be allies, though, were the Shel'ai. At Zeia's suggestion, he'd offered amnesty and protection to any Shel'ai who wished to return and join him in his final push against Chorlga. Most had refused. But a few had returned, dressed in bone-white cloaks that now bore a new sigil: a hand of purple flame.

Though these Shel'ai had been vital allies in helping him track Chorlga from one end of Ruun to the other, their presence had caused no small amount of unrest in the army. Once Chorlga was gone, Rowen had no doubt that most of the Shel'ai would disappear again.

Most... but not all.

There were still matters to attend to in the Wytchforest as well. But first, he had to deal with Chorlga.

Rowen glanced east, far out beyond the ice, where a line of ships was just barely visible. One of them was the *Winter Prayer*, commanded by his old friend, Hráthbam. While Kilisti and the Sylvs patrolled to the west, Hráthbam and a small host of Soroccan sailors did the same to the east, bolstered by Sang Wei, a squad of Isle Knights, and a handful of the best archers the Queshi had left. But Rowen doubted any of that would be necessary.

He turned to face the Dragonward again. "It'll end there, with me," he said wearily. "I'm going on alone."

"Wrong," Jalist said.

"Right," Rowen said. He squeezed the Dwarr's shoulder. "For once, listen to me. Stay here, my friend. You're in command while I'm gone."

Jalist gave him a sour look. "Presuming that even half these people will listen to what I say, what should I do if Chorlga attacks us? I don't remember hearing about axes and arrows being of much use against a Dragonkin."

Rowen smiled slightly. "Chorlga is weak now—weak enough that it wouldn't take magic to kill him. But he won't attack you, because to do that, he'd have to get past me. And he won't."

Jalist and Igrid exchanged looks. "Fine," Jalist said finally. "I'll stay with this camp of rabid Locke-worshippers and stave off frostbite while you two go give the Dragonkin a proper burial."

Rowen turned to face Igrid. "No."

Igrid flashed a crooked grin and said nothing. She just turned north and started walking. Jalist chuckled. Rowen swore. Then he hurried after her.

"When we find him, stay behind me," Rowen said.

"I don't need a bodyguard," Igrid snapped.

Rowen touched Knightswrath's hilt. "I know. But you can be set on fire. I can't."

Igrid raised one eyebrow. She rapped her knuckles against his armored left arm, where the skin from shoulder to elbow had been left permanently red and wrinkled from Chorlga's wytchfire. For some reason, Knightswrath could not heal the itching, sometimes maddening burn.

"That's different," Rowen insisted.

"If you say so." Igrid faced north again. "But if you want to be my shield, Sir Fey, feel free."

Rowen gave her a sour look. "I wish you wouldn't call me that." She'd been using that name sporadically ever since she'd heard Prince Saanji use it.

"At least I don't call you that in front of your men."

"Actually, you do."

Igrid shrugged. They continued in silence for a while, then she stopped. Her expression turned deathly serious. She pointed.

"I know." Rowen squeezed her arm and stepped in front of her. One hand rested on Knightswrath's dragonbone pommel. He started forward again, easing toward the cloaked figure.

Dressed in a gray cloak, Chorlga stood motionless, back turned, nearly invisible against the ice. As Rowen drew closer, the Dragonkin still did not move. Rowen did not draw Knightswrath despite the growing heat of the hilt.

Chorlga stood so still, facing the silent, roiling wall of fire that was the Dragonward, that Rowen began to wonder if the Dragonkin had fashioned a new Jol in his own image. Then Chorlga lowered his hood and turned. Despite himself, Rowen winced.

Chorlga's face remained burnt, his features ruined and twisted. He grinned nonetheless. "Good evening, Sir Locke. It seems you have found me at last."

Rowen took one step forward, then another. He heard Igrid moving a short distance behind him. He was glad that for once, she'd listened to him and stayed back. He flexed his fingers around Knightswrath's hilt, ready to draw it the moment Chorlga moved to attack.

But Chorlga tucked his burnt hands back into the sleeves of his gray robe. "After Cadavash, I went to Godsfall, then to the Dead Shores."

"I know," Rowen said. "I followed you."

"I thought I could get the Olgrym to fight for me," Chorlga continued. "They followed Fadarah. They followed Shade. Why not me?" His grin faded. "But no one would listen. Even those who were afraid of me. Why do you suppose that is?"

Rowen eased even closer, turning his eyes slightly left, then right. He searched their surroundings for some sign of a trap. He saw only bare, empty ice.

"I'm surprised the wytch is not with you," Chorlga continued. "The one with no hands."

Rowen thought he caught a hint of admiration in the Dragonkin's voice. "Shall I deliver a message for you?"

Chorlga appeared to seriously consider it. "No," he said finally. He removed his hands from his sleeves. Rowen tensed, but the Dragonkin merely lowered his arms to his sides. He regarded Rowen in silence then slowly turned westward. "Twelve centuries I've walked this wretched continent, and this is to be my last sunset. Strange that it ends here, on the Wintersea. Fitting, though, I suppose."

Rowen measured the distance between them. He was nearly close enough to slash the Dragonkin in a quick draw, but he hesitated to step any closer because that would also leave him less room to defend himself if Chorlga attacked with wytchfire. Besides, he didn't just have to defend himself. He had to protect Igrid, too.

But I can't let him get away. I can't let him get past me.

Rowen waited. Meanwhile, Chorlga stared, unblinking, into the sunset. Then the Dragonkin closed his eyes and tipped his head back. The grin returned. Slowly, he turned back to Rowen. He opened his eyes. This time, the pupils looked as gray as granite.

"Well fought, Sir Locke."

Without waiting for a response, Chorlga turned toward the Dragonward, raging just a few yards beyond. He stretched out his arms and walked forward. He kept walking. As Rowen watched, Chorlga stepped right into the Dragonward.

Pale purple flames washed over him. Chorlga shuddered but did not scream. He kept walking. The flames brightened. Chorlga's whole body shuddered then withered into ash. For one moment, his ashes flared in the Dragonward like stars—then they, too, burned away.

For a long time, Rowen stared.

Finally, backing away, he wrested his hand off Knightswrath's hilt. He reached down and took Igrid's hand. "Let's go," he said, unable to say more.

EPILOGUE

IGRID SAT ON A STONE bench in a newly planted grove of dogblossom trees, watching the children play. She disliked seeing them play so close to the fissure, despite the stone wall—gated and guarded—that now separated Cadavash from the outside world.

Though all the children but Thessa had violet eyes, they seemed to welcome the Hesodi girl easily enough. In fact, the only untrusting stares came from the faces of the Isle Knights who guarded the new gates into Cadavash.

And my face, probably.

A tiny scream drew her gaze back to the infant in her arms. Sariel had woken again. The infant writhed ferociously in her blanket but stilled the moment Igrid looked at her. Violet eyes stared back. Squelching a feeling of panic, Igrid hummed a lullaby and smoothed back the infant's platinum hair, tucking it behind her tiny, tapered ears.

Sariel smiled, yawned, and went back to sleep.

Igrid stood, readjusting the infant—whose name, according to Rowen, meant *Echo*. As she emerged from the circle of dogblossom trees, she saw Rowen heading toward her. He was scowling. Before he had a chance to speak, Igrid pressed Sariel into his arms. "Hold your damn daughter," she said, not unkindly.

Rowen blinked then obliged. Sariel woke, stared at Rowen with wide, purple eyes, and opened her mouth to cry. Rowen kissed her forehead, and the infant went back to sleep.

Then he directed his gaze back at Igrid. "You don't have to do this. Briel sent nursemaids—"

"She doesn't frighten me," Igrid lied. Staring at Rowen, though, she wondered once again what Knightswrath had done to him. He had not worn the sword in months; still, though, he had nightmares. And more than once, she thought she'd heard him call Silwren's name in his sleep. She wanted to hate him for that, but after Chorlga's defeat on the Wintersea, she'd confessed her own sins: that she'd tried to steal Knightswrath from him once before, and Silwren had intervened. He'd been quick to forgive her. In fact, he confessed that he'd sensed as much when he'd found her in Hesod and healed her. She did not know whether to feel relieved or enraged, though she could not say why—only that sometimes, she wished he'd hated her for a while.

Shaking herself, she said, "What's wrong?"

"Word from the Lotus Isles," Rowen answered. Sariel began to stir. He smiled at her then lowered his voice. "From Aeko."

"About Crovis?"

Rowen nodded. "He's more powerful than ever. He has the whole Council and the Noshans convinced that he alone saved the Lotus Isles. And he's angry that I haven't gone back."

"Angry that you didn't give him Knightswrath, you mean." Igrid thought of the sword, locked away deep in the sorrowful depths of Cadavash, near Namundvar's Well. As far as she was concerned, it could stay there.

"Well, Aeko says he's trying to force his way into King Shigella's tomb. She says he thinks there's something in there... maybe another sword like Knightswrath."

Igrid felt a knot of panic. "Is there?"

Rowen shook his head. "If so, Chorlga never mentioned it. Neither did El'rash'lin. And nothing was ever written about it." He paused. "There must be *something* in there, though. Nobody can break through the stone. The whole thing's sealed by some kind of magic. Zeia said it isn't Shel'ai, either."

"You've been there. What do *you* think?"

Rowen hesitated. "It felt... older. Dragonkin, I think. Maybe Nâya built it. I don't know. I've told Matua to learn all he can about it."

Igrid nodded. She'd seen the cleric of Armahg weeks ago, and still marveled that he'd survived his encounter with the Nightmare—an encounter that had reduced half the Scrollhouse and a good portion of Atheion to ash. But Matua had not escaped unscathed. He'd lost one arm, and half his face had been burned to the texture of rippled silk. Yet, thanks to Rowen's invocation of Knightswrath's power, he could at least live without pain.

Thessa stopped playing long enough to wave.

Rowen waved back then studied the Isle Knights in the distance. "I have one hundred Knights here... maybe half of whom I trust. I have Aeko and Sang Wei back on the Isles. I have Jalist back in Lyos and Briel in the Wytchforest. And the Shel'ai."

Igrid glanced at the cloaked figures speaking in the distance, milling near the gates, their white robes emblazoned with the hand of purple flame. They seemed to sense her scrutiny. Turning, they nodded at her, stone faced.

Igrid nodded back, suppressing a shudder. She was tempted to ask about Zeia and Saanji, if Rowen had any further word on their campaign since they had unexpectedly refused Rowen's help in battling the Red Emperor. She decided she did not want to know.

Instead, she touched Rowen's burned arm, left bare by his sleeveless tunic. When he turned, she kissed his forehead. As an afterthought, she forced herself to kiss Sariel's forehead, too. "And me."

Rowen smiled. "And you." Shifting Sariel to one side, he leaned in and kissed her. As he did so, Igrid felt the cold, brass pommel of Rowen's new sword press into her belly. She shifted. Sariel cried.

Igrid winced then smiled. "It's going to snow soon," she said.

Rowen nodded. "I know. Come inside. I'll build a fire."

ABOUT THE AUTHOR

Michael Meyerhofer grew up in Iowa, where he learned to cope with the unbridled excitement of the Midwest by reading books and not getting his hopes up. Probably due to his father's influence, he developed a fondness for *Star Trek*, weight lifting, and collecting medieval weapons. He is also addicted to caffeine and the History Channel.

His fourth poetry book, *What To Do If You're Buried Alive*, was recently published by Split Lip Press. He also serves as the poetry editor of *Atticus Review*. His poetry and prose have appeared in *Asimov's Science Fiction Magazine*, *Brevity*, *Ploughshares*, *Hayden's Ferry Review*, *Rattle*, and many other journals.

He and his fiancée currently live in Fresno, California, in a little house beside a very large cactus.

www.ingramcontent.com/pod-product-compliance
Lightning Source LLC
Chambersburg PA
CBHW051514250626
47156CB00001B/88